THE BENE LUMEN CHRONICLES:
SAMHAIN SCHOOL OF ANCIENT KNOWLEDGE

BY
JOHN R. MCCORMICK

Ink Smith Publishing
www.ink-smith.com

ISBN: 978-1-939156-28-0

Ink Smith Publishing

P.O Box 1086

Glendora CA

PROLOGUE

THE UNLEASHING OF OROCHI

It was a dark night made even darker by grayish clouds that covered the moon hiding it away like a stolen pearl. A lone figure walked along the rocky edge of Cape Elizabeth stopping to stare down at the rough waters below. The waters seemed to be in more turmoil than usual with the waves slapping hard and loud against the rocks, as if they were trying to send a warning. Siobhan CuCullen had left her two young sons at home so as to perform a duty she wasn't sure she was capable of handling but knew she couldn't avoid. Reaching deep into herself touching the core of her special talents, she looked up at the sky in order to focus all her powers. Slowly, almost imperceptibly, the gray clouds began to part exposing that hidden white moon. It seemed for a moment as if someone turned on the lights in a dark room, as the glow of the moon appeared in the sky. Now Siobhan could see properly the terrain.

Turning away from the water she continued walking along the rocky promontory of Two Light State Park in Cape Elizabeth, Maine. A short distance away she could see a lone figure standing with arms raised to the sky. From her vantage point she could feel the awesome power of this figure. As she got closer she recognized the figure: it was Baal. He was the reason she was here. It was her duty to stop him, a so-called Boss demon, from raising the snake demon Orochi in this genesis ground of evil, which was Cape Elizabeth, Maine. It was her duty to do this or to die trying. This was an oath she had made a long time ago and her people took oaths seriously. Noticing the lithe and beautiful figure of Siobhan CuCullen walking towards him, Baal lowered his arms and turned to face her. He was an attractive man dressed for a cool autumn evening.

"Good evening, Siobhan," he said in an inviting voice. "I wish it was Brian who came tonight instead of you. I would have preferred to slay him than you. It would have been so much more fulfilling."

"I can't let you bring Orochi into this world from the next, Baal," she stated defiantly.

"Too late for that; he's on his way," he said then looked at a spot on the rocky ground beside him. The rocky patch of ground turned to liquid. A green scaly hand with long talons reached out of this liquid and grabbed at the hard ground until it found a grip then a second green scaly hand did the same thing. With great effort Orochi pulled himself out of the dark liquid and onto the ground. He was horrible to look at, a man snake with yellow eyes, green scaly skin, and a red tongue that licked at its missing lips. Baal helped this demon to its feet.

"I'm sorry about this, Siobhan, but you are too late to stop me. It is done," Baal said.

With those words the human face Baal showed the world dissolved away and was replaced by a red face with a rocky ridge along his brow. His eyes turned from an attractive blue to a deep burning yellowish orange. Now standing before Siobhan CuCullen were two demons capable of killing her husband, a man who was difficult to kill, let alone killing her. Lowering her head she reached out to nature asking for its assistance. She felt the spark of power begin to flow through her, a feeling of power that gave her hope and focus in her fight.

In the graceful, slithering way of a snake Orochi began to move forward on two feet, but suddenly hands of rock reached up from the ground and grabbed him holding him in place for Siobhan to attack. With a roar of anger he began to fight at these elemental rock hands, but the rock proved to be too strong for him. Baal turned to help him, but before he could assist him a rumble of thunder shook the ground around him and a clap of white-hot lightning hit him square on the chest sending him flying back onto the ground.

Siobhan turned her attention back to Orochi directing several bolts of crackling hot white lightning at him. One after another they hit him, as more powerful hands of rock reached up to hold him in place. Orochi screamed in pain as he tried desperately to break the rock bonds that restrained him. As he continued to strain and exert himself several of the rock hands crumbled away under his strength, but as one hand crumbled another emerged from the rocky ground to replace it and hold the snake demon back.

"Well, Done. I expected nothing less from a Triune Conjurer of your powers, Siobhan," Baal stated then unleashed a bolt of blue energy from his mouth that was aimed at her.

Siobhan barely dodged the bolt of negative energy he released as a weapon, which hit the ground where she stood exploding the rock under her feet and sending it flying in all directions. A few shards of this rock shrapnel lodged itself in her left thigh, as she rolled away from the destruction and a few more in her side. Reaching down to her thigh she felt wetness. The blood on her hand looked almost black in the moonlight. She ignored the pain and kept rolling away from the area of destruction and got slowly up to face Baal, who had freed Orochi from his earthen bonds.

"That looked painful," he said to her but she didn't answer him. "Join us, Siobhan. The Illuminatii can always use a talented Triune Conjurer. You could become Morgana's right hand woman. You could perform great feats and accomplish unimaginable things and live your life without rules or interference from those with little imaginations. Doesn't that sound like more fun than living by rules and dying a painful death?" With another bolt of lightning hitting him in the chest Baal clapped his hands together sending waves of negative energy towards Siobhan. She attempted to dodge these waves but as she ducked one, another would hit her sending a concussion of horrible pain throughout her body. But she did not succumb to it. Instead of falling in defeat she sent back several bolts of lightning at Baal, who did his best to avoid them. As they fought the rock tomb cracked wide open and Orochi burst out of it. He was breathing hard and his already demonic looking yellow eyes expressed a ferocity and hatred that frightened Siobhan. Nothing would satisfy this creature but her blood now.

Siobhan was now in pain, bleeding from several wounds, and completely exhausted from the fight. She felt her power waning, as her ability to partner with nature needed concentrated energy and focus. Although she was a Triune Conjurer, as were many in her bloodline, she was not as powerful a one as her cousin Sian, who was considered the most powerful of this time. But more than her powers were dissolving; she also

3

felt her hope waning, which was even worse for her. Hope was a powerful tool for a Triune Conjurer because it allowed you to stay in balance with nature. She needed her husband Brian here to push her on through the pain and self-doubt, to give her someone to protect and someone to support her.

"Let me kill you now and maybe I won't go to your home and kill your children," Baal said petulantly.

"You know my answer, Baal," she said.

"Oh, yes, your husband and children, you don't want to desert them because you love them, don't you? How sweet, yet also how predictable," he started to finish what he was saying when a giant rock tomb engulfed Orochi completely and a bright white bolt of lightning hit Baal sending him to his knees and angering him.

With those words Siobhan dug deep into herself and summoned up a whirlwind, which was about to grab Baal, but Orochi jumped into its path and began to battle the whirling twister in the air flailing away with it. He battled the wind itself. As quick as she could adjust she sent another white, hot lightning bolt at Baal. Bolt after bolt the lightning struck at him, and he fought it until finally he unleashed another bolt of blue negative energy, which partially hit Siobhan causing her excruciating pain. She fell to the ground lying there still.

Since Siobhan had concentrated most of her attention on Baal, Orochi finally defeated the whirlwind but was tired and Baal looked as if he had expended a great amount of energy fighting Siobhan. He stopped the snake demon that wanted to rush recklessly forward after her. Baal stared Orochi down calming him and regaining control of him and the situation.

"Siobhan, let the snake kill you painlessly and I give you my word that I will not kill your children once we are done here," Baal said in a soothing, charming voice.

"How can I trust you, Baal?" she desperately asked, as she slowly got up.

"You can't trust me. But you have weakened both of us and I am willing to bet that your children are protected by the best Ardal Cathal you have left in this area, though not the best you have," he said. "If we continue this battle in the end Orochi and I will prevail and you will die. Yes, you will cause us more trouble, more pain, which will in turn make both of us even more angry than we are now. If this occurs I will gladly help Orochi do away with your children's protection then watch him devour them whole. But if this was up to him..."

Siobhan faced turned white at the thought of her children being devoured by Orochi. Baal noticed this. He returned himself to his human form in order to present a normal face to her then continued speaking: "let me kill you then and we will both leave this place and be on our way to where we must go. Your children will not be harmed."

Siobhan was completely exhausted now beyond putting up a good fight. She stood up and for a moment thought of continuing the battle, but she knew she couldn't win. She could feel her body weakened and shaking; the energy to even summon another lightning bolt was way beyond her now. Her children, though, she couldn't let them down, but could she trust Baal to keep his word? She looked at him. He nodded his head, as if he was responding to the thoughts in her mind. She nodded back at him, thought of her children whom she loved, then of her husband who she hoped would not allow her death to change him then let Baal know that she was trusting him with another more pronounced nod in his direction.

"It is a deal then, Siobhan. You have made the right choice. I'll do this myself," he said then unleashed a bolt of blue negative energy hitting her squarely on the chest and sending her off the promontory and into the rough water below.

"Let us kill her children as revenge for her attack on us. I'm hungry; I want to eat them," hissed Orochi.

"No, I gave her my word," Baal said.

"But she is Bene Lumen and we are Illuminatii," hissed Orochi.

"That doesn't make a difference to me. I may be evil but that doesn't mean I can't keep my word now and again."

"I shall kill her children without your help then," Orochi hissed.

"I forgot that you are a snake," Baal stated lazily then hit Orochi with a bolt of blue negative energy sending him into his back. "Now go crawl away on your belly."

Orochi got up off the ground quickly and looked at Baal with hate. But he didn't attack him. Baal was too powerful to attack when he expected an attack. Orochi knew this and knew not to push his luck against Baal.

"I said I gave her my word, which means you will not touch her children. Not unless they grow up and become a problem then I will gladly help serve them to you for dinner," Baal stated. "Now let's be gone from here."

With those words he cast a spell on Orochi turning him into a human looking male, not as handsome as himself, but appealing. As they turned to leave dark storm clouds once again covered the moon hiding it away from sight, then with a loud rumble of thunder and a clap of lightning, it began to rain. Baal looked up at the sky as if to check if this was nature's way of mourning Siobhan CuCullen. Torrents of rain fell hard to the ground quickly forming puddles. This just might be nature's way of mourning, he thought. He laughed and continued on his way.

CHAPTER 1

It was a bitter cold Wednesday in March. Even for a New England state, which was known for the month of March coming in roaring like a frozen lion and settling down like a spring lamb; it was cold. Seven adults and two boys gathered together on a stark rock promontory at Two Lights State Park in Cape Elizabeth, Maine overlooking the rough waters of Casco Bay. A sharp wind, that felt as if it could cut right through the skin and penetrate to the bone, blew hard and constant leaving those gathered chilled, as they stood there on the rocky promontory. Above them the gray sky, which was filled with ominous and darkening storm clouds, threatened to release buckets of cold rain adding to the bleakness of the day.

The gathered individuals were an odd looking mix of people. The oldest in the small crowd was a craggy, rough faced man with white hair and black eyebrows named Mallory Fergus, who was dressed in a gray Savile Row overcoat covering a gray Savile Row suit. He had come from Scotland for this understated and eccentric funeral ceremony because of the importance of the dead they mourned there. Coming along with him from Scotland was the burly, tall, dark haired and pockmark faced Boris Diaghilev, who was dressed in a heavy black coat with a gray fur coat and a gray fur hat he liked to call his Cossack's hat; the always regal and austerely beautiful Sian Boru, who was dressed in a fur lined brown cloak with a hood that covered her head and obscured her face; the slight bodied, though self-assured, Rabbi Jacob Justiz, who dressed in a simple black suit with a simple black overcoat and black fedora covering his mousy brown hair; the slightly pudgy bodied and fair haired Father Michael Mueller, who was dressed in his black priest's clothes along with a Roman collar with a simple black overcoat protecting him from the chill and holding a golden urn in his right arm; and the long salt and pepper hair, which was tied back by a single strip of buckskin, and passive faced Graham Stonefeather, who was dressed in a thick buckskin jacket worn on top of a red ceremonial shirt that was decorated by Native American jewelry and beads and a pair of faded blue jeans.

The last adult member of the group was Brian CuCullen, a handsome dark haired man with the easy and lithe physique of an experienced athlete. He was dressed in a heavy Cumberland jacket, which covered an Irish knit sweater and blue jeans. Beside him stood his two sons, Kieran, the oldest at sixteen who looked much like his father in facial and physical appearance, and Liam, a thin, wiry, copper haired twelve year old. They were both dressed like their father. Unlike the rest of the group who traveled from afar, they lived in Cape Elizabeth.

Two from the group of visitors walked to the edge of the promontory. Father Michael Mueller carried the golden urn gently in his hands, which held the ashes of Paulette Goode, and Graham Stonefeather gently shook two handmade and hand painted for this occasion large ceremonial rattles. Sian Boru dropped the hood of her cloak exposing her high cheekbones; raven black hair and dark blue eyes to the elements. By any standards she possessed an ageless captivating beauty that made most men feel slightly uncomfortable in her presence. Kieran, who looked to be almost overwhelmed by her attractiveness, stared at her with his mouth slightly open, while Liam, who was just getting to the age where he noticed such things as someone's appearance, looked at her with great curiosity. There was something about her, beyond her obvious beauty, which drew his complete attention, though. He felt as if he knew this person without ever having met her before. Liam watched her closely as she lifted her face to the heavens and looked to breathe in deeply and then silently mouth some words.

Suddenly, he felt an odd surge of energy, which felt like a heavy dose of static electricity, flow through his body starting at the base of his spine and moving up into his brain then the biting wind that made this spot so uncomfortable to stand at stopped. It was not the first time he had felt this odd surge of energy flow through his bones. The very first time he felt it was during a blizzard when he was just eight years old. Kieran and he were playing in front of their house when the wind suddenly picked up to the point where he was frightened that he'd be blown away by it. Unexpectedly, as he wished that the hard winds would stop that exact odd feeling of energy surged through his body and the wind astonishingly died down enough for him and Kieran to run into the house and avoid the storm. He always had a distinct feeling that the odd sensation he had felt was caused by excitement or a rush of adrenaline, but this time was different from other times this time he knew that feeling of energy was caused by Sian Boru, who had ignited something in him. She turned her dark eyes in Liam's direction and offered him a smile, as if to say that he had understood what she had done, then she turned her gaze to Father Mueller, who cleared his throat. Graham Stonefeather stopped shaking his rattles.

"Did you feel that?" Liam whispered to his brother.

"Feel what?" Kieran whispered back not taking his eyes off of the raven haired woman whose natural beauty had him enthralled.

"I don't know, you know, the thing that just happened with the wind a second ago. It was strange."

"Shut up, midget, the priest is going to talk. Dad warned us about being respectful," Kieran quietly told him.

"Paulette vas special, but all of us vho are here knew dat," the priest said with a very thick and rough German accent. "Her strength vas impressive, but she vas far from da strongest of us."

Liam could see his father shift his weight slightly from one foot to the other when the priest made this comment. The old man with the craggy face looked over at his father nodded at him and smiled gently. It was an unexpected smile because it was so pleasant and made the harshness of his face completely disappear. Their father nodded in return but did not return the smile.

"But even more impressive than her strength vas her spirit," the priest continued. "Dis vas vhat made her zo special. She had indomitable spirit, which drove her to be zo important to our society. I remember vhen she vas furst told that she'd be coming here to Cape Elizabeth. Her brown eyes grew bright and a genuine smile of pleasure broke out over her face. She knew vhat it meant to be assigned here, yet she wanted dat burden. She vanted to play a role, which few of us vould want und it vas because of her spirit; her strong and joyful spirit, dat she vanted to play da role, which she had been chosen for. Vas a remarkable voman she vas. I vill miss her."

All of the mourners shook their heads in agreement, except for Kieran and Liam, who only knew Paulette as a sometimes houseguest. When Paulette did stay with them she spent all her time huddled with their father asking him endless questions, which they weren't supposed to hear, and listening to advice from him, which they were also not supposed to hear either. She was nice enough to them, but she never came to see them only to see their father, who treated her like a teacher treated a student, even though they appeared to be the same age. Liam continued to look from person to person wondering who they were and how their father knew them. When each of these people saw Brian CuCullen they treated him as if they had known him a very long time. Although they had never seen any of these people before, they knew his and Kieran names without being told who they were and even knew personal bits of information about them, like how Liam liked video games and Kieran was a good athlete. As for Kieran, he just seemed to stare at the beautiful dark haired woman throughout the whole funeral.

"Paulette vas a friend to all of us here, a loyal und devoted friend. May Got bless her soul," the priest broke the silence with these words.

Liam stood by his father on his right hand side checking out these strangers he had never seen before. For the CuCullen's Two Light State Park was always thought of as a sad place since it was from these rocky headlands that Siobhan CuCullen fell to her death some ten years ago leaving Liam and Kieran motherless and Brian CuCullen a widow. Liam remembered when their father told them about how their mother must have fallen while taking a hike on a dark night. Since he was only two years old back then he couldn't understand why he just didn't kiss her booboos and she'd be all right, but his brother Kieran, who was six years old, immediately understood what a fall from the headlands into Casco Bay meant: it was death. Liam recalled how he began to cry and didn't stop until well into the night. That was the last time he saw his brother Kieran cry.

Shortly, after their mother died Paulette Goode arrived in Cape Elizabeth and moved into their old large home which was not that far off from Beckett's Castle, a mansion that was said to be haunted. They moved into a new place not too far from the water in a small Cape Cod house. Once their mother died their father quit whatever he did for a living, the two boys were never sure what that was either, and bought a boat and took up fishing, actually he took up trapping lobsters. Now that he had turned twelve he wanted his dad to take him out to check the traps, but he wouldn't. He wouldn't let Liam do anything which he thought was too dangerous, or in which he could get badly hurt. Brian CuCullen was overprotective of both his sons never letting them close to any physical danger if he could help it. Their father was even against Kieran joining the football team, though Kieran did it anyway and now was the star running back.

"Now before ve give her ashes to da vind," the priest said who placed the urn down on the ground, "because as ve know her spirit is already at rest, Mallory would like to say a few vords."

The older man walked towards the urn. Since the wind was gone his white hair remained undisturbed making it seem as if they were actually standing inside instead of outside. Liam stared at his face. He wasn't ugly so much as extremely weathered, Liam thought. Some of the older fishermen he had seen in town had faces like this, except their faces were less weathered. It was as if this man had the weathering of several lifetimes on his face. And unlike most old men that Liam saw, even the ones that still were active pulling traps and such, this one didn't have a hesitant, pained, or feeble walk, but strode surely and strongly to his destination. Everything about this old man seemed to be imbued with some sort of strength, or power, as if he once upon a time had been a very powerful man, who had not lost all of his power in old age. He gracefully bent down and picked up the urn. After staring at it for a moment he knotted his thick black eyebrows then held it delicately in his left arm. Once a few moments of silence had passed he turned his thick nose, which looked as if it had been broken several times, and tough features towards the mourners. His gruff expression suddenly turned soft and gentle, and even tears began to appear in his gray eyes.

"Paulette, I daresay was one of my favorite students. I hate to admit this, especially in front of so many of my old students here today, but it is true," he said in a clipped English accent. "Why was she one of my favorites? The answer is so simple that it is almost embarrassing to say aloud: because Paulette loved to play Scrabble with me."

Several of the people in the funeral party softly laughed at this comment. Even their father laughed noticed Liam. He was somewhat surprised at this because his father seemed so upset at Paulette's death that he thought he would never smile again when he heard her name. What's so funny about Scrabble, he thought to himself, I've never even played it.

"Yes, Scrabble. Young Mr. CuCullen there, another one of my favorites," he said nodding at Brian CuCullen, "would play chess with me for hours, trying to pick my brain for strategies and tactics, but never would he play me in Scrabble. Words meant nothing to him back then. He had no time for anything that did not further his studies. How times change. But Paulette would gladly indulge me in a game, and on top of that she would even let me use archaic and ancient words then take my word for it that they were correctly spelt or even existed in the first place. How delightful to find such a trusting soul in these difficult days, who kept her gentle humanity no matter what she faced. And now this soul has been taken from us; so sad to see her taken before her time. But how many can we say that about? So few of us are able to reach my ripe old age, or would even want to reach my age."

The old man now looked down at the urn in his left arm and patted it with his right hand. Looking at the mourners Liam noticed that most of them had tears forming in their eyes, including their father who he had barely seen tear up since their mother died. For the first time he realized that Paulette's friendship must have been really important to him. She was a better friend than Liam had understood she was. Kieran didn't notice any of this because he continued to sneak glances at the raven-haired woman. It appeared that she was the only thing on his mind at this funeral.

"Rabbi, will you please do the honors with the urn," Mallory said and held the urn out with his left hand.

Rabbi Justiz came walking slowly forward. He had a gentle face that Liam thought should have a smile on it not the frown, which dominated it at the moment. Reaching Mallory he took the urn in his two hands then walked to the edge of the promontory and began to open it up. Before he could open it completely, though, the beautiful woman once again lifted her face to heaven and mouthed some silent words. Again Liam could feel an odd surge of energy rush through him, but this time the surge left a tingling feeling behind, a tingling feeling tinted with a bit of darkness, though he wasn't sure where the dark feeling came from. It was as if he had released some of this energy himself. The wind suddenly reappeared, but instead of blowing in their faces like it had before, it blew out towards to the rough blue water of the Atlantic. The Rabbi opened the urn and began to pour the ashes out of it. Instead of flowing from the urn to the ground the ashes of Paulette Goode flew into the air and were carried away by the wind towards the ocean. Everyone bowed their head in silent prayer, except Liam who exchanged stares with the woman again. This time her smile was different from before, this time her smile seemed to be a smile of satisfaction instead of friendship.

"Well, let us find somewhere warmer in order to talk over good times, and even some not so good times. I believe that Mr. CuCullen has offered us the use of his home where we may enjoy something warm to drink and a little nosh before we prepare for our trip back. Now is the time to remember Paulette as she was and as we should remember her: a wonderful human being who performed her duty with courage and grace," Mallory said.

Everyone turned from the promontory and started walking away from the water. Brian CuCullen hesitated for a few moments remaining to stare at the remnants of the ashes as they drifted on the breeze seemingly being carried gently by the wind out onto Casco Bay. Both his sons looked at him at the same time. Their expressions asked him if it was time to leave so that they could go home and warm up.

"Come on boys, let's go back to the house. We have guests to take care of," Brian CuCullen said solemnly to his sons.

"They are behind in their studies and completely ignorant of the truth of their situation, of what they were born to become and do with their lives. Luckily, Liam will be entering the first level so he should be able to deal with his ignorance easier. But he has no idea about the truth of us or what we do, or why we even exist. It will take special effort to get him adjusted properly. Brian, it is wrong that he is ignorant of our history and our mission. You and Siobhan are both part of that mission and history. You should have told them the truth. And as for Kieran, he must start at the fourth level because of his age, which means he is woefully unprepared for the tasks ahead of him. This late a start might keep him from fulfilling his full potential and we know what that means. You may have deprived us of something special in him," Liam heard the man called Mallory say to their father in a voice that sounded like a rebuke. "I wish that they both had been enrolled at the proper age, especially considering how potentially important they both are to us."

"I never expected to enroll them at all, regardless of their potential importance to the society, Mallory. Paulette's death, though, has changed all that. Her death changed everything, didn't it? Her death was like a marker being called in. I now have to payoff that marker, don't I?" Brian CuCullen responded to the rebuke.

"Her death was a tragedy but, at the very least, it made you come to your senses finally and rejoin us. Good can come from evil. We need you. Paulette will have served a final great purpose if this had made you realize that you had to return to us, that you were needed. You should never have left us to begin with that was wrong headed of you," Mallory stated with a biting tone.

"I...," Brian CuCullen started to say then noticed his youngest son standing behind the kitchen door and listening in on them.

Mallory and Brian were standing in the kitchen alone while everyone else mingled near a buffet table with had on it lasagna, ham, potato salad, quiche, assorted grilled vegetables, and an angel food cake with chocolate frosting located in the small dining room of the modest house. Since Kieran was fascinated with everything that Sian Boru said or did and wouldn't talk to his brother, Liam decided to hide out in the kitchen. When his Father entered with Mallory, he hid behind the door hoping that they would only be in the kitchen for a few moments. He didn't mean to be there when Mallory and his Father started to talk seriously, but he was. The fact that he was there was not his fault, but the fact that he hid behind the door and listened to them was.

"He has been there since we entered the kitchen. Liam has big ears, I think, which is a good thing and a bad thing. Big ears mean you learn about things you shouldn't know, which is good. It also means you learn about things which you aren't prepared to know about, which is bad," Mallory said with a voice that betrayed his amusement.

"You should have told me he was there," Brian CuCullen said to Mallory, who ignored him then he turned to his son. "Get in the room right now, young man. I need to talk to Mallory in private."

"Don't blame your son for the fact that your skills are rusty, Brian," Mallory stated. "Ten years ago you would have noticed him there the second we entered the kitchen. Ten years ago you would have heard his breathing, smelled his scent, felt his presence without even seeing him. You need to get that rust off before you resume your duties."

"I am not rusty."

"You didn't notice him behind the door. That is proof of your rust."

"I missed noticing him because I've grown so used to him being where he shouldn't be that I've become blind to him," Brian CuCullen stated half in frustration and half in amusement. Mallory nodded his head in disapproval, as if he thought Brian CuCullen was deluding himself.

"Dad," Liam interrupted their argument.

"Yes, Liam Xavier," his father answered in a voice which showed he was irritated that his son had embarrassed him.

"Are you taking us out of school, Dad? Are we leaving Cape Elizabeth?" he asked quickly.

"Maybe, yes... I don't know. What am I saying...I can't lie to you? Yes, I am taking you out of school and you are leaving Cape Elizabeth," his father answered, though he could tell he didn't want to answer him.

"Why?"

"Because it's time that you and Kieran get some proper schooling and when I mean proper schooling I am talking about learning skills and tools you will need to deal with the unique challenges that you'll face in this life. Challenges I had hoped that you would never have to face."

"Kieran won't like this, Dad," Liam said. "He's the star of the football team and he's got a new girlfriend. He won't want to leave Cape Elizabeth. Dad, he loves it here."

"Your brother has a girlfriend," Brian CuCullen said in a voice that was brimming with surprise.

"Yeah, sure. He doesn't go out with his friends every night, you know, most of the times he is going out with her. He and Karen..."

"Her name is Karen?" his father asked.

"Yeah, Karen Maloney. I think you know her father. You know Mr. Maloney. He owns the coffee place you go to all the time. You love that place."

"Yeah, sure I know him. He's a nice guy. Why didn't your brother let me know that he was dating? He should have told me about her."

"He didn't want to give you the chance to say no to his dating, dad. You know that you don't like us to do anything without your permission and Kieran is tired of that," Liam answered honestly.

"You are very rusty indeed, Brian," Mallory added finally breaking his own quiet.

"What you are witnessing is not rust, it is the byproduct of raising two young boys by yourself," Brian CuCullen defended himself.

"When will you bring them to us, so they may begin their training?" Mallory asked.

"Around the beginning of August at the earliest. That should be enough time for you and whomever you've chosen to give them some special attention before start of school. I want some of the summer with them," CuCullen answered.

"Good enough, Brian. I will prepare tutors for them. They have a lot of catching up to do, especially Kieran. As do you, also, Brian. Ten years of inactivity isn't easy to shake off. Once you drop them off, I expect you to report to Avalon for some training," Mallory warned.

"I guess all of us will have to work hard in the coming months," Brian CuCullen said then turned to stare at Liam. "No mentioning of a new school to your brother yet, okay? I want to tell him when the time is right. Understood?"

"I understand, Dad," Liam replied. "Where is this new school?"

"Ahhh, it is some place where only those who belong there can find or even enter. It is a place where only those who are chosen can seek, or know about. It is a very special place," Mallory answered instead of his father.

"Where's that? New Jersey?"

Mallory laughed at this question. Even Brian CuCullen laughed at his son's misguided question. Liam could feel his face turn red with embarrassment. He didn't mean to say something amusing; he was actually being serious. Wasn't New Jersey where his father said he had to go every time he took a trip that he and Kieran couldn't go on? At least that was where his father told him he was going. Now he doubted that was true.

"I can see this one is going to be a delight to oversee and teach," Mallory said with a hint of delight. "He is so much like Siobhan in looks and I am willing to bet in gifts, also. You have two very special sons, Brian. You should be proud of them. You are very lucky man."

"I'm not sure about that, Mallory," Brian CuCullen replied showing his annoyance.

"Sian told me that she could feel him this morning at that lovely park where we had the funeral for Paulette. Yes, she could feel that he has the gift. She was very impressed by the depth of his power, too. He does come from a special bloodline and we know how strong a bloodline that is."

Liam listened closely willing himself not to ask questions because he knew his father would end the conversation. He did feel something strange back at Two Lights State Park; he felt something odd when the woman... when the woman stopped the wind. Yes, she stopped the wind. It didn't stop on its own, but she stopped it. Unable to explain it rationally, even to himself, he still knew that she stopped the wind.

"Is she sure?" his father asked Mallory.

"Positive."

"Who will tutor him then?" asked Brian with some concern in his voice.

"I believe she may do it herself. She told me that she has a feeling about him, that he will need special tutoring and help in fulfilling his full potential and that potential may truly be exceptional," Mallory said.

"Oh," mumbled Brian CuCullen.

Liam couldn't control himself any further. He needed to ask because he needed to make sure he was right.

"She stopped the wind from blowing this morning, didn't she? She controlled the wind back there, didn't she?" Liam quickly blurted out not wanting to leave the kitchen.

Mallory simply smiled at this observation by Liam. But his father didn't find it a smiling matter, as he was frowning. Liam had seen that frown on his father's face before, too. It appeared every time either he or Kieran did something that made them stand out in a crowd, made them seem above average. Their father never seemed to want them to stand out in a crowd or to be too far above average. He often felt as if his father wanted him to hide.

"And he is smart, too. I'm not sure about Kieran, though I have a feeling about him, but my feelings have been known to be wrong over the years. This one, though, I think will be a very special student. He is smart and he has gifts," Mallory stated with a smile on his lips.

"Too smart for his own good," Brian CuCullen said in a voice that sounded sad.

"Being smart is good. Smart people can end up doing great things," Liam stated defiantly.

He had been told too many times by his father that he was too smart for his own good. Liam knew this was meant as a criticism, but he chose to take it as a compliment, a badge of honor to live up to, like being a jock was something Kieran wanted to live up to. He wanted to be too smart for his own good. Kieran was the jock, but he had curiosity.

"You are right about that, Liam CuCullen," Mallory agreed. "The Society has need for smart, above average people like you. We need all the gifted students we can get so that we can fulfill our mission."

"What mission, what society?" asked Liam.

"I will tell you its name since you asked and you are so bright, I know how torturous it is for bright boys and girls to wait for answers, but that is all I will tell you for now. You cannot tell anyone the name of this society, not even your brother who you admire so much. The name must be kept secret for now. We are part of a society called the Bene Lumen. How best do I describe the Bene Lumen? Ahh, yes, we stand in the way of the darkness, which wishes to spread throughout the world. Your father is one of us and you and your brother were born one of us, even though for the longest time your father didn't want you to be part of it."

"But..."

"But no more questions," Mallory said in a tone that made Liam not want to ask any more questions.

"You must be hungry. Go get something to eat in the dining room," his father ordered then ushered him out of the kitchen and into the dining room of their small house. Everyone had moved from the dining room to the even smaller living room, except for Graham Stonefeather. He stood by the table staring at the food looking as if he couldn't make up his mind.

"Your father did this on purpose, I know he did," he said as Liam walked over to the plates and picked one up.

"Huh?" he mumbled.

"He baked a honey ham, as well as made a thick, cheesy lasagna. He knows I love them both and can't resist them. But he also knows that I have to watch my weight, so I can only have one of them. He's got an evil side, your dad does. He must be a real pain in the behind to deal with," he said with plenty of good-natured humor in his voice.

"Yeah, I guess so," Liam said with his mind still preoccupied by everything he had just heard. But most of all he wrapped his mind around the fact that the beautiful woman had made the wind stop and what was the society of Bene Lumen.

"Okay, I'm going with the lasagna. You can't get good lasagna where we are," he stated.

"Where's that?" Liam asked quickly as his mind snapped away from his thoughts.

"So you want to know where I come from," Stonefeather said. "Well, it's a place where you can only find if you're supposed to be there."

"The old guy said something like that in the kitchen," Liam blurted out.

"The old guy? Oh, Mallory, or I should say Mr. Fergus to you. Well, that's the best answer you'll get from any of us," Stonefeather said with a smile.

"Why?"

"Because it's the truth. Now do you want a piece of lasagna or the ham? I recommend the ham, so I can pick a piece or two of it off your plate?"

"I'll have the ham," Liam answered.

"Good answer. You may not believe this, but you just made a good friend," Stonefeather said as he piled five slices of ham onto Liam's extended plate.

"Thank you," Liam said automatically.

"And polite. We should be very good friends when you get to school. Now how about some potato salad," he said as he piled a large mound of potato salad onto his plate. "And take two forks— one for you, and one for me for when I steal some of your ham and potato salad. You see I'm looking out for my weight and I find it better for my weight to steal food off of others plates than to pile it up on my own plate."

"Why?" Liam asked.

"I feel less guilty."

"Why?"

"Sometimes the correct answer to a question is not why but why not," he said with a smile then took one of the forks off of Liam's plate and sampled a piece of ham. "Good ham."

CHAPTER 2

"I am not yelling at you. You're the one yelling at me and you don't even know it, so don't try and spin it that I'm yelling at you," screamed Kieran from behind his closed bedroom door.

The summer had passed quickly away and mostly without problems, but it was now nearing August and it was time to break the news to his oldest son that he would be attending a new school, especially since Kieran was now excited about upcoming two-a-day football practices. He had spent most of the summer hanging with his friends and girlfriend, who he had to now break up with, as well as working hard getting into shape for these football practices. This was going to be the year he won all the awards and set all the records. By the end of this coming football season, he was going to own every running and touchdown record for a single season in the state of Maine. Brian knew he had to end that dream for him now and forever. Life had something different to offer Liam and Kieran than sports records, something more important. But he knew his son would take some time to recognize that.

As for Liam the summer passed a little slower than for his father and brother since all he could think about was how that raven haired woman had stopped the wind from blowing and how he had actually felt it; he had felt her inside of himself, at least that's what he thought that tingling energy was. Liam chalked up that slight feeling of darkness in the tingling energy as just a byproduct of someone sharing energy with him. Each day he thought of that funeral for Paulette Goode with a mix of curiosity and apprehension. He just couldn't get that day out of his mind because he knew that his life had somehow drastically changed that day, even though he wasn't sure how and how much. Whenever he had the chance he stowed away in his room and went on the Internet to search everything he could about magic and people who could really perform it, as well as searched for information about the Bene Lumen.

Unfortunately, several months of research on the Internet and the library had left him with the feeling that he must have imagined what she did; that the wind had stopped on its own, and that he misunderstood what his father and Mr. Fergus talked about in the kitchen. Most of the websites involving magic either just sounded phony or were about black magic, or the black arts, and made him sort of uncomfortable reading them. These websites almost scared him because they offered ideas and concepts that went against what Liam knew was true and right, so he never lingered too long in them. As for the society called the Bene Lumen, for the first time in his life the Internet had absolutely failed him, as it showed nothing on the organization, not even rumors or innuendos about it.

Liam found this extremely frustrating since the Internet had all known knowledge, in his opinion, stored on it as long as you knew how and where to look for it. Yet, he didn't mention his frustration to either his father or brother or ask any questions about the Bene Lumen. He wasn't even sure if his father would answer any questions, anyhow, about the Bene Lumen or anything else, so he kept his inquiries to himself. It didn't help that Brian CuCullen had been in a foul mood for most of the summer, and acted now like he regretted that the summer had ever started or had to end.

For his part Brian decided at the end of July, after he had sold his fishing boat, traps and everything else he used in his trade, that it was finally time to let Kieran know that he was not going back to Cape Elizabeth High School, but that he was now enrolled in a new school along with Liam. He had been apprehensive to do this because of how much Kieran enjoyed his time at the high school and how many friends he had in Cape Elizabeth, but they had to get their passports renewed and a few other things to do so he had run out of time. He dreaded this moment because he knew it was going to strain an already strained relationship between him and Kieran. Last year Kieran had become a bit of a local legend with a two hundred yard rushing game and leading his team to playoff victories. People would stop him in local stores and talk to him about Kieran and his athletic feats. They would tell him how excited they were to see what he would do this year. It was now time, though, to pack up the house and their belongings.

For the past few months a strange looking man and woman named Ned and Noreen lived in Paulette Goode's old house. Liam saw the man and woman occasionally, as they would come by the dock periodically to have discussions with his father as he worked on his boat. The man was extremely tall, almost seven feet tall, and looked to be all muscle with a large baldhead. He spoke with a strange accent, which Liam couldn't place, though he sure he wasn't from the U.S. The woman was small, barely over five feet, and delicate looking, as if a stiff wind could knock her over. Her accent sounded as if she came from the South.

Everyone in the town seemed to be slightly afraid of the odd looking pair who mainly kept to themselves. Liam couldn't blame people for their reaction, either. Every time he saw them coming to see his dad for whatever reasons they had, he kind of got a shiver of fear down his spine. It wasn't so much that they were mean or rude because they were always polite and seemed gentle up close, but they were such a strange looking pair that they made you feel a little worried about their intentions. The man never seemed to look anyone in the eyes and it wasn't just because of his height. He was always searching the sky and the area around him with his eyes, as if he was expecting someone to arrive at any moment. And the woman appeared to be saying prayers or chanting or something like that under her breath, when she wasn't talking. But now their father would be moving back to Paulette's house soon and the strange looking couple would be gone.

"Get down here right now, young man, or I will come upstairs and bring you down here even if you don't want to come," screamed Brian CuCullen to his son.

Having his son locking himself in his room was the end result of finally telling Kieran that he was going to a school in Scotland with his brother. There was an eruption of anger and self-pity by Kieran that his father had hoped not to see or has to deal with, but lately Kieran appeared to enjoy disappointing his father's wishes. It seemed that once he turned twelve years of age Kieran decided that it was his duty to disagree with his father at every turn and to find him inadequate in comparison to his dead mother. Brian CuCullen decided to allow Kieran his rebellion in the hopes that it would eventually burn itself out and go away, but it never did. He and Kieran had become adversaries more than father and son.

"No," was the answer.

"Kieran Fergus CuCullen get down here right this minute before I go up there and drag you down the stairs and force you to listen to me," he yelled in his strongest, loudest voice. For the first time Liam realized that Kieran's middle name must come from the old man he met.

"Do it now," he screamed in a terrifying voice.

They had never really heard their father yell this loudly or sound this angry before this moment. He had always tried to sound calm when dealing with his sons, even when punishing them. It was as if he was afraid to completely lose his temper with his sons and now Liam knew why. Their father sounded and looked very frightening at the moment, like a man who could rip the house apart by his hand leaving nothing more than rubble in his wake. From the living room Liam could hear Kieran unlock his bedroom door and start to walk to the stairs. When he got to the bottom of the stairs, he stopped and stared defiantly at his father. Brian CuCullen stared back at him with equal defiance.

"Get in this living room right now," his father said in a cold, emotionless voice.

Kieran slowly walked into the living room showing his father as much defiance as he could. Liam noticed that his brother looked almost as angry as their father. Going over to their father's favorite chair he plopped himself down. Their father came into the room and sighed heavily when he saw his son sitting in his chair. He saw this act of defiance for what it was a statement that Kieran was Brian's equal and didn't have to listen to him. Even though he could almost hear in his head Siobhan's voice as clearly as when she was alive telling him not to fight every battle but to pick his battles, Brian CuCullen was not going to let this stand. It was in his nature to fight every battle, even battles best left alone.

"Get out of my chair, Kieran," he said in a quiet, cold voice that scared Liam.

"Your name isn't on the chair, is it?" Kieran replied just as coldly.

Without any more words exchanged between them, Brian CuCullen walked over to the chair and easily lifted his nearly two hundred pounds of muscle, six foot one inch son out of the chair and tossed him effortlessly across the room and onto the sofa. Kieran bounced off the sofa and landed hard onto the floor. As quick as a cat he got off the floor and stood in the middle of the room looking as if he was considering picking his father up and tossing him onto the sofa in retaliation. He was so angry that he didn't even take the time to think about how easily his father had done what he did to him. Son and father stood there glowering at each other, while Liam held his breath and hoped for the best possible outcome.

"Don't even think about it, or I won't be so gentle with you next time," his father told him as a warning.

After a few moments considering his alternatives Kieran sat down on the sofa beside his brother. He slumped back in the sofa and glowered at his father. Liam didn't know whether to laugh or cry by what he had just seen. He decided that it was best for him to do neither, but instead to just sit quietly and let them fight it out. Right now it would be dangerous to get in between the two of them, he realized.

"You are going to this new school and there is nothing more to be said about it. We leave in three days for Scotland to drop the two of you off," Brian CuCullen told his son.

"But... But I'm the star of the football team. What will the team do without me? I'm their best player. Does this place even have a football team?" Kieran asked.

"No, they don't, Kieran. They do, though, have other kinds of challenges waiting for you there at this school. Son, I know how upsetting this is..."

"No, you don't," interrupted Kieran. "You don't know how I feel or what I'm thinking. You don't know anything at all about me."

"Kieran, you will understand this better when you get to the school, but you are not meant to play football, or live a boring normal life. You are meant to do something very important in your life. And this school will prepare you for that."

"Something special, like being someone who catches lobsters for a living," he retorted sarcastically.

"I will no longer be doing that after I drop you off. I will be going back to my old job," their father said then took another heavy sigh. "When your mother died I decided to leave my old life behind me, to take up a normal life. I thought she would want me to raise you two ignorant of what we did and who we were. She and I had talked about allowing you two to have a simple normal life. But life, or God, doesn't always let you to live out your plans, especially when life has its own plans for you."

"What about Karen? Do you expect me to break up with her just because you've enrolled me in a new school and ruined my life?" asked Kieran.

"I'm sorry about that. You'll be home during the summer. Maybe you and her..."

"She won't want a long distance boyfriend. No one wants that. Don't you understand anything? If I'm gone from Cape Elizabeth, so is our relationship," bemoaned Kieran.

"What did you and Ma do for a living that you didn't want us to know anything about it?" asked Liam trying to change the subject.

"When you get to this school, you'll find out about that and much more," he answered.

"But I'm the starting running back. I have a chance to be All-State this year and maybe after another good year next year I can get a scholarship to Notre Dame or USC. I don't want to go to this place in Scotland. I mean... they play soccer or whatever they play there, not football. I'm a football player, real football," his son pleaded.

"Kieran, you have no choice in the matter. It is my choice not yours and you have to go along with it until you are an adult and can make decisions for yourself," Brian CuCullen told his son.

"Ma would have given me a choice on something this important to me," he said then got up and bolted up the stairs to his room. He slammed the door shut and turned on his stereo playing his father's old Clash album, which he recently bought on CD, deciding to play the song *London Calling* louder than he was allowed to play his CD player. Brian CuCullen looked at his son Liam, who sat quietly and without an expression on his face.

"I've really mucked it up with your brother, haven't I?" Brian asked his son in a voice that sounded as if he wanted to take a long nap.

"Yeah, Dad, you have," Liam answered honestly as he always did. "Kieran is like you. He doesn't really like to be told what to do with his life. He's stubborn."

"Well, he better get used to people telling him what to do because they will be telling him what to do at Samhain," said Brian pronouncing Samhain as 'Sah-win.' "He won't get away with that kind of behavior there."

"Sah-what? What are you talking about?"

"That's the name of your new school. It's what the old Celtic Druids called Halloween, but it's more than that really. Samhain is where we are headed. It's run by the Bene Lumen, you know, the society Mallory Fergus told you about."

"Sounds like a funny name for a school," Liam said.

"Now do me a favor and go upstairs and start to pack up your room up because if I have to do it, I will throw everything you own away. Okay?"

"Sure, Dad. Oh, Dad, can I bring my Gameboy and games to this

Sahwee or whatever it's called?" he asked his father.

"It's Samhain, pronounced Sah-win not Samwee, even if it looks like it should sound like Samwee. Believe me son when I tell you that Samhain will change your life forever in so many ways and on so many levels. It will be a name you will remember for the rest of your life. Now as for you bringing a Gameboy and some of your games, I don't suppose that having something familiar with you will hurt you too much. It might even make you feel more at home. I know that it took me awhile for Samhain to feel like home. Yes, you can bring your Gameboy and games."

"Cool," he said and got up off the sofa and ran up the stairs to his room so that he could pack his room up and his bags for his new school.

Brian CuCullen sat down in his chair. His bones felt heavy and tired as if he had been supporting the weight of the world on them. He wasn't sure that he was doing the right or wrong thing with his boys, but he knew that he had no alternative. He couldn't avoid the truth about who they were any longer. Most of all he wasn't too sure about himself, though. So much time had passed since he was part of the Society of Bene Lumen, too many years had passed since then. Ten years had passed. Was going back to the Bene Lumen the right thing for him? Did he still have what it took to be the man he was? He just wasn't sure, but he no longer had the luxury of wondering about that. The Bene Lumen had called him back and he could not refuse them now.

The CuCullen family's itinerary was guided by one simple rule: get to their destination as quickly as possible without much rest and with no sightseeing. The long airplane ride from Boston to Heathrow in London was a quiet one for the whole family. They sat three seats across with Liam in the middle and Kieran and his father on either side of him. Liam played with his Gameboy until he finally fell asleep somewhere over the Atlantic Ocean, while Kieran sat with his Red Sox hat pulled down over his eyes, his new iPod player, an unappreciated gift of reconciliation, blaring music in his ears and pouting the whole trip. He seethed with resentment at having to leave Cape Elizabeth High and not being able to play football blaming his father for everything bad that had happened to him in life. Brian CuCullen attempted to read a book, ignoring his oldest son's extended pout, but the negative energy emanating from Kieran kept making it impossible for him to concentrate on his reading.

This silence between Brian CuCullen and his oldest son continued in the cab ride from Heathrow Airport to Euston Railway Station, a white building that looked as if it had been built with a Lego erector set, where they caught a train to Glasgow. There was no stopover to sightsee the famous sights of London or to stay in a nice hotel so that they could catch up on their sleep and deal with their jet lag. This was going to be a long continuous trip for them, their father told them up front before they left. Whatever sleep they got it would have to be on the plane, or train, or car, depending upon what mode of transportation they were taking at the time.

This was a trip Brian CuCullen never wanted to make with his sons. After Siobhan was murdered doing her duty, he swore that his sons would never have to perform such dangerous duty as their parents, that they would live lives free of certain obligations and certain duties, especially those duties that led to being tossed from the rocks into Casco Bay. But his plans and life's plans, God's plans, were not the same, at least that was what Father Mueller had told him long ago.

"This is kind of cool," Liam mumbled as he stared out the window at the passing terrain which even though it had trees, grass, and hills just like Maine, it was all so foreign to him, so unlike the familiar vistas of Maine.

Brian CuCullen looked over at his youngest son, whom he knew was excited and happy about this trip. Unlike his brother he had never found a clique or a group of friends he wanted to hang with back at Cape Elizabeth. He was a bit of a loner, who preferred being with his dad than with kids his own age. Here he was going to a new school, a school that was wrapped in more than a little mystery, and he found it utterly exciting. How much he was like his mother, he thought then he stared across from himself at Kieran, who still had his Red Sox cap pulled down and now dozed. Kieran was much like him he suddenly realized, as he gazed at his son. When his parents turned him over to Mallory Fergus to take him to Samhain, he didn't say a word for days on end. All he did was pout and brood. Instead of seeing the excitement of something new, enjoying the sense of discovery, he brooded and felt sorry for himself. Kieran was definitely more like him than his mother. Too much so, he thought.

Wasn't he a sullen youth, a bit of a loner, until he finally discovered friends and a started to become more self-confident at Samhain? Josh Morley, Francis Philby, Moira Postlewaite, Vladmir Gregarien, and Siobhan were some of his best friends in the world that he made there. All of them taught him how important friendship was and what he could be if he just let go of his anger and believed in himself. And one of them taught him more than the mysteries of friendship. Siobhan taught him how to love and how to be loved. But they were all dead now, all dead. Yet, Nagura Hideki was still alive, though. Nagura was always a good friend. And now was a teacher at Samhain. It will be good to see him, thought Brian CuCullen, good to talk over old times before I have to leave my sons at Samhain and return to my old duties.

"Dad, will you be able to show us around the school when we get there?" asked Liam breaking his father away from his reverie of things past.

"No, not really. I'll only be able to stay the night then I have to leave to go to somewhere else for a week or two before I go back to Cape Elizabeth and take up my duties," he answered.

"Just one night with us?"

"Actually, the very moment we are on the school grounds you are in the care of the school not me. I will only be a visitor there, which means I'll spend only as much time with you as they allow. And I suspect Mallory will start you off on your education from day one. You two have a lot of catching up to do. I'll probably only see you in the dining hall for dinner and that's all," he explained to Liam.

"That kind of sucks," Liam stated.

"Sounds good to me. I'm starting to like this school a little better now," mumbled Kieran from under the bill of his hat.

These were the first intelligible words he had spoken in almost a day of travel. And they were negative ones towards his father. Brian CuCullen could only hope that his attitude towards him would change with time and experience.

Brian CuCullen decided it was best to pretend that he didn't hear his son's sarcastic comment. Instead of responding and starting yet another argument with Kieran, he patted Liam gently on the head and closed his eyes. He realized that sleep was impossible, too many thoughts swam around aimlessly in his mind and too many fears crept up and down his spine, but he wanted to rest and conserve his energy. The Society had promised a clean and easy journey, but those the society fought liked to make life difficult for members of the Bene Lumen, especially for someone with his reputation. Now that he was back in the game, he was a target.

He thought he had broken off full relationships with the Bene Lumen when Siobhan died. It was a painful break, too. Yes, he did a few odd errands for them now and then, especially when asked by Mallory or Sian as a favor, but he was an outsider when he did these odd jobs. And when he talked to Paulette and advised her, it was like a retired police officer talking to a still active colleague giving them insight and hints from his own experience. He understood what she was going through and could advise her on what to do, but it was all in the past for him until now.

"Dad," Liam piped up once again tore away him away from his thoughts.

"Yes, Liam."

"Where we are going, you know the place you told me the name of..."

"Yes, Liam."

"Well, did Ma go there, also?"

For the first time in days, Kieran moved and raised the bill of his hat because he was interested in what his father had to say about his departed mother. When his mother died he was only six years old and somehow felt it was his father's fault that she died. After the funeral he even went into his father's bedroom late that night and said as much to him, that it was his fault that his ma was dead and it was him who should have died not her. His father didn't argue with him, either. He just gave him a gentle hug and returned him to his bed.

"Yes, she did. It's where I met her, where we fell in love, even where I asked her to marry me," he answered.

"You never talked about this with us before. Why not?" Kieran demanded.

"Because it was your mother's and my history, not yours. She and I talked about telling you two when you were old enough, but once she was gone... once she was gone, they were memories I shared with no one else. And I still don't wish to share those memories with anyone else, so I tell you two this once. Your mother and her cousin Sian, the dark haired woman at Paulette's funeral, were the two most beautiful girls at school when I was there. We started dating in our fourth year and we married right after I graduated. That is all I will tell you. Now go make your own memories," Brian CuCullen said softly, as memories of Siobhan and happier days flooded into his mind.

"But she was our mother, we deserve to know," demanded Kieran in a voice that was verge on yelling.

"Oh, you'll learn about her life at school. You can't help but learn about her once you are at school. The two of them were tops in their class. Sian teaches there. The old man, as you like to call him, Liam, Mallory gave her away at our wedding since her father was deceased. You'll learn plenty about your mother at school," Brian stated calmly.

"Then maybe this place won't be a complete waste of my time after all. I wouldn't mind learning more about Ma since you don't talk about her very often," Kieran commented.

"Let's hope that you aren't a waste of Samhain's time, son," his father added with sarcasm and immediately regretted that he took his son's bait.

"Yeah, sure, like I'm a waste of your time, right," Kieran retorted in a dismissive tone to his father's jibe then pulled his cap bill back down over his eyes and went back into his world of silence. Liam looked over at his father to see his reaction to Kieran. Brian's face was stoic, except for his eyes, which looked sad to them that Liam had seen too often in his father's eyes.

CHAPTER 3

After several hours of traveling on the train from London they finally arrived at Glasgow Central Railway around dusk. Checking out the platform through the window, Brian cursed to himself over the setting of the sun. They would arrive at their destination under the cover of the night, which was not a problem but was an inconvenience because he knew how much Liam hated the dark, feared it even. Ever since his mother died nights were filled with nightmares of abandonment and creatures trying to grab him and take him away. Besides a nightlight Brian CuCullen had given his young son permission to join him regardless of the time of night in his bed to sleep. Liam took advantage of that permission several times a week.

Samhain was best experienced with a clear and open mind and daylight was best for that. Unfortunately, they probably wouldn't have daylight on their side when they got there. After rousing both his sons, who had fallen asleep, they grabbed their bags. Kieran lugged his own three bags, two of them he easily slung over his shoulder and one he carried in his right hand, while Liam carried the smallest of his own bags, as his father effortlessly carried Liam's other two and his own one bag. Through the fairly crowded rail station they finally exited its stony facade and stepped out into an evening, which was cooling down after a warm day.

Stopping on the sidewalk outside of the station Brian CuCullen searched for a familiar face while his two sons scanned the unfamiliar faces and buildings of what little they could see of Glasgow, Scotland. Like London all they would be able to see of this city was a few city blocks, a few sites passing quickly before their eyes as their father sped them along to their final destination. There was no time for even stopping at a local fast food place to get a quick meal that tasted better than the food on the plane or train that they ate.

According to their father it was important, very important that they get to the school as quickly as possible and without getting into any trouble. Neither one of his sons argued with him, but for different reasons. Kieran didn't argue with him because he didn't want to talk to his father, as he was still seething at leaving behind Cape Elizabeth, football, and his new girlfriend. It was all Brian CuCullen's fault in his son's opinion. Liam on the other hand wanted to get to this new school as quickly as possible in order to satisfy his curiosity, which was gnawing away at him.

Finally, seeing what he was searching for Brian lifted the bags he was carrying off the sidewalk and started off in the direction of a strange looking man. Standing in front of a black Mercedes Benz, an older model, a tall, thin, dour faced, silver haired, pale faced stranger looking as bored as if he was staring at laundry being done in a laundry mat stood waiting for them. What made this strange man strange, though, wasn't his appearance, or even how bored he appeared, but the way he dressed. He wore a gray London fog raincoat that was too short for his well over six-foot frame. Under the London fog he wore a pair of striped white and blue pajamas and a pair of galoshes on his feet. It was as if he had just gotten out of bed and didn't have time to change.

"Hey, Ivan," their father greeted the man. "Still like to dress for the occasion I see."

"I find social conventions too boring to observe, CuCullen," this man, Ivan, answered their father in a slow, bored Russian accent. "Anyway, my specialty does not call for much field work such as this."

"I can see that," Brian CuCullen said as he reached Ivan. He put the bags down and shook the man's offered right hand. They grinned at each other as they shook hands.

"Knights offered their sword hands to rivals in order to show that it was empty, hence the handshake," Ivan stated. "You would think we would have grown beyond such a quaint act by now."

"You're lucky my sword hand is empty," Brian CuCullen said with a tone that made Liam believe that his father knew what it was like to hold a sword.

"It won't be for much longer now that you are once again a Tiarnán,"

Ivan stated.

Both Kieran and Liam looked at Ivan with great curiosity when he said the word Tiarnán. Neither one of them knew what the word meant, or had even heard it used before. Kieran decided to ignore it chalking it up to some European thing he didn't understand and didn't want to understand, but Liam suddenly wished he hadn't packed his laptop so securely in his clothes bag. He'd love to connect wirelessly with the Internet and look up the word to see if he could find out the meaning.

"The car is all gassed up with petrol and ready for the trip. You shouldn't have to make any stops from here," Ivan said then took car keys out of his left raincoat pocket and handed them to Brian CuCullen and nodded to a beat up burgundy Mercedes Benz 300 SE.

"Can I drive you home, Ivan?" their father asked the strange man.

"No, I enjoy the opportunity to take a walk among people. It gives me time to think about important matters while getting some fresh air."

"You'd think that thinking wouldn't be an enjoyment for you," their father said to the man.

"Why? Because I have to do thought experiments about what our adversaries are up to? I am Russian, I enjoy thinking horrible thoughts," he said then strolled away not paying any attention to any of the citizens of Glasgow who stared at him.

"He's strange," Liam stated.

"He grows on you once you get to know him," his father replied.

"What does he do?" asked Liam.

"You might say he thinks for a living. His specialty is thought experiments. He imagines what others are up to," Brian CuCullen said, "now let's get in the car.

"I'm hungry," said Kieran in an annoyed voice.

"We have a three hour drive then you can eat. I bet Mallory will have some food waiting for you when we get there. And I bet that he will want to talk to the two of you, also," their father stated in a voice that told them not to complain.

Liam had filled up on nuts and tuna salad sandwiches that his father bought for them on the train. He was too excited to be hungry now, anyway, as they were getting closer and closer to their destination. And he was starting to wonder what was wrong with his brother. Why wasn't he excited, or at least more curious, at how this trip had gone so far? It just seemed like Kieran was determined to act bored by the whole thing in order to annoy their father. But it wasn't working. Their father now seemed too preoccupied to be annoyed.

After their father put all of their bags in the roomy car's trunk, they got into the Mercedes Benz. Liam instinctively got into the passenger seat beside his father while Kieran took over the back seat stretching out and making himself comfortable. Without any further conversation Brian started the car up, pulled boldly into the traffic, and drove off from Glasgow Central Railway Station.

"This is lame," Kieran mumbled from the backseat.

"Why?" asked his father hoping to engage him in a conversation rather than a fight, as they were closer to their destination than their home, he was hoping Kieran would start to change his attitude. There was no going back.

"Because I'm hungry," he answered then turned his head and began to stare out the window.

"Dad," Liam piped up not wanting to give his father a chance to get into a fight with his brother.

"What?" he answered gruffly as if he was starting to get more than a little annoyed by his oldest son's behavior. Yes, he could understand his anger, his brooding, but at some point he had to accept his decision to send him to a new school.

"What's a Tiahhrnon, or whatever it was that guy called you just now?" Liam asked, even though he knew that the chances were that his father wouldn't answer him.

"I am a Tiarnán," he said pronouncing it teer-nawn.

"Okay, I got that much now. But what is that, what does it mean?"

"It is what it is."

"Okay," Liam said trying to think of another way to get information from his father. "Is there more than one Tiarnán?"

"Yes," he answered with a slight smile breaking out on his face. He admired his son's constant curiosity.

"Okay," Liam said again. He knew that his father wasn't going to make this easy for several reasons. Kieran had put him in a bad mood to start with, so getting information about the Bene Lumen and everything to do with them was virtually impossible, and his father never really liked to easily share information in the first place.

"How many of them are there?" he asked.

"Like days of the week, the number of days it took God to create the world, the number of Deadly sins, the number of genesis grounds for great evil, the Wonders of the Ancient World, the Wonders of the Modern World, and the number of dwarfs, there are officially seven of them," he answered.

Liam was surprised that his father gave him a fairly straightforward answer, though one cloaked in a way not to tell him what a Tiarnán was. This meant that his father was either getting in a better mood, or was in such a bad one that he didn't care what he talked about just as long as it wasn't about Kieran. Either way, he wanted to take advantage of his mood to find out more.

"Have there always been seven of them, seven of these Tiarnán?" Liam asked.

"That's an interesting question. No, not initially, there have been times in history when they weren't even known as Tiarnán, yet they still existed in some manner. And they have existed in all cultures, too. But it has become tradition for the Bene Lumen and a necessity that there are seven now, not that I can tell you why. I always felt we needed one or two more. Someone else can explain that to you," he replied.

"Would I know the names of any other Tiarnán? Like are some of them famous?" he asked.

"Yes, you would know a few of the names of past certain Tiarnán."

"Like who?"

"Okay, I'll answer this question. But it is the last one you get until we get to school. Okay?"

"Okay, Dad," answered Liam.

"Thank God," interjected Kieran from the backseat.

"Do you have a problem with me that you want to talk about?" Brian CuCullen asked his oldest son.

"Yeah, sure, I do. All this talk is lame and doesn't make any sense."

"That is because you have a closed mind, Kieran. But that is your problem, not mine."

"Well, it's better than being out of my mind like some people in this car are," Kieran goaded his father sounding if he wanted to start a fight with him. The closer they got to their destination the more he seemed to want to fight with their father. This seemed kind of crazy to Liam because it wasn't like his father was suddenly going to change his mind and return them to Cape Elizabeth, but Kieran was determined to be difficult during this trip. Since his life has been ruined, he was going to ruin everyone's in the family life.

"Dad, Dad, forget about him," Liam interrupted him. "Tell me some of the names of these Tiarnán. You said I know some of the names."

"Okay, I promised to tell you ones that you knew, so let's see who can I chose. I might as well stick with Celtic ones, since I've told you about Celtic mythology and history myself... CuChulainn, Fintain McCoul, King Arthur, Brian Boru, Queen Boudicca, I think that about covers your sphere of knowledge," he stated.

"Fintain McCoul... King Arthur.... Brian Boru. Dad, they are all..."

"This is nuts," Kieran exclaimed from the back. "He's pulling your leg, Midget."

"Are you, Dad?"

"No. I am telling you the truth, Liam. They are all real people not myths or legends, and they were all Tiarnáns, even if they weren't called by that name."

"Bull," declared Kieran who returned to his silence.

"Dad, they are all mythical, I mean, except for Boudicca and maybe Brian Boru, who I think are somewhat historical."

"No, they are not myths; they are all real. Legends and myths have grains of truth, as do some urban legends. Now, no more questions from you, just like you promised me," he said then went as silent as his oldest son.

Liam felt like he wanted to jump up and down in his seat. Stopping the conversation right when they did was almost painful to him. His father just named great mythical warriors. How could they be Tiarnán? Of course, he wasn't allowed to ask now because he promised not to ask. He'd have to wait until they got to Samhain. So was his father some sort of great, mythical warrior? And if he was, was he one, too? He was his father's son, though it was true that Kieran took after their father more than he did.

Yet, his DNA was the same as his father's, or at least he had pieces of his father's DNA floating in his blood. Just like he also had some of his mother's DNA in his blood, too, which he always took as a great comfort because it meant that she was never completely gone. She was still partially inside of him. What was his mother, he asked himself. Was she some sort of mythical warrior, also, he mused? Dad always treated Ma as his equal in all things. Would a great warrior treat a not so great one as his equal?

Suddenly, he wanted to ask his father about his mother, about Samhain being a school for warriors of some sort, about a million different things that entered his mind, but he knew better than to do it now. When his father said no more questions that meant no more questions. If there was one thing about his father that Liam could rely on, it was that when he made up his mind, it took almost an act of God to change it.

Kieran was just like their father, too. They both were stubborn, hardheaded even, which was why they had such a hard time getting along most of the time. Well, that and the fact that Kieran blamed their father for their mother's death. It was childish, but Liam knew that Kieran needed to blame someone. He blamed no one, but he was always different from Kieran.

One hundred and forty-one miles on the road and they arrived at the town of Fort Augustus on Loch Ness. Brian CuCullen sighed deeply as he drove carefully through the once familiar surroundings during a black night. Fort Augustus with its population of six hundred and some odd number of souls was one of the most picturesque and quiet places he had ever visited in his life. Even in the height of tourism season when people came from all over to see if they could spy Nessie swimming in his loch, Brian felt it would be a perfect place to raise children. He and Siobhan often talked about living in Fort Augustus, one of the prettiest and charming either had ever seen, when they both gave up their vocations. Both thought that eventually they would had given enough to the Bene Lumen and would retire in peace to maybe teach at Samhain, but that dream was long dead. She ended up giving her all, and he ended up giving up.

Driving through the town, past the little town pub that still looked to have locals imbibing spirits even at this late hour, passing everyone and everything until he got to a rough, worn dirt road that led them towards the Loch. Once on the dirt road the car responded to the bumpiness of the unpaved and rougher road. Both his sons, who had been sleeping, were startled awake.

"Where are we?" Kieran asked as he adjusted his eyes to the blackness of the night. Like his father his night vision proved to be better and more accurate than people's day vision normally was. He never thought about this, but merely accepted it as a freak of nature that he and his father could see like cats in the dark.

Liam merely stayed quiet since his night vision wasn't that great and the blackness of the night frightened him more than he was willing to admit to. Even now at twelve he still had a small night light on in his room to make sure his bedroom wasn't completely dark at night. And this was the blackest darkness he had ever experienced in his short life. Not even the many stars and a crescent moon above them could lighten this darkness enough to make him feel comfortable.

"We are just outside of Fort Augustus, which is on the famous Loch Ness. In other words we are almost at our destination. Not long before we are at Samhain," Brian said.

"There is a school around here?" Kieran asked in a voice filled with doubt that any school could be in this area.

"Yes, there is," he answered then pulled the car off to the side near a footpath that led to the water.

"Come on, boys, lets get your bags out of the trunk," he said and then opened the car door and went to the back of the car and opened the trunk.

Neither boy moved. They both thought their father had gone a little mad. Maybe Kieran was right maybe Dad was crazy, thought Liam. There was no school around here.

"Come on, boys, we are not quite there yet. We still have a ways to go," Brian CuCullen yelled for his sons.

He stood holding Liam's bags in his hands. His expression was sharp and he looked to be checking out every tree and bush in the area, as if he expected something dangerous to jump out from behind them. Liam and Kieran got out of the car slowly. Immediately, Liam almost tripped over a stray branch, but his brother grabbed him by the arm and led him to his father.

"I'll take care of your brother, Kieran," Brian CuCullen said, "while you get your bags."

Kieran did as he was told then he followed his father as he walked down the footpath to a smallish rowboat that was waiting for them by the shore. The whole time Liam held his father's right elbow, as if he was blind and being led across a street. When they got to the rowboat, Brian dumped his and his son's bags into the smallish boat. Kieran did the same with his own bags.

"Well, get into the boat," he said to them.

"Why?" Kieran asked in surprise.

"So we can get to the school."

Kieran looked out onto the placid waters of the large loch. Other than what appeared to be a smallish island there was nothing out there except water. He shook his head and laughed to himself then looked over at his brother who looked nervously at the water. Liam hated the dark and it didn't help that their mother had drowned, so he wasn't that found of water either. His father always told him that the dark held no secrets, which could not be conquered, but Liam always felt night held too many secrets that he was afraid to know.

"Where is it?" he asked.

"It's where it has always been and will always be," his father answered cryptically.

"Dad, are you sure about this?" tentatively asked Liam.

"Yes, Liam, I am sure. Trust me."

Liam got clumsily into the rowboat and sat down on the middle seat. Kieran, not wanting to be look like a coward compared to his brother, got in and sat in the front. Brian CuCullen gave the rowboat what appeared to be a gentle push and sent it gliding into the water. He gracefully mounted the boat before it got too far away from him. Once in the rowboat he took the oars that lay on the bottom then sat down and began to row in strong even stokes. The rowboat was pushed gracefully by the oars and with some speed moved towards the middle of the lake.

"Dad, this is kind of strange. I'm getting scared," Liam said quietly as he looked about in the dark.

"That's your fear of the dark talking. Don't worry about anything happening to you, I'm here. This is strange right now and it will only get stranger, but you'll love it and I think your fear will be conquered by your curiosity soon," he replied.

"Yeah, I bet," Kieran, blurted out in a tone of complete disdain.

He was starting to believe that his father had gone completely insane, that he lost what was left of his mind. First they had to go leave their school for a school in Scotland, and now they were looking for that school in the middle of an empty lake. He wasn't going to let this go on for long, he decided then he noticed something on the water. It was as if the water was on fire, not a blazing fire, but a smoldering one that caused lots of thick white smoke to form in one spot. The white smoke began to grow larger and larger in volume, too, as if it was starting to reach out for them, as they got closer to it. Instead of rowing away from it, they were headed right for it.

"Dad, what is that?" Kieran asked with his voice finally losing its negative aspects and becoming concerned for what he assumed was his father losing his mind.

"Your school," he answered.

Liam tried to stand up in the boat in order to see what they were talking about as his nervousness about the night lost a battle to his curiosity, but he almost fell into the loch. Kieran grabbed him and settled him back down in his seat. For the second, though, he thought he saw white, billowing smoke drifting on the water.

"Dad, shouldn't we turn away from this before something bad happens to us in that fog?" asked Kieran. "I don't think you'll be able to see anything in it."

"Just trust me and don't worry," Brian answered and kept rowing hard for the white smoke.

It didn't take long, only a few minutes for him to reach the smoke. The rowboat touched the smoke. Once it did this, the smoke appeared to grow even larger and quickly swallowed up the boat. Both the boys jumped out of their skins once this happened. They had never seen smoke act this way before, as if it had a purpose. Both of them thought of covering their mouths so they didn't breathe in the smoke, but when they caught a whiff of it they changed their minds. It smelled of cinnamon, rosemary, thyme, and even a hint of wild flowers.

"What is this?" asked Liam.

"The mist is a kind of a door that we just passed through and this is Samhain, school of ancient knowledge and training ground of warriors and other members of the Bene Lumen," answered his father.

Kieran couldn't speak because he saw a clearing in the smoke and a shoreline. It wasn't the shoreline of the other side of the lake, but the shoreline of a large island that appeared out of thin air. On the shoreline a pyre burned and it looked as if two men were waiting for their boat.

"I don't believe this," Kieran said aloud.

"Open your mind and believe it, Kieran," his father told him with a voice that had more than a little excitement in it.

The rowboat continued to this shore hitting the bottom of the shoreline and stopping. Brian CuCullen dropped the oars and jumped out of the boat then pulled it all the way onto this large, unexpected island. One of the men walked towards them with a torch in his hand. He was wearing a black flowing robe with red trimming that had a gold and red dragon's crest on its right breast. The man was Mallory, who was at Paulette Goode's funeral.

"Glad you could make it, boys," he said in a friendly tone his clipped English accent as crisp as ever. "Welcome to another isle that hides in the mist, though this one is not Avalon. This one is called Samhain."

"What in the fu..." Kieran started to say.

"I know that it is a dramatic way to make entry into your new school but, like Avalon, Samhain exists just beyond the veil of human senses, just beyond life as most people know it. There is no other way here but through the mist," Mallory interrupted him.

"You mean that Avalon really exists and it's like this place," Liam said. All his apprehensions and fears disappeared as his curiosity took command.

"No, actually, Avalon is a larger mist isle with far more interesting architecture than here. Samhain merely has schoolhouses, dormitories and halls, worship areas, playing fields, a small forest, an arboretum and training fields. Everything needed to train the young in their skills to fulfill their vocations," Mallory explained.

"How did we get here, I mean, how is this place here?" Kieran asked.

"The mist you traveled through is the doorway between Samhain and Lock Ness. When you enter the mist you leave behind your dimension and enter this one. Once you are here on Samhain you are hidden behind the veil. No one from the shore, or the water, or above can see us. If a boat was to come towards us right now, we would be able to see it, but it would not be able to see us," Mallory told them in a calm reassuring voice.

"You mean it would pass through us?" Liam asked.

"No, not really. As this hypothetical boat would be about to touch Samhain it would disappear from our view then reappear after it had passed through us. We would lose sight of it once it entered our space then see it on the other side of Samhain after it passed through us. The boater on the other hand would only see water," Mallory continued to explain.

"I... I don't get this," Kieran said.

The second man came walking towards them now. Liam noticed him before Kieran. He was Japanese, about their father's age, and dressed in a samurai garb with a samurai sword tucked firmly in his black clothed belt around his waist. Over a red samurai robe he wore another robe that was the color of summer wheat and had a black and orange crest on its right breast. He gave a friendly wave to their father.

"Hey, Brian, it is good to see you again my friend," he said without the trace of an accent in his voice.

"Hideki, it's been years, too many years," Brian said.

"Yes, eleven of them have passed. I'm sorry I never made it to Siobhan's..."

"Don't worry about it, Hideki, I understand that your time is not your own. You serve the whims of others not your own," Brian interrupted him not wanting to hear the words Siobhan's funeral uttered.

"Master Nagura, why don't you and Mr. CuCullen take the boys' bags to their proper houses then enjoy the rest of the evening catching up on old times. Young Liam will be in Morgana House and the strapping young Kieran will be in CuChulainn House," Mallory told them.

"It will be my pleasure to catch up with an old friend," Brian CuCullen responded.

"Sure. It will give us a chance to talk about things. I am very excited that you have returned to us," Nagura said.

"I hope you have a bottle of honey wine somewhere and some food," he retorted as he grabbed half the bags out of the boat while Nagura grabbed the other bags.

"Of course. You'll be staying in Tamo House for the night with me."

"So you're the head of a house now," their father commented.

"I am teacher and guide of young minds and bodies in search of enlightenment," he said with a broad smile breaking out on his face at the end of his statement.

"I'm impressed. Goodnight boys," Brian said turning to look at his sons. "I'll see you two in the morning in the dining hall for breakfast.

The two men walked away carrying the bags and talking to each other. Both Kieran and Liam were left dumbfounded with part of them wanting to call after their father not to leave them alone and part of them wanting to get back in their rowboat and leave before it was too late. Mallory stood smiling at them.

"I have some food waiting for us in my private study, nothing extravagant just a nice snack. We will be able to talk there without interruptions," he told them. "I..."

"Save your questions for when we eat and talk. Outdoors at night is for discussing the moon and love not school and other boring things," Mallory said then turned and began to stride strongly away.

Both the boys followed closely behind Mallory as he strode up a path made of smooth stones. Each stone was a slightly different shade with some tending towards lighter colors and others blacker. As their feet slapped the slate they heard a barely audible thud sound, but Mallory's feet made a louder, stronger thud sound. The two young boys could barely keep up with the old man as they entered through a large black wrought iron gate that was attached on either by a eight foot high stone wall that seemed to reach a great distance in both directions and encircle what was the school.

Once passed the gate their way was lit by what appeared to be street lamps powered by gas, though Liam wasn't sure gas was keeping the street lamps alight. The school was made up of many two to four story brick buildings all connected by sidewalks and streets. It almost looked like one of those English Public Schools, Liam thought, that he had looked up on the Internet when he was told that they were going to school in Scotland. They were walking on what seemed to be the main street, which led them to a large brick house with black wood shudders and a large oak plaque on the front door that read Headmaster.

"This is my office as well as my abode. I should think after today when you are called to see me here, it will cause you great consternation," Mallory said then opened the door and let them into his office and home.

As they entered the house it appeared to be lit by gaslight, the first area they hit was the front hall. Besides a line of pegs where up to twelve people could hang a robe or a coat and several bookcases of what appeared to be very old books, the hallway had one truly remarkable feature. It was an impressive feature because it was a life sized marble statue of a kind looking man who wore a robe not unlike Mallory's. Looking at the base of the statue both Kieran and Liam read but a single name: Merlin. They looked at each other.

"On the right hand side is my office door," he said and nodded towards a closed wooden door, "and on the left is my downstairs study where we will find the food."

He entered the study and they followed him. It was a large room filled with bookcase after bookcase of ancient looking books. Towards the back right wall there was a large oak desk with two comfortable, padded wooden chairs in front of it. On the desk sat a tray of sandwiches and small cakes, as well a decanter of an amber colored liquid and three long stemmed glasses. With his right hand Mallory ushered them along to the chairs where they sat down. He looked at the plate of six sandwiches with great consternation as he sat down behind the desk.

"Excellent roast beef, very rare with some of its juices intact just like I like it, and hot spicy mustard on the sarnies, or sandwiches to you boys. This is one of my favorite nighttime snacks," he said then picked one up and took a generous bite.

"Try one," he said in a muffled voice as he chewed his sandwich.

Kieran picked up a sandwich and took a bite equal to Mallory's while Liam took a much smaller bite from his. He was feeling a little unsteady and unsure of himself, almost as if he was afraid he was imagining the whole evening. Mallory poured each of them a glass of the amber liquid.

"This is pomegranate wine. Though you are too young to drink in your world, here you are allowed pomegranate wine. It has many holistic qualities to it that the body enjoys, as well as a very low alcohol content. Now honey wine is much, much stronger and only those in sixth term are allowed to drink a glass or to on special occasions," he said and took a sip of the wine.

Kieran took a long sip drinking half his glass of wine. It was as if he was taking the opportunity of letting the wine soothe his nerves. Liam merely took a small sip. Like the food he wasn't sure if he wanted it or not because his world was so upside down at the moment.

"Now while you eat I will do the talking," Mallory said then took another generous bite of his sandwich. After a few quick chews he swallowed the sandwich then washed the remains of his bite down with another sip of wine.

"I expect you both are a little overwhelmed right now, so I won't expect you to be able to answer anything I tell you on a quiz tomorrow," he said with a smile that seemed to imply he was amused even if they weren't. "The Society of Bene Lumen was started by Merlin over 1800 hundred years ago during a time when druids still lived out in the open and evil didn't bother to hide in the shadows. You see he realized back then that evil succeeds because most people do not know how to combat it properly, and some don't even recognize it. After training Arthur to see him defeated by evil, he knew that one enlightened and highly trained soul was not enough to change the world and defeat the evil that made this world its home. So being a highly skilled Druid priest and Triune Conjurer, he started the Bene Lumen."

"Triune Conjurer?" asked Liam, as he took another small bite. His appetite was slowly returning.

"Yes, a Triune Conjurer. You see there are conjurers, they use nature and the powers of nature to perform their magic for lack of a better expression; charmers, they uses potions and charms to perform their feats; and casters, they use words to perform curses and enchantments. But only a Triune Conjurer can perform all three aspects of a conjurer, a charmer and a caster."

Liam and Kieran ate and drank as Mallory explained Merlin to them. For Kieran this was like some dream that he was having and enjoying, but for Liam this was a dream come true.

"Now usually women have greater druidical powers than men, but

Merlin was the exception to that rule. His powers were truly unique. In fact his powers, well, his powers were legendary. He was a truly great conjurer, the greatest in some opinions. And he was much, much more than that. But let me get back on the point I was making to start with. Once he had started the Bene Lumen, a prodigious task to begin with, he then decided that his society needed a school in which to train students so that the Bene Lumen didn't go the way of the druids or Arthur, so he started Samhain. You see it was fortunate he did this, too, because evil often has its own inspired ideas and in this case, its idea was called the Illuminatii. At least, that is what they are called now. They have been known by other names in the distant past, though. You see the Illuminatii is sort of an evil Bene Lumen, a group of human beings and others trying to fulfill the desires of their masters, upper level demons of great power and hate. We have waged war with each other in the shadows, mainly outside of most people's sense of reality in those places where they don't want to look. So when Merlin opened this school some 1800 years ago, he assured that the Illuminatii would always have competition in this world. This war between us has been a constant ever since then. Samhain is part school and part boot camp."

"You mean this school has been open for over 1800 years?" asked Kieran as he reached for a second sandwich.

"Give a decade or two," replied Mallory.

"This is unbelievable," commented Liam.

"Yes, but it is simply true. Now where was I? Oh yes, would you like to know the meaning of our school's name?" he asked.

"Yes," answered Liam excitedly.

"Samhain is the word for November in Irish and Scottish Gaelic. The same word was used for the first month of the ancient Celtic calendar, and in particular the first three nights of the month, which was a festival marking the beginning of the winter season. Elements of the festival are continued in the traditions of All Souls Day and Halloween. In this way the Samhain celebration survived in several guises as a festival dedicated to the dead. In Ireland and Scotland, Feile Na Marbh, or the festival of the dead, took place on Samhain. Samhain Eve, in Irish and Scots Gaelic, Oidhche Shamhna is on the principle festivals of the Celtic calendar, and is thought to fall on October 31st. It represents the final harvest. Samhain, November, was also Merlin's favorite month. Hence, he called this mist isle school Samhain."

"That's amazing," Liam interjected.

"So Merlin created the society and the school to combat evil, but not just garden variety evil, the kind we face every day in many respects, like answering machines and automated tellers, but to fight truly depraved and supernatural evil, such as demons, evil spirits, werecreatures, human who have sold their souls, and the others which you will learn about. You see evil, true supernatural evil does exist and the Bene Lumen has fought for centuries to keep the Illumaniti from getting stronger. If we didn't this world would eventually fall completely to its influence and we can't have that, can we?"

"How do you combat it?" asked Kieran.

"Several ways. We attempt to be the ying to their yang in some respects doing good where we can, but mostly we fight it in combat, kill it, return it to its otherworldly home. In many respects we attempt to keep a balance in this world."

"How?" Kieran asked again.

"With Aongus Cathal and Ardal Cathal; with conjurers and charmers and casters; and with those with other talents that have either been honed here or by us somewhere else. We stand in the way of the Illuminatii. We hold the line against them," Mallory stated.

"Aongus Cathal? Ardal Cathal? What are they?" asked Liam.

"The Ardal Cathal is made up of a group of trained valiant warriors, wonderful warriors. From them come the Fiach, who are hunters of evil, the Niall, who are strong and loyal fighters and bodyguards, and the Eadach, who are warriors who patrol the waters and waterways. Now the Aongus Cathal are the strongest warriors we have. Am Aongus Cathal is born to be the strongest. They are our frontline troops. From them we get our greatest warriors: the Tiarnán. As you can see we have many uses of Celtic words which are particular to our argot. Now how does one describe the Tiarnán? Do either of you like football?" he asked.

"I love football. I was a running back on my high school football team," answered Kieran.

"Oh, no, not American Football, but real football. What is it you call it in North America?" he said to himself more than to them.

"Soccer," offered Liam.

"Yes, soccer. That is an ugly name for a beautiful sport. Well, in football there are the good players and then there are the superstars, those who can almost carry a team on their own. The Tiarnán are the superstars. There are only seven of them at a time for reasons that will be explained by someone else. When one falls in battle or decides to leave the field of battle, an Aongus Cathal, who has trained to temporarily replace them until a new Tiarnán can step in, replaces him or her. But a true Tiarnán is difficult to replace, a true Tiarnán has more than physical skills, though that is great, they have the ability to lead."

"Paulette Goode replaced my dad as a Tiarnán," offered Liam.

"Correct," Mallory said excitedly as if he was very pleased that Liam figured that out on his own. "Paulette was a highly trained and skilled Aongus Cathal of great courage and skill. She replaced your father when he decided to step down and she herself would have been replaced when we had another fully trained, true Tiarnán to replace here. Only an Aongus Cathal can be a Tiarnán but few Aongus Cathal are born to be a Tiarnán. We have been short on Tiarnán lately for reasons that are both sad and complicated. How did you know that your father was a Tiarnán?"

"That guy, Ivan, called him by that title," Kieran stated.

"Well, it was very bright of you, Liam, to put the pieces together," Mallory said looking at Liam with a gentleness that seemed out of place on his gruff face.

"Mr. Mallory..." Liam started to ask.

"The name is Mallory Fergus, Liam, at least that is what I've called myself for many years now. Before that I had another name, which I won't share with you yet. After tonight you will call me Headmaster or sir, unless I give you permission to do otherwise."

"Okay. Mr. Fergus, how does the Bene Lumen, I don't know how to ask this, but how is it that the Bene Lumen are still around after all these years without everyone knowing about them?"

"Through the ministrations and help of those we call Giolla, normal people who support us financially and other ways," he answered.

"Do you have any names that sound normal, I mean that sound like names I'd understand without having to ask what it means?" asked Kieran.

"Well, not really. You see Merlin came up with all the names for us all himself and being a Druid he mainly used Gaelic names. The only reason he didn't use a Gaelic name for the society was he also liked Latin and he was trying to make the society appeal to Christians who he thought as a natural ally in his war."

"Oh," Kieran mumbled then drank the rest of his wine. Mallory drank down his wine then refreshed all three of their glasses.

"So Giolla know about the Bene Lumen, but are not Bene Lumen. Maybe they have had family that was, or somehow interacted with us and offered their fealty. You see from the Vatican to China, from politicians to businessmen, we have people who support us. They provide cover, jobs, money, information, and their power to help us in our mission to fight evil."

"So you aren't just druids here, you're from many different religions and cultures. I mean the guy that was with you was a samurai," said Liam.

"Good observation, Liam. That is Master Nagura and he is head of Tamo House. Tamo House is where many Ardal Cathal are, as well as thinkers and others of different skills. CuChulainn House houses Aongus Cathal and some of the top Ardal Cathal. Morgana House is where potential conjurers, charmers, and casters live. And finally is Sybil House is the home of potential seers and prophets. No, we aren't just druids. We are from many cultures and many religious backgrounds, some ancient and some newer. Though the teachers and students here come from many faiths, we respect each of our beliefs. Yet, we have one thing that bonds us together and that is we all accept and understand that true evil exists and must be fought."

"Oh, wow," said Liam. Kieran remained silent as he sipped his wine. Mallory took this opportunity to take another bite of his sandwich and another drink of his wine.

"As of tomorrow you enter this school officially, a little before term, but officially. Since your father chose to leave you ignorant about us and about yourself, I am providing you both with private tutors for the rest of this month and the rest of this term. Your private tutor will help you catch up. I am also assigning you spiritual council. We call a spiritual advisor a maol. It is a term of respect. You see, boys, you are both important students here because of who your parents are and were. Siobhan Griffin had the bloodline of Merlin flowing through her, which means that you, Liam, probably have the ability to be a triune conjurer just like your mother. You see Triune Conjurers are rare, but they run throughout Merlin's bloodline."

"Wow," was all Liam could utter as he thought of his mother being a triune conjurer and a descendent of Merlin.

"And as for you, Kieran, your father is a Tiarnán, true, but he is not just any Tiarnán. He was one of the best and strongest we had. For ten years he performed brilliantly then, well, then your mother died and he left his duties behind him to raise you boys. Usually with a Tiarnán of his strength and ability some or sometimes all of his or her traits are passed on to the first-born. That is you."

"You mean I may be a Tiarnán like my father is. That is what you are trying to tell me," Kieran said, his voice sounding as if he wasn't sure if he wanted that or not.

"Yes, Kieran, you may be a Tiarnán just like Brian CuCullen, or maybe even greater than him, only time will tell. Unfortunately, you are very behind in your training and studies. You will have to work harder than any student here just to become passable. It is a herculean task standing in front of you, but I think you can do it. Now, let's eat and drink up then have dessert. Then I shall take you to your houses and you'll get a good night sleep. In the morning you will meet your tutors."

CHAPTER 4

Even though Morgana House was pitch black and empty, except for Liam and whoever was the head of house, Liam slept soundly through the night, not even caring that there was not even a hint of a nightlight in the large dorm room. Between traveling all day and the dinner with Headmaster Fergus, jet lag, and excitement had really taken it out of him, leaving him exhausted. When he was awakened at six-thirty in the morning by a loud reverberating gong that rang twice and no more, he felt completely refreshed, although he didn't get as much sleep, as he wanted. He was too excited by all he had learned from Headmaster Fergus to get too much sleep now. His brain was filled with thoughts of a shadow war between good and evil and he was chosen to be on the side of good. It was overwhelming, yet he accepted it because he knew he had been chosen for this honor since birth. He just knew it; he felt it.

Since he came into the dorm room so late when he was brought to his bed by flashlight by Headmaster Fergus, he had no real idea what the area looked like in the light. Suddenly, his curiosity overcame his sense of awe over the idea of being part of this shadow war, so he began to scan the area. Looking about him he saw that he was in a plain dormitory room without much personality and not a single other occupant. No one else was in the room with him, no nightlight could be found, yet for the first time in his life he slept without fear. He assumed that the pomegranate wine had something to do with that, since it didn't bother him or cause worry to sleep in a large room with nineteen similar but empty beds and no nightlight.

He lay there in his bed staring at the large empty room. The walls were white, the beds all the same, large ceiling lamps hung down, and there were no signs of personality, pictures, or posters. This made Liam wonder if they even allowed students to put up pictures or posters in the dorm room. When he didn't get out of bed five minutes after the clanging sound awakened him, a smallish man, no more than five foot three inches tall, in a emerald green robe with a blue and green world crest on his right breast appeared at the foot of his bed. Draped over his left arm was a similar looking robe, though smaller, to the one that he wore. After a moment of just staring at Liam who didn't know he was there and was attempting to fall back asleep, the man cleared his throat rather loudly. Liam sat straight up in his bed with his heart racing.

"I am Diarmund O'CuChulainn, teacher of Druid mysteries and arts, as well as demonology and head of this particular house. Each house has one House Master and one House Mistress. The master is in charge of the boys and the mistress is in charge of the girls. Our House Mistress is Janell Besheba. She has not returned to school as of yet. I believe she is visiting family in Africa. Now I've come to chivvy you out for breakfast. You are Liam CuCullen, I take it," he said in a lilting accent. It was a friendly voice, though Liam thought he detected a bit of aloofness in it.

"Yes, Mr. O'CuChulainn," Liam said.

"You may address me as Master O'CuChulainn, or Tadhag O'CuChulainn, which is an old term which means Scholar O'CuChulainn, or just use plain old sir, if you prefer, but don't call me mister. Mister is reserved for assistants, adjunct faculty, students and those who are not faculty at all but work here in various jobs. You will address all your teachers as Master, Tadhag, Mistress, sir, or ma'am, unless they give you permission to address them otherwise. Formalities are important because they endow order, both physical and mental, and order allows for easier learning. Now I have your new house robe for you. I will provide you with a winter robe later as the weather becomes colder," he said then tossed the robe that was draped over his arm onto Liam's bed.

"Colder? Does it get cold in Scotland, sir?" he asked Master O'CuChulainn.

"Believe me, young man, it gets cold enough in Scotland for my taste, but on Samhain we get more than just cold. We have quite a chilly winter. You see Merlin liked snow for reasons I have never understood since I myself do not enjoy frozen water falling from the sky. So whereas Avalon's

51

weather is either summer, spring, and autumn, we have all seasons and an especially cold and snowy winter."

"I never thought you could actually do that," Liam said to himself.

"Do what?" O'CuChulainn asked.

"Control the weather that precisely, sir. I thought that was impossible. Maybe there will be science, you know satellites, to control weather in the future, but I didn't think it was possible now."

"Well, it takes a truly powerful Triune Conjurer's enchantment to control the weather with that much accuracy. Not many have ever been able to do it precisely or well. Merlin, of course, was an exception to most rules and did it very well. He could make a thunder clap shake the ground and lightning strike an enemy. You see Merlin was a not easy to define individual who seemed to be born for a purpose, which only he and his particular deity understood. Now please get dress in some clothes, put on your new summer robe, and get ready for breakfast. This dormitory room's bathroom is at the end of the room behind that closed door. I will wait for you outside the door."

Diarmund O'CuChulainn turned and left the dormitory room closing the door behind him. Liam grabbed the robe at the foot of his bed then bolted out of his bed. He noticed that his bags were at the foot of his bed pushed slightly underneath it. Grabbing the largest bag, he unzipped it and pulled out a pair of chinos, a summer shirt, a pair of white socks then ran into the bathroom to clean up, as quickly as possible.

The bathroom was vast in size by Liam's standard of bathrooms. Every bed in the dormitory had a corresponding sink, bathroom stall, and shower. There would be no excuses about getting to class late because you had to wait to use the shower. Rushing as quickly as he could Liam accomplished in six minutes what usually took him twenty to do every morning. Pulling on his emerald robe, which fit him perfectly in that its hem stopped at his ankle and the sleeves stopped at his wrist, he ran to the door of the dormitory flung it opened and went out into the hall. House Master O'CuChulainn was waiting patiently in what appeared to be a state of prayer.

"Ready, sir," he said.

"That was quick young man. I like that, Liam. It means you should be able to do everything quickly including learning your lessons and following orders," O'CuChulainn said with a look of amusement on his face.

"Yes, sir. I guess that's true, sir, though I thought it merely meant that I brushed my teeth quickly," Liam answered not knowing what else to say.

They continued to the wooden staircase, which Liam vaguely remembered walking up last night, and walked down into Morgana House's front hall. It was decorated with beautiful statues and paintings extolling nature and the seasons. Master O'CuChulainn nodded to a closed door off to his left when they got to the bottom of the stairs.

"Behind that door is our house's lounge or common room. You will find several chess sets, a conjurer's maze game, tarot cards, backgammon set, Chinese checkers, and several bookcases full of what I believe are informative and entertaining books. It can be used as a place to unwind after a difficult day or to study and do your top school, though the library is a better place for that since it is much quieter," Master O'CuChulainn explained in his lilting accenting.

"Top school, sir?"

"Oh, yes, you're an American, aren't you? You would think your accent would be enough to remind me of that fact. Let's see now, what is the proper phrase for you Americans: homework. Yes, homework. Many students like to do their top school in the common room."

"Oh," sighed Liam then he followed O'CuChulainn out of Morgana House and cobble stone sidewalk outside. It was a beautiful summer's morning, not too hot or too humid, but warm with a slight breeze with the air smelling of freshly cut grass.

"These many red brick buildings, though you will find a couple of white brick buildings including the hospital building, but mainly it is red brick that make up the majority buildings on Samhain. We used to have earth and wood buildings but they were done away with around 1850. It was decided to use red brick then. They are our houses, school rooms, common rooms, library, eating hall, and the rest," explained O'CuChulainn as they walked along the sidewalk. "Architecturally it is a little dull, sort of British Public School, but it is a homely pleasure..."

"I don't think its ugly at all, sir," interrupted Liam defending the look of the school.

"Ha, ha, hee," laughed O'CuChulainn. "Not homely as in ugly but English slang homely, as in pleasant and comfortable. I find Samhain very comfortable and pleasant to live at, especially since druids are no longer welcomed in the world as they once were."

"Sorry, sir," Liam replied.

"No need to apologize, Liam. You are learning about your school and its idiosyncrasies of custom and language, such as every year, except the first year level, one boy and one girl from each house and each year is chosen to become a monitor. These students wear a black beany on their head and are able to give out a certain amount of demerits or credits. Now we are headed for the eating hall where all meals are served. Breakfast is served promptly at seven and will continue to serve until eight. Lunch begins serving at noon and stops at one-thirty, and dinner is served for all at six on the button. If you are not seated at six, you are not allowed to eat."

"Does everyone eat together at the same time in the hall, sir?" asked Liam.

"At dinner, yes, the school eats together. Teachers sit at the three tables near the walls encasing the room and students, by house, sit at the tables in the middle of the room. Altogether there are sometimes over five hundred seated for dinner," answered O'CuChulainn.

"Will there be many there today, sir?" Liam asked another question.

"No, only a few of us. I think we can forego protocol and allow you and your brother to sit at the same table even though you are not in the same house."

"Good," said Liam to himself.

"Now that building," O'CuChulainn said pointing to a rather modest size red brick building that appeared to have everything from books, to games, to candies in its window.

"That is our student store..."

"You mean I need money, sir?" asked Liam.

"No. You purchase items based on how many credits you have earned. A credit is given for either a good deed done out of class, or a good answer given in class, or homework well performed, or a lesson or instruction well followed. They are also given on special occasions for success in a game or a competition. Your head of house will keep a tally of your credits. They receive a notice at day's end from each teacher on credits and demerits. You see along with credits, there are also demerits. Demerits are black marks on your record and if you earn enough of them you have to perform JUG."

"Jug, sir?"

"Yes, JUG: Justice Under God. A Jesuit who taught here many years ago started it. The JUG Master will decide on your punishment. Ahh, we are here at Chang Hall," he said and nodded to a large single story red brick building.

"Chang Hall, sir?"

"Yes, Chang Hall. Like many of the buildings in Samhain they are named after famous Bene Lumen. Chang Tan was a Tiarnán who died over six hundred years ago while battling a truly nasty demon by the name of Choronzon. You see Choronzon was a demon of the abyss who was terrorizing Hong Kong. Though he defeated Chang, he so badly injured Choronzon that he had to return to the abyss to heal and has yet to resurface. Chang is honored for his act of courage and heroism. Sometimes the best we can hope for in our battles is a draw and in that we have a victory of sorts. Chang symbolizes that lesson."

Liam decided to ask no more questions but followed him up the four bricks stairs to Chang Hall. O'CuChulainn opened the door to reveal a large hall filled with tables along three of the walls that sat up to ten and many tables in the middle which at up to twenty. He immediately noticed that his father sat with Master Nagura who wore his yellow colored robe, the woman who was at the funeral who was an emerald colored robe like Liam's, the Native American man he talked to who was a lavender colored robe, a Catholic priest who was in a lavender colored robe, a rough and tough looking man who was in a maroon colored robe, and Mallory, wearing a plain black robe, at what he assumed was the lead table of the dining hall.

At one of the tables in the middle of the eating hall sitting all by himself was Kieran who was in a maroon colored robe. Liam left O'CuChulainn, who was continued on to the lead table, waved shyly at his father, who proudly returned the wave, and joined Kieran at the table. He noticed that the crest on the robe was the same dragon as Mallory's. Kieran had a plate of food in front of him that was piled with two sunny-side up eggs, some fried potatoes with onions, fried tomato slices, several sausages, and two pieces of toast.

"Hey," Liam said to him.

"Hey, midget," Kieran replied then shoveled one of the eggs into his mouth. "This is too weird to believe, isn't it? Tough place to get used to at first, but the wine last night sure helped. I slept like a baby until someone woke me up with a gong. Weird."

"Yeah," Liam responded as he watched a middle aged man with a large paunch around his middle carrying a plate of food just like Kieran's limp towards their table. The man placed the plate in front of Liam and then limped away. On the table in front of the boys was two empty glasses beside a large white ceramic container. Liam reached for one of the glasses and the container. He poured himself what appeared to be a red juice.

"Give it a taste and tell me how it is," Kieran ordered him.

Liam tasted the red juice. It tasted like the pomegranate wine from last night but was sweeter, less tart. He took another drink of it, but this time it was a long one, which emptied half his glass.

"I think its pomegranate juice. It sort of tastes like the wine we had last night, but sweeter and without that warm feeling going all the way down the throat and into the stomach," he told Kieran.

"Pour me some then. I guess I'm thirsty from that wine last night. I think I drank too much of it," Kieran said and continued to eat.

Liam poured his brother some then began to eat his breakfast. He was far hungrier than he expected to be since he had eaten two sandwiches and a honey cake before going to bed last night. Picking up his toast, which was already heavily buttered, he noticed that it was burnt on one side. He stared at it as if there was something wrong with it.

"It's an English thing," his brother commented as he noticed Liam staring at the toast.

"Oh," he said and took a bite. Although he didn't like burnt toast, it was the best piece of toast he had ever tasted. His face must have told that fact to Kieran.

"It's the butter. It's sweet and is like no other butter I've ever tasted. I can't wait to put it on some fresh rolls," he told Liam.

"This place is really strange. I mean it looks kind of normal, as long as you don't look at it too hard then all the strangeness starts to show through," Liam pointed out.

"Yeah, I know what you mean. That guy in the maroon robe over there awakened me this morning. He said that he wasn't the head of the house, but he would act as head until Master Diaghilev came back to Samhain then he tossed me a similar robe and told me to get ready for breakfast because the headmaster will be annoyed if we're late. Who cares what people think?"

"I bet that you'll have to care or you'll get demerits," said Liam.

"Demerits?"

"Yeah, black marks on your record. Get enough of them and you have to perform a kind of punishment called JUG. It was set up by a Jesuit..."

"Well, I don't care. Even Mallory said that the chances of me succeeding here are very low. I'm too far behind the rest of my class. If I play this right, maybe I can get kicked out of school and be back in Cape Elizabeth before the Christmas break. Yeah, I'll miss football this year, but I'll be able to play next year if everything goes the way I think it will,"

Kieran confided in his brother.

"I don't think it's going to be that easy for you."

"Why? Is it because our father is someone important? That doesn't mean anything to me," Kieran stated sounding as if he had half convinced himself that this was true.

"Well, the Headmaster also said you probably had the makings of a Tiarnán. I don't think they'll give up on you that easily, don't you think?"

"What does he know," Kieran mumbled then put a sausage in his mouth and began to chew.

Liam looked over at his father, who was deep in conversation with the dark haired woman and Headmaster Fergus. He had not seen his father look so at ease, or even almost happy, in years. The last time was when he was eight and Kieran was twelve and they had a happy and uneventful Christmas. Both of them got all the toys and games they wanted and their father actually looked happy as if everything was all right in the world.

"I wonder what Dad has to do once he leaves here today," Liam said to Kieran.

"I don't know."

"I bet it's dangerous."

"I guess so, midget," Kieran said in a tone that didn't hide the fact he didn't care.

"Did you know that this place is named after a Tiarnán who died while fighting a demon?"

"No, I didn't and I don't really care to know," Kieran said while he continued to eat his breakfast.

"I wish Dad wasn't a Tiarnán. It's bad enough Ma died, I don't want to lose him."

"Midget, he is who he is and you can't change that. Only he can. Just like you are who you are and I am not staying at this school for long."

"But, Kieran, I don't want to be here at this school without you," admitted Liam.

"Sorry, Midget, but I don't want to stay. I don't belong here and I think they know it. I'm too old to learn this stuff."

Before they could continue to their conversation any further, Mallory stood up from his chair. He was holding what appeared to be a big coffee mug. Taking a sip of his drink he looked over at Kieran and Liam.

"Since we are so informal this morning I thought we could take care of some business quickly then finish up our meals and get to work, as some of us here have a great deal of work to do," he announced.

Everyone at the teachers' table stopped eating, putting down their knives and forks and gave Mallory their full attention. They did this in way that gave the impression they would have given Mallory their attention, even if he didn't ask for it. Kieran and Liam did the same.

"When I say your name please just stand for a moment so that the boys have a face to put the name to," he said to the other teachers. "Well, first off let me introduce you to the most attractive person at this table, Sian Boru."

The beautiful dark haired woman stood up gracefully, looked at the boys with some interest then sat down in her chair. Liam noticed that their father seemed to be interested in her not taking his eyes off of her. Kieran for his part didn't notice because he couldn't take his eyes off of her as well.

"Sian is the deputy headmistress, though she has told me countless times that she would never want to be the headmistress of this school if I retired. Pity for the school, I think. She will be Liam's private tutor," Mallory stated then turned his attention to Liam. "This is a great honor, Liam. Besides being the most beautiful creature at this school as the senior Druid priestess at Samhain and a powerful Triune Conjurer in her own right, she only takes on the best students for private tutoring. Like you, Liam, she has the bloodline of Merlin. There are less and less of you with that bloodline every year."

Liam looked over at Sian Boru. She smiled at him. It was both a friendly smile and a smile that told him she was going to challenge him in many ways. He blushed with his cheeks turning the same color almost as his copper hair.

"Your maol will be Graham Stonefeather, who is a shaman and a spiritual guide of the astral plains. I must admit that the astral plain sours my stomach when I enter it, but it appears to agree with Master Stonefeather," continued Mallory, as Stonefeather sat up and then sat back down laughing as he did. "Next we have Kieran's private tutor, Mr. Donovan Talbot."

The large, almost six-foot five inches, rough looking man with the maroon robe and hair the color of sand stood up. Though his face wasn't unattractive by nature, he made it unattractive with a constant grimace. He glanced at Kieran then sat down looking at the tabletop in front of him.

"Donovan is the lead assistant to Boris Diaghilev who is in charge of the Cathal program and personally trains all Tiarnán candidates. Talbot trains the Ardal Cathal. Mr. Talbot was once an Aongus Cathal, whom many thought had the makings of a true Tiarnán. I myself thought that and I was a

Tiarnán of some reputation for many years, actually, for too many years when I come to think of it. Donovan should be addressed as sir or Mr. since he doesn't teach a class, but only assists in physical training. Beside him is your maol, Father Michael Mueller, who is also head of Sybil House, as well as a learned demonologist and a decent seer, or prophet, if you prefer that term. Father Mueller once warned me not to give my trust to a teacher who later turned out to be a great disappointment. I have taken his council seriously ever since then."

The Catholic priest in the lavender robe stood up looking almost embarrassed at having to stand and speak. He smiled at both the boys and then quickly sat back down.

"Now that you boys know your tutors and maols, I can round things out. Next is Diarmund O'CuChulainn. He is head of Morgana House and is a fine teacher and druid priest of some skill and power. He is also a demon at chess, so if either one of you want a good game, I would ask him. He is also an expert at Conjurer's Maze, which is a game I've never played because of my lack of supernatural gifts and never wanted to play," said Mallory as O'CuChulainn stood and sat back down quickly.

"And finally there is Master Nagura Hideki. He is head of Tamo House, a master samurai of great skill, and an Ardal Cathal. His specialty is as a Fiach, a hunter, though he is also a renowned Niall, warrior. Master Nagura can track just about anyone or anything, so if you need to take a tracking class I would consider him. When it is time for sword lessons, I also recommend you take his class because I have only ever seen one or two who can handle the blade better than him," said Mallory, as Nagura half stood up, gave the boys a wave, then sat back down. "Now that we are all introduced finish up your food and then say goodbye to your father, who will be leaving us very soon, and then you are in the hands of your tutor and advisor."

At the finish of his introductions and announcements, Mallory sat back down and the conversation resumed at the teachers' table. Kieran went about finishing his own breakfast then pouring himself another glass of pomegranate juice. Liam stared at his plate. Though, he was almost too excited to eat, he started to force himself to eat. There was no telling what the rest of the day would be like, or how much energy he would need.

"You boys listen to your teachers. Besides the fact that they know what they are doing trust me when I say that life will go easier here if you listen," Brian CuCullen told his sons as they stood on the shore beside the rowboat he was about to get on.

Liam stared at his feet with tears starting to burn at the corners of his eyes. He didn't want to see his father leave. If he could only stay another day or two, until he was completely adjusted to the school, then he wouldn't mind so much his leaving. Unfortunately, Brian CuCullen told his son he had no choice. He was already scheduled to be somewhere else. Kieran merely looked down at his sneakers as they said their goodbyes, occasionally kicking at the sandy ground.

"Won't people notice you appearing out of nowhere in a rowboat during the day?" asked Liam while looking at the rowboat.

"One minute the water will be empty and the next I'll be rowing through it. If done with style and assurance, no one will notice, or if they do, they will discount it after a moment or two. Cameras won't even pick me up coming out of the mist. It's magic," Brian answered with a smile. "Now I have to go."

"I'll really miss you, Dad," said Liam while Kieran remained silent.

"I'll miss you, too, Liam," he said trying to hold back the emotions he felt. It was not proper for a Tiarnán to cry in public, or so his old trainer taught him.

"Where are you going now, Dad?"

"To Avalon to do some training and get back into fighting shape. Being a Tiarnán isn't easy work and I've lived an easy life these past few years. When I left here at twenty I was a formidable Tiarnán, too, but that was twenty years ago. And the last ten all I've done is boss you two..."

"I know," Kieran interrupted his father finally looking up from staring at the sand.

"And pull lobster traps out of the water. Hard work, but not the kind of work that prepares you to slay demons and other evil creatures," he continued ignoring his oldest son. "I have a lot of catching up and training to do. In some ways for the next month we will be doing the same thing - catching up."

In one swift motion he lifted Liam off the ground and gave him a firm hug. Once in his father's arms Liam hugged him back not wanting to let go since he knew that it was time for his father to leave. Brian CuCullen released his youngest son then offered his oldest one his right hand to shake. Kieran did it grudgingly. He then pushed the rowboat off the shore and got into it and began rowing away.

As the white smoky mist appeared on the water Sian Boru, Graham

Stonefeather, Donovan Talbot, and Father Mueller joined the boys on the shoreline. Stonefeather placed his right hand on Liam's shoulder and gave it a little squeeze. It was his way of telling him that he understood his feelings.

"When I was a boy, my father brought me here. Even though he was a great shaman he was a giolla and not a member of the Society, but he had no problem with me joining. He understood the importance of the Bene Lumen, even if I didn't. I actually considered diving into the water and swimming after him but right before I was about to run into the water, Mallory pointed out to me that the Loch Ness monster is real and that it is actually a water demon, a dragon called a tannin, who the Illuminatii placed here to try and kill some of us when it could. He has become lazy over the years, Nessie, but you never know when he might get riled up again. Nessie is a demon. You can't trust demons."

Liam swallowed hard when he heard that, not that he contemplated swimming after his father, but the thought that an actual dragon, a demon, existed in the water. He heard Kieran chuckle at Stonefeather's story.

"Of course my father didn't tell me that last little part about old Nessie. I was afraid to go near the water for months after that until the Headmaster explained Nessie to me," Stonefeather added.

"Vat est zo funny?" Father Mueller asked him.

"I just think its funny that so many people come here wanting to see Nessie. I wonder if they would if they knew it was a demon," Stonefeather answered.

"People often don't know vat is best for them. They are told that somezing est fun, so they do it vithout much thought. Thoughtful people do not make as many mistakes, or if they do then they at least learn from it," Mueller commented.

"We should begin your training now," Sian Boru said in an elegant Irish accent. "Donovan, take young Kieran wherever you need to and Liam follow me and Master Stonefeather."

With her robe gracefully trailing behind her, Sian walked towards a little forest of trees just outside of the school walls. Stonefeather ambled behind her with Liam trailing behind him. Donovan Talbot and father Mueller stayed on the shore with Kieran.

"We are going to the obstacle course to see what you are made of," Talbot told Liam.

"But before dat I vant to speak to him," Mueller added.

"Go on, Father, talk to him for as long as you need to then he is mine to train."

"It is obvious dat you do not vant to be here. Dat est unfortunate because our verk here est God's verk. In his divine will he has chosen certain people fur certain tasks, yet He has alzo given us free will. Even if you are chosen you still must choose fur yourself. Evil has become more and more powerful as da centuries pass, too powerful. It est only with our vork that a balance remains and ve need balance for humanity to fulfill its destiny. I hope dat you come to see dis since you have great potential," Father Mueller said solemnly. "I vill pray fur you to see dat. Now Donovan vants to put you through the paces and I vould only get in the vay, so I vill be off."

Father Mueller walked away leaving only Donovan and Kieran on the shoreline. Donovan looked him up and down as if he was sizing him up and finding him lacking at the same time. Kieran stared back at him with a look that found Donovan lacking. The larger man finally shook his head as if he asked himself a question and the answer was no.

"Come on, the obstacle course will give me a chance to see if you have any skills or if you are a complete waste of my time," Donovan commanded and marched off towards the schools gate. Apprehensively, Kieran followed him, but as he did he looked over towards the trees where his brother was. As he shuffled his feet behind Donovan he caught a glimpse of Sian Boru, Liam and Graham Stonefeather standing still as statues with their heads rose to the sky.

"At Samhain we mainly teach the druid arts, the preternatural arts found in nature, though we include certain shaman arts, like Maol Stonefeather's, Eastern arts, and certain juju. There are other supernatural arts, but most of them are tied to the dark arts, or they are so similar in their approach to the Druid arts that we feel it is easiest to use only one as the main art. Breathe in the air, allow the sun's rays on your face, for the breeze to cool your skin, for the gifts of nature to caress your body and touch your soul," Sian Boru broke the silence. "Nature is a conjurer's ally. We become one with nature, make peace with it, and it becomes a friend, unlike a necromancer or a mage, users of the black arts, who try to manipulate and control nature. We of the Bene Lumen, we of the blood of Merlin, do not use nature, but we partner with nature. This allows for balance and harmony, which are to be strived for at all times."

She lowered her head and walked over to Liam placing her left hand on his diaphragm to check his breathing. When she did this, he started to breathe faster and faster almost hyperventilating, as he took in too much air.

"Don't have kittens, Liam. I'm only checking your breathing to check how calm you are," she said.

"Sorry, ma'am," he said.

"Don't be sorry, Liam. You don't have to apologize unless you truly did something wrong. And wrong answers are not worth apologies. They are an expected as part of learning and nothing more," she said.

"What a nice day it is. I might just take a nap under a tree," Stonefeather said as he walked away from them and sat under a tree. He knew it was time to give her some alone time with Liam.

"Relax, Liam," she said.

He stood at ease lowering his head to look down at his feet. For reasons he could not easily explain he felt uncomfortable with Sian Boru. She reminded him of the fact that his mother was dead. But he also knew that he had to get beyond that feeling.

"At the funeral I felt your power," she started to explain. "As a matter of fact I borrowed some of your power to help me shift the wind's direction."

"Really," he blurted out excitedly.

"You felt it, didn't you?" she asked him.

"Yes, ma'am, it felt like a tingling electric charge going through my body. I wonder what that was," he told her.

"That were your nascent powers working," she stated.

"Really," he said in awe.

"Yes, really," she said with her dark blue eyes looking admiringly at him. "I knew that power would be there because I knew your mother so well. Your bloodline is very strong, very strong."

"You knew her..."

"Yes, I knew Siobhan Griffin. We were second cousins or some such thing, not really close relatives but we became fast friends when we met here at Samhain. She was a wonderful student here. We both turned out to be triune conjurers. It is unusual to have one, let alone two, triune conjurers in a class. We were inseparable during our time here and afterwards we were always close friends."

"I don't remember my mother, ma'am," Liam admitted. "Kieran remembers her better than me. Sometimes at night I can see her face, I think it's her face, in my dreams, but it is never very clear."

"I'm sorry that you don't remember her because she was an exceptional person, Liam. But we will have more time later to talk about her. Now let me explain a few important things to you. Liam, I do not take many, private tutoring jobs on from year to year. I only do so when it is a potentially powerful student who I believe would benefit from my help, and once I take you on as a private student, you remain my private student until graduation. You are that kind of student."

"Really, ma'am," he said in surprise.

"Yes, really, you are. I have no intentions of filling you in on our school history or what you do or don't know about the Bene Lumen like Mallory expects. I will leave that for others to do. My intention is to bring out your full powers, to make you a triune conjurer like me and like your mother. Do you know what happened to your mother, do you know how she died?"

'Yes, ma'am, My mother fell from some rocky headlands in Two Lights State Park into Casco Bay and died. My father told us it was an accident, though I was too young to understand what that meant," he answered.

"Brian Malloy CuCullen, you are an idiot," she yelled his father's name in a fury, which made Stonefeather open his eyes and look at her. Out of nowhere a cold breeze came up out of nowhere and chilled them to the bone. Stonefeather looked over at Sian Boru with an expression of amazement and amusement. As suddenly as the wind came up, it died back down and so didn't Sian Boru's fury with Brian CuCullen.

"Excuse me," she said. "Strong emotions in a conjurer of some power can sometimes cause an unexpected reaction in nature. I once made it rain when I lost my temper. Your father didn't tell you the truth because he wanted to protect you but what he has ended up doing is slowing your progress."

"What do you mean, ma'am?"

"I am going to tell you the truth about your mother because you need and deserve to know the truth. Siobhan Griffin was murdered by a demon named Baal. It was her mission to stop Baal from bringing a powerful and depraved demon into this world. Since your father and his team were battling another demon somewhere in the Ozarks, she faced him alone. Baal was the one who sent her off the headlands and into the water."

At first the words made no sense to Liam, but then they suddenly struck him with the power of a hard slap to the face. His mother didn't have an accident but was murdered while doing the work of the Bene Lumen. She had been taken from him by a demon not by chance. Sian Boru was right. This was something he needed to know and deserved to know.

"ma'am, can I sit down on the grass because I feel dizzy?" Liam asked.

"Of course," she said and helped him to sit on the grass.

Once he was down on the ground, Stonefeather came over to sit beside him. He placed his left arm around Liam, who wasn't sure if he wanted to cry or to scream in pain. Liam nodded his head, as if to tell Maol Stonefeather that he was okay. Stonefeather took his off of Liam's shoulder and then inhaled and exhaled.

"I tell you this because your father should have told you this long ago. Just as your father should have told you about the Bene Lumen and the gifts you were born with. Your father is a strong, brave man, but when it came to Siobhan he loved her so much he couldn't stand losing her. Her murder made him not want to expose his sons to the work of the Bene Lumen, but that was a silly choice. And now that you know the truth, I think you know why I have decided to take a personal hand in training you."

"So I can kill Baal," Liam whispered.

He felt Stonefeather's grip on his shoulder tightened. Taking his own hands he started grabbing a handful of grass almost ripping it from the earth.

"No, that is not the reason. The actual reason is so that you can protect yourself. By not exposing you to the Bene Lumen Brian wasn't protecting you but endangering you. Those in league with evil know his name and know who his children are. Paulette died keeping a minion of Baal from visiting your family. That is why he finally agreed to come back into the Bene Lumen. Paulette's death awakened him to his obligations, made him see some of the truth, even though he still fights accepting the complete truth."

"Life is difficult, Liam," Stonefeather spoke. "We have many choices to make and your father made a choice based on wanting to protect you. It did not work out, though. You must not blame him for his choices. He blames himself for your mother's death."

"I don't blame my Dad; I blame this Baal, whoever he is. He killed my mother not my Dad," Liam said.

"That is very enlightened of you to able to accept that both mentally and emotionally," Stonefeather commented. "I am afraid your brother would not react the same."

"I know. Kieran blames Dad for everything in his life that he doesn't agree with or like, including being here."

"Will you tell, Kieran, what I have told you here today, Liam?" asked Sian Boru.

"I don't know," was his honest answer.

"I recommend that you don't tell him," Stonefeather stated.

"I agree," Sian added.

"Kieran should know, but I don't think he is ready yet, so I'm not sure what to do."

"Liam, Kieran needs time to mature," Sian told him, "he is still angry over your mother's death. He needs to deal with that."

"Oh, that's not it," Maol Stonefeather interrupted her, "he's a man of action, a warrior, not a shaman. Kieran has the soul of a Tiarnán, just like your dad. He will need to kill Baal and he isn't ready for that yet. Is he, Liam?"

"No, he isn't."

"Tell him when he is ready," Stonefeather, said.

CHAPTER 5

"You call that running fast, Bampot," cried Donovan as he outraced Kieran on the sandy covered track. "You are just not top caliber material. I don't care what Fergus says or feels about you. I see nothing special about you. You shouldn't be in the Aongus Cathal program, or in CuChulainn House, or maybe even in the Ardal Cathal program. I'm not sure that you even belong here at Samhain."

It wasn't that Donovan merely beat Kieran in a footrace, which Kieran couldn't believe since he was the fastest runner in his school at home, but that he beat him by several lengths, and he didn't even appear to be giving it his all. Even with a hot sun beating down on them Talbot had not even broken a sweat. After five full days of criticism and being told that he was slower than expected and weaker than expected, and that he had poor instincts and inadequate agility, Kieran was feeling the overwhelming effects of demoralization. His body felt tired in the morning when he woke up and continued to feel tired all day. And he had another day's worth of torture tomorrow with only Sunday as a day off. At Cape Elizabeth he was considered a great athlete, maybe one of the top high school athletes in the state, but now he was considered slow, weak, and incompetent. It was a lot to get used to for him. His emotions, as well as his mind, had trouble accepting that he was not even average.

"You have grown up allowing your muscles to do just enough as they needed to do in order for you to get by. Most humans use only between twenty to twenty-five percent of their muscles abilities because their bodies are unable to take using anything higher without their muscles and body ripping itself apart. The brain regulates the muscles usage to make sure there is no damage, but we are not normal. An Ardal Cathal can use fifty, even sixty percent of their muscles capabilities without stress on the body, and an Aongus Cathal can use sixty to seventy percent of their muscles capabilities without stress to the body. Do you know that a Tiarnán can use up to ninety percent of their body's muscle capabilities without stress? Your muscles have accepted using twenty percent, which is foolishness. Our physiological systems are such that we even live longer than normal humans. It is your inherent laziness combined with the limitations you have imposed on yourself, which hold you back. Didn't you ever feel that you could run even faster if you wanted?"

"No, not really," said Kieran in a gasping voice.

"Your muscles and you are lazy to the point of making you weak. Your muscles have never truly been pushed to their limit, have never felt what it feels like to work at peak condition with your mind not thinking about obstacles or limitations, but working freely and at their fullest. You have never broken through your muscle's barriers. And worst of all, you also think too highly of yourself, so that you are unable to see that you can break through your muscles barriers," Donovan lectured to him.

"I...uh...uh...I don't think highly," he inhaled some air trying to get as much oxygen to his lungs as he could, "of myself right now."

"Yes, you do. And you don't deserve to think that highly of yourself. Follow me," he said disdainfully then walked towards the obstacle course.

Kieran lifted his head, which he had been trying to place between his knees. His whole body ached from work and creaked from tiredness. At dinner last night he didn't even have the energy to talk to Liam, who rambled on and on about his lessons with Sian Boru. But all he could do was eat his Shepard's pie, drink his pomegranate wine then crawl off to Cuchulainn House and his bed to sleep knowing full well that he'd have to get up at six in the morning for more of Talbot's torture.

Maybe he might have thought of himself as something special just a few days ago, but now he felt as if he was third rate, not even second rate, a has been before he even turned eighteen. Donovan was headed back to the obstacle course that had destroyed his body all day yesterday. At his top speed he could perform this obstacle course in no less than twenty minutes, which made Donovan scowl and shake his head. He told Kieran that an average Aongus Cathal could perform this obstacle course in fourteen minutes flat, an Ardal Cathal in fifteen minutes, and the best do it in ten minutes, someone once even did it under nine minutes, then he proceeded to question why Mallory had enrolled Kieran in the Aongus Cathal program. It must be because of your father, Talbot decided.

Kieran couldn't believe that anyone could do that obstacle course in that amount of time. It was just too formidable, too difficult, even for an Olympic athlete. First you had to run 300 yards then jump over a water pit that was twelve feet in length. Next up he had to pick up a large round stone which weighed somewhere between 250 and 300 pounds, carry it nine feet, not roll it, to a six foot marble stand and place it on top of the stand then return and to that to another stone. After that you had to run at full speed through what appeared to be a jungle gym made of thorn branches where you had to duck, jump, and step aside the branches or had the thorn rip your skin. His arms and face today were covered in bandages as a reminder of just how hard it was to get through the jungle gym without a scratch. Next up you had to climb up a slippery rope as fast as you could until you got to the top of a tower that Kieran estimated as four stories high then cross of rope to the other tower than climb down.

Donovan told him to run as fast he could across the rope between the towers, to trust his skills and his balance and to run instead of walking across at such a slow pace, but Kieran was afraid of falling to his death and told him this. Donovan Talbot merely laughed and said that fall wouldn't kill a real Aongus Cathal. Was he that weak, Talbot asked him in a voice filled with scorn? This made Kieran start to believe that Talbot was insane. How could he fall four stories from a rope and not be killed? Even if he had his father's bloodline, he was still human. Maybe everyone on this island was insane, he considered.

After the towers he had to run 400 yards to a pit which was half a football field long where you could only cross by running across pole tops that were no more than six inches wide. If you slipped, you fell hard on either onto one of the poles or in the pit that was laid with sharp stones at the bottom. Once past the pit you had a long run to your final obstacle, a series of hoops set at varying heights, some which were at least eight feet, which you had to dive through, roll and dive through the next hoop until you got to fifteen foot wall that you had to get over without a rope or any other help, then ended with a long mile long sprint around the outside of the course.

On top of all this Kieran had to put up with Donovan yelling at him and using slang, like wean, bampot, nappies, and prat, which he had no idea what they meant. He had thought two a day football practices were difficult, but this was torturous and he was sure he'd never be able to do a single one of these tasks up to the level that Talbot thought they should be performed. Yet, he also was bothered by the fact that his father had performed these tasks once upon a time better than him. His father had not alone performed them, but had done them so well he had become a Tiarnán. Kieran didn't like to think that his father was better at something than him.

"Donovan," the familiar voice and accent of Father Mueller cried out.

Donovan Talbot stopped walking towards the obstacle course and turned to see the pudgy priest walking towards them. He waved at them in a friendly way with his right hand and carried what appeared to be a picnic basket in his left hand. Kieran stopped, also, and again lowered his head between his knees. He had been at this for strenuous, gut churning hours and needed a rest. Father Mueller finally caught up with them.

"Donovan, I vish to talk to Kieran for a little vhile," Mueller said calmly.

"Of course, Father, I'll be glad to let you have him for as long as you need him. It doesn't seem like I am getting through to him," Donovan responded.

"I thought ve could have lunch," Mueller said in his thick German accent to Kieran. "Are you hungry?"

"I'm not sure," Kieran answered honestly.

"Vell, we shall see. Follow me," Mueller told him then started walking towards an area of shade provided by a grouping of trees. Kieran gladly followed him relishing the chance to get away from Talbot.

Father Mueller sat down with his back up against a tree with rough bark. While he unpacked his picnic basket, Kieran dropped down on the grass in front of him in what could be described as a sloppy attempt at the lotus position. Placing down a small cloth, Father Mueller placed two apples, two wrapped sandwiches, two brown bottles of something to drink, and two small sweet cakes down on the cloth.

"Zo I take it dat you are having a difficult time mit Donovan," Mueller gently stated.

"Uh huh," was Kieran answer as he picked up an apple and took a bite. It was sweet, chilled, and juicy. After several hours of running through Talbot's paces he was hungrier than he thought. His stomach began to make a low grumbling noise.

"Ahh, you are hungry after all," Mueller commented sounding pleased with himself.

"I guess so, sir," replied Kieran.

"Call me Vater Michael or just plain Vater, or even maol, if you wish, though I prefer Vater. It reminds me that I am in accord with the Holy See in my duties here."

"Okay, Father."

"Zo, difficult vork, huh, this becoming an Aongus Cathal, becoming a warrior of the Bene Lumen est very hard?" Father Mueller asked taking a bite of his apple.

"I don't think I can handle it, Father. It's too hard for me. I'm not good enough to do this stuff like he wants," admitted Kieran sounding truly depressed.

"Really," Father Mueller said with amusement then handed him one of the wrapped sandwiches. Kieran unwrapped it. It was a roast beef and spicy mustard on freshly made bread. He took a big bite of the sandwich and started chewing it. Father Mueller then handed him one of the brown root beer bottles.

"It is real root beer brewed by our school's brewery from the best and freshest ingredients," Mueller told him.

Kieran twisted off the cap of the bottle and took a long drink of the root beer. It was sweet, cold, and invigorating, nothing like any root beer he had ever drunk in his life. This root beer actually seemed to give him energy, not from too much sugar, but from something natural and good for you.

"Have you ever vorked zo hard before in your whole life?" Father Mueller asked him.

Kieran thought about it. Working out for football, getting in shape, he worked hard, but not that hard, not so hard that he felt empty at the end of the day. He ran and lifted weights. And during two a days and regular football practice he worked hard, but never this hard. He had never done this much work over a five day period, or pushed himself this hard or this far and not accomplished what he wanted to accomplish.

"No, Father."

"Yet, you are able to handle it. Donovan throws everything at you, but you handle it. All dings considered dat est impressive for someone who vas never trained to do dis. I think if one of your teammates vas here, they vould not be able to even stand up right now I think," he pointed out to Kieran.

Kieran thought about it. Could Tommy Foley spend four straight hours getting his hump busted by Talbot, who was worse than any coach he had ever met, or could Clyde Simmons do it? No, they probably couldn't do it. But Kieran had been able to do it so far.

"No, probably not, Father," he answered.

"You are stronger than you realize, Kieran, much stronger than you realize. You are more capable than you know and you must learn to trust that you are more capable than you think," Mueller told him.

"But, Father, I don't think I will ever be able to do as well as Talbot tells me I should be doing," Kieran said honestly.

"Dat est Mr. Talbot, Kieran. He est your tutor."

"Yes, sir. Mr. Talbot," Kieran repeated.

"Mr. Talbot expects much from you because he understands vat it est vat you must do. Shall I tell you something about, Mr. Talbot?" asked Mueller.

Kieran took another bite from his sandwich. It tasted good. His stomach appreciated the fact he was feeding it. He nodded in the affirmative.

"Vell, Donovan Talbot vas a highly thought of Aongus Cathal student. Many thought he vould become a Tiarnán, even he thought dat. Master Diaghilev pushed and pushed him, pushing him to break your vater's own records in the obstacle course..."

"My father has the obstacle course record," Kieran interrupted the priest sounding as if he couldn't believe it.

"Yeah, he set it. I believe the time is 9 minutes und 19 seconds."

"But... but... that is impossible. I'm doing it in 20 minutes and 3 seconds."

"Est your vater so much better than you, Kieran?" asked Father Mueller.

"I... no, he isn't better than me," answered Kieran not wanting to admit to himself or anyone else that his father was better than him at anything.

"No, he est not. Now back to Donovan Talbot. Mr. Talbot never broke your vater's record, but he came close and vas vell respected. Vhen it came time for the Tiarnán test, which est very difficult and dangerous, though, he failed. No one could believe it. He could not believe it. He failed because he did not believe in himself as much as he thought he did. Because of his failure Mr. Talbot thought he vas less of a man than he truly vas. He lost faith in himself and vhen dat happens you are never able to be as goot as you should be. Losing faith in yourself stops you from fulfilling your true potential. Don't let your inability to do as Mr. Talbot says make you lose faith in yourself, Kieran. Trust that you have great potential to fulfill and let things take their course," Mueller told him.

"You know, Father, I'm not sure that you aren't a motivational advisor instead of a spiritual advisor," Kieran said as he started to feel slightly better about himself because of what Father Mueller said.

"Well, Kieran, the spirit occasionally needs to be motivated, as well as moved," he said with a sly smile. "Now let's enjoy our lunch and forget about our troubles."

"Father, can I ask you something?"

"Surely."

"What is a bampot?" he asked wanting to know the meaning of the word that was constantly used to express Mr. Talbot's frustration.

"A bampot," Father Mueller repeated. "I gather you are having trouble with some of the slang you hear coming out of Mr. Talbot's mouth."

"Yes, I am. I won't ask him what it means because... well, just because, but I'd love to know."

"Well, a bampot est a person who is clumsy or an idiot, or a clumsy idiot. I believe it is a Scottish slang. Has Mr. Talbot called you a bampot?"

"No," answered Kieran not wanting Mueller to tell Talbot to take it easy on him.

"Of course he has. He est the type dat would call students dat because he expects zo much from them. You know vhy he calls you dat?"

"Because he has low self-worth," Kieran answered.

"No, because you are probably a bampot on the obstacle course. Twenty minutes, Kieran, Gott in hiemel," he said then started to laugh. For a split second Kieran felt insulted then he realized Mueller was right. He was a bampot on the obstacle course and he joined Father Mueller and laughed. Although he didn't want to be here, he was damned if he remained a bampot in Talbot's opinion.

In the small forest Sian Boru and Liam strolled along with their eyes such allowing nature to guide them, to warn them of problems, to stop them from hurting themselves. She told Liam that by doing this exercise he should be trusting in nature and nature would return that trust. Coming to a stop by the sound of a small pond, she opened her eyes. Liam continued to walk until he was beside her then he stopped and opened his eyes.

"Tell me what you just felt," she ordered.

"I...I...it's almost impossible to describe. I felt as if nature was talking to me but it wasn't in any language I've ever heard, or one that even exists. It's a language without words but with feelings instead. I mean I was going to step in a hole and suddenly I knew not to put my foot down in that spot, so I didn't. Then I felt around in front of me with my left foot and I felt the rabbit hole that I was going to step it. I knew it was there because nature told me," Liam explained.

"Excellent," she said with a smile. "In less than a week you have already met nature and offered it your trust and it has accepted your trust. That is wonderful, Liam. It usually takes weeks for a potential conjurer to get to this point. Nature trusts you."

"Really, ma'am?" he asked.

"Really. I am afraid that I have made your first few weeks of school into a bore for you, though. When classes begin you will already be ahead of your housemates and classmates, and I expect that my tutoring will keep you ahead of them the whole year. But my job is not to make life easy for you, but to get you to fulfill your potential. How did you enjoy this exercise?"

"It was wonderful," said Liam, "I never realized how much nature had to offer. Yes, it is beautiful and scary, but I never realized it offered more."

"Of course you didn't, you lived in the modern world. You lived in a world that believes science's job is to decipher nature, to understand it, and surpass it. Your scientists want to raise themselves above nature. God, or the Gods if you are druid, has given us nature to learn from and to partner with. Scientists do not look to partner with nature, to befriend it."

"What does nature have to teach us besides partnering with it?"

"Liam, nature holds cures to illnesses, solutions to problems such as poverty and good health, but you cannot take those cures and solutions from nature and expect nature to respect you and offer you more. No, you must ask nature for its help and be surprised at what it offers you in return. Besides asking for the wind to stop, I can request a lightning bolt to strike someone or something? Or I can ask a tree or a patch of grass to grab an animal or person for me and hold them? Nature's powers are great."

"Really, you can do that," he said in surprise knowing seeing what a conjurer could do if probably trained and in communion with nature.

"Yes, really. I have asked flood waters to not take a town; I have asked the sky to rain when people needed it; I have asked nature for a cure to insomnia and it has offered me a plant or an herb to take; and I have asked nature to protect someone I loved who was in trouble and it did."

"How did you protect this person?" asked Liam not in a voice that told her he would not be denied.

Thinking of his mother and how she died at the hands of Baal, he

74

wanted to know all the ways to protect those he loved. Sian Boru looked as if she was considering how much he should be told about this person and what she did. It had been many years ago and that someone she loved, and still loves, didn't know just how much she loved him.

"All right I will tell you, but this is a secret between student and teacher and in druid tradition that is a bond not to be taken lightly. A druid priestess and their private students are bonded together, they become family and family never betrays each other. Do you believe that, Liam?"

"Yes, ma'am. I won't tell anyone any secret you share with me," Liam said.

"Good. Werecreatures, such as a werewolf or weredog, can be very dangerous to deal with for conjurer. Since we trust nature and nature trusts us, our instincts tell us that we can deal with these human animals by reaching out to their animal half, their natural half. I have many times asked a wolf for directions when I was lost and it has supplied me with them, but these creatures are abominations of nature, not nature. These creatures are unnatural, not natural. We classify them as abominations. A weretiger, one of the most powerful and dangerous of these werecreatures, attacked this man and I while we were seeking a high priest in India. This weretiger took us by surprise because at the same time we were attacked by the weretiger, we were attacked by a real Bengal tiger."

"Couldn't you communicate with the real tiger and stop it from attacking you?" asked Liam.

"No, unfortunately, I couldn't stop it. It was under the power and influence of this weretiger. The man I loved saw that I was unable to communicate with the tiger so he broke off his battle with the weretiger and tackled the tiger as it leapt for me. Taking advantage of this the weretiger was about to attack the man. I could not let this happen because he saved my life and I loved him. I had to stop the weretiger, even if only for a few seconds to let this man get to his feet. So I reached out with my powers and joined with the tiger part of this half man half tiger. It was a foolish thing to do since such an abomination has a will power that conjurers are unable to influence, yet I did it. It was horrible. I felt its fury, its bloodlust, its hate, and its evil nature. I was almost overwhelmed by these feelings, these truly unnatural feelings. But it stopped its attack because of me... my presence trying to reach out to its animal half caused it pain, made its hatred grow even greater towards me than towards the man. I gave this man just enough time to kill the tiger, an unfortunate act, then he pulled this weretiger off of me right before it ripped open my jugular and drove a blessed saber right through its heart."

"Did the weretiger bite you?" Liam asked.

"Yes, it did," she answered with a smile impressed that Liam thought of the importance of the bite.

"Didn't that make you a weretiger?"

"If treated within three days, a werecreatures bite can be counteracted, though certain effects are left behind. Yes, the bite polluted my blood, but, luckily, the priest we were seeking was a powerful charmer. He was able to brew a potion of herbs and plants to remove the beast's pollution from my blood. The effects that are left behind, though, I have learned to deal with," she told him. "To protect someone I love I am willing to die, Liam. This is something you must know because as one of my special students and son of my dearest friend Siobhan, you are someone I love.

This touched Liam. He never had a woman in his life say that to him. He never had a woman acting as a motherly substitute for his own deceased mother. There was a void of female caring and understanding that he had grown up without. No soft arms cuddled him to sleep when he was upset or rocked him to sleep when he woke up in the middle of the night feeling deserted. His father tried to fill that need, but he never really felt that comfortable with emotions or empathizing. He specialized in fixing booboos and problems and lecturing his sons on how to overcome an obstacle.

Sian Boru, the mighty and aloof druid priestess, loved him, though. She told him so, told him that they were bonded as druid priestess and special student, and as the son of her close friend. He wasn't sure how to react to this, other than to give her a hug. Stepping close to her, Liam put his arms around her waste, drew himself close and hugged her. Sian Boru hesitated for only a moment but then she returned his hug. Strongly and warmly, she returned his hug. They stepped apart.

"Thank you," Liam said softly.

"You're welcome, Liam," she replied. "Now let's return to your trust exercises with nature. You show a true empathy, but that is not enough. You must trust nature enough to join with it. Next week I hope to teach you how to start communicating with nature, so that you can request something and nature will answer you. You see nature is always speaking to us, but few of us can understand its language."

"ma'am, what happens when you force nature to do something it doesn't want to do?" he asked.

Sian Boru looked into the eyes of Liam for a moment. He thought she was searching for something in his eyes, a clue to his thoughts or maybe insight into his soul then suddenly she patted him gently on his left cheek.

"Liam, if one of us decided to force nature, to manipulate it, then we would be opening ourselves to true evil. We possess the power to force nature to bend to our ways, Liam, but if we chose to do that, if we chose to use those powers wrongly, then we cease becoming nature's partner. When we cease becoming a partner, we become a master. That is wrong. Only God, or the Gods, depending upon your beliefs, can hold dominion over nature. To attempt to become God leads to evil because God is the supreme power. Liam, you should never want to possess the power of God because we cannot handle that much power. Look at humanity we become corrupt with less power."

"ma'am, have there been Bene Lumen who have become corrupt?" Liam asked.

"I am afraid there have been," she answered.

"But have there been Illuminatii who have turned away from evil?" he asked.

"Liam, none of my special students have ever asked me that question before," she stated then took a moment for some introspection. She thought about the question for a few moments as Liam quietly stared at her. "There was one that we know about, a vampire, but only the Council of Guaire, Mallory, and very few others know all about him. He is unique. He is the exception to the rule."

"I'd like to meet him," Liam said.

"You have a lot to learn before you do that," Sian stated.

From the outside, the building looked as if a giant black marble had been cut into two pieces, and a beautiful lake placed one semi-circle piece and it had a doorway craved into it. On the inside this black marble mausoleum was where the body of Arthur laid. Brian CuCullen stood quietly in front of Arthur's white marble tomb which had but one single Celtic word craved on it: Ualgarg. Ualgarg was a famous and fierce warrior. It was a succinct, though incomplete, description of the man who lay in that tomb. On one side of the tomb in the black mausoleum stood a statue of Merlin, not unlike the one that stood in Mallory's hallway. Like in life Merlin stood beside and watched over his favorite student. On the other side Excalibur stood stuck in a boulder that had been rolled into the tomb. There it was to stay, unused and trapped by the stone, until removed by another

Arthur, another great hero and Tiarnán.

Standing at Arthur's tomb, his Druid Dolmen, in prayer was a pilgrimage all Tiarnán, Aongus Cathal, and Ardal Cathal took when they came to Avalon. It was more than a sign of respect it was a request for strength. When he first arrived back on Avalon, Brian CuCullen fought tradition eschewing a trip to the tomb of Arthur. Deep down he felt as if he wasn't worthy of being in Arthur's tomb, in the tomb of a man who had given his life standing up to evil and following the code of the Tiarnán. The code of the Tiarnán was a simple one: Never surrender to evil, never retreat from evil, and never succumb to evil. He had retreated.

The Lady of the Lake Una Boru, the eldest of the six Boru sisters, had convinced him, though, that Arthur deserved his respect more than he deserved to feel self-loathing or self-pity. So Brian CuCullen found himself doing his duty, paying his respect, and standing in front of the Arthur's tomb. He felt a slight shiver go down his spine. Because the mausoleum was made of black marble, it always felt a bit chilly inside of it. Another shiver went down his spine. But this one wasn't because it was cold it was because someone was watching him.

"CuCullen, are you done gathering hay?" asked Master Mifune in his Japanese accent that was now slightly changed by years of living on Avalon.

Master Mifune was a mystical samurai who lived on Avalon as one of its protectors. All who knew him respected his skills and powers. Over thirty years ago he refused an opportunity to become a Tiarnán in order to live on Avalon as a protector. Today his task was to sharpen the skills of Brian CuCullen.

"I am done here, Master Mifune," replied Brian and turned to face the aging, but not old samurai, who dressed in red as a protector of Avalon.

"Good. We may begin our work," he said with his strong lined faced looking Brian up and down then he turned and left the mausoleum with Brian following him.

Out of the mausoleum the sun shone brightly and warmed the earth. Not too far from the black marble Dolmen to a fallen warrior was a clearing by the edge of the lake. In the background Brian CuCullen could see a view of the forests and mountains of the Cumbria area, since Avalon was now located on the waters of Windermere Lake. When Arthur fell Avalon relocated from its original spot near Glastonbury. Mifune pulled his katana, his samurai sword, from its sheath and took a warrior's attitude. He waited for Brian to attack him, as he wanted to find out how much work they needed to do to get him back into form.

Brian CuCullen wore his specially made hybrid sword in its sheath across his back. The sword was forged and designed by Francis Timlin, whose family had made weapons for Tiarnán for eight generations. Its blade was a cross between several different styles and blessed by four maols. The hilt was a lightweight version of a broadsword the blade combined the sharpness, weight and strength of a katana with the metal of Calibur metal. Few knew the secret of Calibur. Of course, few knew that Calibur metal was only found on Avalon, yet most everyone knew the name of one famous sword that was made completely from Calibur: Excalibur.

Instead of immediately taken a warrior's attitude, Brian pulled his sword from its sheath and twirled it about testing its weight and balance in a series of elaborate and showy swordsmanship. Once he was satisfied he stopped these flourishes and took his attitude, which was a unique combination of many fighting styles.

"I see you still are a bit of a showoff," stated Mifune in a voice that let him know that he was not impressed.

"Master Mifune, it is more of a habit than showing off when I wield my blade."

"What is the difference?"

"A habit can be broken, but showing off is a weakness that can be exploited," he answered.

"I hope that is true and it is only a habit then," said Master Mifune.

The two men charged each other and exchanged seven blows and passes then they backed away from each other. Mifune raised his katana almost above his head and charged Cucullen, who took this opportunity not to charge but to do a forward roll in the grass passing just under Mifune's blade and coming up behind him. Once standing he slashed at Mifune who parried his blade without even turning around. Then Mifune turned and took a defensive attitude.

"That was a habit I take it?" he asked derisively as if to tell Brian that he expected that move.

"So I am predictable in my movements and actions to you," Brian said.

"You have fallen back on that which worked for you in the past. You must be constantly evolving as a warrior. You must never be satisfied with your skill."

"Thank you for the lesson," Brian CuCullen said with a hint of anger in each vowel. Even though he was rusty, he hated being lectured by the old samurai. Yes, Mifune was a master swordsman, but he was one also. Or, at least, he used to be one.

"You are welcome, Tiarnán," he said.

"Am I that rusty?" asked Brian.

"Not so much rust, though, you have forgotten that your sword is part of you, an extension of you. It is not merely a weapon to use; it is part of your soul, part of your body. You need to regain respect for your weapon and for yourself."

The words were true. Again the two men clashed with their blades exchanging slashes, blocks, and parries until they once again backed off of each other. Brian CuCullen was breathing heavily, winded from their exchange. Mifune did not seem to be winded or tiring, though. He stood with his katana now resting at his side but slightly away from his body.

"Difficult work?" asked Mifune gruffly.

"Tiring work for someone who hasn't trained in many years like myself," Brian replied.

"I think you have forgotten that surprise is the greatest weapon a great warrior can have. Surprise is the one thing an opponent cannot study or train for," Mifune stated.

With his left hand Mifune quickly grabbed his wakizashi, his small blade, from its place on his belt and threw it gracefully and fluidly at Brian CuCullen. The blade flew quick and true and it was only because of the quick reflexes that CuCullen blocked the wakizashi sending it off towards some trees that were some distance away. Coming up quickly to take advantage of CuCullen being out of position Mifune slashed his katana at Brian, who barely got out of the way of the samurai's blade.

Brian CuCullen's maroon robe now had a long rip in it from Mifune's blade. In a desperate move Brian did a backwards roll then bolted to his feet and coming up in a defensive attitude. Mifune closed in on him and began to strike vigorously at CuCullen, who blocked each and every blow. Brian could tell that each stroke of Mifune's blade was not meant to exercise him but to draw blood. The old master was intent on teaching the Tiarnán a painful lesson.

After one hour and thirty-five minutes of nonstop, arm tiring, graceful blade work, Mifune finally backed off. Brian felt his lungs burning as if he had just run a very long race at top speed and his concentration had been tasked to its limit. It had been a long time since he had exerted himself to this level. Even Mifune appeared to be slightly winded after this difficult exchange.

"You are still a talented opponent, CuCullen, and I believe you will be able to return to form. I am satisfied with your work here today," Mifune stated nodding his head as if he agreed to his own statement.

"Thank you," said Brian trying to take in a breath without seeming to need to do it.

"I would say that three weeks of training under me and you will be able to return to your duties as a Tiarnán, and you may even be a better swordsman then you were before," Mifune stated then elegantly placed his katana back in its sheath and straightened his kimono.

He strode forward his sword hand extended. Brian sheathed his own blade and took his hand and shook it. After the two men stopped shaking hands, Mifune gave Brian a gentle hug.

"After we retrieve my wakizashi, I have some honey wine, freshly made rice, vegetables, and fish waiting for us. We can eat, regain our calm and energy, and talk," Mifune said.

"Sounds tempting."

"You have been here two days, did you think that you could avoid me forever, Tiarnán?" asked Mifune.

"Not avoid you, but to put you off until I was ready to face you. I am aware how unprepared I am to resume my duties. And I know that it is your duty to prepare for the resumption of those duties. My apprehension is based on my inadequacy."

"Good answer and that is a good start for now," he said as the two men walked towards the trees. "In three weeks you will have worked harder than you have been worked in ten years. I will once again make you the best Tiarnán among the seven, one of the most talented Tiarnán of many generations, and then I expect you to remain the best for many, many years, though not as many as Fergus."

"I was never the best Tiarnán," Brian said.

"You were the best in many, many generations, Brian. You were a great warrior; a Ualgarg equal to Takeda Shingen, or even King Arthur. If you had not left your duties, you would have been worthy of a tomb such as the ones built for Arthur or Takeda. Then again there is still time for that. You have many years left in you to prove yourself as great as them."

"Your compliment is unnecessary."

"No," Mifune said, "I tell you the truth. But they would never have deserted their duties like you did, Brian CuCullen. They would never have allowed love to make them weak. Love is best when it makes us stronger. You were selfish, Brian CuCullen, over Siobhan's death. She was loved by many, she made many of us stronger from having known her."

Brian CuCullen didn't say a word in protest because Master Mifune was correct. He had allowed his love for Siobhan to make him weak instead of strong. And now he had to make up for that mistake.

"Love definitely has made you stronger, Master Mifune. Una Boru is almost as beautiful as her younger sister Sian, though not quite," Brian noted letting the master know that he had seen the way he looked at the Lady of the Lake.

Out of the corner of his eye, Brian noticed that Master Mifune's cheeks had slightly blushed. For most people it would have been almost unnoticeable, but a slight blush on the old master was as noticeable as fireworks on a clear night. Mifune's love for the Lady of the Lake was a secret, which everyone knew about. Because of her exalted position, though, she could never take a husband. This meant Mifune was forever an ardent and loyal protector but also an unrequited lover who was forever faithful and loyal. He turned and looked at Cucullen.

"You notice much, maybe too much, my friend. But that is what made you a great Tiarnán. You must find love again. You are too young to be without it. And love can keep you young and strong," he commented.

"I'm not sure about that."

"I am," Mifune said with a bit of humor in his voice.

"How come I have the feeling that you are laughing at me somehow," Brian commented.

"I could have been a Tiarnán. I also notice things that others do not notice."

"Like what?"

"Like there is a woman around who still loves you after all these years, a woman who has never stopped loving you, and a woman that you may still love, if you didn't feel such guilt over your wife's death," he said.

"I don't know whom you are referring to, and I don't want to know," Brian said with his cheeks turning slightly red.

"If you say so, Tiarnán. But I think you know who I am talking about."

They continued walking towards the tree to look for the samurai's smaller blade. Was love still possible, Brian CuCullen asked himself, or did he even want to find out?

CHAPTER 6

The lithe, raven haired and beautiful Nadia Nabakov was the finest Aongus Cathal in Kieran's year. This was a fact that did not surprise anyone who knew her or her family background since she was the daughter of Boris Diaghilev's youngest sister, the daughter of the Tiarnán Ivan Chekov. Even when she was a child Diaghilev saw that she had great potential to be a future Tiarnán, especially since she already had the genes for it, so he personally took over her training and education at the age of five in order to breakdown the mental and physical barriers of her muscles and develop mental strength, pushing her to use a greater and greater percentage of her muscles until she was a top Aongus Cathal. When the imposing Boris Diaghilev showed up to check on Donovan Talbot's training of Kieran, he had his impressive and competitive niece in tow with him. This was not so much to intimidate Kieran, though he knew it might which wasn't a problem in his opinion because working well under pressure was part of being Aongus Cathal, but because she traveled with him all during summer, so that he could keep an eye on her training. Her training never stopped, not even during what was supposed to be her vacation time.

As they approached the training fields, Kieran instantly noticed the young girl. When he left cape Elizabeth he left his girlfriend Karen behind him. She was his first girlfriend and he hated breaking up with her just because his father was sending him to Samhain. Karen was sweet, if not a little too willing to be liked by others, yet he missed her. Seeing Nadia made Kieran unexpectedly feel relieved that he had broken up with his girlfriend and that he was now free and unattached. Not that he wanted to ask her for a date or anything, but being unattached meant he could ask Nadia if he wanted to, or, at least, felt like he could ask her.

She wore the same loose fitting gray workout clothes as he did, and she had her long black hair pulled back to keep out of her face. Even though she walked beside, the imposing, Diaghilev with his salt and pepper colored hair and unmistakable scar that ran from his forehead to his jaw line, which was given to him in a training accident, Kieran found that he only saw her. If Sian Boru captivated him because of her pure and natural beauty, Nadia drew his attention because of her athletic grace and burgeoning attractiveness, which she attempted to hide by not wearing any makeup and by always dressing as if she was ready for training.

"Have you started sword training with him yet?" Boris in a rich Russian accident that was sensuous yet easily understood asked Talbot as he came up on them.

"No, Master Diaghilev, he is not ready yet for the sword," answered Talbot as he came to rigid attention at the presence of Diaghilev. "He is a slow student who hasn't learned how to trust even his most rudimentary skills yet. Being Brian CuCullen's son, we know he has the genes for this, but he doesn't know it yet. He hasn't even begun to push himself past his barriers. I thought it best to keep training him on the obstacle course, since it works his muscles to their peek and increases his skill level."

"I find that it is hardly ever the student's fault but the teacher's when a student is thought to be slow to learn, or to make little real progress," Diaghilev commented putting emphasis on the word teacher as if it was an indictment of Talbot's ability.

Kieran could see the change in Talbot's body language from confident and in control to an insecure man without authority now that Diaghilev had shown up. For the first time in weeks he felt sorry for Donovan Talbot and thought about the story that Father Mueller told him about. Boris brought out all of Talbot's insecurities.

"I am Boris Diaghilev," Diaghilev introduced himself to Kieran. "And this is Nadia Nabakov. She is the top Aongus Cathal in your year and my niece. Please, do not think of her as my niece, but rather as your competition even though you are not much competition for her yet. Nadia's skills are honed beyond anyone in her year. I have personally honed them. You, Kieran, have a some way to go before you are on her level, though you might make it someday considering who your father is."

"Yes, sir," Kieran responded. For the first time since he had been there, he addressed someone as sir without feeling silly about doing it. Calling Boris Diaghilev sir was like calling his football coach 'coach.' It just seemed like the right thing to do.

"Nadia, get two of the training swords and give one to Kieran," Boris said and she ran off towards the training shed to retrieve the swords.

"So, Donovan, what is his best time in the obstacle course?" Boris asked.

"19 minutes and 4 seconds," he answered.

"Well, he has never trained for it I suppose, so it can't be expected for him to be good at it yet," Boris said almost to himself. "It will have to improve by year's end to at least 13 minutes and 30 seconds or he will be placed as an Ardal Cathal for next year, even if his father is Brian CuCullen. I can't have an Aongus Cathal who is that slow, even one with his pedigree. There are standards that must be kept."

"Headmaster Fergus has faith in him, Master. He thinks he is something special and you know how the headmaster can be about a student he believes in. He is a tenacious supporter," said Talbot sounding just a little annoyed.

"And you?" asked Boris.

"My job is to train students not to have faith in them, sir," replied Talbot.

"I see. You are still not the teacher you should be, Donovan, and that is probably my fault. I have been hard on you thinking you could take it and learn from it. It has made you hard but has not made you the best teacher you could be," replied Boris as Nadia came running towards them carrying two wooden training swords.

"Nadia, I want you to run the obstacle course in order to show young Kieran what is possible when you give yourself over to your instincts and break the barriers of your muscles. He has never trained for it and is having problems with it," Boris directed his niece.

Following Nadia over to the obstacle course, Kieran stood on the sidelines and watched as she stretched her muscles and prepared to run the course. He didn't like that idea that he was going to be shown up by a girl, but he had no choice but to watch her. Donovan Talbot walked up beside Kieran. His lips were tightly perched over his teeth in a grimace, as he also watched Nadia ready herself.

"When you are ready, Nadia," Boris stated.

Stopping her stretching routine Nadia nodded her head. Boris Diaghilev took a stopwatch from his left pants pocket and looked down at it.

"Go," he yelled.

She was off. With a speed and lithe beauty that he had never seen before, Nadia took off reaching the water jump in what seemed like mere seconds and hurdling it as if it was nothing more than a puddle. She continued onward only slowing down to pick up the stone and carry it to its pedestal, returned for another stone and did it again. Nadia treated the course that had taken Kieran so much time and struggle with such ease and grace. Next up was the thorny jungle gym, which she easily ran through without even a scratch. She continued on to the slippery rope climbing up slowly but surely until she got to the top of the tower. Now Kieran watched as she ran across the rope to the other tower without hesitation or fear and at a speed he doubted he'd ever attain. It was magnificent to watch.

Boris Diaghilev smiled as he watched his protégée. She had turned out to be everything he knew she would be, a true Aongus Cathal and a potential Tiarnán. All the training and hard work had been worth it, he thought as he watched her gracefully and elegantly execute the course. Down the second tower she climbed and then sprinted as fast as she had in the beginning reaching the pit. Slowing up she got her feet into the right rhythm to cross the pit on the pole tops. Once across she sprinted to the last set of obstacles. Diving through the hoops with ease she passed the last obstacle and continued on to the end of the course and the wall, which she looked to almost run up and over with ease. Kieran heart sank as she finished her mile run and the course.

"Ten minutes and 28 seconds," Boris declared as she crossed the finish line and double backed to join her uncle. "Very good, Nadia. I think you still have another fifteen or so seconds you can take off of it this year before you try and break Brian CuCullen's mark next year."

Kieran was crestfallen. If this display was supposed to encourage him, it had the exact opposite effect. He was now sure that he was incapable of ever doing what she had just done. Standing beside him he could hear Talbot breathing heavy, as if he was trying to control his temper. Boris and Nadia walked over towards them.

"Why don't we introduce young Kieran to the sword to see what his instincts are like," Boris said to Donovan in a disappointed voice then turned his attention to Kieran. "Did you know that a blessed sword is the best weapon against a demon or an evil creature? Guns are useless against them in most cases, but a good blade will send them back to where they belong."

"No, sir, I didn't know that," Kieran answered.

"Well, the sword, the arrow, and the knife are all ancient weapons. When made and blessed properly they are the best tools we have to fight evil. Of course, the right sword is the greatest weapon to have. It is the most important weapon any Cathal carries and you should be introduced to it earlier otherwise you will be too far behind your class to even train with them."

"Yes, sir," Kieran replied.

"Nadia," Boris said handing her one sword and Kieran the other one, "take it easy on him. He is new to all this and we don't want him hurt too badly. Treat him as if he is younger than you."

"Yes, sir," she replied.

She assumed the first attitude of attack, judging your opponent. Raising her wooden sword chest level and slowly circling Kieran she began to judge him, to seize up his skills and potential as an opponent. Kieran was unsure what to do, so he decided to keep his sword in a defensive position in front of him and attempt to keep her in front of him. They began a dance of sorts, a prodding, testing dance.

Nadia jabbed her sword at him a few times to check his reflexes, which were quicker than she expected though not up to Aongus Cathal level. Kieran hoped to stay on the defensive knowing that he didn't have the skills to go on the offensive. He thought of his football coach telling him that when in doubt a good defense will keep you in the game. Even though Kieran played offense in football he understood the need for good defense. This was the time for a good defense.

"Interesting, Donovan, young Kieran knows not to attack her right away. That is very good. He is aggressive, you can see that in his eyes, but he is smart. You can't teach aggressive but you can smart. You can teach tactics and strategy, but not the instinct to attack yet the intelligence to know to wait. Nadia would disarm him in seconds if he did that. This at least shows some good instincts for battle. We can work on improving those instincts and getting him to turn himself over to them," Boris explained to Talbot who didn't say a word.

Noticing that Kieran was paying more attention to what her uncle said than to her, Nadia took the opportunity to attack him. Assuming the third attitude, slashing attack, she moved with great speed at Kieran while her sword seemed to slash at him from every direction all at once. He blocked and parried as best he could, but his inferior knowledge of using the sword left him with bad footwork and in a vulnerable position. Nadia brought her sword hard across the left side of his head just above the year. He stumbled at first, not wanting to fall down, but the world appeared to darken for a split second and when the lights came back on he was sitting on the ground.

"Interesting," Boris commented, "I think he could be a decent swordsman in the end. No knowledge or skill at the moment, but he actually blocked eight of her attempts before she hit him with one. Not bad, not bad at all. I know one or two in her year who couldn't do that."

"Yes, sir," said Talbot.

"Do you need a break to catch your breath, young Kieran?" asked Boris.

"No, sir, I'm fine. I can continue," Kieran answered as he slowly got back up onto his feet.

"Well then, let us continue with this exercise until you no longer wish to continue," Boris Diaghilev ordered and then continued.

For ten more passes and ten more hard hits to the head and torso Nadia attacked Kieran. Each time he stayed on his feet for as long as he could before either dropping down on one knee or onto both knees, but each time he got back up and said he was ready for another pass. Boris Diaghilev watched quietly, slowly becoming impressed with Kieran's determination and ferocity of spirit. Fergus was right; he was special. But Diaghilev didn't want to let him know that just yet. Kieran had far to go first.

"Have you had enough now, Kieran, or do you want to continue?" Boris asked Kieran.

"No, sir. I can still do more, I'm learning a great deal fighting her," Kieran answered.

"You are learning to lose," she stated simply sounding as if she thought Kieran wasn't worth her time, yet she hated to admit that she was impressed with his perseverance.

"Maybe, maybe not, but I say you should take a rest," Boris said then turned to Donovan. "Let us talk."

Boris Diaghilev and Talbot strolled away so that they could speak without being overheard. Kieran dropped down to his knees and began to rub his ribs, shoulder, and head where Nadia hit him. When he brought his right hand down from his head, he noticed that he was bleeding.

"I am sorry that I cut your head with my sword. It was an accident of course. I sometimes get carried away in battle and can't hold back. Boris has told me that I need stronger control," Nadia came up to him and said.

He noticed for the first time that she had a slight Russian accent, not as much as Boris had but it was there in her voice. Spying her from his position in the ground he also noticed that she appeared to be refreshed as if the swordplay between them was merely a warm up.

"No need to be sorry. You were just doing what you have to do in battle," he answered.

"Yes, I know, but it is still unworthy for a superior opponent to torture an inferior one. When you have an inferior opponent you should make a quick clean kill. That is mercy. It made me feel uncomfortable beating you so much here today," she stated.

"You weren't torturing me, you were schooling me. You were doing me a favor and that's all. In some ways you were preparing me to beat your ass, eventually," he corrected her.

"It felt like I was torturing you, which I see no favor in that."

"That's only because I don't know what the hell I'm doing with a sword yet. I know a little more now after fighting you. The next time I might not be as inferior as this time and there will be a time when I won't be inferior at all."

"If you say so," she replied.

"Well, it's true. Once I learn how to use this thing, you won't school me that bad ever again. I don't mind losing just as long as it teaches me something."

"If you say so," she replied again then sat down on the ground in front of him. "Is it true that your father is the Tiarnán Brian CuCullen?"

"Yes," he reluctantly answered. "You've heard of him?"

"Of course I have. He has set most of the school records for Aongus Cathal. Did you know that after the two year training program for Tiarnán, he became a full-fledged Tiarnán at the age of only twenty? I think of him as an example to follow and emulate. You father is an inspiration for me. I want to be a Tiarnán."

"I didn't know any of that stuff about my father."

"He became the Cairbre..."

"The cairbre? What is that?" asked Kieran.

"A leader, the one in charge of an area which has a birthing ground of evil," she answered him in a tone that told him she thought he was a little dense. "He became the Cairbre of the Americas and as Tiarnán was headquartered in Maine, which is one of the seven genesis grounds of great evil, one of the places where demons can more easily enter into our realm."

"Maine is a genesis ground of great evil?" Kieran asked incredulously.

"Of course. Haven't you ever read Stephen King?"

"Yeah, sure, but he is a fiction writer."

"He didn't make it all up," she told him.

"Nadia, come here," Boris called his niece. "We must see the headmaster."

"Yes, sir," she said and got up and joined her uncle.

"Remember what I have told you, Donovan. No one will think badly of you if you stepped down as his private tutor and let me take over," Boris said to Talbot.

Kieran had not enjoyed Donovan Talbot's training methods or him in general, but the fact that Boris Diaghilev wanted him to step down as his tutor, his trainer, annoyed him. It wasn't that Diaghilev thought of Kieran as inferior, he thought of Talbot and him as inferior. All his competitiveness was coming out in him. First he had been schooled by one of the prettiest girls he had ever met and now he was having his trainer taken away because he was so inadequate. Kieran had enough. He was going to improve and improve with Talbot's help.

"I would think badly of him, if he did that, sir," Kieran said as he slowly stood up and looked at Boris Diaghilev.

"You wouldn't, would you," Boris said sounding quite amused by him.

"Yes, I would, sir. He is my private tutor and I don't want another one. Mr. Talbot is doing fine with me and my training," Kieran stated.

Donovan Talbot, who had fought against being made the private tutor of an untrained and uneducated newbie that was behind his class, who was behind every class, now wanted to be his tutor. He would be honored to be his tutor because Kieran showed him loyalty.

"You do not know any better, young Kieran. Another teacher would be better. You don't want him. Do you?" Boris asked.

"Yes, I do, sir. I may not be skilled at what you considered skilled, but I have had sports coaches. My football coach always told me that it was his job to bring out the best in me, and Mr. Talbot is trying to do that. He knows I'm behind everyone but he is pushing me. Look I've already lowered my obstacle course time from over twenty minutes to less than twenty minutes. I never thought I'd be able to do that in just two weeks."

"Well, we have three weeks until school starts," Boris stated. "I will give you until then to bring your time to 18 minutes or I will replace Mr.

Talbot as your tutor. Is that agreed?"

"Yes, sir," replied Kieran.

"And you, Donovan."

"Yes, sir, I will have his time down by the start of the year," said Donovan.

"Good. Let's us go," Boris said to Nadia angrily.

They began to walk away towards the buildings and the school proper. As she walked Nadia Nabakov turned her face just enough to catch a look at Kieran. He wasn't sure if he had seen a smile on her face, but he thought he did. Donovan walked tentatively over to Kieran, who wanted to sit back down on the ground. He fought the urge, though, as Talbot approached him. They had a great deal of work ahead of them.

"Why did you do that? Why did you stand up for me?" Donovan asked him.

"Because I don't like being told what to do, sir," Kieran replied.

"Neither do I. I've been told that is a weakness I have. It looks like a share of weakness with you, Kieran," he said using his name instead of calling him a Bampot or a prat for the first time in a week.

"I want to get my time down, sir," Kieran stated.

"When we are training together call me Talbot, Kieran. I do not like being called Donovan. Boris calls me Donovan," Talbot told him. "I guess we are partners now."

"I guess so, Talbot," Kieran responded.

Talbot and Kieran walked over to the obstacle course. They now had only three weeks to get another minute or so off of his time. It wasn't impossible, but it would be difficult, especially since he now had to learn how to use a sword, too. Kieran considered these as challenges now, instead of unattainable goals. He was determined to put Nadia Nabakov onto the ground just like she had put him there. She had schooled him this time, but eventually he would school her. And it wasn't because she was a girl who admired his father, but because she was the prettiest girl he had ever seen and he wasn't about to let her best him.

"Talbot," he said.

"Yes, Kieran."

"Can you teach me how to use a sword, too, as well as she used one?"

"In time, I will teach you how to wield a blade," he answered with a smile on his face. "In time I will teach you skills which will let you defeat Nadia."

On his third week of training with Sian Boru her other two private students showed up to begin their private lessons. One was a blonde haired beauty just coming into young womanhood whose name was Dani Weiss and the other was a dark copper haired, freckled faced, plane looking girl named Brigid Cochran. Dani was in the same year as Kieran, while Brigid was only a year ahead of Liam. They all wore the same colored emerald green robes signifying Morgana House. Without letting them speak to each other Sian Boru had them all meet by the oldest tree in their small forest. Of course, she didn't tell them which tree that was.

In some ways this was a difficult test for her students. A good experienced conjurer, or a charmer, could tell the age of a tree by sensing the age more than any other trusted and true method. It took a deep faith in your skills and experience. Conjurers could even ask the age of the tree if need be, but a talented charmer had the ability to sense the age of plants, herbs, flowers, and trees because the advance age of these manifestations of nature added to their power when used as an ingredient in a potion. She staggered each one's departure from the school's gate, so that each would have to find the tree on their own. As the youngest member, Liam was last to leave the gate.

Following these voices speaking a newly learned language, which he had just begun to understand, he walked past tree after tree until he came to a gnarled, slightly bent tree with moss growing up its craggy bark whose branches were growing in such a way that some even looked to be turning on each other in order to fight. The trees in their shared language told him that he was looking for this one and no other. This was the oldest tree, so he sat down beneath it and waited for everyone else.

"Very good, Liam," Sian Boru said to him as she came into view. "I am usually the first to find the tree when I do this exercise, especially since I already know where it is. You are the first to ever beat me here. That is remarkable."

"Really, ma'am, I beat you," he said but it was more of a question than a statement.

"Yes, you beat me and I knew where I was going. Now let's hope Dani and Brigid show up soon," she said then joined him beneath the shade of the tree.

Within ten minutes Dani, sixteen years of age, came walking into their view. When she saw them, she waved and ran the rest of the way to them. Her cheeks were as red as a cherry with excitement as she got to them.

"Mistress, I would have been here sooner, but the trees weren't very talkative today," she said to Sian Boru.

"Why?"

"Because I wanted to be first one here so I demanded their cooperation. It took me sometime to attain balance with nature after that."

"I hope you learned a lesson from that," Sian Boru stated then noticed Brigid, thirteen, coming into view. She was carrying an armful of sunflowers that she smelled as she walked. When she saw the three of them beneath the tree she gave them an apprehensive wave.

"Sorry I'm late but I saw these perfect sunflowers and had to pick a few of them. It took me a little of time to figure out which were ready to be picked, which were ready to die," Brigid said in a lilting Irish accent similar to Diarmund O'CuChulainn.

"I thought there might be some excuse like that, Brigid. You too often stray off track when I give you an assignment. You still haven't learned to finish one thing before you start another," Sian Boru told her.

"Sorry, mistress," she replied.

"Don't be sorry. It is in your nature to follow new paths and go in the wrong direction in order to find the right place to be. You have a gift and it should not be ignored. Now I have saved the formal introduction until we got here. I want you to start by stating your name, your year, where you are from, what is your major power, if you have a minor, and finally, what you did this summer. Dani, please start," she said.

"My name is Dani Weiss. I am a fourth year student. I am from New York City, Eastend Avenue to be exact, right across from Gracie's Mansion. My major power is as a conjurer, though I have shown a minor talent as a caster. But I find it difficult to cast spells with ease or confidence. Oh, yes, and what I did this summer was hang out on the beach at the Hamptons while my father worked a few business deals and my mother fretted about me coming back here. She hates that they are Giolla and I am part of the Bene Lumen. If it wasn't for Rabbi Justiz, I'd never be allowed to return here."

"Sounds like a very relaxing time you had," Sian Boru commented.

"I'm glad to be back here. In some ways I've started to think of Samhain as my home more than New York. Don't get me wrong, I love New York, but this place is home," the young girl stated.

"Next is Brigid," Sian Boru prodded pleasantly.

"Oh, yes, me," said Brigid Cochran as she stood up to speak. "My name is Brigid Cochran. I am a second year student. I come from Donegal, Ireland. My major power is as a charmer, and I enjoy my power. Besides that, I believe Mistress Boru has told me I have an aptitude for conjuring, though I'm not too sure of it, and a slight, underdeveloped talent for some casting, though not enough to ever be a true Triune Conjurer. As for this summer I went on a pilgrimage to the grave of Nimue near Glastonbury. She is buried in the trunk of a beautiful old tree that protects her and entraps her. I cried when I saw it. I consider Nimue a role model."

"Who is Nimue?" asked Liam knowing he had heard the name before in Arthurian legend but forgetting who she was.

"Go on and tell him, Brigid," Sian Boru prompted her.

"In Merlin's time Nimue was also a triune conjurer, just as Morgana was, and like Merlin was. Of the three some say that she was the strongest, but she gave her life for Merlin's. She loved him. Her death and the death of Arthur led Merlin to begin the Bene Lumen."

"Who killed her?" asked Liam.

"Morgana," she said in a tone that seemed shocked that Liam didn't know any of this.

"Liam was raised completely ignorant of our history and our ways. His father is Brian CuCullen and his mother was Siobhan Griffin. He carries the bloodline of Merlin in him, even stronger than I do," explained Sian Boru.

Both the girls seemed impressed by these facts about him, but Liam felt suddenly and unexpectedly out of place in their company. Even though he was starting to feel his powers, he still wasn't sure if he belonged there. For a minute he wanted to do the obstacle course like his brother rather than being in the company of his fellow classmates Dani and Brigid.

"Morgana," Sian Boru started to explain, "was once a good, druid priestess and potential Lady of the Lake, which means a potential leader of all druids, but she became an atrocity to our kind. She who understood and once partnered with nature perverted nature by stopping her own aging process and making nature bend to her whims. You see she didn't want to lose her beauty, so she manipulated and perverted nature. Morgana still lives today and is an active member of the Illuminatii."

"But our house is called Morgana House," Liam said in confusion since he was told that the houses were names after heroes.

"True. Unlike the rest of the houses which are named for those who exemplify the best of their powers we chose to name our house after Morgana to remind us that we, and our powers, are susceptible to perversion and atrocity if we are not vigilant and true to our best nature. Her name is a reminder of what we may become if we stray from the true path and crave power more than truth and goodness," Sian Boru said. "Now tell them about yourself, Liam."

"My name is Liam CuCullen. I am going into my first year. I come from Cape Elizabeth, Maine. And my power is... what is my power exactly?" he asked Sian Boru.

"You are a young, uneducated, yet possibly a very, very powerful Triune Conjurer, Liam, which means you are a unique student here. The first true Triune Conjurer we've had since your mother and I were students here," Sian Boru answered him.

Both the girls seemed impressed by this fact. Their whole demeanor towards Liam changed from superior to awe inspiring. Here was someone who knew nothing of their ways, or had not even completed one year of school, and Sian Boru had declared him a triune conjurer.

"Are you sure about that, ma'am?" he asked her.

"Positive, Liam," she answered.

"But... How...can I be?" he asked.

"Liam, you are because the powers of the three flow through you completely and truly. I have introduced you to the powers of the conjurer, and you have even felt that you have that power. Next we shall explore the power of the charmer. You see anyone can mix herbs and flowers together, or chose an object to endow it with a power, but only a charmer can make a potion or a charm work because they add a piece of themselves to their work. Maybe it's some spit, or blood, or a piece of hair or two, or even some skin, but without this addition the potion or the charm wouldn't work at all. The charmer carries their power in their skin, blood, hair, and even spit. All we do is add to their knowledge of nature and what is possible. I have felt that power in you, too."

"But, ma'am, I... I didn't realize you could tell I had that power," he said.

"I can. Finally, there is the power of the caster. They cast enchantments or curses with words or with thoughts if they are powerful enough. Now do you think it's the words that have the power, Liam?"

"In some ways they do, ma'am," he answered.

"You are right. In some ways words have a kind of power, but to utter an enchantment without having the power to enchant embedded in your soul then all you would have are the words. The power is supplied by the caster's soul. It comes from their very depth," she said.

"And I have that power, too?" he asked.

"Yes," she answered then turned to Brigid and Dani and smiled. "And you will help me bring out all of Liam's powers and together we shall help him fulfill his greatness."

Dani raised her hand in a high five motion to Liam, who slapped it instinctively. Brigid for her part merely smiled at him and nodded her head in the affirmative. Liam wanted to exchange high five with her, but she didn't raise her hand. Sian Boru stood up from her spot beneath the tree.

"It is time for us to begin our journey. By helping Liam, you, Dani, will strengthen your conjuring powers and explore how far you can develop as a caster. Dani, you are born to be part of a Tiarnán's team, his fealty, because you are a battler. Liam will learn tenacity and courage from you. And you, Brigid, you who are the most gifted charmer I've seen in many years, and you will be able to test conjuring and try casting. I feel, Brigid, that you have the soul of a truly great teacher. Liam will need your guidance in learning about many things. Together, I believe you three will be able to do great things at Samhain. And now as my private students you are bonded to each other. We are all family now."

CHAPTER 7

Master Mifune first served Brian CuCullen and then served himself some sashimi and rice seasoned with a hint of rice wine vinegar along with some tempura vegetables that he dished into separate small, delicate ceramic bowls that he had made himself. He used making his own pottery dishes as a form of relaxation from the burdens of being a warrior. Master Mifune extolled the art of pottery making as a way of keeping his focus and energy focused on the important things in life.

They sat on the floor of a small cottage that Mifune kept as his own private resident forgoing a place in the palace where the Lady of the Lake and her attendants stayed. As the Lady's lead protector, he would be honored in the palace, but Mifune preferred to stay in his own abode. The palace was too soft and comfortable for his old warrior's taste. As a warrior who believed in perpetual vigilance, he shunned easy comfort just like he shunned those who flattered him too easily. A samurai should not trust compliments because they are worthless pay, he once told a much younger Brian CuCullen.

This was going to be their last private meal together after three weeks of hard training, as Brian was almost ready to leave Avalon and return to his duties in Maine. Tomorrow Master Mifune planned a final test for Brian CuCullen. It was a simple test of having him go through the Mifune attitudes of the sword, showing his grace, and his control of his blade. The Lady of the Lake would be viewing him and afterwards there would be a goodbye feast. No more battling one to five swordsmen for hours at a time, or testing and strengthening his muscles in a series of exercises and drills which a normal man would be unable to do. No, his last test was the simplest one, yet it was also the hardest one because it would either show how his skills had improved or expose them as still rusty. Mifune was sure they had improved.

"This is delicious, Master. It has been a long time since I've had rice prepared correctly for sushi or sashimi," Brian told Mifune as he shoveled some of the rice into his mouth with chopsticks.

"I once considered becoming a chef instead of samurai. You see I was always very good with a knife," Mifune reminisced. "As a boy my mother used to have me slice the fish and meat for her when she was preparing meals for our family. She took pride in my skill with a blade. It is a gift to be able to make a good clean, true cut."

"I've noticed that, Master Mifune."

"So, is it good to be back in the saddle, so to speak in your American slang?" Mifune asked him as he ate some of his sashimi. "I'm a more of a mariner than a cowboy. I prefer boats to horses," Brian responded then smiled. "I'd forgotten how beautiful Avalon was. It is an eternal oasis from the harshness of the modern world, a true paradise. If people in the world knew it existed, they would destroy it by making it a tourist spot to be ogled. The Lady of the Lake should be commended for being able to keep it anchored to this plane of existence. I can't imagine a world without Avalon. And as for Samhain... well Samhain holds more fond memories for me than almost any other place in the world."

"Yes, but are you glad to be back in your position as a Tiarnán?"

Brian ate some more of his rice then sampled some of the vegetables that were filled in Mifune's ceramic bowls that laid on the table. The food was delicious and was made even more satisfying after a long day of training. Shifting his legs, which were getting a little cramped underneath of him, as Mifune had no chairs in his hut only pillows for sitting on the floor, Brian considered if he was glad to have returned to his role of Tiarnán.

"I'm not sure about that yet. I guess time will tell on that note," he finally answered.

Mifune reached over and grabbed the white ceramic bottle that was filled with Saki. He filled two small white cups, handing one to Brian CuCullen and keeping one for himself.

"Saki?" Brian asked him.

"Yes, warmed as it should be, too," answered Mifune with a smile on his face. "I once visited New York and had Saki that was cold. It was an offense to my taste."

"And this is quality stuff," he said after taking a sip. "Where do you get it from?"

"I have couriers from Japan bring me some bottles whenever they come to Avalon and seek advice or council from the Lady of the Lake. Though, she refuses to take a position in the Bene Lumen or in the Council of Guaire, her council is often sought by them. She has great wisdom and insight."

"Why doesn't she join the society outright instead of staying just on the outside of us?" he asked him.

"Because the Lady of the Lake must not be under the authority of anyone but the Goddess Cerridwen, the Celtic Goddess of nature, or so she has told me many, many times over the years. I think she just doesn't like the idea of leaving Avalon too often, and they would insist she sit on the Council of Guaire if she official joined. Yet, she and all who follow her are loyal to the Bene Lumen."

Brian CuCullen took a sip of the strong alcohol. It had been years since he had Saki, the last time being about seventeen years ago or so when Mifune surprised him in Maine with a visit upon hearing that Siobhan was pregnant with a son. They finished that bottle together in one night then had another. Mifune was sure that Brian would have a son who would be a great warrior.

"You have not answered my question," Mifune pointed out to him.

"I'm not sure how to answer it. Being a Tiarnán is an honor but it is also a great burden," he said.

"Yes, a burden which you believed cost you your beloved wife's life. Am I not correct?"

"I should have been with Siobhan when she faced Baal in Cape Elizabeth instead of leading a team to fight another demon, a lesser demon, one that didn't need my personal attention," Brian CuCullen stated harshly. In his words all the pain he felt at not being there when his wife was murdered flooded back. Ten years was not enough passed time for him not to feel the pain.

"But you had been ordered to pursue that demon by Fiona Philbin, is that not right?" Master Mifune asked.

"Yeah, Fiona headed the Council of Guaire back then. She thought Azeral was more of a danger than Baal and everyone on the council agreed with her because of her position as Supreme Councilor. I'm kind of glad that she is retired from her position now because I would have trouble taking orders from her," said Brian.

"The council believed a fallen angel needed the attention of a Tiarnán-- so much for the insights of those who allegedly know best. They too often make mistakes yet hardly ever admit to them. Of course wisdom doesn't come from admitting to mistakes, it comes from learning from them," Mifune observed.

"I agree, Master Mifune. The Council of Guaire had me take my fealty, my best team, and confront Azeral when I knew that Baal was the real danger. I told Fiona that but she wouldn't listen to reason. We confronted Azeral all right. I sent him and his few minions back to whatever nether hell they inhabit. Meanwhile Siobhan attempted to stop Baal from raising Orochi, the snake demon, by herself. Combined they were powerful. It was suicide to stand up against them. She was no match because..."

"Because her heart was too kind," Mifune finished the sentence for him. "She needed to protect someone to be at her strongest and being alone she had no one to protect, so she was not at her best."

"You understood her, Master."

"Yes, I did. Remember, that the Lady of the Lake sent me to Samhain to instruct you during your two years of Tiarnán training. She thought so highly of your talents that she demanded you have the best tutors, which included me. As I got to know you, how could I not get to know Siobhan? She was... a gentle soul," he said.

"She was my better half, Master Mifune," Brian CuCullen stated.

"Why did you not pursue Baal to kill him like the warrior you are?" asked Mifune.

"That answer is simple: the boys, my sons. They needed me. I couldn't leave them without a parent after having just having lost their mother. Siobhan was an only child and her parents died when she was at Samhain. As for me, my mother and father gave me to Mallory when he came and told them about me. Neither one of them was Bene Lumen. My uncle, though, was and my grandfather was a Tiarnán. He died in battle and my father always blamed the Bene Lumen for taking his father's life, even though it was not their fault. As for my mother, she was afraid of all things Bene Lumen. Anyway, they had my brother Thomas and sister Eileen. Both of them were model children."

"In other words the Bene Lumen was your true family," said Mifune.

"I guess they were. I guess they are."

"Which is why I ask again, are you glad to be back as Tiarnán?"

"I just might be, Master Mifune, but it is too early to say honestly. My sons are safe at Samhain, though, which I am glad for. They are learning things they never imagined were real or that they were capable of... but Baal is still out there. I still owe him... and Orochi."

"Good, I am glad to hear that you owe them," Mifune said and raised his cup. "I toast Brian CuCullen, a Tiarnán I trust and believe in, who someday will vanquish Baal and revenge his wife's death."

They touched cups and drank down their Saki. Mifune placed his cup down and picked up his bowl then began shoveling rice into his mouth. He ate as if they were about to go into battle and he only had a short time for his meal. Brian picked up his bowl and did the same.

"You will be given a special mission to perform in order to test you, to see if you are ready to return to your post," Mifune told him as he ate some sashimi.

"How special?"

"A werewolf."

"A werewolf," he said in a dubious tone since he had killed many werewolves in his time.

"Yes. We are not sure who it is but we are sure that there is a werewolf in New York City, who has decided he doesn't feel the need to hide his kills any longer. The New York Police think they are tracking a serial killer, but it is a werewolf and a dangerous one, too, from what I've been told. The police are unprepared to stop this real cunning and dangerous werewolf. I mean, how can you stop something you do not believe exists?" Mifune told him.

"Are we sure about this? Humanity is capable of great evil without the help of those we fight. It could be a serial killer in New York."

"The Bene Lumen has a giolla in the New York Police Department who is working the case. He is sure that it is a werewolf. He knows what signs to look for since he has had some training."

"What does it mean that he has had some training?"

"His mother was an Aongus Cathal. She died in the line of duty fighting a vampire. He never attended Samhain, but since he was an only child without a father, she shared much of her knowledge with him, including many of our ways and secrets. He knew all about the battle that waged in the shadows and squarely stood on the side of the Bene Lumen."

"Oh, I see. He's never attended the school or even was sent away for a retreat or two?" asked Brian.

"No, he has never been to one of the Bene Lumen retreats or training camps. Though he has met with some Bene Lumen stationed in New York City and offered his loyalty to them, but he prefers not to be tied to the Bene Lumen since he is a Police Officer."

"The Council of Guaire trusts him of course," Brian CuCullen said trying not to show his lingering disrespect for the council.

"Of course," replied Mifune.

"So I am to track the werewolf down and slay him then I can return to Maine and resume my duties as Tiarnán and Cairbre," Brian CuCullen stated.

"Exactly, Tiarnán."

"Have arrangements been made for my departure to the Big Apple?" he asked.

"Yes, you will leave Heathrow in three days and arrive at JFK Airport thereafter. At the airport an Aongus Cathal by the name of Jennifer Sult will meet you. She will take you to the Chelsea Hotel. There you will meet with the police detective, Sgt. Darrell McGavin. He will fill you in on everything you need to know about the police investigation."

"Sounds like everything has been thoroughly arranged already," Brian CuCullen agreed then drank some more of his Saki.

"I know you will do a good job in New York," Mifune stated then drank his own Saki.

Brian CuCullen was glad that Mifune thought he would do a good job because he still wasn't sure of himself. Ten years was a long time between battles, and even Mifune's training and tasks couldn't prepare him for real battle. If he wasn't up to battle, he could die, and he knew it

Headmaster Fergus, Sian Boru, Master Nagura, Father Mueller, Maol Stonefeather, Master Diaghilev, Master O'CuChulainn, Dani Weiss, Brigid Cochran, Nadia Nabokov, Liam and Donovan Talbot all gathered at the obstacle course to watch Kieran run the course for the last time before the start of the new year. It was all the talk during breakfast since it was Kieran's first chance to show that he could live up to a challenge. Kieran would have preferred if they had all decided not to watch him run the course today, since his best time yesterday was still only 19 minutes flat. This was a far cry from what he needed if he was going to show Master Diaghilev that Talbot should remain his private tutor for the year. 18 minutes was the time he needed, a full sixty seconds better than what he was doing now. He doubted he could make up that time today.

As he stretched out his muscles and ligaments at the starting line, Donovan Talbot, Master Diaghilev, Nadia Nabokov, and Liam strolled over to check on him before his run. Liam gave his brother a quick wave as they approached while Nadia Nabokov nodded to him in that way he was beginning to recognize as her unstated way of saying hello. The two older men merely remained impassive in their facial expressions and manner watching Kieran as he stretched out his muscles.

"Hey, Bro," Liam said then began to reach under his robe, "I brought you something for good luck."

He took out from the back pocket of the jeans, which he wore under his robes, Kieran's red and blue Red Sox hat. His father bought him this hat when the Red Sox won the World Series breaking the Curse of the Bambino, which Liam had found out was placed on the Red Sox by a necromancer, an evil conjurer, not for trading Babe Ruth but for winning the World Series and losing a bet for him. The curse was broken when this necromancer was finally destroyed. Kieran took the hat from his brother and gave him a smile.

"Thanks, midget," he said and put the cap on fixing it on his head just the way he liked it.

"I thought that the more luck the better for you right now, though, I know you will surprise everyone and do great," Liam said.

"You didn't do anything to the hat, did you, anything, you like making it into a supernatural good luck charm?" asked Kieran leery of the answer.

"Nay, that hat doesn't need to be made into a charm. It's already lucky for you. Remember you wore it when the Red Sox broke the curse."

"Okay, midget," Kieran said and firmly patted his brother on his right shoulder.

"You have a lot of time to make up, Kieran," Nadia Nabokov stated using his name, which meant that she accepted him as a friend. Over the past few weeks Nadia had come by to watch Talbot train Kieran and encourage him in her fashion. Kieran had gotten used to her form of encouragement, too. It was never a rah-rah-rah or a pat on the back, but a nod and a few suggestions about how to improve. He also had gotten used to seeing and being with her.

"I know."

"If I were you, I would concentrate on one section of the course which you are very bad at and try something different. There is no reason to try and improve at every section since it is too late for that. I think you can find sixty seconds at the end where the hoops and wall are."

"Really," said Kieran slightly surprised that she had waited until now to tell him this.

"Yes, you tend to hesitate at the hoops trying to gage each one as you go then when you get to the wall you have left yourself without momentum. The hoops, you should treat the hoops as one obstacle not many and find a rhythm then you need momentum so that you can almost run up the wall," she told him.

"I'll remember that."

"Good," she said then nodded and went to stand at her uncle's side.

Donovan Talbot now sauntered up to Kieran as if they didn't have a care in the world. He was trying to look calm and reassuring, but Kieran could see sweat breaking out at his hairline. It was too cool a day for sweat without exertion. As much as Kieran wanted to succeed today, Talbot wanted him to succeed more.

"She gave you good advice just now," he said then leaned in close to Kieran so no one could hear him. "Think of a song and fit the rhythm of the hoops to that song. You know - *Sitting on the dock of the bay...*"

"I'm not really an Otis Redding fan," Kieran commented.

"It's doesn't matter what song it is, so long as you pick one you know and find the right beat in order to jump through the hoops," Talbot told him.

"Why didn't you mention this earlier in our training?" Kieran asked.

"Because I wanted you to improve as much as you could without tricks or shortcuts, so that you would push yourself as hard as you could. Now is the time to use a trick or two, when you really need one."

"You think I'll make 18 minutes today?" Kieran asked Talbot.

"I bet Diaghilev that you would do 17 minutes and 30 seconds," he answered.

"17 minutes and 30... have you gone off your freaking rocker?" asked Kieran.

"Naw, I know you can do it, Kieran, you have it in you to be an Aongus Cathal, maybe even more than that," he said then turned to Liam. "Come on and believe. Let's go watch your brother surprise us all."

The small group walked back to where the rest stood waiting to watch Kieran. When he was ready, he was supposed to raise his right hand in the air and when he was going to start drop the hand and Diaghilev would begin to keep time. Kieran stood and began to visualize the course. He saw himself running through without a problem, no hitches or mistakes, and then running across the finish line in record time. Raising his hand, he took several deep breaths then once he felt his lungs had enough air he dropped his hand then began to run.

Faster than he had ever run in his life he dashed to the water jump and cleared it easily. Next was the heavy stone, which slowed him down as he had yet to trust his strength. After the stone he saw that pitiless jungle gym made of thorns. Holding his breath he ran through it trying to dodge the sharp thorns. A rip of his gray workout shirt, a slash across his face, and several thorns stuck in his hand, he finally got through and ran as hard as he could to the towers.

As always the slippery rope caused him problems. It slowed him down, which caused Kieran to lose his temper. He hated the idea of everyone seeing him struggle up the rope. Just the thought of Nadia Nabokov seeing him flail away trying to get up the rope drove him to get angrier and angrier with himself. Finally, he started to make headway up the rope until he got to the top of the tower and faced his nemesis, the tightrope that connected the two towers.

No matter how many times that Talbot told him to screw his courage and just run across, he could never trust himself to ran across the rope. Just like every time before, he slowed balanced and walked himself across the rope losing precious minutes. Down the rope of the second tower he went and began running as fast as he could to make up time. 200 yards later and he reached the pit where he had to balance across on the tops of poles.

Like the tightrope, the pit always caused him to lose time. The thought of completely trusting his physical gifts without thought just did not come easily to Kieran. It didn't matter what he did, football or helping his father haul lobster traps he put thought into the activity. But Talbot constantly told him that he shouldn't think about the tightrope of the pit, he should just trust his instincts and his physical gifts. It just didn't seem right, though, to him. But he had no choice now. Across the pit he went, hopping from pole top to pole top as best and as quick as he could until he was on the other side.

The last set of obstacles faced him. Again he tried to make up time with his foot speed but he was starting to doubt that he was going to make the time Diaghilev had set for him. As he saw the hoops coming, he began to hum to himself *London's Calling*. To the beat of the Clash he began to drive, roll, stand, run, drive, roll until he passed through all the hoops then he ran as hard as his legs could pump towards the wall. He ran and kept running until he was half way up the wall then he used his leg strength to catapult him up enough so that his hands grabbed the top of the wall. Pulling himself up and over the wall he fell to the ground, scrambled to get up then ran and dove over the finish line.

Once across the line Kieran dropped to his knees and began to take in big gulps of air. As he knelt there, he swore he could hear applause from those who watched him. Tentatively, he lifted his head to look at those who came to watch him. Everyone seemed to be happy, even Nadia Nabokov who was nodding her head appreciatively. Kieran couldn't help but stare at her. And she returned his stare. This continued until Liam and Donovan Talbot came running up to him. Both of them had big smiles on their faces. Kieran couldn't understand why they were smiling since he knew he couldn't have done better than 19 minutes.

"Kieran, Kieran, that was amazing, Bro, really, really amazing," Liam yelled as he ran up to his brother side.

At first he was going to give his brother a hug, but Kieran didn't look in any condition to be hugged, so Liam offered him a hand to get up and Kieran took it. He stood on wobbly legs and waited for Donovan Talbot's comments. Kieran assumed that he was going to tell Kieran he did his best and that was all that counted.

"I guess we are stuck with each other for the time being," was Talbot's comment.

"What do you mean by that?" Kieran asked.

"I mean you did it, Kieran. You passed the test that Master Diaghilev set for you to pass."

"Really? I did it," he said sounding surprise. He knew he had run better than he had ever run this course, but he didn't feel like he ran it that fast. "What was my time?"

"Well, I won my bet with Master Diaghilev, so that should tell you everything. You did it in 17 minutes and 29 seconds. That is a great improvement, Kieran," Talbot stated.

"17? Really? It couldn't have been that fast, not that fast. I meant I stumbled and did horrible across the tightrope and the pit..."

"Kieran, you did it. You still don't trust your instincts completely enough, but you are starting to trust yourself," Talbot said.

"What was your bet?" asked Kieran.

"That he has to teach first year conjurers, charmers and casters in physical education this year. I usually do that," Talbot said then shrugged his shoulders. "Sorry, Liam. Master Diaghilev is a much harder teacher than me when it comes to non-Cathal."

"That's okay," Liam said then looked closely at his brother. For the first time he saw that there was blood on his right cheek just below his eye and blood dripping from his left hand. "Hey, Bro, you need some bandages."

Talbot looked closely at Kieran's wounds now. He didn't even think to check for injuries because he was so happy his student had done as well as he had.

"Let me see your hand," Talbot said and Kieran showed it to him. There were two thorns stuck in his palm.

Taking Kieran's hand into his left hand gently with his right hand he pulled the two thorns out then he ripped off part of his robe and used it to bandage his hand. Kieran had never seen Talbot be this gentle and concerned for him.

"I remember when I first did something better than I thought I could do it. Master Diaghilev told me that I should get used to it because it is the job of the Aongus Cathal to perform better than they thought they could. Today, I tell you to be proud of what you did because you have come farther than you thought you could and you have done it like a man," Talbot said to him with a voice filled with pride.

"Thank you, sir," Kieran responded.

"Now everyone expects you to get cleaned up and meet them in the eating hall. I think lunch is a planned celebration for you. Master Diaghilev was impressed with you. He still doubts that you'll be able to get your time low enough to remain a Aongus Cathal," Talbot told him.

"We'll see about that," Kieran replied then he took his cap off and wiped the sweat off his forehead.

"In two days school starts. Our private tutoring will be every Saturday morning from nine in the morning until noon. Starting this Saturday we will begin learning how to use the sword properly, so the next time you face Nadia she doesn't have such an easy time with you. All that she has on you, Kieran, is experience, nothing more than experience. Master Nagura has promised to be there, too. I am okay with the blade, competent enough to teach you the basics and a little more, but he is an artist with a blade." Talbot said and started to mend his wounds.

CHAPTER 8

At the Hall of Heroes, the great gathering spot that was used for special occasions and where stood statues and hung paintings of the great heroes from Merlin and Nimue to Serge Vladmir and Siobhan CuCullen, the new and old students as well as teachers gathered for the placing of new students into their house depending upon their gifts. Gathered in the black marble pews with the first two rows filled with teachers and the next four filled with the newer students, everyone waited as Mallory in his headmaster robes and M'Tenga with his great shaved bald, brown head in his lavender robes came to the front of hall. Standing beneath the twenty-foot high white marble statue of Merlin whose arms were spread wide as if to greet the students, Mallory began his introduction.

"Welcome old and new students to the beginning of the school year at Samhain," Mallory greeted them. "I hope you all had a pleasurable summer, but now it is time to get back to work. Sixth year Aongus Cathal will end the year with the trial of the Tiarnán to see if any will partake in the two year Tiarnán program. Fifth year conjurers, charmers and casters will be tested at year's end to see if any will qualify for Mistress Boru's advanced classes in the sixth year, otherwise they will have to settle for just a normal sixth year class load of seven classes and two trials. But, of course, it will not be all hard work for you. We will have a Conjurer's Maze tournament for those who think they can rest the cup from Rhianna George. And there will be the Ruadh League, of course, which the whole school enjoys to cheer along their favorite team. Last year Nagura's Ruffians of Tamo House won the championship. I believe those who saw it will not forgot their defeating Cuchulain's Chieftains in the semi-finals then beating Diarmund's Cathal in one of the closest finals we have ever had in Samhain. It was a rousing year in Ruadh. I expect Nagura's Ruffians will want to defend their title against the best and strongest again."

Kieran, who sat beside a female student around his age in a Lavender robe and a younger student in a yellow robe, wondered to himself what Ruadh was. Was it anything like football, or any sport he knew or ever saw? If it was then maybe he could join the league just to pass the time.

"Now for first year students, I have some rules for you to follow. Your house robes must be worn during the school day and at school events, unless otherwise advised not to. When not in your robes, you may wear whatever clothing you have brought with you to Samhain. Those are the rules that I find important. As for all other school rules either your housemaster or mistress will inform you about them. Remember, though, that school monitors hold a place of honor and they must not abuse that honor. Last year one Douglas Doogal of Sybil House relied on his emerging powers as a seer to give demerits to students before they had committed their offense."

Everyone either sitting next to Douglas Doogal, a towheaded fifteen year old in lavender robes, or who knew Douglas, looked at him. With his red face making his blonde hair and black beany stand out, Douglas tried to sink down as low as he could in his seat.

"This is not fair," Mallory continued. "Monitors, especially those endowed with either prophet or seer powers, should not rely on their gifts in order to give demerits to other students; they should rely on the actions of their fellow students instead. Now, except for the one student who has already been placed in their appropriate house and the one student who enters the school as an older student and has been placed, will all new students come forward so that Master M'Tenga can place you in your proper house."

With a small amount of chaos and noise a gathering of twelve year old boys and girls came forward to stand in front of Master M'Tenga, who would lower his head, place one hand on the top of the students head then call out for a robe form whatever house he saw they belonged in. A robe would then be brought out from a room, which was situated behind the statue of Merlin by Wanda Dumas. The aged Ms. Dumas with dyed black hair and a pin cushion filled with hundreds of pins on her right wrist had been the seamstress for Samhain thirty-six years and could pin a robe for hemming in a matter of seconds. After pinning the first robe Ms. Dumas would stand beside M'Tenga and her assistant Clarence Cobble would bring out the next robe while M'Tenga would call the next student to be placed and pinned for their new robe.

This placing of students and pinning of robes lasted for over an hour as one by one all the new students, except Liam, were put into their proper house. Last year from a gathering of eighty-six new students only twelve were placed in Morgana House. The house that did the best was Tamo with thirty-eight new students. The rest of the students last year split themselves between Sybil House and CuChulainn House. This year there were ninety new students to place, not including Liam. M'Tenga called out the first students name and began the ritual placement using the crystal to test their powers.

"James Allard," he called out in his commanding voice.

The young boy came rushing up to M'Tenga who placed his left hand on the young boy's shoulder in order to calm him. He then placed his right hand, which held the crystal, against the boy's forehead. M'Tenga nodded in appreciation then said: "Sybil House."

Ms. Dumas called for a Sybil robe and began to measure the young boy. Once the robe arrived, she put it on him and pinned it then took it off of him, tagged it with his name, and sent the robe back to be sewn later. M'Tenga called the next student.

By the end of the ritual Sybil received ten new students, CuChulainn got 18, Morgana 22, and Tamo received the rest. Now that the placing was finished, the now harried and exhausted Ms. Dumas returned to the backroom while M'Tenga took a seat in the front row. Mallory once again readied himself to speak.

"Now that we are all placed in our proper house based on your natural skills and inclinations, it is time for each new housemate to get acquainted with their house. We will break for the rest of the day until dinner when you are all expected to come to the dining hall unless excused. After dinner we will march as a school to the cloister for a religious ceremony thanking whomever it is each of you thanks for all that you have received. Tonight the ceremony will be officiated by Father Mueller, Rabbi Justiz, Maol Stonefeather, Taoist Brother Zheng, Druid Priestess Boru, and Maol M'Tenga. We must never forget why we are really here and learning the skills we learn. You are all dismissed," he concluded then began to walk down the main aisle in order to greet some of the new students.

Aside for the newer students, teachers, and sixth year monitors, whose job it was to make sure the new students got to their house, everyone else filed out of the Hall of Heroes. Unlike Liam, who had Brigid and Dani as new friends, Kieran felt at a loss and even a little jealous of his brother who had already made friends, and one of them, Dani Weiss, was even cute. Everyone in his age group already knew their classmates, had made friends, cliques, and bonds. He was adrift merely following everyone in maroon robes back to CuChulainn House. As he walked a handsome brown haired boy with sad brown eyes along with a striking, African boy who had his thick curly black hair cut close to the scalp came strolling up along side of him. Both the boys were in his year.

"My name is Philippe Renoir," the brown haired boy said with a French accent.

"And I am Jean Pierre Tutu," added the baldish African boy with an accent that mixed his native South African with French, as he had been educated in France as a child.

"Hey," said Kieran.

"You expect us to know your name I guess," Renoir commented in a tone that showed he thought Kieran was rude.

"But we do know his name, Philippe. He is Kieran CuCullen and we have come to talk to him," Tutu stated.

"Son of Tiarnán Brian CuCullen, I know that, but he doesn't know that we know that, does he," Renoir said.

"Does everyone know me just because of my father and his history here?" asked Kieran.

"No, there is also your mother. She is also famous," Renoir replied.

"Didn't you see her portrait in the Hall of Heroes this morning?" asked Tutu.

"No, I didn't notice it. I was too busy being bored," Kieran responded. He had not bothered to look at the portraits or the statues, or even ask why these people had been honored as a hero. He assumed it was because they were great in life and were now dead. But now that he heard his mother was a hero, he wanted to go back and find her portrait so he could stare at it and remember what she looked like. Lately, he had forgotten what she looked like.

"You have a brother, don't you?" Renoir asked.

"Yeah, he's in the first year in Morgana House."

"I heard a rumor that he is like your mother in powers, maybe even more powerful than she was. That is impressive. Within five minutes of returning to Samhain, the rumors about new and old students are already stirred and making the rounds, you know. There is also a rumor that you and Mr. Talbot get along well. No one gets along well with Talbot. He is very difficult," confided Tutu.

"He is a sour egg," said Renoir.

"That is a bad egg, Philippe," Tutu corrected his friend. "Do you get along with him, Kieran?"

"I guess that I do. He is my private tutor," Kieran replied.

"I guess that makes you a bad egg, too," Renoir goaded Kieran.

They came up to CuChulainn House and began to file orderly into their building. Some of the students automatically went into the common room while others sought out other nooks and lofts of the house. Kieran began to walk to his dormitory with Tutu and Renoir following behind him. Entering his dormitory he headed for his bed and sat down. Tutu sat down on the bed to his right while Renoir sat down in the bed on Tutu's right.

"Can I help you two with something or are you just bothering me because you have nothing better to do?" asked Kieran.

"These are our beds so we can be here if we want to be," stated Renoir argumentatively.

"Let's not argue," Tutu said. "Kieran, we want to start a Ruadh team and we thought..."

"We thought you would be a good teammate," interrupted Renoir.

"Why me?"

"Because your...."

"Because my father was good at it," Kieran interrupted Renoir.

"Yes, he was a champion in the sport. His team won for three straight years," Tutu said.

"We need a team of four. We now have interested Gunthar in joining us, but we need a fourth person to make up a team. We thought it could be you who will be our fourth person," Renoir said.

"I have never played Ruadh before. I have no idea how to play it," said Kieran.

"So? Have you ever seen a Ruadh field, or even seen a game of Ruadh?" asked Tutu.

"No."

"Let us show you," Renoir added.

"Come on and see what a Ruadh field looks like," Tutu said as he got up out of his bed.

Renoir joined him. Since he didn't have anything else to do, Kieran decided to follow them. Once they exited CuChulainn House Tutu and Renoir began to run in the direction of the playing fields. This was a part of the campus that Kieran had not seen yet. So far he had spent all his time either in the dining hall, or CuChulainn House, or the training fields. But the playing fields meant nothing to him. Samhain didn't have an American Football team and that was his game.

After a short jog they got to the Ruadh Field. Surrounded by viewing stands, that looked as if it could hold the whole school, was the Ruadh playing field. Some fifty yards in length and forty feet in height, a jumble of bars, balancing beams, and rings with what appeared to be a small net at either end comprised the Ruadh field. Kieran was fascinated by all the equipment on the field it seemed more like a gymnastics course than a place to play a sporting event. Now, he was more intrigued by Ruadh than before.

"This is it?" he asked.

"It is," Renoir stated. "Is it not the most inspiring field you have ever seen? Football, rugby, American football, field hockey, none of them can equal Ruadh for its speed, complexity, and difficulty."

"The hardest game you will ever play, Kieran. I like to think of it as the first great X game team sport ever invented. It will challenge you and..." added Tutu.

"It will cause you great pain, if you are not careful," Renoir completed his friend's sentence.

"How do you play?" Kieran asked.

"Two teams each with four players play two 30 minute halves with a 10 minute intermission and try to score as many goals as possible by placing the corb in their opponents' net," explained Tutu.

"What is a corb?" asked Kieran.

"It is sort of like a grapefruit sized ball but dense and heavy which really hurts when you get hit by it. Last year I got knocked out by the corb," Renoir answered.

"Okay, okay. Let me guess how you do this. You swing and jump from the bars and beams and rings passing the corb and working your way down to the opponents' net where you toss it into the net," commented Kieran.

"The other teams tries to knock the ball away from you, or block passes, or...."

"Knock you off the bars with a hit in the head," added Renoir as he rubbed his head in memory of how he landed.

"A judge tries to keep opposing teams from killing each other with fouls or to make sure that the play doesn't get too rough, but things happen. If you play a little too hard against your opponent, you will be given a penalty and your opponent will get a penalty shot. Get four penalties and you're out of the game then it's four on three for the rest of the game," Tutu said as a caution.

"Is there an open net with the penalty shot or can someone try and block it?" asked Kieran.

"The four on the opponent team choose which one of us will guard the net for the penalty shot. They usually score," Renoir explained.

"I have never played this game, and when we run the obstacle course next time, I guarantee I will either finish last or next to last. Why would you want me on your team?" asked Kieran.

"Because we need a fourth person," Renoir said.

"Also, we understand that you are new to all this stuff, to training as Aongus Cathal. We think you will only get better in whatever you do. Kieran, your bloodline is strong, so we are betting that you will end up a good player after you get used to the game," explained Tutu. "We don't care if we win the league, we just want to be part of it. We want to be a team."

"Let me guess, no one would pick you two for their team," Kieran stated.

"I played on a team in my second year and was knocked off the bars and hospitalized for weeks. No one wanted me the next year because they thought I was clumsy," Renoir told Kieran.

"And I lost an important game for my team last year," admitted Tutu.

"What about Gunthar?" asked Kieran.

"Well, she is a difficult person to get along with. Jan doesn't like many people or get along with many people, but she likes Jean Pierre," said Renoir.

"She?"

"Yes, she," Jean Pierre Tutu said defiantly sounding as if he liked her in return. "And she will be the best player on our team."

"Until, we think, you come into your own and become a strong Aongus Cathal," added Renoir.

"Okay, I'm in. But you guys have to teach me how to play," Kieran said.

"It is a deal," said Tutu.

"We need a name," added Renoir.

"How about Aongus Misfits as a team name," replied Tutu.

"You've been thinking about that name for a while, haven't you?" asked Kieran.

"I embrace what happened last year. It was a learning experience and I refuse to be punished for my mistake," Tutu replied.

"I like the name. It sort of suits us. I must admit that Jean Pierre, Jan and myself are misfits and have been since we came here," Renoir offered his opinion.

"Why do you three think that you are all misfits?" asked Kieran.

"Because each of us has either failed at something important or refused to accept the invitation to join one of the important student clubs," explained Philippe.

"No, really, what makes you a misfit?" asked Kieran of Philippe.

"Besides the incident playing Ruadh where I was put in the hospital, I am the slowest Aongus Cathal in my year," he admitted.

"Until me. I'm the slowest now," Kieran said.

"I guess," Philippe responded.

"And you," prompted Kieran of Jean Pierre.

"Well, there was last year's Ruadh game then there was the time I accidentally knocked Master Diaghilev out with a wooden training sword. I was swinging it about, even though I knew not to, and Master Diaghilev had his back turned and was telling some of us how we need to concentrate better on our technique. Master Diaghilev was out cold for several minutes before regaining consciousness," Jean Pierre told him.

"Knocked out cold, really? I wish I had seen that," Kieran said with relish.

"It was funny," Philippe said, "but everyone started to think that Jean Pierre was bad luck, especially after what happened in Ruadh."

"What about this Jan Gunthar, what is her real story?" Kieran asked.

"She refused to join the Champions' Club. It is prestigious to be asked to join it. The Champions' Club is one of the oldest in Samhain, only the best Aongus Cathal are invited to join it. It is for those who everyone accepts as the best of the best. She said no to it. She told them she is not a joiner of clubs. Ever since then everyone treats her like some kind of a misfit," Jean Pierre explained.

"This place sounds just like any other school I've ever been to," Kieran commented.

"I guess so," interjected Philippe.

"Well, if it is okay with this Gunthar, then that will be our name for the team. Aongus Misfits. I kind of like the sound of that. Sign us up for the league then," Kieran told his new teammates then turned and looked at the Ruadh field. Maybe there would be something at Samhain that he could be good at. All he had to do was try his best and not give up.

"This is great," Tutu stated with great excitement.

"I hope so," Philippe added.

Meanwhile Brian CuCullen in New York...

At the airport Aongus Cathal Jennifer Sult, a smallish in height and built mousy haired woman with the body of a long distance runner, held up a sign that read Brian C. After exchanging passwords to make sure that she was Bene Lumen and niceties, she walked Brian to her beat up red Volkswagen Rabbit then drove them to the Chelsea Hotel where Sgt. Darrell McGavin, an athletic man who looked like he could handle the rigors of being an Aongus Cathal, just like his Jamaican mother had been. After Brian CuCullen checked into his hotel room, he dropped his bags off in his room and they wasted no more time and went searching for the werewolf. McGavin brought them to the rooftop where the last victim was found dead.

The rooftop was in what they used to call the Hell's Kitchen section of Manhattan, but what they now called the Clinton neighborhood. Even though city planners and politicians liked to sell this neighborhood as Clinton now as a way of raising rents and property value, a little of the Hell's Kitchen mystique remained. Many in New York City thought it was nicknamed Hell's Kitchen because of gang wars and Irish Hoodlums who made this their territory, but the real reason was those streets on the Westside of Manhattan in the fifties were long ago cursed. Brian CuCullen wasn't surprised when McGavin brought him and Jennifer Sult to a rooftop near Fifty-fourth Street and Tenth Avenue in Hell's Kitchen. Cursed areas were cursed areas and those who followed darkness always felt more comfortable in those areas.

"This is where she was found on the roof of her apartment building," McGavin said as he pointed to where the stain of the victim's blood remained on the rooftop.

"Tell me as much as you know about her," said Brian as he knelt down beside the dried blood.

"She was an actress, or to be precise, an aspiring actress since she had only auditioned for parts and hadn't yet snagged one. Her name was Karen

Hill, twenty-two years old, from South Carolina. She graduated from NYU and lived off of a trust fund while she pursued her acting career," McGavin recited the facts. "The coroner said the killer used animal claws and teeth to... well, to do what he did to her. I think you know what a werewolf does to its victims. The FBI and local CSI investigators think he is a serial killer who thinks he is a predator hunting prey, or maybe someone who is into primal animal killings, but we know better, don't we? Their profile changes daily since they really have no idea what they are looking for."

"Definitely a werewolf," Sult stated as she looked over Brian's shoulder.

"And one that doesn't care to keep his tracks hidden, which means he is very sure of himself, arrogant even, maybe even a little crazy, which isn't good for us. It's easier to track when you have a predictable werewolf, though, but one this arrogant we will have other problems in dealing with it," Brian CuCullen stated.

Brian CuCullen stood up and looked around the neighborhood at the other rooftops. The buildings were all similar in height, four or five stories with some more and some less, and mainly brick buildings. After killing the poor young girl, the werewolf must have run across the other roofs, maybe even jumping across the street to the roofs on the other side. A fully developed werewolf in full rage would be able to make that jump easily, Brian told himself.

"Are all his victims female?" he asked McGavin.

"Yes, so far," McGavin answered.

"The other victims were found in a different neighborhood than this one?"

"The other vics were all killed in Astoria Queens. This one being in Manhattan has investigators a little confused. Some even think this is a copycat crime and not done by the same unsub, though I doubt we have two werewolves on the loose," McGavin answered.

"Considering this area, Hell's Kitchen, and its history with the Bene Lumen, I would say he makes his home right here. The Illuminatii are attracted to areas with a history of evil or a cursed area like this one. I heard that some have said that they can feed on the residual evil. He must have found the victim on the roof, a willing easy victim and decided to prey on her instead of hunting elsewhere. She is a victim of opportunity outside of his usual hunting ground," CuCullen explained.

"Should we stake this area out with some Ardal Cathal?" asked Jennifer

Sult.

"I haven't decided yet," Brian CuCullen said then smelled something, a scent, floating in the air. It was a familiar scent, even though he hadn't smelled this particular scent in years. The scent was a mix of human and animal sweat, wet fur, and blood. It was the smell of a werewolf. He turned quickly to see the outline of a creature with the characteristics of a wolf, fangs, claws, glowing yellowish eyes, and bristling fur, with the body of a man on one of the roofs across the street from them. It was bent low trying not to be seen, but he saw it.

Not waiting to explain or even thinking too much about what he was doing, Brian CuCullen walked towards the middle of the roof then stopped and began to run at full tilt towards the edge of the roof pointed in the direction of Fifty-fourth Street. Coming to the edge he pushed himself with all his muscles and former training as hard as he could and sailed over Fifty-fourth Street until he was able to reach out and grab the roof across the street with his hands. He then pulled himself onto the roof, did a forward role and came up holding a retractable bladed sword that he had kept under his raincoat. A growl came from the gray furred werewolf that now stood up from its crouching position and began to run skipping from one roof to the other and continuing down towards Eleventh Avenue.

"That's impressive," McGavin exclaimed.

"I have skills and I wouldn't try it," Jennifer added admiringly as she watched Brian.

Brian CuCullen followed the creature with his sword in his right hand running at his top speed. The werewolf fell to all fours, which made him quicker than Brian, but Brian continued running after him without thought for waiting for backup. When the werewolf reached Eleventh Avenue, it stopped for a moment, as if it was contemplating leaping the greater distance between buildings on an avenue, but then it changed its mind and started running along the rooftops towards Fifty-third Street. Brian was hot on its trail.

Jennifer Sult and Sgt. McGavin didn't wait on the roof for Brian CuCullen to either return or not return. They both knew that if there were going to be action it wouldn't take place where they were standing. Heading to the roof's exit, they opened the door and headed down the stairs as fast as they could. Once they got to the first floor, they ran into the street. In the street both of them began to search the rooftops to see if they could follow them as the abomination and Brian CuCullen ran and jumped from rooftop to rooftop. Sult, who also had a retractable sword under her jacket, did not take her weapon out. She knew that it would bring too much attention to them if she ran down the street with a sword, even in Manhattan.

When the werewolf got to Fifty-Third Street it started to head along the rooftops back towards Tenth Avenue. Brian did not lose any speed in his pursuit. He was determined to catch this creature before it killed again. As he turned down towards Tenth Avenue he saw what the creature was headed for, a young Latino couple who were on the rooftop of one of the buildings on Fifty-Third Street. They were frozen in their tracks from fear as the werewolf headed straight towards them with its fangs bared and growling ferociously. Suddenly, the young man woke up from his fear and stepped in front of his girlfriend, as if to protect her, but the werewolf merely grabbed him and then tossed him off the four-story roof onto the pavement below. Now the werewolf could move in on the young girl, who began to scream hysterically.

Without even looking at where the young man landed, Brian CuCullen knew that he was dead. Brian saw the werewolf bite the young girl on the shoulder once and was about to bite her again but this time in the neck, when he took his sword and from the distance of one rooftop away threw it at the werewolf. The sword flew through the air and hit the creature a slicing blow on the back of its left shoulder just under the shoulder blade. The werewolf howled in pain then dropped the young girl and turned to face at Brian CuCullen, who was still charging forward even though he no longer had his sword for battle. Its yellow eyes, which almost seemed to glow in the dark, were trained on Brian as he came running towards it. Blood dripped from its canine teeth as it glowered at Brian. There was something about his demeanor and body language that made this creature think twice about facing him at this moment and instead of charging him, it merely growled out the word, "Tiarnán," and started running towards the edge of the building so that it could make a great leap over Fifty-third Street.

Once on the other side of the street the werewolf disappeared from Brian's sight. He was no longer concerned with the creature, though, but with the young girl. Getting to her side he saw this frail looking girl, no older than fifteen, with her dark hair and dark eyes staring up towards the heavens, as if she was asking for help. He immediately applied pressure to her shoulder wound.

"What is your name?" he asked her.

"Oh, God, what was that thing," was all that she said.

"What is your name?" he asked her again.

"Selena," she answered.

"Selena, I'm going to help you. My name is Brian," he said then reached into his raincoat's left pocket and took out a small plastic bag, which had a mix of herbs and crushed flowers, as well as the small essence of a charmer, in it. Before he left he asked a charmer to give him a mix to sleep on the plane, and she did. But once he was on the plane, he decided not to use the mix and still had it in his pocket. Now he gave it to Selena. Placing some of the mix in her mouth, he made her swallow it. Within only a few seconds Selena was asleep.

"Is she dead?" asked Jennifer Sult with great concern as she came up behind Brian.

He turned to look at her. She was holding his sword that he had thrown at the werewolf. As he stood up to address her, she held it out to him and he took it back. Retracting its blade, he put it back into his raincoat's hidden sleeve.

"She's alive. We need to get her back to my hotel room somehow without being noticed and then we need to get a charmer to address her wound so that she doesn't become a werewolf," he stated then noticed McGavin was nowhere in sight. "Where's McGavin?"

"Checking the young boy's body out," she answered.

"He's dead. There's nothing to check out. We need to concentrate on the living right now," Brian told her.

"I know but he also wanted to make sure that he was dead. McGavin is just doing his duty as a police officer," she explained.

"The creature tossed him over the side without a thought. He doesn't care for male prey. He wants female prey. The poor boy never had a chance. My concern is for the living right now, though, not the dead. We can revenge all the dead later. It wanted the girl more than him. I would say our werewolf is a predator of women even when he is in human form, which means he probably likes to pick woman up in bars or clubs. He is also not subject to lunar changes, as tonight is only a crescent moon, which means he is a fully matured and powerful werewolf. I place him at least at hundred years old, and one that has a deep bloodlust that he indulges often," Brian stated.

"You... you really are a Tiarnán to be reckoned with. That jump you made across the street, I never saw a human jump like that not even at Samhain, and then I saw you throw your sword at the creature and hit it.

You continued after it, too. I mean the werewolf saw you were disarmed but it still ran away from you, Tiarnán. I've never seen anything like that," she said in awe of him.

"I wasn't fast or good enough to stop it from biting her, so there is nothing to be proud about tonight. That damn thing shouldn't have gotten away," he said looking down at the poor unconscious girl.

"But you stopped him from killing her..."

"Let's get her off this damned roof and out of here. I want to take her to my hotel room and then we need to have her treated as soon as possible by a charmer. I refuse to see her turn into a werewolf," he commanded.

"I'll take McGavin and we'll get the car pulled outside of this building," she said then left quickly to follow out his orders.

Brian CuCullen bent down, took off his raincoat, wrapped it gently around her then he picked up the light body of Selena, as if she weighed but mere ounces. He carried her towards one of the other rooftop exits because he wanted to make sure that no one stopped him. The young girl needed the attention of an expert charmer now, not a doctor.

CHAPTER 9

Brother Zheng, a bald and unassuming in appearance and manner Taoist monk, stood in front of his class of first year students, which included Liam CuCullen. They were there to begin studying the undead. For many first year students this turned out to be one of their favorite classes since they usually knew most of the undead creatures from books, video games, and movies Tadhag Zheng discussed, unlike in Introduction to Demonology where they were solemnly instructed on the character and powers of Grigori, Azarel, Lucifer, Baal, and Lilith by Tadhag Beesheba. But in this class it was almost like discussing a horror film they had seen over the summer on TV. The upswing of this was that they had foreknowledge, but the downside was that they almost treated this subject like a film class.

"Good morning class, I am Tadhag Zheng," Zheng introduced himself in his neat schoolroom, which had only a chalkboard for him to write on. He had no need for books since his knowledge of the undead was thought to be encyclopedic. The students sat on bleacher style benches saving the long desks.

"We are here to learn about the undead. Yes, the undead, as in not dead, but, of course, that does not mean that they are not alive. The undead is a creature that should be dead but isn't because of either a curse by a mage or a necromancer, a necromancer's enchantment, or a pact made with a higher level demon necromancer, such as Humunculus Sawol, who is half human and half demon, or through fulfillment of a dark ritual. When you encounter the undead, it is always best to make them permanently dead," he said then laughed gently.

"I will teach you about the undead and by the end of this term you will have some basic knowledge on how to deal with them. There will be only one test in my class at the end of term. It will be inclusive of all we have learned. Other than that I expect you to listen, answer questions when asked, but most of all to learn about the undead. They are a reality we in the Bene Lumen have to deal with. Now the undead are broken into two categories: corporeal and incorporeal. I will begin first with corporeal since you will face them more than the other. Can anyone name an example of the corporeal undead for me?"

Several boys and girls shot their hands up in the air waving them about like flags in the wind. Liam looked about at his classmates. So far he had felt a satisfaction at Samhain that he never felt at Cape Elizabeth. It was not that he no longer had to learn English, math, and science, because he did along with the Undead, Conjuring, Casting, Charms, and Beginning Demonology, but that he understood the purpose for his learning now. He understood why he needed to learn everything taught here and more.

"Miss," Zheng said then closed his eyes as if he was checking a seating chart in his mind, "Hansen."

A blonde haired girl with yellow robes on who sat in the row above Liam stood up. She looked thrilled to have been picked by Tadhag Zheng.

"Zombies," she answered.

"That is correct. You do not have to stand when you answer my questions by the way. I prefer to maintain a relaxed atmosphere," he said gently. "Zombies who come from the negative part of the Voodoo tradition. Yes, there is a positive part of the Voodoo tradition. Samhain has had Voodoo priests and priestess as maols and so hasn't the Bene Lumen. Anyone else have an answer? Let us try Mr. Hamad."

"Ghouls," the brown haired boy in the Lavender robe answered.

"Correct. Ghouls are known to us from Arab folklore they are, indeed, real. And they are ghastly and dangerous creatures and you must be careful when you face them. Now, Mr. Chung, please give me another one."

"The hopping vampires of China, sir," the dark haired boy in emerald green robes answered.

"Yes, the hopping corpses, or hopping vampires, of China. They are exceedingly blood thirsty and vicious creatures with very bad tempers. They don't care about being caught in their atrocities because they enjoy attacking and battling. Who else should I call on? Ms. Milford."

123

"Draugrs from Norse mythology, sir," Molly Milford a dirty blonde haired girl in maroon robes called out.

"Of course, the Draugrs very strong, indeed. The Norse always had to pit themselves against strong opponents to test their own mettle, as much as test their opponents. They can be bear-like, cannibals, and are always difficult to dispatch. It is merely the way of the Viking to like a tough opponent. Ms. Shultz, do you have one for me?" asked Zheng of a timid young brown haired girl in emerald robes.

"Werewolves, sir," she said unsure of her answer.

"No, that is not correct. Werewolves are abominations, men and women who take on the characteristics of wolves through curse or ritual, but they are alive. Of course, there can also be other werecreatures, such as tigers, lions, dogs, and such. Many European countries and cultures have stories of werewolves, including France where they are called Loup-garou; Greece were they are called lycanthropos; Spain hombre lobo; Bulgaria vulkodlak, Czech Republic vlkodlak; Russia oborten, Poland wilkodlak, Ireland foaladh or conriocht, Italy luop mannaro, even Portugal where they are called lobison. It may seem sometimes that werewolves and their like bred like wererabbits," he said with almost a giggle of amusement.

Everyone in the class listened as Tadhag Zheng closed his eyes and smiled as if he had come on to a happy memory in his mind. For a few moments he stood in deep thought smiling. He then opened his eyes and looked at the students.

"There are those who say certain undead creatures become werewolves when they are destroyed but that is not true. There is myth, which is often true, and legend, which is hardly ever true. That is a legend. Werewolves are their own creatures. Some trace the werewolf back to the ancient story of Lycaon in Greek Mythology. Lycaon was transformed into a wolf as the result of eating human flesh. Virgil even mentions men who change into wolves in his writings. In Satyricon Gaius Petronious has one of his characters tell a story about a man who turns into a wolf when the moon is full. The werewolf has an old, rich, and fascinating history. But you will learn more about that in your Abominations Class, which I also teach. I am somewhat of an expert on these particular creatures. Mr. CuCullen, can you name another corporeal undead for me?"

Liam felt his heart jump into his throat. He had not expected to be called on by Tadhag Zheng. But, of course, he should have expected it, he thought. Sian Boru probably spoke to Zheng about him and told him to make sure I was challenged. She told him that she expected a great deal from him in all his classes.

"Um, um... vampires, sir," he said.

"Exactly, vampires. They can be found in Europe, America, Asia, everywhere actually. Some call them the kings and queens of the undead because of the extent of their powers. Like werecreatures they become more and more powerful the longer they exist. Most have lost their souls, which are in servitude to a demon or another vampire, though some posses their souls because they were so evil in life. They are some of the most dangerous undead you will ever face. Did you know that Vlad Dracul, or Vlad the Impaler, really did become a vampire? He is not known as Dracula, as he is mentioned in film and books, but is known to us in the Bene Lumen as Vladmir Dragon. So many times he has slipped away from us, too many times. He is a very powerful adversary indeed. But we are not through with the undead, are we? Can you, Ms. Simon, name another?"

"Um, would that be revenants, sir?" answered a shy young strawberry blonde haired girl in emerald green robes.

"Correct. Revenants. Stories of revenants first come to us from medieval chroniclers, who write of these undead attacking caravans of crusaders. They took them very seriously. They are the recently dead who have been raised, so to speak, in order to seek revenge on those who were responsible for their death. They are truly bitter and petty creatures that merely want to bring as many souls with them as possible when they return to their state of being dead. I believe I will take one more answer. Mr. M'benga," said Brother Zheng.

"I do not think that wights have been mentioned, sir," answered the strong jawed brown skinned and bald M'Benga who wore a maroon robe.

"Very good. They have not been mentioned."

"What is the difference of a zombie, a revenant and a wight, sir because they all sound like they are the same?" asked one of the students in the back row, a boy blonde haired wearing a emerald green robe, who looked like a smaller version of Donovan Talbot.

"Well, Mr. Talbot, a zombie is the body brought back to life in order to act on the will of its master. It has no soul, though it may be enchanted to seem to have a soul, nor a mind of its own, but does only as it is commanded. They are slow in movements and in wit, but are difficult to stop or dispose of. A revenant has no soul, but does have its mental bearings, though not fully. It can think, but of course it thinks only of revenge as it is obsessed with killing those it blames for its death. A wight, though, is different from the other two in that when it is revived by an extremely powerful necromancer it has its evil soul returned to its body and its mind is completely intact. In many ways it can pass itself off as a living human being, except for certain telltale signs, which you find with all undead. A wight even needs to eat if it wants to avoid becoming emaciated like other undead," he explained.

"What are the signs, sir?" asked Mr. Talbot.

"Ahh, first off there is bad breath," Zheng said and everyone in the class began to giggle. "Oh, not just normal bad breath but the worst breath you have ever smelled. Remember this creature is undead, which means it should be dead. Its insides are rotting away. Next, since its blood ceases to flow through its body, its skin is pale, which burns easily in the sun, and ice cold. Now bad breath along with pale skin that easily burns in the sun and feels ice cold can be concealed with some effort, but one thing cannot be concealed. If you get close enough to an undead to place your head against its chest, you will notice that it has no heartbeat," he said.

"Those are the only ways to tell it is undead, sir?" asked Simon quietly.

"No, there is another way," he said then reached under his robe and took out a clear crystal, which was hanging from a chain. Tadhag Zheng dangled the crystal so that everyone could see it then he moved to one of the male students in the front row and placed the crystal close to his skin. A bluish light began to glow from the crystal.

"You see this is a soul crystal. If Mr. Chirac here was undead the crystal would glow red because it senses a lack of soul," explained Tadhag Zheng.

"But what about a wight, sir," blurted out Liam as he had become fascinated with this talk of the undead.

"Ahh, yes, a wight. It has a soul, but an evil soul. If I was to place this crystal near a wight then a black light would glow from it," he said pleasantly then put his soul crystal away.

"Where can you get a soul crystal, sir?" asked M'Benga.

"Your uncle M'Tenga has one I believe," said Zheng. "He got his from a charmer of some skill. A charmer needs to find the right type of crystal then he or she can endow it with this power. They are not easy to come by."

The bell ending their lesson rang. Everyone in the class seemed apprehensive to leave. Tadhag Zheng had made the time pass quickly with his style and knowledge. They all wanted to stay and listen to more, but the class was over.

"I want you all to think about what we have talked about today. The Undead are fascinating but they are also deadly and evil. The man whose body was used to make a zombie may have been good, but that zombie is evil. Remember that, especially if you_are ever to encounter someone you knew and liked in life that was turned into an undead you have to remember they are evil, even if they tell you otherwise, they are evil. That above all you must remember from this class. The undead are evil. I can only think of one exception and that exception is exceptional, so he does not count. Next class we will discuss incorporeal undead, such as ghosts and poltergeists."

In New York CuCullen gets a charmer...

Brian CuCullen watched as the charmer, Brother Thomas Zane, who Jennifer Sult had called in worked on the young girl, worked with the victim. The first potion he administrated to her was one to aid her body in replenishing the blood she had lost. After that he began the work to remove the pollution, the contamination, of her blood by the werewolf. It was now going on three days and it was getting nearer to the point of no return when the young girl was either cured or would need to be destroyed before she could became a werewolf, too. With the help of Sgt. McGavin they had gotten the young girl into his room. McGavin gave the clerk all sorts of trouble as Sult and Brian CuCullen got the young girl into the smallish elevator that the Chelsea had and took her up to his room, which overlooked Twenty-Third street, on the fifth floor.

Selena Maria Limos, as they had found out was her full name, was put into a healing trance by Brother Zane with a special potion. He had never encountered such a powerful bite before, which wasn't surprising because the good Brother had seen only few werewolf bites. His initial potion did not draw out all the abomination's pollution from her blood. Now he brewed another potion, which he hoped would remove the rest of the werewolf's pollution.

"She's become a front page story for the New York newspapers," McGavin pointed out then showed Brian the front page of the Daily news, which had a large picture of Selena Limos on the cover. "What do we do?"

"I'm not sure exactly," Brian answered.

"Well, if Brother Zane can cure her, we return her to her parents somehow," Jennifer Sult stated.

"It's not that simple. Once you have been bitten by a werewolf and survive, there is a lingering effect that never goes away. You become sensitive to werecreatures, to all evil, you can feel their presence when they are near, sense their emotions and thoughts. Some who survive their bites even become sensitive to evil in general. It is almost as if they can see it in a person. She will have to be taught to deal with this power," Brian CuCullen explained.

"But what about her family?" asked Sult.

"She will need to understand what happened to her; she will also need to be trained to deal with her ability to sense werecreatures. I am afraid that if Selena Limos survives she will need to be sent to Samhain for training," Brian told them.

"But she is only fourteen, she's got family here," interjected McGavin.

"Yeah, what about her family?" asked Sult.

"She is dead to them now. She will not want to be near them because she will feel that she is a danger to them," Brian said.

"I'm not sure about that. I don't think she'll feel that way," said McGavin, who never truly understood why his mother had to battle evil to the point that she died doing it.

"Yes, she will," Brian, said. "Surviving a werewolf bite changes you in too many ways. You will never be the same."

"He is right," added Brother Zane who had completed giving her his newest potion. "Coming that close to such a depraved evil makes you understand the battle we face better than most people, even some in this room. In some ways she will understand evil better than any of us, except maybe the Tiarnán here. And in understanding this evil, having come so close to it, so close to becoming like them, she will have the overpowering need to hunt such evil and fight it. Young Selena Limos, if she survives, will become Ardal Cathal from an act of desecration that almost took her soul from her."

"You see a victim of a werewolf bite, even if they are cured of the bite, have already experienced the creatures bloodlust and sense of joy at having killed while the creature was biting it. They can even sense the creature's emotions and memories of its last few kills as their teeth sink into them. You cannot just forget such a thing. It stays with you forever," Brian stated.

"You know a werewolf bite survivor?" asked Brother Zane.

"Not a werewolf, but a weretiger's bite. To this day she can sense most evil when it is near. Only those whose skills can truly hide their debased nature go unnoticed by her," he answered. "This poor girl's life is changed forever. She will now have an overpowering need to save others from her fate and to destroy evil such as she experienced. Her whole sense of the world, the innocence she had before the attack, will be gone. She will see the world as a place of good or evil and her mind will be open to the shadow war that wages all around her. She can never go home again."

"But what about her family, they will be worried about her?" asked Sult once again.

"I saved her, so I will be her family from now on. Her own family cannot help her, or train her for the life she has now been born into," he said looking at the young girl who lay on his hotel bed. She was fourteen falling right in the middle of Kieran and Liam. Even if she wasn't his biological family, she was now family.

"I need a spirit guide so that I can contact Samhain through the astral plain," Brian ordered.

"I'll call one I know and have her come here," Jennifer said then took out her cell phone and dialed a number.

"I still don't like this," said McGavin.

"Once you found out that all those creatures that you thought were just imaginary creations by writers and film makers were true, how did you feel?" asked Brian CuCullen.

"It scared the living daylights out of me."

"Exactly," Brian interrupted him. "And it was only through the help of your mother and the Bene Lumen that you were able to come to terms with this knowledge and its importance, otherwise you'd be in an asylum somewhere wearing a coat that ties in the back. She now not only knows that they exist but she can sense evil, she can feel the presence of evil when it is near."

"Yeah, but..."

"Do you think her parents will be able to deal with her nightmares where she dreams of biting into people and ripping their flesh with her claws? These nightmares will be true, as she will be tapping into the supra unconsciousness of werecreatures all around the world."

"I...I don't' know," answered McGavin.

"Do you think a psychologist will be able to make those dreams go away with his Freudian or Jungian theories when they are real and she knows it? No one will know how to help her deal with this, except us."

"Nay... but," then McGavin fell silent as he thought about what Brian had said. This young girl had seen a werewolf, felt its teeth sink into her skin, then felt what that creature felt when it killed. She was now sensitive to these creatures and could even sense them. He just needed to know one more thing. "CuCullen, will werewolves and their like know that she can sense them, too?"

"Yes, they'll know it. She'll be marked as someone who survived a werecreatures attack for the rest of her life, and they don't like those who survive their attacks and are not turned because it makes them vulnerable."

"I don't believe this," McGavin said with a sigh, "of course, she has to go to Samhain. She's a sitting duck otherwise. She has to learn how to deal with..."

"The spiritual guide is on the way," Jennifer Sult interrupted McGavin.

Before any other words could be exchanged, the young girl began to moan loudly. Brother Zane and Brian CuCullen moved to her side. Slowly, the moan evolved into screams, as all the horrors the werewolf bestowed on her came rushing into her conscious mind. She sat up in the bed. Brian sat down beside her and took the small girl into his arms. Her screams dissolved into sobs as she grabbed onto him.

"Oh, God," she cried, "It was so horrible. Blood and pain, that's all he wants is blood and pain. He has to be stopped now, right now."

"It's over," he said to her in a calm voice.

"No, it isn't. They are out there, he is out there still killing, wanting to kill more," she said pulling away from him so that she could look into his eyes. "He has to be stopped. And everyone like him has to be stopped."

Brian stared into her brown eyes, which were filled with pain but also determination. Just as he knew it, surviving a werewolf bite had permanently changed her. Without the training or bloodline, it made her into a Bene Lumen for life. Brother Zane made her lie down then became to examine her. He took out a blue crystal from his pocket and held it to her forehead. When the crystal didn't change color, he smiled and turned to the rest of the people in the room.

"It's passed. She's safe from contamination," he stated.

"Father," she said looking at Brother Zane.

"I'm a brother not a priest," he told her.

"Brother, please pray for this beasts victims. It's horrible what he does to them. He causes them pain and terror before killing them. He feeds on their terror and pain," she said.

"I'll pray for them. I will pray for them and for all of us who must stop the creature."

"He's afraid of you," she said looking at Brian CuCullen.

"I know he is," Brian answered.

"I want him to be afraid of me, too. I want his kind to hate me. Help me do that," she said.

"Don't worry, he will be someday. He and his kind will fear you someday. I promise you that. You are now part of my family, do you understand what that means?"

"I can't go home. They would kill my family," she said with large tears forming in her eyes.

"I will be your father now, not your flesh and blood father, but one that will be able," he said, "to protect you."

"Brother, please pray for my family. Pray that..." she started to say.

"Please drink this," Brother said to her as he put a small bottle of orange liquid to her lips. She drank some of the liquid and quickly became calm then fell asleep.

"I wish I had some of that stuff on the nights that I can't sleep lately," Sgt. McGavin quipped.

"Believe me it works," Sult told him.

"She needs to sleep, to rest," Brother Zane stated then got up and collected his things. "I need to go now. But if you need anything else from me, Tiarnán, just have Jennifer call me."

Brother Zane nodded his head then went to the hotel door, opened it, and left. Brian CuCullen returned the bedside of Selena Limos.

"When will your spiritual guide get here?" he asked.

"Give her another fifteen minutes. The village isn't that far away but she was busy when I called her," Jennifer Sult replied.

"What are you going to do with her?" McGavin asked about the young girl.

"Tell Headmaster Fergus to get ready for her then make arrangements for her to go to Samhain," he answered.

"Fergus... I remember my mother saying that the headmaster of Samhain when she was there was a Mallory Fergus. Any relation?" asked McGavin.

"It's the same man," answered Sult.

"Really, you got to be kidding me, the same guy? Huh, he's got to be old," McGavin, said.

"He is old, very old, older than any of us even know," replied Brian.

"Geez, you people are a real trip," McGavin said more to himself than anyone else.

For the next ten minutes they sat quietly waiting for the spiritual guide to arrive. Jennifer Sult sat staring half in awe and half in frustration at Brian CuCullen. He was a Tiarnán, which meant whatever he said was final. She couldn't argue with him and after seeing him pursue that werewolf she wasn't sure she wanted to argue with him. Sgt. McGavin sat by the French doors, which faced the Twenty-Third Street and read the Sports Page.

Finally, there was a knock on the door. Jennifer let the spiritual guide into the room. The spiritual guide was a young woman, no older than twenty-five, with long auburn hair and dark blue eyes. Brian CuCullen noticed that she dressed in what his son Kieran would call earthy crunchy, sandal woody kind of way.

"Everyone this is Delia Malone," Jennifer introduced her.

"Hey," said McGavin as he looked over the top of his newspaper.

"Hello," Delia replied.

"Hello," Brian said.

Delia stared intensely at Brian for a few moments. When she was done staring at him, her expression on her face became soft. She moved close to him and offered him her right hand.

"I believe warriors offer their sword hands to each other. Ivan once told me that," she said.

He took her hand and shook it. When he did this, he thought he felt a volt of electricity pass between them. He ignored it, though, since he wasn't sure why it had happened.

"You are the first Tiarnán I have met. Your aura is amazing, filled with power, strength, burdens, and great sadness. Your presence sort of brings out the fullness of my powers, too. Trippy! This is a rush," she explained to him the volt that passed between them.

"It's okay. Certain Tiarnán auras can have that effect on spirit guides," he said. "I need you to contact Maol Stonefeather at Samhain and have him arrange an astral plain meeting between Mallory and my sons and me."

"My pleasure," she said. "This will only take me a few seconds in your reality, though in my reality it will take some time. When I return, you will need to prepare to enter the astral plain with me."

"I understand. I've done this before," Brian said.

Without explaining herself Delia Malone sat down on the floor assuming the lotus position then she closed her eyes. Suddenly, the lights in the room flickered and Delia's body became rigid.

"See people don't have to worry about me telling others about you guys because no one would believe me in the first place," McGavin said. "You people are definitely the you-gotta-see-to-believe types."

"I've been part of this since I was twelve and I still don't believe it sometimes," commented Jennifer.

As quickly as her body went rigid, it returned to a more natural state. Delia Malone was back from the astral plain. She stood up and stretched for a second then faced Brian.

"Stonefeather is getting everyone together on his end. He said to give him fifteen minutes to get them ready for the astral plain," she said.

"Can you read her aura?" Brian asked Delia Malone about Selena Limos.

"Yes, I can," she answered then stared intently at Selena for a few minutes. Finally, she closed her eyes and when she opened them there were tears in her eyes.

"She has been touched by evil," she said. "Her life will never be normal again. She will have a desire to seek out evil and destroy it. That is the weakness of evil, you know, it creates its own mortal enemies by its depraved actions."

"Will she understand my sending her away from her family?" Brian asked her.

"Yes, she will. She would never want to expose her family to what she saw in that creatures mind. She would want to protect her family from that and from herself. The poor girl doubts her goodness now. Samhain will be a good place for her to learn and heal," she said.

"Good. Let's prepare for a trip to the astral plain," he said then sat down on the floor in the lotus position. Delia sat down on the floor in front of him in the same position and took his hands in hers.

"I take it you've done this before?" she asked him.

"Oh, yes," he said.

"Good. This will be easy then," she said "We must become one in spirit. You must concentrate on me and when you feel my soul, you must connect with it and allow it to guide you. Now concentrate."

For several minutes they each concentrated on their separate tasks until Brian felt her soul. Years of practice had allowed him to be open to this. He connected his soul with hers and allowed her to take him out of his body and to the astral plain. Feeling his soul suck out of his body, it followed her soul to that place of liquid colors, flexible solids, smells that he could taste as if they were food, and a sense that all dimensions met here on this plane. No matter how many times someone attempted to describe the astral plain, it always fell short. You had to experience it to truly understand it.

Leading him through this plane, Delia finally stopped where astral representations of Stonefeather, Mallory, Kieran and Liam waited for them. The representations were colorful with auras surrounding them. They both looked like the person in real life and a drawing of the person at the same time. Since on the astral plain time had no meaning, Brian realized that it might have taken his sons hours to achieve this plane or minutes. It didn't matter.

"Brian, it is good to see you," Mallory said.

"Mallory, Stonefeather," Brian said their names to greet them then he turned to his sons. "I told you I had other ways of keeping in touch."

"Dad, this is fantastic. I can't believe we can meet like this," Liam said.

"I don't know. It kind of makes me a little sick to my stomach being here," Kieran admitted.

"I used to be like that, too," Brian said. "Let me make this quick then, so you don't spend hours vomiting when you return to your reality. I saved a girl from a werewolf but not before she was bitten. A charmer saved her but..."

"But she, of course, is one of us now. How old is she?" asked Mallory making this easier for Brian CuCullen then it should be.

"Fourteen. I need to make arrangements for her to come to Samhain," Brian said.

"I will make all those arrangements for that, Brian," Mallory said. "You have a werewolf to slay."

"Could you also make arrangements with a few well-placed Giolla for Selena to be quietly adopted by me. You know - false paperwork and the rest. I saved her, so I am responsible for her now," Brian said.

"Of course, I understand the obligations of power. I will do that, too," Mallory replied.

"Boys, I want you to take care of her. She will be an outsider there, you know how that feels," Brian said to his sons.

"Why are you adopting her?" asked Kieran.

"Because she needs us, Kieran."

"I understand, Dad," said Liam. "I'll explain it to Kieran."

"You understand, Liam?" asked Brian.

"Yes, Dad. I understand in a small way what she will need us now. She is bonded to you and to us now."

"He does understand, Brian. He is strong and powerful. Sian believes he is a Triune Conjurer like Merlin," Mallory said putting a little emphasis on the name of Merlin. "Ancient knowledge exists inside of him."

"Mallory, does Sian protect him?" asked Brian.

"Yes, she does. She has a small group placed around him to help him fulfill his potential and to protect him," Mallory stated.

"Boys, when Selena gets there, she is your sister. You must protect her like she is your flesh and blood. Now Stonefeather can lead you two back, I need to talk to Mallory without you," he said.

"Goodbye, Dad," Liam said but Kieran said nothing. Stonefeather led his sons away.

"Yes, Brian," Mallory said.

"A Triune Conjurer," said Brian CuCullen.

"Yes, and maybe more than that. He may be something truly special. It happens now and again."

"How special?" Brian asked.

"So special that if the Illuminatii knew about him, they would stop at nothing to kill him."

"Mallory, we are talking about my son. How can we know if he is this special, how can we find out?"

"Sian has a way. During Halloween she will test him," Mallory replied.

"If he is a truly special Triune Conjurer, he will need extra protection. I want him..."

"I know, Brian, but there will be no Ardal Cathal acting as security on Samhain. He is safe here at Samhain. And let us not forget that his father is a Tiarnán and his brother may be a Tiarnán, and he has a teacher like Sian Boru," Mallory stated. "He is well taken care of. Now you should find that werewolf and kill it."

Stonefeather returned for Mallory and led him away. Delia Malone took Brian CuCullen in hand and led him back to his body. Once securely back in his own body Brian bolted up off the floor. His son had the potential to be another Merlin.

"Tiarnán, I congratulate you on your youngest son. He sounds truly remarkable," Delia said to him as she stretched out.

"You know not to mention this fact to anyone," he responded to her congratulations.

"I will not. And I should be going," she said.

"No, do not leave yet. There are some things that need to be done.

Jennifer, I want you and Delia to gather together all the Bene Lumen in the New York City. I also need a Fiach to hunt. This werewolf will go underground now. Until he thinks it's safe he'll feed off of those who won't be missed, such as homeless and runaways. We need to look out for these people," said Brian CuCullen.

"What about me?" asked Sgt. McGavin.

"I want you to do the same with all the Giolla in NYC. We need to keep an eye out for his new feeding ground, so that I can confront him," he stated.

"What about her?" asked Jennifer Sult.

"Mallory is making arrangements for her to be transported to Samhain," he answered.

"I don't agree with this. You can't separate her from her family."

"Her family thinks she is dead," Sgt. McGavin said. "There was so much blood on the roof, all of it hers, that everyone will assume she's dead and will be looking for the body."

"But she isn't dead," stated Jennifer Sult angrily.

"She is to them," replied Brian CuCullen in a voice that allowed for no more argument. He turned and looked at the young girl. She was sleeping comfortably and would remain asleep for several more hours. When she awakened, he would spend hours talking with her, preparing her for what was to come next. He would also tell her that she was now part of his family and that his sons would look out for her at Samhain. If she could survive a werewolf's bite, she could survive this upheaval in her life.

CHAPTER 10

It was the first Ruadh game of the season for the Aongus Misfits, and they were not sure they were ready for the game themselves. After three weeks of practicing as a team, three weeks of bruises, bumps, falls, and Talbot trying to tutor Kieran in Ruadh, as well as sword play; Jan, Philippe, Kieran and Jean Pierre had to face Tamo's Titans. Like he felt the first time he ever played football in front of a crowd, Kieran was so nervous he couldn't eat before the game. He scanned the large audience checking to make sure that Liam was sitting with Selena by his side. He finally found them in the first row on the Aongus Misfits side. Liam was sitting with Dani, Brigid and Selena cheering him on.

Although when he first heard his father tell him to take care of Selena he couldn't believe that he wanted Liam and him to accept a stranger as a sister, his attitude changed after meeting her. When he met her and saw in her eyes the pain she felt, he couldn't help but feel protective of her, wanting to make sure she was taken care of. Without admitting to it, he agreed with his father's decision. Over the last few weeks since her arrival both he and Liam went out of their way to treat her like family and to make sure she felt protected, even to the point that he asked if she could be placed in CuChulainn House, so that he could keep an eye on her. Mallory, who obliged him for now, seemed pleased with his request, as if it was a sign that Kieran was slowly accepting who he was and what that entailed.

"All right guys lets huddle up," Kieran called the team together.

Kieran was the official team captain. Jan, who was the best player, did not want to be captain nor did she care who was. All she wanted to do was play. Jean Pierre and Philippe agreed that as friends they didn't want to be in the position to boss the other around, so the job of team captain fell to Kieran. He didn't want the position of captain and thought he was the least qualified for it because he had no experience with Ruadh and was probably the least physically capable member on the team. But he was selected captain against his own wishes anyway. Kieran assumed it was because he was the son of a Tiarnán. Everyone huddled around him.

"Okay, it's a long season so let's not go crazy over the first game. If we lose our first couple of games as we get used to each other, it won't knock us out of contention for the playoffs. There are twenty teams and we have to play every team at least once, so let's just play hard and improve each game and we'll do fine," he stated.

"You call that a pep talk. I am French and I could even do better than saying don't worry if we lose because we will get better," Philippe commented disdainfully.

"Philippe, don't start with him right now," Jean Pierre said.

"Who takes the face off?" asked Jan.

"You do," Kieran answered surprised that she even asked. "Let's go."

The four teammates ran towards the Ruadh playing field, climbing onto the bars. Jean Pierre climbed his way towards the goal, where Kieran had him posted. Jan acrobatically swung from bar to bar making her way towards the center where the judge and the opposing team player waited for her. Kieran and Philippe took their positions not too far from where Jan was, where they would wait to see who would win the face off.

"Okay," the judge, a lecturer in Bene Lumen History, said. "Any really dirty play will be penalized with the immediate loss of the ball, and if I see any truly nasty plays that cause intentional injury I will penalize the player with the loss of ball for his team and a card against his team. Three cards will add up to the loss of one point from your score. Are you ready to play?"

Both the players nodded in the affirmative. The judge tossed the corb up in the air and swung away, as Jan and the player from the Tamo's Titans flew after the corb. Jan got to it first, but the opposing player slapped the ball so hard that it flew out of her hand towards a Tamo's Titan's player. Philippe pursued the player, even though Kieran had told him that it would be better when the opposing team had the corb that they took up defensive positions rather than chasing them around without a plan or line of defense. Already his team was not following his orders. They were freelancing and acting as individuals instead of as a team.

Within seconds the opposing team scored to the enthusiastic cheers of the crowd. The game went, as Kieran feared it would, with his team not playing with any sense of a game plan. By the end of the half his team was down sixteen to five, and four of those five points were scored by Jan without much help from her teammates. When the judge blew the whistle for halftime, Kieran debated whether he should forfeit the rest of the game, but chose instead to talk to his team like the captain he was.

"Well, that wasn't pleasant at all," said Kieran.

"No, it wasn't pleasant at all," agreed a dour Jean Pierre.

"We are getting our ass kicked out there. Should we forfeit the game now and take the rest of the afternoon off?" he asked them.

"No, we shouldn't," answered Jan. She was angered by the question.

"Okay, then we should keep playing. But can we play as a team instead of as strangers and can we play as best as we can without thinking about our own individual stats or reputation?" Kieran asked.

"Are you insulting me? What do you mean by that?" asked Philippe.

"I mean everything we practiced and talked about, we have done the opposite. We are playing like four individuals out there. There is no communicating and team play. Jan is our best player and she is out there waiting for one of us to set her up for an easy goal. Let's realize what our strengths are and play to them. But instead we are trying to do everything on our own."

"I don't know what you are talking about, Captain," Philippe stated.

"Yes, you do," Jan said. This was the most she had said in all their practices and meeting as a team. Kieran was pleasantly surprised by Jan's fired up attitude.

"We are playing like four strangers, which we cannot do and expect to accomplish anything except last place in this league. I do not want to be in last place at the season's end," Jean Pierre pointed out.

"Exactly. Now let's play like a team and see if we can improve in the second half. We may be too far behind to win this game, but that doesn't mean we can't play hard and use this as a way of getting ready for our next game," he told his teammates.

"Let's go and do what our captain said," Jan declared then they broke towards the Ruadh playing field.

The second half went better than the first half for Aongus Misfits. During stretches the Misfits played as a team with Jan benefitting from their better passing and communication with a few easy scores. Kieran was starting to believe that he could even play this game. Towards the end of the game with only a minute left the score was 29 to 20, which was a victory of sorts for the Misfits to close the score, Kieran finally felt his own play improving to the point that he started to understand the complexities of the game. As Tamo's Titans were coming down towards the Misfits' goal, Kieran could see the passing lane in his imagination. Maybe it was instinct, or maybe it was just coming to understand the game, but he knew where the next pass was headed.

Dropping from the bar that he had been hanging from Kieran grabbed the pole below him by wrapping his knees around it then swung himself forward with his hands free so that he could catch the corb as it was thrown. Jan, seeing Kieran's move, began to swing as fast as she could towards the Titans' goal. Kieran caught the corb then in one motion twisted in midair and threw the corb towards Jan. It was an acrobatic move that he wouldn't have dared try at the start of the game. She caught the corb and threw it into their goal. The judge blew the final whistle.

With that goal Kieran knew exactly how the game should be played and that he was capable of playing it. He had the physical and mental skills to do this. All the doubts he was having about Ruadh and being at Samhain were unnecessary because he did belong here. All the players swung their way off the bars and headed towards their own bench. In the crowd Kieran could see Liam waving to him. He waved back then waved at Selena, who smiled at him.

"We got better," Philippe declared.

"Yes, we did," agreed Jean Pierre.

"Next time we can win if you play like you did at the end of the game," Jan said to Kieran.

"It will take more than me playing well for us to win," he replied.

"No, it will take you playing as well as you can," she said. "Together, you and I can be an offensive force. I knew what you were going to do I saw it just like you saw it. We could be a successful pair. Other teams will have trouble stopping you and me when we work together like that."

"But Jean Pierre and Philippe have to be..." Kieran started to say but she cut him off.

"They play as well as they can, and will play better when you play up to your best. You are just starting to play well. We will go as far as you can take us, Captain Kieran. You lead and we will follow," she stated then walked away towards the locker area so that she could change out of her uniform.

"I agree with her," Philippe said.

"Sorry, Kieran, you are the key to our success as a team," Jean Pierre added.

"Yes, you are. So let us all agree if we lose, it is your fault and if you win, it is our victory. I like the sound of that," Philippe stated.

"He is an egotist but he has a point. You are the captain and the leader," Jean Pierre said to Kieran.

"I am not the leader," he said but they didn't listen and followed Jan to the locker room.

Back in Manhattan...

"The werewolf is now staying close to Spuyten Duyvil," said Paul Mecouri. "I finally tracked his scent there. He has easy access to the Bronx, Manhattan, even Yonkers from there. At night I believe he takes off from his hiding spot, maybe an apartment in the area, does his hunting of those who no one will miss then returns to his spot which is there somewhere in Spuyten Duyvil area. He's a smart beast, too, because I can't get a complete bead on where his lair is, only where his territory is."

Mecouri was the local Fiach. Having graduated from Samhain twelve years ago his hunting prowess was considered impressive and needed to be with the werewolf they were tracking, who so far had been able to keep his tracks cold for three weeks. The local Bene Lumen and Giolla were able to keep a few steps behind him by tracking the homeless and runaway population, which the werewolf was now feeding on. They did this by befriending the population, noting who made what area of the city their home, keeping an eye on runaway shelters and homeless shelters, and documenting as many of them as they could. When a particular homeless man or woman disappeared they would search for signs of them. They did the same with runaways. So far they had documented the death of eleven homeless and three runaways. And the city didn't notice these deaths because of who the victims were. This was an unfortunate byproduct of a large city.

"Spuyten Duyvil," Brian CuCullen said the name aloud. He turned to Jennifer Sult who had become his top lieutenant. "Give me a history of the area."

"In pre British Colonial times when New York was still New Amsterdam, there was a horn player by the name of Anthony Van Corlaer who would blow his horn whenever Peter Stuyvesant wanted to call together the Dutch people for whatever reasons. One night, Peter Stuyvesant received word that the English were going to attack New Amsterdam to wrest it from the Dutch. He sent Anthony to warn the Dutch people along the Hudson in order to prepare them to fight for their land. It was a stormy night, though, and when Van Corlaer reached the tip of Manhattan Island, there was no ferry waiting there to take him across the tide water creek which connects the Harlem and Hudson Rivers. Allegedly, Van Corlaer played his horn over and over again trying to call the ferryman, but there was no answer. Conscious of the importance of his mission and the need to gather people for the cause, he decided he would swim across that creek in spite of this devil, which the Dutch people thought lived in the water there, or as they said in spuyt den duyvil," she explained to Brian.

"Well, the Devil heard him calling for the ferryman, and when Anthony had swum into the middle of the creek, the Devil caught him by the leg under the water and started dragging him under the water to his death. Van Corlaer pulled out his horn and he blew a terrific blast, louder than he had ever done before, so loud that it was louder than the wind. This sound startled the Devil so much that he let go of his leg letting him swim away. People who had gathered on the other side of the creek they could see him coming towards the land, but Van Corlaer did not have strength enough after his battle with the Devil to swim the rest of the way across and he drowned. Since then that area of New York has been called Spuyten Duyvil. The creek is called that, too."

"Then we need an Eadach because it sounds as if there is a water demon hiding away in that water. An Eadach can keep the water demon occupied in case it comes to the werewolf's defense," Brian CuCullen said.

"I'll make sure one is with us when we go after the werewolf," Sult said to him.

"He's gone from Hell's Kitchen to Spuyten Duyvil; from one evil hot spot to another. This creature gains power from being around areas in which evil thrives, as if he uses that evil to supplement his already strong powers. It must draw healing or strength from it somehow. This is a very smart creature," Brian CuCullen said aloud as if he was merely thinking.

"Should I let the NYPD know about this, tell them that I had an informant give me some 411 on a potential location of the serial killer?" asked Sgt. McGavin.

"No. It would only get too many cops killed if they got in the werewolf's way. Bullets, blessed or not, aren't going to stop this one. This calls for a blessed sword, made of Calibur, to give him a deathblow. He's too smart and too powerful for anything else. I'll take care of this the only way it can be done and that is with a blade to the heart or to cut his head off. The old ways are still the best ways when it comes to certain creatures and demons."

"How big of a fealty should I prepare for this hunt?" asked Jennifer.

"Seven, it's a lucky number. I'll take a Fiach, an Eadach, a conjurer, three Ardal Cathal and me," answered Brian.

"Well, I'll call in a conjurer, and two other Ardal Cathal," she said.

"Not you, Jennifer. You are Aongus Cathal. I don't want you to come with us," Brian told her.

"Why not me?"

"Because in case I fail, I need someone competent to continue the hunt and that is you," he said.

"But..." she was taken aback by his comment. This Tiarnán trusted her enough to leave her in reserve in case he failed. There was no insult there, only a compliment.

"New York seems to have a lot of hot spots, so if we don't get him here, know that he will merely move on to the next one," Brian told her.

"It doesn't have as many as Maine," Jennifer Sult responded defiantly.

"What about me?" asked Sgt. McGavin.

"You should be in the area in case we succeed. Make sure one of my people has your cell phone number and we'll call you if all goes well, so that you can clean up the mess we leave," he explained. "Now let's get this show on the road."

New York City at night had the quality of being a beautiful city, as well as a frightening one, a seductive city as well as a decayed one, a courageous city as well as a weak one. Amongst the architecture that mixed those buildings which seemed to be striving towards the heaven along with those squat buildings, some of which were decorated with gargoyles and others in need of great repair, the battle between good and evil played out, and evil appeared to be winning. In the passive acceptance of evil's slow victories, victories that made the twentieth century a hundred years of slow progress for fostering malevolence's cause, the people had compromised their willingness to recognize evil and call it by its actual name. They backed away from absolutes and in doing so they embraced the gray where evil's degeneracy found solace and room to grow. But some recognized that the battle, which had been fought since the beginning of time, a battle documented in mythologies and histories, still waged around them. Some continued to fight the good fight.

In a white cargo van Brian CuCullen and his fealty, six chosen Bene Lumen, were being transported to the area named Spuyten Duyvil. Through the parts of Manhattan, which urban renewal and high rents had not yet revisited, the cargo van worked its way up through Midtown, Lincoln Center, the Upper Westside, Harlem, Washington Heights, until it finally made it into Inwood section of Manhattan, which ended Manhattan Island. Through one section of Manhattan after another they could see through the front window of the van the effects of how some parts of humanity chose to ignore other parts of humanity based on economics seeming to only take notice when the real estate interested them.

The Van pulled over near the stadium that housed Columbia University football team. Before crossing over the Broadway Bridge to the other side of the Spuyten Duyvil Creek, Brian CuCullen dispersed his fealty. Mecouri would do most of the beating of the bushes, telling everyone where to go, except for the Eadach and the conjurer who would make camp on the Manhattan side of the creek making sure no aid would be given to the werewolf by whatever water demon lived there. Once they had dispersed, the van's driver continued over the Broadway Bridge and dropped Brian off near the Spuyten Duyvil public playground.

Brian CuCullen made his way to the playing field, hopped the fence and took a stand in the middle of a baseball field. This was where he wanted to face the werewolf, in a place where neither of them would have an advantage, where they had no choice but to battle until one of them was dead. It was time to end this. He knelt down on one knee, resting his sword arm on his right thigh. Under his raincoat his sword with the retractable blade waited to be pulled out for battle. Everything was set, and then Brian wondered if he should pray.

It had been years since he had prayed, the last time being at Siobhan's funeral. Siobhan was a druid priestess, but she agreed to raise the children as Catholics, like their father was. There were few true practicing druids left. Her reasoning was simple for raising her sons Catholic, but in its simplicity there was a profound understanding of the universe. Through the auspices of Merlin and Arthur many druid customs had been subtly adopted by Catholics, so that she understood that many of her beliefs were laying in the foundation of this religion. She herself found comfort praying to the Virgin

Mary. But Brian gave that all up with her death. Yes, he made his sons go to Mass and receive the sacraments, but he abstained.

Yet, now he had the urge to pray. It was as if by accepting his role in the Bene Lumen again, that he was saying he needed spiritual help. He bowed his head solemnly for a moment, made the sign of the cross, and began to recite words long ago learned by rote now unsure in his head. These words had meaning that he was no longer sure of, yet they still had a certain comfort for him. He waited and prayed.

For what must have been more than two hours, he waited. It was now well past midnight but not quite coming up to cockcrow and the reappearance of the sun, when he heard and smelled the werewolf. He looked up from his spot and saw the gray furred body running towards him on all fours. Once again he made the sign of the cross then he stood up quickly and took his sword out, retracted its blade, and waited for the werewolf to come to him.

"Hey, what's going on here," a man's voice said from behind him. Brian's focus was so trained on the werewolf that he hadn't noticed someone had come up behind him. He turned his head slightly to see who it was. It was a police officer, about fifty years old and nearing retirement, with gun drawn and aimed at him.

"Get out of here," Brian ordered.

"You can't tell me what to do," the cop said.

"Yes, I can. Look over my shoulder," he said and the cop did. He saw the ferocious werewolf running towards them. A low growl could be heard coming from it, a growl that was getting stronger as it got closer. Suddenly, the werewolf went from running on all fours to running on its hind legs, so that it could use its front legs as weapons.

"What the fu..."

"Get out of here now," Brian told the cop in a voice that left no room for argument. "When you have your wits about you call Sgt. Darrell McGavin. He works out of Manhattan. He will be able to explain this to you."

The old cop didn't say another word, but holstered his gun and ran away. Seeing a werewolf in the park was too much for him to handle. Brian CuCullen now gave the werewolf his full attention. The creature never slowed down but continued at him at its blazing full speed choosing to dive at him when it got close enough. Brian easily sidestepped it and its claws. Thank you, Master Mifune, he thought, knowing that old Samurai had honed his rusty skills. He was able to give it a nice cut on one of its back legs before resuming his defensive squatting position. The werewolf rolled on the grass then readied itself for another attack. Instinctively, the creature knew that its best chance was to take Brian out quickly, so it again sprang at him in a fast attack hoping that Brian would drop his defenses. This time Brian rolled underneath its attack and gave it a good cut on its belly causing it to howl in pain. The werewolf landed on the ground with a wound that bled badly. It was ready for the deathblow.

Regaining his feet, Brian CuCullen prepared an attack of his own this time. He held his blade high as if he was going to wait for the creature to attack him again. When the werewolf began to ready itself for another of its attacks its sinews began flexing under its fur, Brian saw this movement of muscle and knew that it meant it was ready to leap at him, so he spun around and released his sword in a mighty throw catching the werewolf in the middle of its chest shredding its heart. Again the creature howled in pain, though, this time it fell dead after its blood, curdling cry.

By the time he got to the werewolf to retrieve his blade, the bone crunching transformation from creature to human was taking place. He watched as the fur retracted and the shape of the man returned to a human one to reveal a middle-aged, fairly good looking blonde man with a Nazi swastika tattoo on his left shoulder. Bending down to examine the man, Brian noticed that under the tattoo was a date: 1937. As a creature, he was a werewolf, but as a man, he had once been a Nazi, and had been one for the last seventy years. Hitler loved the occult, he must have had more than one werewolf as a pet, he thought, and this must have been one of them. He wondered how many more of Hitler's abominations were still out there in the world doing evil wherever they could.

In the distance CuCullen noticed Mecouri hopping over the fence and come running. Looking back down at the dead man, he saw that his body was beginning rapid decay. Mecouri came up beside Brian.

"It's over," Mecouri stated.

"Uh huh," Brian CuCullen answered.

"What should we do next?" Mecouri asked.

"For the next week or so we need to canvas the city to make sure that none of his victims have been turned into werewolves like him. I have my doubts that he turned any into his fold. Something tells me that he would only make someone a werewolf who was up to his standards of evil," Brian told him.

"Understood," Mecouri said. "I'll put together nightly hunting parties for a few weeks. I know his scent and anyone he made would have his scent. What else?"

"Well, I'll put my affairs in order here and then return to Maine to take my place as Tiarnán."

"Glad to have you," said Mecouri then looked at the body. "That was a nice clean kill you made there."

Brian CuCullen stared back down at the quickly decaying body of the man he just slain. For the first time in a very long time, he felt a sense of pride filling him up and giving him a sense of his proper role in the world. Pride had been lacking in his life for some time. Yes, he did a job and took care of his sons, but for years he had not been living up to his duty, to his vocation, to what he was meant to do. There was no denying he had been born with abilities and skills beyond the normal for a purpose. And he had not been taking these gifts and doing his true duty with them these last ten years. His duty was to fight evil, to slay beasts, to maintain the balance between good and evil, a balance that had shifted too much lately towards evil's success. But he was back doing his duty and was filled with pride because he knew that he belonged on the front line doing this job.

CHAPTER 11

So far during his time at Samhain the only activity that Kieran truly enjoyed was playing Ruadh. Though it still hadn't replaced football for him as his favorite sport, it was a game, which both challenged and exhilarated him at the same time. Even as he improved with each and every practice and game, he still knew he had a long way to go before he was in the top tier of players. And he wanted to be in the top tier. Everything else at Samhain was a struggle, which seemed to have no real payoff for him, especially since he still secretly hoped that he would flunk out of school and return to Cape Elizabeth. On top of his academic woes he was getting demerits every day.

But solace was found for him in Ruadh since it was an athletic competition. He understood sports because there were winners and losers, and he could see improvement in himself by the play of the whole team, as well as his own play. After their first loss, they did better in the second game, but it was still a loss. The third game the Aongus Misfits had their first victory over Morgana's Maniacs. Unfortunately for Kieran, his celebration over their first victory was short lived. That Monday after the win he received three demerits by a sixth year monitor for not knowing the definition of a wight which put him over the limit and sent him to his first JUG of the year, though he doubted it would be his last one he received at Samhain.

Rabbi Justiz was overseeing JUG that day. Along with Kieran there were two other students attending this particular Jug session. Monica Balducci, a comely fifth year student from Tamo House, who had compiled enough demerits because of a bad memory and forgetting to keep appointments, hand in assignments, and address teachers by their proper titles, and Jace Gracia, a sixth year student from Sybil House who had managed to find himself in JUG by breaking one of Headmaster Fergus' windows with a cricket ball, also were in attendance. Rabbi Justiz's form of punishment was to have Kieran, Monica, and Jace read a chapter from a book on demons and then write a fact sheet about what they had learned. It wasn't a difficult task, though Kieran would have preferred a more physical form of punishment.

Once he was done with his punishment, he had to then report to Master Diaghilev to practice running the obstacle course. Since Nadia was in the process of training to break Brian CuCullen's record, she needed a training partner, someone to keep her company more than push her considering no one came close to her overall time in their year, or in any year. Diaghilev chose Kieran for this job. He didn't explain exactly why, only that he had to show up at four o'clock ready to push Nadia and keep her company as she trained. There was no way out of this request, which he disliked more than having to do JUG. Nadia beating him easily in the obstacle course just didn't help his own confidence in ever running it very well.

Kieran rushed through his reading and wrote his fact sheet on wights as comprehensively as he could write. He then handed it in to Rabbi Justiz, who had him stand by his desk while he carefully read it. Once he was finished, Rabbi Justiz handed the paper back to him.

"Here, Kieran," he said, "I recommend you commit this to memory. There is some important information here, which may someday come in handy considering your particular set of skills and talent. Demons are a hazard in your line of work."

"Is memorizing this part of my punishment, sir?" Kieran asked dolefully.

"No, it is a recommendation and nothing more, so don't sound so glum. I was talking to Father Mueller the other day and he mentioned that you show little interest in learning about demons, abominations, spirits, devils, and the Illuminatii. He told me that all your effort is on becoming a better Ruadh player and a stronger, faster, and more capable Aongus Cathal in the physical skills."

"It's not that I show little interest, sir, but I'm so far behind in everything that..."

"That you have decided that some things are more important than others. I can understand that. All students tend to believe those things that they feel that they are best at are more important than those things that they struggle with. But a truly enlightened student discovers that they must keep their mind open to learning a little of everything, so as not to be caught by surprise because you didn't know what your enemy was capable of," Rabbi Justiz completed the sentence for him and then some.

"Yes, sir," he replied.

"Kieran, I realize that you feel that you are more behind in the physical aspects of your training and schooling than in learning about what you will face in battle, but I have a question for you? If you catch up in the physical aspects, what good does it do you when you won't know the powers and weaknesses of a vampire, or a wight, or even a human member of the Illuminatii?"

"I... I suppose I'd just deal with it as best as I could. I mean, sir, from what I can tell an Aongus Cathal basically hacks away at their enemy with a sword or some other blessed weapon until their enemy is defeated."

"If only it was that simple, Kieran. Every creature has their strength and a weakness. You need to know that. The older a vampire gets the more its powers increases, which means the more formidable a foe it is. A truly old vampire is best faced in the day when it is weaker due to sunlight rather than at night when it is stronger. A wight is far harder to slay than a zombie because it has a functioning intelligence. This allows it to attack and counterattack and learn its opponent's weaknesses. What would you do with a necromancer? Do you understand their weaknesses and their strength? It is one thing to have physical gifts, but it is another thing to use those gifts intelligently and well. Do you understand what I'm telling you?" he asked Kieran.

"Yes, sir. Besides being able to do something, I must be able to realize the best way to do it. Having the skill to defeat a demon doesn't mean I have the knowledge to defeat it. I got it," he answered.

"Yes, that is correct. Now go run along to the obstacle course and practice your less intellectual skills. I believe Master Diaghilev will be waiting for you with the always intimidating, yet exquisite to look at, Nadia."

"Thank you, sir," Kieran said then took for the obstacle course.

Bolting out of the schoolroom then out of the schoolhouse, he ran and pulled off his robe as the same time. Underneath his robes he wore his gray workout clothes. As he ran a feeling of dread began to turn his stomach.

Boris Diaghilev thought Kieran was a lost cause spending too many years not working to bring out the extraordinary gifts he was born with. Of course, Diaghilev didn't blame Kieran, he blamed Brian CuCullen, which turned Kieran's stomach even more. In Kieran's opinion his father had nothing to do with him, so he shouldn't be blamed for Kieran's problems. He was in charge of himself, so if it was anyone's fault that he had not developed his skills or muscles fully, it was his own fault.

As he came up to the training fields, he saw Master Diaghilev waiting patiently, along with Nadia and Selena, who sat nearby under a tree. Selena had become attached to Kieran in a very short time. Whenever she had free time she spent it with him, and he allowed her to do so. Headmaster Fergus told him it was probably because of his resemblance to his father, the man who saved her life. When Kieran asked her why she enjoyed being with him so much, all she would say was that she felt safe with him. Considering what she had gone through he couldn't refuse her, though he tried to tell her that he was the least menacing and powerful Aongus Cathal in school. She'd be better off finding protection from anyone else at the school.

Nadia was stretching out her muscles preparing for training by sitting on the ground and grabbing her feet with her hands and touching her head to her knees. Kieran tossed his robe beside Selena, gave her a friendly wave as she looked up at him then joined Nadia in warming up.

"Good to see you, Kieran. I was looking forward to your company today," she said as she pulled her left leg in order to stretch out the hamstring up so high that it was above her head. To Kieran this looked not only impossible but down right painful.

"I hope your Uncle isn't mad that I'm late but I had JUG and couldn't get out of it. I know he wanted me here on time in order to begin being your training partner," he said as he began to stretch out his hamstrings.

"He did not want you as a training partner for me," she stated in a matter of fact tone, "I wanted you as my training partner, Kieran."

"Why?" asked Kieran, as he stopped stretching and stood still, half in shock and half enjoying the fact she wanted him as a partner?

"Because you do not give up even when you are overpowered by an opponent. You are tenacious of spirit and burn with a fire that you do not even have to stoke. I can learn that from you," she said.

"Not that you should take this wrong, but that just sounds silly coming from someone like you. You're the best Aongus Cathal in our year, maybe one of the best they've had in this place and you think you can learn from me," Kieran told her confused.

"Yes, but I can still learn from you. My Uncle has taught me that you can always improve. From you I learn that I could be better and should not doubt myself," she admitted though he almost thought it impossible for her to train harder or to be more diligent in her work. And the thought that she considered him tenacious completely floored him. He was one of the slowest to run the obstacle course, his swordsmanship had improved but not enough for him to defeat anyone, and he was a veritable dunce in class. She considered this a don't-give-up-attitude.

"I think you are nuts. You're the best there is. I can't keep up with you," Kieran said.

"But that won't stop you from trying to keep up, will it," she told him then stopped her stretching and stood up. "You have come a long way in a very short time. I think you will go even farther once you realize that you can be one of the best, just like me, if you allow your body to overcome your mind. Right now you are working hard just to catch up, but once you catch up... you will realize you can be great very great."

"You sound like Talbot," he said.

"Mr. Talbot has become a much better trainer and teacher because of you, Kieran. He is turning into the teacher my Uncle thought he could be. You have taught him as much as he has taught you. That is a good partnership and one I want to have with you."

"I still say you are nuts," he countered, but she didn't flinch from her opinion.

"We shall see," she said then jogged over to Diaghilev who waited by the starting line of the obstacle for them. Kieran joined her.

"We shall work on the first two obstacles only today. I want you to run them over and over again and each time I want you to think less, trust your muscles more and push yourself to be faster. You will run the first two obstacles, run back to the starting line, take two minutes to allow your body to remember what you have done, then run them again. You will keep this up until I blow my whistle for you to stop. Do you understand?" he asked Kieran and Nadia.

"Yes, sir," they both snapped to attention and answered at exactly the same time.

"Good," he said ruefully then raised his hand, "get ready set and go."

Side by side for the first fifty feet they ran as hard as they both could run then Nadia pulled ahead of him. Kieran concentrated on keeping up with her, but she flew away from him. Inside he felt his confidence sagged. Deep down it still annoyed him that a girl, and a pretty girl at that, kept beating him in a footrace, not to mention being stronger and more agile. He had a hard time getting used to that.

She ran the first two obstacles then returned to the starting line, waiting two minutes then did it again. Trailing behind her, Kieran did the same thing as her. Over and over again they did this, pushing their bodies and their minds, imprinting the obstacle course into their muscles' memories. At first, Nadia pulled ahead of him to the point that she was passing him on the course with ease, but as time progressed passing him became harder and harder for her. He got stronger as they progressed through the first two legs of the obstacle course. Even as she tired, he got stronger and stronger, a fact only the most discernible eye could see. Diaghilev shook his head with appreciation. Mallory was right about Brian CuCullen's oldest son; he was special. And he didn't even realize it yet.

Finally, after what seemed an eternity but was only an hour, Diaghilev blew his whistle for them to stop. Nadia dutifully pulled up when she heard the whistle blow, but Kieran didn't. He had just started another go at the first two obstacles, so he continued with his run ignoring the whistle. Trying to push his body harder than ever, trying to go faster than he had ever run in his life, he completed the first two obstacles then dropped to the ground.

"Very good, Kieran, very good. That was your fastest time run yet," Diaghilev yelled in support. Selena came running up to him and sat down beside him. As usual she didn't say a word, but just wanted to be near him. Soon thereafter Nadia joined Selena and sat down on the ground.

"Good work," she said.

"Yeah... sure," he replied as he inhaled and exhaled deeply.

"No, really, you are getting much better, much faster, than you realize. I am impressed with your improvements. Training with me will be good for you and you will be good for me in some ways," she told him.

"Do you need anything, Kieran?" asked Selena shyly. "I can get it for you if you do."

"No, sis, I'm fine right now. All I need is a new pair of lungs and faster legs," he answered. After her first few days with him at Samhain, he had taking to calling her sis as in sister. She seemed to like it, so he made it her permanent nickname. Now Jan, Jean Pierre, and Philippe even called her sis when she came to practices or to watch them play games.

"Very good, Kieran," Diaghilev said as he strolled up to where they sat on the ground. "If you keep this up, you just might make it as an Aongus Cathal after all. I would hate to have to send you down to Ardal Cathal."

"He is an Aongus Cathal," Selena said defensively.

"Ahh, you are a fierce protector of your new brother, huh," Diaghilev said to her. "That is noble and loyal of you, young one. It speaks well of you, Selena, it speaks very well of you. You will make a great Fiach some day. Brian CuCullen saved a lioness the day he saved you. A lioness always protects her pride from predators and dangers."

She did not say a word to him, but instead kept her attention riveted on Kieran. Kieran stood up and faced Boris Diaghilev, who gave him a friendly nod of the head.

"Sir, if I am here next year, it will be as an Aongus Cathal or not at all. I do not intend on becoming an Ardal Cathal. I'm prime time or nothing," he told the large man.

"Ahh, I have already learned not to bet against you, Kieran. But you still have a long way to travel before you can be sure of what you will be next year," replied Diaghilev in a slightly condescending tone. "Now Nadia, you must go and clean yourself before dinner."

"Yes, sir," she said then stood up and began to trot silently away. As she left with her uncle, Kieran noticed that she twice glanced a look at him over her right shoulder. He wasn't sure how he felt about Nadia Nabokov, other than she was still the prettiest girl his age that he had ever seen in his life.

"Today's lesson is on those mysterious and powerful undead called vampires," Tadhag Zheng told Liam's class. Many in the class appeared to perk up when he mentioned this subject. In the imagination of children, vampires were one of the ultimate monsters, one of the ultimate evils. They were part of nightmares and ghost stories told around a campfire. Maol Zheng stared out at his now captivated audience. In his many years as a teacher and as a priest, he had faced many vampires, and they always fascinated him. Vampires were seduction and power mixed with decaying evil and the ugliness of pure selfishness.

"Vampirism is the practice of drinking blood from a person, or an animal if the vampire chooses, in order to gain preternatural powers and a long life, some even say an eternal life. This is evil spawned by ritual and a pact long ago made with certain powerful demons. It is an ancient pact that had spawned many vampires, many of these creatures, which care for nothing but their own pleasure and lives. Vampires are said to mainly bite the victim's neck, extracting the blood from the carotid artery, though I have known some to drain the blood from the veins in the wrists or inner thigh."

Zheng continued to speak of tales of the undead. "Vampire-like spirits called Lilu are mentioned in early Babylonian demonology, and the bloodsucking Akhkharu are mentioned even earlier in the Sumerian mythology. These female demons were said to roam during the hours of darkness, hunting and killing newborn babies and pregnant women. One of these demons, named Lilitu, can also be found in Jewish demonology as Lilith. Lilitu, or Lilith, is sometimes called the mother of all vampires. There is a well-known vampire still around today named Lilith, Lilith Isis. She is believed to be one of the first vampires, a truly powerful and hypnotic creature. Many Bene Lumen and others have died trying to kill her. I would think that her death would be a great blow to the Illuminatii. Questions?"

No one in the class asked a question or stirred as he lectured them. They were enthralled by this subject, which had taken on an almost romantic aura in movies and books. Vampires were mainly presented as sympathetic creatures now, but they didn't sound worthy of sympathy when Zheng explained them. Liam listened intently to Tadhag Zheng mesmerized by the older man's depth of knowledge. He wondered if he would ever know as much.

"The Ancient Egyptian goddess Sekhmet in one myth became full of bloodlust after slaughtering humans and was only sated after drinking their blood. In Homer's Odyssey, the shades that Odysseus meets on his journey to the underworld are lured to the blood of freshly sacrificed rams, a fact that Odysseus uses to his advantage to summon the shade of Tiresias. Roman tales describe the strix, a nocturnal bird that fed on human flesh and blood. The Roman strix is the source of the Romanian vampire, the Strigoli and also the Albanian Shtriga. In early Slavic folklore, a vampire drank blood, was afraid of pure silver and could be destroyed by cutting off its head and putting it between the corpse's legs or by putting a wooden stake into its heart in order to bind it to its grave. Medieval historians and chroniclers Walter Map and William of Newburgh recorded the earliest English vampires in the twelfth-century. Many vampire legends also bear similarities to legends regarding succubi or incubi, which are incorporeal undead."

He stopped lecturing for a few moments and looked out at his class full of young minds. Zheng waited for a question, or even a comment, but none came. The whole class continued to be mesmerized by their teacher's subject matter. Maol Zheng merely smiled then continued his lecture.

"As they are dead, Vampires do not need most normal things required for human life, such as oxygen or food. They are often described as having either a pale or ruddy appearance, and are cool to the touch from the perspective of humans, as they have the body temperature of a corpse. Some vampires are sometimes considered to be shape shifters. We have come to find that only older vampires can shape shift, though. Some vampires can fly. Yes, they can really fly. Again, the older more powerful vampires can do this and not the younger ones. Sometimes this power is supernatural, other times it is connected to the vampire's ability to turn into flying creatures, such as bats or owls, or into lightweight forms, such as dust or smoke then they create winds as a means of propulsion. Because of a lack of soul, or having an evil soul in some cases, vampires cast no reflection in Holy objects. Yes, you can see them in a mirror, but they cast no reflection on a blessed blade or blessed mirror. Generally, though, Vampires' powers are often limited during the day or in daylight and in some cases sunlight can kill younger vampires who have not developed enough power yet."

"How do you ward them off, you might ask yourselves. Apotropaics are objects intended to ward off vampires. These items include garlic, as they hate the smell; wild rose, again the smell; and all things sacred from holy water and crosses to sacred objects from all faiths. Remember, the object needs to be blessed by a holy man or woman for it to be effective. I have used Shinto seals to ward them off myself. Of course, you must have faith in the objects holiness for it to be empowered."

Again he stopped to see if any of his students had a question or a comment, but none of them did. This was often the effect that his lecture on vampires had on young students. He thought the reason for this was because up until this very lecture, vampires still were more fiction than fact to them, more movie than actual creature of the night. But once Tadhad Zheng lectured on them, they became real. He smiled at his class.

"There are three main ways to destroy a vampire: a consecrated weapon through the heart, decapitation, or incinerating the body. Yes, but how do we deal with such a powerful creature in order to do such a thing to them. Well, incapacitate them. There are some vampires, which suffer from what modern psychologist call Obsessive Compulsive Disorder, or OCD. They are fascinated with counting. When millet, or poppy seeds, or even rice are dropped in front of these creatures, they have to count every grain. You then can kill them while they are counting."

"Are they OCD as a vampire because they were OCD when they were alive?" asked Liam.

"Excellent question," said Tadhag Zheng. "They are OCD as a vampire because they are conflicted with their fate, though not conflicted enough to retain their complete soul or humanity, more like confused by what has happened to them. You see some vampires are made into vampires unwillingly. People punished by vampires by being turned into vampires themselves. Most of them get over this state eventually, but some do not."

"How do we know this, sir?" asked Liam.

"Because I have a close friend who is a vampire and he has explained this to me," he answered.

Several of the students gave a big inhale of surprise. If Tadhag Zheng had their attention before, he had it even more now.

"My vampire friend was made into a vampire over three hundred years ago in Newport, Rhode Island. He was a sailor, a first mate to be exact, who found that his ship, which was off the coast of Rhode Island and heading into Newport, carried an evil cargo of four vampires in its hold and began to destroy them as best as he could. Unfortunately, the last vampire was able to attack him before he could complete his work and as punishment it turned this brave man into a vampire."

"How has he lived with himself this whole time?" asked the blonde haired Talbot.

"With great guilt and by feeding only on small animals and such. This vampire is one of the Bene Lumen's greatest allies and one of the greatest enemies of all other vampires and Illuminatii. He hates them for what they have done to him and believes that he is the way he is because his God wants him to battle them. I believe he is a truly great man," explained Tadhag Zheng.

"Sir," Liam once again piped up, "does he still possess his true soul?"

"Yes, he does, Liam," he answered with a smile that showed his appreciation of Liam's question. "That is why he has not turned evil all these many years. This man possessed a great soul, a good soul when he was normal. It is his soul that has kept him from being tempted by the evil power of being a vampire. But he is not tempted by that power, by that sense of being 'all powerful.' He knows that he is not all powerful."

"What is his name, sir?" asked Talbot.

"I cannot share that with you, young Talbot. If you asked your Uncle Donovan, he would not be able to tell you. It is a closely held secret known by few."

"Why, sir?" Talbot asked.

"Because his burden is great enough without everyone knowing his name and wanting to talk to him," Tadhag Zheng said. "This vampire, this man, wishes to do his work without too many of us knowing his name. I met him when I was tracking a hopping vampire, one of those vile corpses, in Hong Kong. Now as I have told you before the hopping Chinese vampire is a vicious and brutal opponent, who will kill randomly to satisfy its bloodlust. This hopping vampire almost had me because I tried to protect a child from him. I thought I was going to die when my friend saved my life. Since then he and I have been close friends."

"Sir, is he the only one like that or are there more vampires like him?" asked Julia from Tamo House

"There is only him. All other undead are evil and cannot be trusted. He is unique among his kind, so when you face a vampire, do not hold out hope that you can turn them into creatures of light. They belong to the dark."

"Sir, who is the worst vampire you know of?" asked M'Benga.

"Ahh, who is the worst? That is a difficult question as it presupposes that there is a best," he said then laughed. "Well, Lilith is said not only to be beautiful but deadly. There is something to be said about a beautiful but deadly woman to cause fear in a man, even one who is a monk."

Again he stopped to laugh to himself amused by his own little jokes. None of his students appeared to understand what he found amusing. He continued.

"Vlad Tepes, Dracul, or as I mentioned him before, Vlad Dragon, is quite bad. But in my opinion the worst is Lord Byron," he stated.

"Sir, isn't he a dead poet?" Talbot asked.

"Actually, he is an undead poet," chuckled Zheng. "You see Byron was attracted to sin and becoming a vampire, a creature who feeds off of human life, was the greatest sin he could think of. After becoming a vampire he murdered his friend and fellow poet Shelley then sent to Shelley's wife his heart, which Byron had ripped from his chest. History says that Shelley drowned in a boating accident, but history lies in this case. Byron actually killed Shelley."

"Why do you think he is the worst of his kind, sir?" asked M'Benga.

"Because he not only killed a friend he loved, but he turned his back on poetry and on art. He now lives in Paris and Los Angeles and calls himself a jet setter. To this day he feeds off those he seduces and makes them fall in love with him first. A vile creature."

CHAPTER 12

W ith the end of October nearing Halloween preparations had begun at the school. For Samhain this was not just any holiday, but a time of celebration and a re-commitment to their cause, a pledge of fidelity to the mission of the Bene Lumen. Turning this night into a celebration and a chance to show their loyalty to their cause, Samhain taught the students never to fear the other side, even when they were stronger, but to celebrate that you were not part of the other side. All about the school decorations were being hung in windows and from street lamps. They were mainly orange and black in color representing spirits along with skulls to symbolize death. A bonfire was planned in the middle of the training fields this night with most of the school attending then at midnight in the dining hall foods, sweets, mulled wine, and other drinks were being served to all who wanted to indulge themselves.

Students and teachers alike were all in a festive mood at breakfast, which consisted of waffles, pancakes, bacon, sausage, blood sausage, corned beef hash, hash browns, orange juice, watermelon juice, milk, and plenty of fresh brewed coffee. Part of the celebration was to eat heartily and well because this day went late into the night. The only ones who did not have a festive attitude were the chosen maols since All Hallows Eve was the time when the spiritual caul, a barrier, which separated the world of the living and dead and demon dimensions, was at its weakest. These maols held guard during this day and night in order to stop the crossing over of unwanted or malicious spirits from the other side. They protected the students with special prayers and rituals. It was their duty to make sure that Samhain, which was a focal point for the spirit world, especially for malicious ones who wanted to even the score of their demise, remained safe for the students.

Starting the morning of the 31st of October, the chosen maols walked around the school praying to their respective deities for protection and strength. Maol Stonefeather walked the streets dressed for cool weather while beating a small drum and chanting to himself; Brother Zheng walked from schoolhouse to schoolhouse with prayer beads in hand and praying for protection while leaving small slips of papers in each room with an enchantment to keep spirits at bay; Father Mueller worked a rosary bead ring round the index finger of his right hand as he prayed and walked the training grounds making sure that they stayed safe; Diarmund O'CuChulainn with his eyes closed dressed in his druid robes walked through the arboretum praying for protection; Brother Sen held his prayer beads while he prayed at each House for the safety of each and every student; Rabbi Justiz wore a prayer shawl and walked around the training fields chanting a prayer of protection and harmony; and Brother Dolan with black rosary beads in his hands, which he held behind his back as he walked the streets of Samhain, prayed and kept vigil for any signs of weakness from the other maols. Brother Dolan was a healer and one of the strongest spiritualists, so he acted as the protector of the maols. Through their prayers and meditation they held kept these spirits safe on their side of the spiritual caul.

Sian Boru had other plans for her and Liam than her being a chosen maol and celebrating, though. With the permission of the Headmaster, she had exempted Liam from all his assigned work that day, as well as classes, which were few because of the preparation of the night's festivities. On this day she planned to perform an ancient ceremony with Liam. Without any other students in their party, including Dani and Brigid who balked at the idea of not coming, Sian Boru and Liam awoke at cockcrow and taking only water, they made their way to the oldest tree in the small forest. When they got to the tree, Sian Boru sat on the ground and motioned Liam to do the same. He did so. Although he wasn't nervous, he was anxious. She had not explained to him the reason or the purpose why they were there.

"First, I apologize to you that you will not be able to join in the festivities today, maybe not even tonight, but I have a more important task for you," she told him.

"I understand, ma'am," he replied.

"Do you, Liam? Do you understand without knowing? Are you that enlightened?"

"I know you wouldn't have me here to perform a ceremony unless it was important. I trust you completely, ma'am," he told her in a serene and sincere voice.

Sian Boru stopped for a second to look at this young boy she had come to know. He had grown up so much in such a short time since coming to Samhain. Liam began this year an untutored yet willing student and she was his superior who could lead him through the difficulties of learning his powers. She was now sure their relationship would change soon. He was learning fast and would be her equal quicker than either would be prepared for. Liam had found his purpose at Samhain, even if he didn't know that yet. But he was about to find out.

"I'm glad of that. You will have to trust me a great deal today because we are going to attempt something today that someone your age never attempted, but I think it is important for you to do this," she explained. "On this day that we have come to know as Halloween, or All Hallows Eve, or as the Celts and druids called it Feile Na Marbh, the festival of the dead, the spiritual caul, the membrane between the living and the dead, is at its weakest. As you know our maols prevent evil spirits from coming through the caul today, but you and I are going to attempt to do something different. We are going to invite someone dead to visit us. Through meditation and fasting, we will spend the next hours preparing ourselves to receive this person."

"Who is it... my mother?" Liam asked with a great deal of excitement.

"No, Liam, it is not your mother we invite. The person we invite here tonight has powers to return back to the world of the dead. This is important otherwise he will be stranded in the world of the living for eternity. This is where ghosts come from. They are souls who crossed during this night and became stranded in the world of the living. Your mother was a powerful priestess but we do not want to take the chance that she would become stranded here," Sian Boru told him.

"Why?"

"Say we invite her and she comes and can't return to the other side where she now belongs. Yes, her spirit, her soul, will be with you now, but when you die, and you will eventually die, she will be stranded here and you will be with the dead. You will be separated for eternity. Wouldn't you prefer to have her with you for the rest of eternity rather than have her with you for your time here while you are alive?"

"You're right. I wouldn't want to do that to my mother, to strand her here without any of us," he agreed. "So who is it we are going to contact?"

"We are going to invite Merlin, himself, to visit us this day, Liam," she replied.

"Merlin, really," his response showed excitement. The idea of meeting this druid priest who started the Bene Lumen and established Samhain, the man who trained and guided Arthur, and fought against evil was making the hair on his arms stand up.

"Yes, Merlin. I believe you and Merlin need to speak to each other; need to share some things. He has some wisdom which only he can impart to you."

"Why?" he asked.

"I'll let him explain that to you, Liam. You have to trust me on this one," she said. "Now I want you and I to completely open ourselves up to nature, to open ourselves up so much so that time no longer matters. If we do this properly, we will enter into a trance that will make hours seem to pass in minutes then as our sense are free and open to the mysteries of life and death we will call for Merlin. If he deems it time, he will visit us here on our plane. Are you ready?"

"Yes," he said apprehensively.

"Let us close our eyes, let go of your consciousness and give yourself over to nature," she said.

Both Sian Boru and Liam got themselves comfortably situated on the grassy ground, closed their eyes and opened themselves up to nature and its calming ways. Although Liam at first had trouble releasing his consciousness over to nature, eventually he allowed for the calming influence of the breeze, trees, water, sky, grass and ground to guide him to the trance state that Sian Boru told him about. They whispered to him, assuaged his fears and offered him a path to take. He listened to them, but hesitated to take the path they offered him. Liam liked journeys but this one was the most intimidating one he had ever been on. He had no time to prepare for it, no time to contemplate it. But nature called persistently to him.

Finally, he let go of his fears and took the path they offered and in doing so he found himself with Sian Boru and entrenched in that trance state. He heard the voice of Sian Boru telling him to open his eyes. Doing as

163

he was told he noticed that it was no longer morning out, not even afternoon, and that a great deal of time had passed. It was dark out, night had fallen, stars twinkled above in the sky and all he saw seemed to be tangible, but slowly drifting between two worlds. It was as if the world of the dead and the living overlapped each other.

"Call Merlin," she said to him.

"How?"

"Just call out his name and if he wants to come he will," she said.

"Merlin, sir? Merlin," he called.

"Is it that time already," Liam heard a rough burr, though somehow calming, voice reply.

"Yes, Merlin, it is that time already. I have brought someone important for you to meet. I am glad you could join us," Sian Boru said.

As if he stepped from out of one room and into a new one, through a doorway, which Liam couldn't see, a strong limbed looking old man appeared in front of Liam and Sian Boru. He was dressed in a robe, not unlike the robes that Liam and Sian wore. His hair was white and longish and he had a short-cropped beard and moustache that still had a hint of red in them. This was the great Triune Conjurer Merlin.

"Sian, ancestor of Brian Boru and of my bloodline via my brother Rudhage, it is lovely to see you again," he said. "How long has it been?"

"Twenty-five years ago from this night," she answered.

"I thought it was that short a time ago. I barely had time to miss you and you have me back for a visit. It must be time for me to meet someone special," Merlin said then gave Liam his attention. "So this is he?"

"Yes," she answered.

"Hello, Liam CuCullen, ancestor of CuChulainn, the great Tiarnán, who was a forefather of Arthur, my King and champion, and also a direct ancestor of me via my wife, Nimue, who died saving my life. Some people have written in their myths about me that she imprisoned me for Morgana, but that's not true. She merely stopped me from falling into a trap by giving me a potion to make me sleep then placed me in a tree trunk for my own protection. Nimue went to this meeting in place of me falling into the trap meant for me. We were married but for such a short time, yet she gave me a wonderful daughter, who I gave to a sweet couple to raise for me after Morgana ensnared her. I never wanted those who hated me so much to know that she existed because they would have tried and killed her. Hmm, forgive me, I am going down a different road now, memory lane, and should return to the right one. Again I say hello, Liam CuCullen. It is a pleasure to meet you on this fine night."

"Hello, sir," he said in response not really understanding the implications of what Merlin said to him.

"Do you know why Sian Boru has had you invite me here tonight?"

"No, sir, I don't know," he answered.

"Stop calling me sir. Call me Merlin. When I hear sir, I feel like turning around and looking for whomever it is you are talking to. In my time I was called Merlin the great, Merlin the magician, and Merlin the devil, but you can call me just plain Merlin, a name I gave myself for history to record," Merlin told him.

"Yes, Merlin."

"Liam CuCullen, I am here to tell you that you have the potential to be another me, so to speak, a powerful Triune Conjurer, yet more than that, like I was more than that. I wasn't just a Triune Conjurer; I was a fulcrum, a focal point of great energy and power, also, and I was able to shape the history of my time as well as effect what came afterwards. We are very rare breeds you and I. We aren't born every generation, but we are born when needed most by humanity. We are a gift from a great power. You have that potential to do as I did, Liam," Merlin told him.

"But...but," Liam stammered.

"But nothing. I know fulcrum doesn't sound like a pleasant thing to be. It may even sound sort of painful, but it is an important thing. It is also a burden that you will have to learn to live with or it will ruin your life. So like me, Liam, you are a fulcrum, which means that I expect no more buts. All I am doing now is telling you a truth, so listen and learn. You are what you are. There is no changing that. But to fulfill your role as a fulcrum, you have a long road ahead of you to travel. You see I need to impart some important ancient knowledge to you that you will need when the time is right."

"What ancient knowledge?"

"Oh, Liam, I am not going to give you this knowledge by telling you about it, I am going to impart it to you, which means I am going to transfer it to you where it will remain in your unconscious until it is needed. This knowledge encompasses many things and it will reveal itself when needed, no sooner or no later than that. You are young and I want you to enjoy your youth as best as you can. To have all this knowledge right now would place a burden on you that the young should never carry."

"How will you give me the knowledge?" he asked Merlin.

"Like this," he said then touched Liam's forehead with a hand that was at once ephemeral and solid. "It is done. Don't you wish all knowledge could be given so easily? You wouldn't need to go to school."

"I like school," he replied.

"I'm glad you do. School has importance beyond learning, Liam. It is also a place where you make friends and friends are needed in difficult times. The right friends will stand beside you when everyone else has deserted you. It is a proving ground, too, where you face challenges and learn to handle them."

"Why do I need this knowledge, Merlin?" asked Liam.

"Because evil and those who fight for evil, the Illuminatii, will fear you when they find out who you are. The war waging between our sides has been going in their direction for the last one hundred and thirty years, but when you come into your complete power, you will be able to help restore balance to this war and they will not like that," Merlin said.

"How will I do this?"

"In time you will understand how. Right now it is your time to learn and grow into your powers," Merlin answered.

"But..."

"But, but, but. There you go again with the 'buts.' You have too many buts, Liam, but then again so didn't I when I was your age. Now listen closely to me because I must go soon. You must also look out for your brother because he is important to you, more important than just being your brother. As a fulcrum, I needed the right Aongus Cathal to help win my battles, to be my hero, to be my champion. Heroes and champions are very important beings, and great heroes and champions are needed in times of war because they can do what others fear or believe can't be done. A great champion, a great Tiarnán, is more than a creature of war he or she is a creature of faith. Now, the Bene Lumen and the Illuminatii have been at war for a very long time. In my time I had Arthur; you will have Kieran. With a mother like Siobhan Griffin and a father like Brian CuCullen you and Kieran were destined to be extraordinary. Kieran is another Arthur, even if he doesn't know it as of yet. Make sure your Arthur fulfills his destiny, Liam, as you make sure you fulfill your own," Merlin stated. "Do you understand what I've told you here on this night?"

"Yes, I think I do understand."

"I think is a good answer. It shows a mind working and that means you will eventually know, even if you don't know right now," Merlin said pleasantly then he turned his attention back to Sian Boru. "Before I leave, I need to speak to you, Sian, for a few moments."

"Yes, Merlin," she said in a cracking, dry voice having quietly listened to Merlin and Liam speak.

"Love, Sian, love is so very important. You don't realize how much I miss my Nimue," he said with a voice that was filled with sorrow.

"Isn't she with you now in the afterlife?" asked Liam.

"No, Liam. Her soul, her spirit, is still in that tree which holds her body, trapped there. When Morgana realized Nimue had saved me from what she planned, she decided to punish us both by trapping her soul. I will not be reunited with my love until Morgana is dead and the curse is finally broken."

"Merlin, I am so sorry for that," she said quietly.

"You need to pursue the love you feel for him, the man who is still in your heart. He is a very strong man, and you think he does not need you, but he needs your love and you need to love him. Do not fool yourself about this," Merlin told her.

"But, Merlin, he... he's back doing his work. We are not together," she replied.

"He will return here someday soon to stay. Mallory knows that he has a role even greater than the one he has returned to do, and when he takes on that role, you will need to offer him your love," Merlin explained.

"I, I..."

"Think about it. Like Liam, you will understand and see the truth of what I have said. Now I must go," he stated then stepped back into that unseen room.

Within seconds of Merlin's leaving, the world around Sian Boru and Liam CuCullen stretched out and snapped back into their own reality. It was night, late at night. Liam felt exhausted as they returned completely to the world of the living. His body was covered in sweat and his muscles felt as if he had been running for hours. He slumped to the ground.

Sian Boru, who was also exhausted, got up and went over to the water containers she brought with her. Opening one of them she took a long drink of water then brought the other bottle over to Liam.

"Drink the water. Your body needs the fluids to bring back our body's energy," she told him.

"What Merlin said... what he said is it true?" he asked.

"Drink now, you are dehydrated and you need the water to restore yourself," she commanded.

Liam opened his container and drank down half the water in it. All the wondrous strangeness he had experienced these last months couldn't begin to compare to what he had just experienced. He had met Merlin. Not just met Merlin, but the powerful Triune Conjurer had imparted ancient knowledge to him and told him that he was a fulcrum. A fulcrum.

"Was that really Merlin?" he asked rhetorically just realizing the honor he had been given.

"It is my second time contacting him, Liam. Each time I understand his greatness a little more," Sian Boru said as she drank more of her water.

"I am a fulcrum."

"Yes, you are," she said.

"And ... my brother is another Arthur," he said.

"Yes, he is. And like Arthur he doesn't have the slightest idea what and who he is. He doesn't think highly of himself and underestimates himself," she stated. "He has a difficult road ahead him."

"Kieran will do fine. I'll make sure of it because I need him," Liam declared.

Sian Boru looked at him with no small amount of pride. She knelt down beside him and gave him a warm hug for a few moments. When she broke the hug off, he looked at her with tears in his eyes.

"What is wrong, Liam?" Sian Boru asked.

"Merlin is correct you need to offer your love to my father. Love, true love, should never be wasted on what ifs or fears," he said.

"How did you know that it was your father I love?" she asked in a voice that was completely shocked. "You can't know this."

"I guess Merlin imparted more than ancient knowledge to me, ma'am. He told me in his way."

"He shouldn't have let you know that I love Brian CuCullen. It is too personal," she said with her voice turning angry.

"He did this because he knows you must tell him eventually how you feel or it will be too late for both of you. I know my father... he needs you," Liam stated.

"This is too complicated a matter for me to even think about right now," she said.

"Love is always complicated, but we should always find time for it, Sian. My father needs to love you and you need to love him. According to

Merlin my father has always loved you, he just loved my mother a little bit more," Liam told her.

Sian Boru looked at the young boy in front of her. He was no longer the little, innocent boy that came here just a few months ago. In just a short time, he had become the equal in his sensitivity to nature of any sixth year student. His powers were growing quickly and strongly and seemed to know few limits. When introduced to charming, he understood its complexities; and when introduced to casting, he understood the nature and limitations of the power. And now that he has met Merlin, a feat that no one else his age could even attempt, he has grown in his understanding and_knowledge in one giant leap. He truly was the fulcrum.

"Liam, I don't want to talk about what Merlin said to me, and I ask that you don't mention this subject to your brother or father," she said.

"Our bond and trust is intact, ma'am. There is so much I have to learn from you, but ma'am, there are things I will be able to teach you. All I do now is remind you that trust should travel both ways," he said.

"Liam, I trust you. I am also overwhelmed by you and your powers right now and need time to adjust to them. Please give me time to adjust," she requested.

"I understand," he replied.

"I know that you do. How could you not understand? Now let's finish our water because we need it and see if any of the festival remains to be enjoyed. I don't know about you but I am hungry and hope there are some cakes left."

"Agreed, ma'am," he said.

"Liam, when we are alone, you can call me Sian instead of ma'am. If Merlin can let you address him by his name, I can also let you call me by my name," she stated gently.

"Thank you, Sian."

Halloween in New York...

Halloween was always a difficult time for a Tiarnán and Cairbre. Besides the possibility of rogue spirits passing through the caul, it was also a time when some beasts decided to wreak havoc, to bring destruction on humanity, or win a victory in their war against the Bene Lumen. For Brian CuCullen this Halloween was going to be a time for him to face a hybrid killer.

"When Grigori, or watchers as some call them, fallen angels turned demons, mated with mortal women their children turned out to be hybrids,

169

half demon and half human. These Nephilim live by feeding on the life energy of human beings. They are rare corporeal incubi. They are physically adept and strong abominations that live until they are killed. The Illuminatii use these abominations as assassins, trained killers, whose work appears to be natural causes or a heart attack, but what they have done is drained the life's energy from their victims," Jennifer Sult read from a Bene Lumen reference book.

After his adventure in New York City, Brian CuCullen had requested that Jennifer Sult be transferred to Maine as his new first lieutenant. Out of loyalty for Paulette Goode, the old first lieutenant of the area asked for reassignment and was sent to Europe to serve under another Tiarnán. Brian chose Jennifer as the replacement. He did this because he enjoyed working with her during their time in New York. She believed fully in their cause, but she also never lost sight of their shared humanity, which was important. When she argued against his sending Selena to Samhain, he heard in her protests the very soul of humanity, in addition to the concern for others. She wanted to think the best of the situation that Selena would not be changed by evil's touch and would be able to return to her family. Within the soul of humanity was to hope for the best, and to want the best for others. He needed someone with the soul of humanity near him.

"I've never seen a Nephilim before. I barely remember them from my advanced abomination class," she stated.

Now that he had returned to his position of Tiarnán and Cairbre of the Americas, he had returned to the home he lived in before Paulette Goode took his place. The home was a large colonial not too far from Beckett's Castle, a haunted mansion in Cape Elizabeth that was built on land with a door between worlds. He always considered this place his home in many ways because he had made so many happy memories there with Siobhan. After Siobhan's death, he regretted having to move his sons to a new home. And now he was back living there but without his sons. He and Jennifer were now in his old library, which Paulette had kept the same not even changing a single book.

"They are stunning looking abominations. Some have become models and movie stars because of their great beauty. Grigori only chose the most attractive and susceptible men and women to mate with, so that they can control their progeny. The males are handsome, athletic, charismatic, and the females are gorgeous, athletic and alluring. They possess incredible strength and speed, as well as healing powers. This characteristic is almost unfathomable considering they appear to be human from the outside. Unload a clip from a pistol into them and they will be back on their feet in a matter of minutes. Blow them up and they regenerate given enough time and the right conditions. The only way to stop them is with a blessed weapon of some sorts. Of course, a blessed sword means getting close enough so that they can touch you. This is not recommended. They suck your life energy out through the pores in their hands," Brian told her solemnly.

"They sound like a real nasty piece of work. They must be difficult to kill, Tiarnán" Jennifer commented to Brian CuCullen.

"I fought one once and ended up needing the attention of a charmer with healing as their specialty along with energy restoring potions for a week. The thing almost sucked my life force out of me just by placing its hand on my chest for no more than 6 seconds. Luckily, as a Tiarnán, I have greater life energies to draw on than the normal human being," he told her.

"So why did you have me read that bit of information?" she asked as she placed the book back on the bookshelves.

"So that you understand why I am going on this mission by myself," he answered. "The Council of Guaire's sources have said that a Nephilim is supposed to kill me tonight when I am scheduled to meet Maol Byrd. I do not want to give this thing a chance to kill any of my people. All of you are too ready to protect me in dangerous situations, to give your lives for me," he told her. "Plus, I have a mission for you and whatever handpicked fealty you chose."

"What is this mission?" she asked with her mood changing from disappointment to interest.

"A Bigfoot, or to be more exact a mountain demon, has been spotted where the Appalachians end. I want you to hunt him down and destroy him," Brian said.

"Where do the Appalachian Mountains end exactly?" she asked sounding, as if she was embarrassed to ask.

"Here in Maine as a matter of fact. Not many people realize that, but they end right here in Maine," he answered.

"And while I go and hunt down this Bigfoot, or one of his overgrown brothers, you will face a Nephilim alone, right?"

"Exactly. You will do your duty and I will do mine. Now get your team together and get going," he commanded, "and if I might make a suggestion, take Paul Lamont. He's a first class Fiach. Although a mountain demon is big and ugly and should be easy to spot, he is at home in the woods and difficult to find."

Jennifer started to walk to the library door. Before she got to it, though, she stopped and turned back to look at Brian. He stared back at her from his position sitting behind a large, darkly stained hardwood desk.

"You realize that Maol Byrd is more than likely dead," she said.

"I know. I knew that when I heard from the Council this morning. We'll mourn her later, though. Right now we will both focus on our missions," he said.

"Why such a bold move?" she asked.

"Killing a maol then pretending to be them," he returned the question.

"No, trying to kill you during Halloween?"

"For one of two reasons. The first reason is simple to explain. If they kill a Tiarnán on Halloween the chances are that certain spirits will be able to wrestle my soul into hell because of the conditions of this night. That's a victory for them having a Tiarnán's soul in hell," he explained.

"My God, that sounds horrible," she interrupted him.

"It would be if it happened. But it won't happen. Now the second reason is more complicated, and I am unable to tell you about the second reason right now."

"Why?" she asked taking by surprise at the second reason.

"For reasons that I cannot explain to you as of yet," he said.

"You don't trust me."

"No, I trust you. I just don't know what the second reason is yet, that is why I can't tell you why. But there has to be one because the first reason is just not enough to go after me. They know that all the rust is off and that I am not an easy target. They have to have a better reason to go after me now. Now get going and find the Appalachian Mountains. I think there are some Maine State maps in one of the drawers in the kitchen," he prodded her in good humor.

"I'll check the Internet for directions," she said then exited the library.

Brian was left alone in his library to contemplate the coming night. There was six hours before he was scheduled to meet Maol Byrd. The Tiarnán and his head maol would meet at a preordained spot on Halloween perform a ritual in order to keep rogue, evil spirits at bay on this unusual. Tonight he was supposed to meet Maol Byrd near the lighthouse, Portland Head Light, at for Williams Park for the ritual. But instead of her he knew he'd have to face Illuminatii.

To pass the time before the scheduled meeting he picked up a book that was on his desk and began reading it. The book was a piece of fiction written by a writer who decided to portray the Illuminatii, as a group of powerful businessmen who had been manipulating world politics since the Enlightenment and into modern times. The businessmen changed from time to time, as they died and were replaced by new blood, but their mission to control the world from behind the scenes continued to this day. It was a surprisingly good yarn written with some competence by a writer who had it half right.

This book of fiction had elements of fact in it, a sign that the author had some insight into this secret society of darkness. The Illuminatii did exist, though they went back further than the Enlightenment, and it did have a world domination agenda just as he wrote. The humans, demons, and abominations, though, behind the Illuminatii and associated with them were not businessmen manipulating commodity markets, politics, and free markets, starting wars for profit, or destroying individuals to stop changes in capitalism, rather they were monsters preparing the way for their masters. And Brian CuCullen knew them well.

He remembered the first time he came up against this society of darkness. It was right after he had been installed as the Tiarnán and Cairbre. It was a great honor to be Cairbre of the Americas. This meant that whenever a Tiarnán was in the Americas they must follow his orders, just like he would have to follow theirs when he went on their Cairbre area. He was green and too willing to prove himself and it showed in his decisions. The Illuminatii until then had been nothing more than stories he had been told at Samhain. They were the bogeyman you never ever see but you fear that they lived in your closet or under your bed at night. But they became real very quickly for him, more than simple bogeymen, as he came up against their economic and violent force.

Since he was young and new to his position they immediately made a move on him to test him and his people in Maine. First they bought the land around his home then they attempted to buy Beckett's Castle, which was an important hot spot of spirit activity. Yet, they didn't know that a certain Giolla had long ago made impossible for them to purchase it. When their financial power failed they killed several of his closest fealty. Within a week four team members were killed, one by a vampire, another by a Nephilim, and two by the work of human scum. He couldn't let this stand without retribution.

First he had his Fiach hunt down the vampire. It turned out to be a fairly young vampire, only seventy-five years old. The Fiach followed the vampire's trail down to Boston where it made its home among an enclave of other young vampires, some newly made and others no more than fifty years as a vampire, on Beacon Hill, a ritzy Boston neighborhood. Fifteen vampires lived in two expensive brownstone houses that were located behind the State House and down the street from Suffolk University. Brian CuCullen and eight Ardal Cathal with the help of one outside ally made short work of these vampires killing all of them, except for three vampires who escaped. He was glad, though, that they escaped, as they would end up telling those in powerful positions what this new Tiarnán was capable of doing.

Next up was the Nephilim. This encounter almost got him killed. But he succeeded in disposing of the Nephilim. After weeks of recuperating he went after the two human members of the Illuminatii. Through Council of Guaire sources they were tracked down in Los Angeles, Malibu to be exact. One of them was a necromancer by the name of Thaddeus Wren, who was the head of a quasi-church that was headquartered in the Malibu Hills. The church was called the Church of Light and Enlightenment and was a front for the Illuminatii out in Southern California. The other human was one of the church's top members and a seer, Dolores Morgan. Neither he nor any of the other Bene Lumen had been able to get close to them. Once he had destroyed and vampires and Nephilim, they decided to never leave the Church of Light and Enlightenment grounds.

Checking the clock he saw that it was almost time for him to leave. Bringing up old memories could eat up the hours, Brian told himself then he got up and went to one of his bookcases. Pulling down a copy of a book about Arch Angels, the bookcase silently moved forward revealing several swords, knives, battle ax, and crossbow and arrows all of them either hanging from racks and pegs or stored behind a glass case. These were all blessed weapons and some of his favorites to use.

The first weapon he took was the retractable blade sword. He tossed it onto the brown leather sofa in his library. Next he opened the glass case and took out three throwing knives. These knives he slid into slits in his belt at the back of his back. He was now ready to go. Walking over to his loose fitting black raincoat, which hung from a peg on a coatrack in his library, he then placed the sword with blade retracted into a sleeve on the right inside of his coat.

He was now ready to meet Maol Byrd, not her but whoever they had replaced her with, at the lighthouse. Instead of driving to fort Williams Park he decided to walk. There was enough time and he was feeling anxious enough that a walk would help. Once out in the open, the chilly fresh air and black night sky put him in the appropriate mood for a fight. Maol Byrd, the voodoo priestess would probably be a shapeshifter, a human abomination whose power came by way of the skills of a twisted necromancer or mage. He had to not think of the woman he knew, the woman who risked her life time and time again against the Illuminatii and had offered him sage advice. Now, she was dead. It was the only way a shapeshifter could be sure to carry this off without being found out.

And as for the Nephilim, he or she will be there, also, waiting in the shadows, waiting to touch him and suck his life force from his body. But he knew their plan because of an informant placed in the Illuminatii, and informant whose life will be sacrificed once Brian CuCullen killed the two creatures waiting for him. Within hours the Illuminatii will know who leaked the information as they proceeded to have an older powerful vampire sample the blood of all those who knew about this mission. When the vampire did this the most recent memories of the person would become the vampire's memories, also. This was one of the pleasures a vampire got from drinking blood. They also could sample all the memories and feelings of their victim as they drank the blood. The more blood drunk by the vampire, the more memories and feelings they sampled.

Was he worth the life of an informant and Maol Byrd, Brian CuCullen asked himself? Many thought he was, but did he believe he was worth those brave lives? He wasn't sure, though, he knew in the end it wasn't important if he believed he was or wasn't. It was important that those who gave their lives for him were vindicated in their beliefs. No Bene Lumen should die completely in vain. Their lives should have meaning, he thought.

Getting to Fort Williams Park, he skipped all entrances, which were closed at this time of night and slipped into the park unnoticed. Slowly he walked in the direction Portland Head Light, which also was now a small museum. Someone lived on the grounds all year round to take care of the things. He hoped the caretaker, Ben Northup, was still alive and hadn't been another sacrifice in this foolish scheme. Enough people had died for the Illuminatii's misplaced mission already, Brian CuCullen concluded.

He could see the lighthouse now, as it stood stoically on a rock landing. From this spot this lighthouse gave guidance and warning to ships. Edward Hopper painted this lighthouse, locals and tourists visited this lighthouse, and now he was going to face Illuminatii there. In the background he could see the cloaked figure of Maol Byrd. But this wasn't Maol Byrd, this was someone who looked and sounded like her only. The short pudgy body, five feet tall and thirty pounds too heavy, and friendly broad face would immediately return to its natural form when he slew her.

As he walked towards the cloaked figure, which stood near the lighthouse, he noticed that the light was on where the caretaker resided. Instead of making him feel that Ben was alive, it made him realize that Ben was probably dead. He continued walking towards her, she turned and smiled at him. She looked so much like Maol Byrd, but he had to remind himself that it wasn't. Whoever this was, he or she wasn't Maol Byrd.

As he got close to her, he reached into his raincoat, took out his retractable bladed sword, extended the blade, and cut her down. As the blade passed through her, the shapeshifter screamed a blood curdling scream then their body began to expand. The night air was filled with bone crunching and muscle snapping sounds as the body returned to its form of a six foot tall, brown haired, pale skinned male. Brian CuCullen walked up to the body and stood over it.

From behind the lighthouse, a tall handsome woman came around the corner. She had black eyes and hair the color of a summer's sun with a face that was filled with a beauty. She had enjoyed seeing such things as a shapeshifter being slain. Brian CuCullen looked up at her.

"Very good, Tiarnán. You are as I have been told, a formidable foe. I like that," the Nephilim stated as she came further out into the open. Behind her the ocean was black and he could here the lulling waves.

"The real Maol Byrd is dead?" he asked.

"You mean the little dark woman, the shapeshifter was mimicking," she replied.

"Yes, I mean her," he replied feeling the bile of hate creeping up his throat.

"She's dead. I killed her. Yum, yum, she was good to eat. She had a wonderful tasting energy, slightly Cajun in flavor, like blackened chicken."

"And the caretaker at this lighthouse?" he asked.

"Both him and the little black woman were very tasty, though I found him a bit salty. Maybe it was all the time he spent living by the sea. I needed to get my energy up to face a Tiarnán. I am now at full of energy and ready for you," she said.

"You know what I like about abominations like you?" he asked her.

"Other than our beauty what do you like about us," she replied with a smile that made her beauty ugly.

"You think too highly of yourself; you're arrogant. It's a weakness that is easy to exploit. I like that," he said with a smirk on his face, which annoyed his opponent.

"Not arrogant, but confident, Tiarnán. I am confident that I will now suck a Tiarnán's life force out of his body and complete an important mission. I won't have to eat for months after this," she stated with complete confidence and disdain for him.

"I'm so glad that you feel that way about this situation," he said then quickly reached behind him where he kept the throwing knives, and he threw one of the knives hitting her squarely in the chest. Her reaction was of shock, as she reached to take the knife out, but before she could remove it, he placed another knife in her throat.

"Arrogant and stupid," he said to the Nephilim as he began to swing his sword around in a flourish, the kind of flourish that Master Nagura would call showing off.

The Nephilim dropped to her knees in great distress. Brian CuCullen walked up to her as she struggled with the blessed throwing knives, raised his sword and then easily and gracefully sliced her head off with a clean cut. The cut head flew off into the air then landed and kept rolling until it fell off the landing into the water below. He then dragged her body to the side of the landing and tossed her body into the water. It was a short drop. He even heard the body make a nice simple splash as the waves slapped at the rocks. Next, he did the same to the shapeshifter's body, which was now completely returned to its male form. His night's work was done. But now he needed to know the second reason why the Illuminatii tried to kill him this night. There had to be a second reason, and he was betting that it was a good one, a better one than just killing a Tiarnán. And he knew of one person who could help him with finding this reason and that was a vampire named Caleb Keane.

CHAPTER 13

Caleb Keane made his home wherever he wanted to be at the moment. Caprice had become his domestic impetus. Sometimes it was Galveston, Texas; sometimes a cottage of the shores of Nova Scotia; sometimes it was somewhere along the Alaskan coast; sometimes it was a humble abode on Prince Edward Island; sometimes Block Island, Rhode Island: and then there were times the enticements of modernity called him and he made his home in Boston, Massachusetts. His choice of home was based really on his emotional needs since his physical needs were very few. A pint or two of animal blood for life, a dark place to rest during the daylight hours so as to re-energize, and the nearness of the ocean to make him feel at home were his only requirements. Interestingly enough, though, emotionally there were times he needed the nearness of humanity, the sounds of human beings living their lives so as to give him the feeling that he still was a human being and not just one of the undead.

Because of a longing, which he had suppressed for years, to see humanity instead of isolating himself from people this winter he decided on Boston for his home. The reason for this was a need to remind himself that he was once human, once a man who loved and hated, who wanted a family and friends to go along with a normal life. At one time his greatest wish was to be giving the position of captain of a ship by the businessman whose ships he sailed on. He made it all the way to first mate at the ripe age of twenty-six before he was turned in the creature he now was. That was literally several lifetimes ago. One of the benefits of having been undead for hundreds of years was that he still owned a building in the Back Bay that he had bought for next to nothing long ago. He had converted the building on Marlborough Street near Mass Avenue into apartments, choosing to keep one the apartments for himself.

Since it was a snowy day Caleb Keane decided to go out for a daytime walk along the Charles River. He dressed for winter with a pair of corduroy pants, an Irish knit sweater given to him by Brian CuCullen as a thank you for helping him in an operation against the Illuminatii, Wellington boots, and a heavy hooded winter coat, which he pulled the hood up over his head just in case some rays of sun made its way through the snowfall. He didn't need the clothes since weather no longer affected him, but he wore them to blend in with people. From extreme cold to extreme heat, it all felt the same to him. He was literally dead inside, so weather just didn't affect him.

Up over the Arthur Fielder Bridge, which he still thought of by its old name of the Longfellow Bridge, he leisurely walked over to the edge of the Charles River. Boston was a good city for him because he had easy access to the Charles River and not too far away was the waterfront and Boston Harbor. The urge to be near the water still was strong in him even after all these years of being alive, so to speak. It wasn't the ocean, but, at least, it was water. Life was perfect for him when he was on a wooden sailing vessel carrying fare and cargo across the Atlantic to England then back again to Newport, Rhode Island. He stared out at the slate gray water of the Charles. Rough water or calm water staring at the water always calmed him, made him feel almost human again because it reminded him of his pre-vampire life.

Across the Charles River stood MIT and Cambridge. Back in 1950 he knew an arrogant professor who taught at MIT. He was a scientist who thought he could disprove the existence of God, as well as prove that there was nothing supernatural to life only those things natural and explainable, with science, some math, and dollops of academic logic. He was a man who believed as strongly in the dominance of science, as a good priest believed in the existence of God. Caleb was never one to put the fear of anything in human beings, especially the fear of God, but this particular professor was too sure of his beliefs and was turning his students into clones of himself, and this offended Caleb's sense of right and wrong somehow. The Illuminatii thrived off of people like this professor. All it took was one nighttime visit to change this scientist's opinions of God and the supernatural, though. He took the good scientist on a visit of parts of

Cambridge he had never seen, such as the Monkey's Paw, a club where abominations and undead mixed with men and women who eventually became their victims.

After scaring all vestiges of surety from his intellect at the Monkey's Paw, he took him to another, even more important stop in Cambridge. Near Harvard Square in a small apartment Thomas Conklin Devlin made his home. Devlin was a Bene Lumen historian, a man who knew all the stories and secrets and kept them for the society. Caleb introduced the scientist who understood the natural world to the historian of all things supernatural. They spoke the same language, understood the same methodology and ideas, even like the same tea, Earl Gray. Devlin introduced the professor to the world of the Bene Lumen and stood beside him when the good scientist became a member of the Bene Lumen, where he remained one until his death in 1971. That was the last time Caleb had decided to take an active hand in the changing of someone's soul. Since then he had remained fairly distant from humanity with only making the odd foray helping a Tiarnán here and there, but, lately, he had the need to mix with people, to sense those whose lives were so short yet so poignant and important.

A giggle quickly turned his attention away from the Charles River. Two college aged young women were rushing towards him. As they walked, almost running but not quite because of the snow and ice of this moderate blizzard, they seemingly talked and laughed and enjoyed all that was around them. That was what he missed the most about being a living, normal soul. When he lost his humanity and became one of the undead, he lost those small moments, the seemingly unimportant moments, such as walking in the snow with a friend and enjoying a good laugh over the trivialities of life.

Turning on his heels, Caleb returned over the footbridge towards his apartment. Within a few hundred yards of the Public Gardens, he pulled down his hood exposing his hair and face to the obscured sun and the harsh wind. If it was a non-stormy day, this simple act of pulling down his hood would have caused him a great deal of pain, instead it allowed his blue and green veins to be clearly seen. As for his hair, once a human died their hair and fingernails continued to grow for a period of time.

For vampires they always continued to grow, so his white and blonde hair now fell to shoulder length. Whenever he looked in the mirror, he saw a man whose age was made virtually unreadable because his body no longer partook in the aging process. He could be fifty or he could be thirty. It was all in the eye of the beholder. What Caleb beheld was a creature that he hated being, a monster that he barely held in check.

Coming to Marlborough Street, he began to walk up it towards Massachusetts Avenue. If a normal human being was to look closely at him they would notice a few remarkable things, which would make them pause, maybe even run in fear. Even though it was below thirty degrees, no steam came from his nostrils or mouth because he wasn't breathing. There was no pulse in his wrists or neck, no heartbeat keeping beat to his walking, no lungs taking in oxygen and releasing carbon monoxide. He was a walking corpse, who didn't even blink because his eyes never dried out like a normal human being. And these eyes no longer looked like the ones he was born with, either. He was born with blue eyes, which his mother always said looked like kind merciful eyes, but now he had yellowish specks mixed in with his blue pupils with an iris that was three times normal size. Why this last thing occurred he never bothered to find out, especially since he tried to blink every few minutes whenever he didn't wear sunglasses to hide them just to make his appearance a little more normal in the presence of normal people.

Yet, how could a man who didn't suffer permanent damage from bullets, knives, swords, or explosives unless they were blessed by a holy man truly appear normal? Well, immune to everything except the explosives. Explosives could destroy his body, but his body regenerated in time. He was old enough a vampire to be able to do that trick, to regenerate his body over time. It was painful, too. He had his hand blown off just fifteen years ago when he was assisting a few Aongus Cathal in killing a horde of vampires in Mexico City. Someone tossed a hand grenade at the vampires. They then tossed the grenades back, but not until Caleb grabbed them in mid-air and went off in his hand. It took three painful months and plenty of fresh animal blood, but his hand grew back and looked normal, too.

Nothing about him was normal, though. His strength was preternatural. If he wanted to he could toss one of the cars parked so snugly against the sidewalk over on to its roof. He could even jump a story high, if he wanted to, or needed to, as well as glide on the wind. All these remarkable, even inspiring, powers, and he'd give them up tomorrow for a few more hours as a normal human being, though. A few hours of being with a woman and not being afraid that his bloodlust would overtake him during contact, or a few hours playing with children, those ever so perceptive miracles, and not being afraid of them noticing that he didn't breath, or his breath reeked of death.

Maybe it wasn't his pure soul but this desire that actually kept him from turning to the dark side and begin to feast on human blood.

Now within eyesight of his front door, eyesight that could see better in pitch dark than in light, he noticed someone standing on his doorstep. It was a man dressed in a navy blue Pea coat with a hood. The hood was pulled up covering his head and face. He closed his eyes and listened closely, blocking out the ripping sound of the wind, the gentle sound of the snow falling on the ground, and focused on the man's heart. Everyone has a distinct heartbeat to a vampire; once heard it was never forgotten. This one was Brian CuCullen's heartbeat.

He opened his eyes and found himself standing in front of his buildings front steps. Brian CuCullen pulled back his hood and looked down at him with a smile on his face. Of all the Bene Lumen he had known Caleb felt a connection to CuCullen. He was also a man uneasy with his fate in life.

"Hello, Caleb," he said.

"Hello, my young friend."

"I need your help."

"I know that. I didn't think this was a social visit, Brian, you have never been that social a person," he said as he walked up the steps and unlocked the front door, which lead to the first floor hallway. Caleb's apartment was the only one on the first floor. He unlocked his apartment door then motioned Brian CuCullen to enter his apartment. He did so.

The apartment was sparsely decorated: a sofa that looked worn but comfortable, several large comfy padded armchairs, a TV with a cable box on top of it that was on a card table, no pictures, paintings, posters, or personal items. In the kitchen all you could find was a few glasses, a microwave to heat cold blood, and nothing more. His fridge was empty but for a gallon or so container of animal blood and his bedroom had a bed with two pillows and a closet full of clothes that he chose without much thought. Most vampires filled their habitats with either reminders of what they considered to be luxurious living, or expensive items collected over the years like some animals collected shiny items for their lairs and nests. But Caleb Keane had no such attachments. Whenever he needed to see something beautiful or inspiring he visited the water.

"So is your Cape Horn fever over yet?" Brian CuCullen asked him then sat down on the sofa.

Caleb took off his coat, tossed it on the floor where it would stay until he needed it then sat down in one of the armchairs. He crossed his legs and stared at Brian with his yellowish blue eyes. A sly smile crossed his lips.

"It was more of a French leave than Cape Horn fever," he answered.

"Six years of avoiding the Bene Lumen is merely a French leave for you," Brian said with incredulity in his voice. "Sounds more like dereliction of duty to me and I should know something about that. I was gone for ten years."

"Dereliction of duty, huh? This is a watch I never asked for, Brian, so how could I desert it?"

"God gave it to you, Caleb, so how can you refuse it?" Brian asked.

"Did He? Did God give me this duty or did he just turn his head for a moment and this duty fell to me? I wonder," Caleb said to himself.

"How else do you explain your never giving into your bloodlust when you were turned in a vampire? Or the fact, that you still have a soul? If I took out my blessed blade, I'd be able to see your reflection in it; if I had a soul crystal it would turn a lovely shade of whatever color they turn when they sense a good soul. A divine presence has looked over you, Caleb."

"I stopped trying to explain such things like that, Brian. Just like you stopped trying to explain why you were born to be a Tiarnán or why that beast Baal killed Siobhan. They merely happened and you go on with your existence as best as you can. At some point in your life you just have to accept it for what it is and stop questioning yourself. Since I'm no rosewater sailor, I do my duties as I see fit, but occasionally you need a little shore leave," Caleb told him in a tone that had hints of pain and sympathy in it, which Brian appreciated. Caleb showed sympathy for few.

"Time heals all wounds," Brian whispered.

"No it doesn't, my friend, no it doesn't. Time heals nothing at all. Time merely passes and when enough of it has passed, you start to realize the absurdity of looking for answers to questions that have no answers in this life. Even when you seemingly have all the time in the world, like me, you realize all the true answers to the important questions lay on the other side," he said.

"I'll have to remember that."

"So what is it you want?" Caleb asked him.

"Your help."

"How original. Are you sure you wouldn't rather have a glass of water?" he chided him.

"I need your help, Caleb, it's important," Brian CuCullen stated seriously.

"No sense of humor, it must be important. You always had a sense of humor before. What is it?"

"A nephilim tried to kill me just a few weeks ago..."

"What distasteful creatures those things are," Caleb said in an annoyed tone.

"They truly are abominations. I abhor them, too, Caleb," Brian agreed.

"No, I don't mean that they are heinous, which they are, I mean that they taste horrible. Their blood is tainted with so much evil it is horrible to drink, though it did increase my strength quite a bit. Yet, I still wish I had never bitten a nephilim. But as a vampire I have only so many ways to kill them. Unlike you I don't carry blessed weapons. So this nephilim tried to kill you..."

"On Halloween," Brian interrupted him.

"On Halloween. How interesting, if not a little prosaic," he responded then fell silent.

Brian remained silent, also. He knew Caleb well enough to know that when he was thinking he wanted silence. While sitting on the sofa, he slowly took off his Pea coat and laid it on the cushion beside him.

"To kill a Tiarnán on Halloween, a night when he is expecting the worst, is a daring move, even for the Illuminatii. You do it for only a few reasons. One, you want control of the Tiarnán's soul; two, you believe this Tiarnán is either lax in his duties or new and will not appreciate the importance of Halloween, or you desperately want this Tiarnán dead and hope his mind is on all those lovely things that can happen during Halloween and will not be expecting a frontal attack. I'd think it would be the last one with you, don't you?"

"Yes," Brian answered.

"But why? You've been out of the game for ten years. You'd think they would slowly test your mettle to see if you had acquired any weaknesses in your early retirement. This is a bold move made for a bold reason."

"Exactly."

"You want me to find out why they desperately want you dead, to discern the larger plot that is at play here, right?" Caleb asked.

"I'm not ready to leave my children orphans. I need to know why they want me dead, other than the obvious reasons, so I can protect myself against them."

"Of course, you need to protect yourself and your children. So you dispatched this Nephilim easily I take it," he said.

"I was expecting it, so there wasn't much of a fight. I was about to let it get close to me. An informant..."

"A white mouse," corrected Caleb preferring an old nautical expression for informant.

"A white mouse told the council the attack was coming, so that I was ready."

"And that white mouse is now in Davy Jones' locker I take it," commented Caleb Keane.

"Yes, unfortunately, the informant is dead. He was a well-buried mole who thought an attempt on my life was worth his own. God knows what made him think that. We were never able to find out the reason why they tried to kill me, though, other than it is part of a greater plan," Brian stated.

"Interestingly enough not everyone converted to vampire or werecreature is sanguine with their fate, but they adjust in time. The urges for blood and death together with their new power cruising through their veins guides them to their fate. They take to this fate too easily and soon begin to enjoy their new powers, and too quickly start enjoying the death and blood. The best way to get them to get information from them is not to appeal to their humanity, which is basically gone like their souls, but to place them in a situation where you will deny them any further evil existence unless they tell you what you want. I will find out the reason for you, Brian. It may take some time, though. A vampire must be very desperate or hungry to tell me what I want."

"I know, Caleb."

"It may take several months. You better keep yourself prepared for battle until I seek you out with the truth of why they want you dead. They will keep coming for you, if they are that desperate to get rid of you," Caleb said in a calm even voice.

"You know what I like most about you, Caleb?"

"What?"

"You make me feel normal by comparison and that is very hard to do."

"Is it my old age or my lack of a heartbeat that makes you feel normal in comparison, or is it my odd dietary habit?" he asked with a slight smile.

"Where are you going to start looking for answers for me?" Brian asked him.

"A place I hate more than almost any other place on the face of the earth, Southern California. It is a wonderful place to find evil."

"Why do you hate Southern California so much?" he asked the

vampire.

"Because the sun is too bright; the people are too shallow; the Illuminatii are too powerful out there; but most of all there are too many people out there who want to be just like me, too many people who romanticize my kind of existence."

"Caleb, I know you don't need to hear this, or even want to hear it, but you are a good man. You don't think, but you are."

"I'm no longer a man, Brian. I am a creature, an undead monster, who hates what he is and would love if God would take away this burden."

"No, Caleb, you aren't a monster; you are a good man who has been given a difficult fate. Don't think of yourself as anything except a good man, Caleb. Hold on to that because I believe it is that which has stopped you from becoming the monster you say that you are."

"If you say so, Brian, if you say so. Now, since it is snowing more than a little I take it you will need a place to stay the night before you return home tomorrow," he said.

"Yes, I do need a place to rest my head for the night. It's a little too cold out there to sleep in the park."

"The sofa you're sitting on is comfortable, at least I assume that it is, but I'm afraid I don't have any blankets for you. Neither the cold nor the heat bothers me, so I don't keep any," Caleb stated.

"No problem. I'll use my coat as a blanket to keep warm. As for dinner...."

"As for food... unless you like rabbit's blood, as in the blood of a rabbit for food, I think it best you get some takeout for yourself."

"Good advice," Brian replied.

"I recommend Chinese food," Caleb commented. "It's been years since I've watched someone enjoy a meal of Chinese food."

"But I was thinking of pizza."

"Come now, Brian, pizza. Have more imagination than that. I can no longer eat food myself but I can enjoy a good meal through another. Allow me a good Chinese meal," Caleb implored him.

"All right, I'll order Chinese."

"Good. Make sure you get some dumplings and egg rolls. They appeal to my sense of smell."

Liam and the Conjurers Maze...

Like Ruadh's purpose was to teach teamwork as well as help to perfect physical skills, Conjurer's Maze was a game with a purpose to teach as well

186

as entertain. Conjurer's Maze tested the innate powers and learned skills of conjurers, as well as casters and charmers, who wanted to test themselves against others conjurers, casters, and charmers and prove their powers were equal to, if not superior to, conjurers. For Liam this was a chance to test his abilities against older conjurers and the better casters and charmers. It was also his way of showing Sian Boru that he was learning everything she taught him. So with a large gathering in the Morgana common room, Liam prepared to face a third year student, Thomas Hollingsworth in a game of Conjurer's Maze.

The Conjurer's Maze board took up most of a large library table. It was an intricate maze, which had two small white clay statues standing at opposite entrances. The maze was endowed with enchantments, hidden options, and certain arcane spells that made it a testing ground for any conjurer who entered it. The goal of the game was to be the first to crack the maze and entered the middle area. To play the game a spirit guide and a conjurer used their combined powers to temporarily transfer the soul of the game player into the clay statue, which would then become animated by the soul becoming in effect the game player.

Maol Stonefeather along with Master O'CuChulainn, Sian Boru, and Maol M'Tenga waited by the Conjurer's Maze gameboard for Liam and Hollingsworth. Also crowded in the common room were as many students from Morgana House from all levels, as well as Kieran and Selena. Dani and Brigid escorted Liam to the Conjurer's Maze board. Before sitting down Liam looked up at Sian Boru, who gave him a serene smile. Thomas Hollingsworth was escorted to his chair by two of his classmates. He sat down, while a few of his pals cheered him on.

"Go on, Thomas, you kick his arse," cheered one of his buddies.

"Thomas, he's an upstart, so put him in his place, show him what a third year can do," another yelled.

Thomas blushed and waved at his friends. He then began to take deep breaths in order to calm himself. They were now ready to play.

"Now that we are all here," Master O'CuChulainn stated, "it is time to play the game. Conjurer's Maze should never be taken lightly because it offers both the players and the audience lessons to be learned. So everyone pay attention and learn for this game as much as you enjoy it. Now I will act as the conjurer for Mr. CuCullen and Maol Stonefeather will be his spirit guide. Mistress Boru and Maol M'Tenga will act to enchant Mr. Hollingsworth. Are we ready players?"

"Yes," they both answered.

"Good. Let's us begin," O'CuChulainn declared in a dramatic voice.

Liam closed his eyes and sat silently in his chair. He was waiting for Maol Stonefeather and Master O'CuChulainn to transfer his essence, his soul, to one of the clay figures, which would then become animated by his presence. He would then have to make his way through the maze to the middle, conquering tasks and challenges, while inhabiting the clay figurine as if it was his own body. This was his third Conjurer's Maze game. In his first one he easily beat another first year. His second game was against a second year that he also easily defeated. Liam wasn't sure why since he had never played the game before, but he was a natural at the game.

Internally, he began to shiver and feel himself detached from his body. It didn't take long for him to feel free of his physical form, floating unattached in the air until he was grounded once again in a body, but this time the clay body. He opened his eyes. In front of him was the opening to the maze. He looked up at the many giant faces, which looked down on him now. In his first game when he saw this sight for the first time he panicked. A combination of anxiety and fear almost overwhelmed him until he looked up and saw Sian Boru's, Dani's and Brigid's abnormally large faces looking down on him. This calmed him and he was then able to enter the maze. This time he had no anxiety or fear, so he returned his gaze to the maze's entrance and entered.

At first this felt no different from the first time he played Conjurer's Maze. He was in complete control of the clay body. It moved easily and at his will. But this time after he took his first few steps, he noticed the body didn't feel right. He stopped in his tracks and looked down at his body. At the clay figures base there were a few cracks starting to form. If the clay figure broke while his essence animated it, his soul would be freed to the air and since it wasn't grounded to his body by a spell he'd be unable to return to his body.

Liam looked up at the large faces watching him. He needed to return to his body immediately as the cracks grew larger and larger in the base of the clay figure. There were two ways to have your soul returned to your body in Conjurer's Maze. The first was to alert your Maol with a request on the astral plain. It took minutes, though, and Liam wasn't sure he had minutes. If during a challenge his figure was damaged he would be returned immediately, but no challenge was taking place at the moment. The second way to have his soul returned to his body was to make it to the middle of the maze. Immediately on entering the maze, your soul was returned, so as to give proof of who got to the center first. Liam needed to be in the middle of the maze now.

All of a sudden, he heard a voice in his head. It was Merlin's voice, speaking to him. The voice sounded as if he was whispering to him, telling him how to solve his problem. As a caster and a conjurer he had the power to teleport himself to the center of the maze. All he had to do was concentrate all his energy and power, visualizing on where he was and where he wanted to be, concentrated on moving from where he was to where he wanted to be and then cast a spell with these words: time and space become one; all locations are one; I am here and need to there. He stopped moving, closed his eyes, and began to concentrate and focus all his energy and power on visualizing where he was and moving to where he wanted to be, then he mouthed the words, cedo transeo, drew on the power of nature, and cast the spell.

Liam had never experienced anything like this before. Time felt as if it stopped completely, not that it slowed down or ceased, but that it temporarily stopped. At the same time the area of the maze he stood in dissolved into nothingness and the middle of the maze began to form all around him. When time resumed, he was standing in the middle of the maze and in seconds his soul was returned to his body.

"Quickly return Thomas Hollingsworth to his body before it's too late for him," Liam yelled surprising everyone in the room. Liam felt the energy of his body ebbing, needing time to rejuvenate. What he had just done was unheard of, except by Merlin, and took a power that few understood. Many of the students gasped in surprise and some in horror. No one could understand how Liam got into his body so quickly. The four teachers stood and stared at him.

"What happened?" Maol Stonefeather finally asked in shock.

"No time to talk, return him now or it will be too late," Liam demanded.

Stonefeather closed his eyes to do as Liam requested, but before he could make contact with Hollingsworth several of the students watching the match screamed. The clay figure crumbled before their eyes releasing the young boy's soul into the air. Sian Boru looked at Liam with fear for him and for what had happened in her eyes.

"Stonefeather get Liam into the head of house office. M'Tenga, O'CuChulainn get the students out of this room. I will try and contact the boy in the maze and see if I can guide him back to his body even though he wasn't grounded," she said then looked over at Hollingsworth slumping body. She knew that it was useless to search for the boy's soul, but she had to try. His soul was gone, unattached to anything, ungrounded and he was dead.

M'Tenga and O'CuChulainn rushed the student body out of the room while Stonefeather rushed a shocked Liam into the head of house office, which was located across from the common room. Stonefeather gently sat Liam on the sofa in the office, patted him gently on the right shoulder then began to pace.

"What happened?" he asked Liam.

"Something was wrong with my clay figure. It was crumbling, falling apart," Liam stated calmly.

"How did you get to the middle of the maze so quickly?" he asked him.

"I teleported myself there," was Liam's simple answer, but it was far from being a simple thing. Liam had done something that no one else could do, not even the best Triune Conjurers. Stonefeather looked at the boy with amazement startled by what he had just heard. In the Bene Lumen history only Merlin had ever teleported himself, and that was considered a myth. But this boy had just done it, too. What was he to think?

"How did you know that Hollingsworth was in trouble, too?" he asked with a mix of concern and wonder in his voice.

"I had a feeling he was in danger. I just felt it," Liam replied flatly. He was too tired and shocked to have emotions.

Sian Boru entered the room. Concern clouded her beautiful face. She looked at Stonefeather, who merely shrugged his shoulders as if to say he couldn't explain anything then she turned her attention to Liam, who looked as if he was tired and drained of energy.

"What happened?" she asked.

"When I started to move in the clay figure, it began to crumble. I knew what this meant then suddenly I heard Merlin's voice in my mind. He told me how to teleport, or as he called it travel in time and space, to the middle of the maze. I did it. It drained all my energy but I did it. Once I was in my body I knew that Thomas Hollingsworth was in trouble, too," he answered.

"Liam, someone tried to kill you," she stated.

"Wait a minute..." Stonefeather began to speak but Sian Boru stopped him.

"It is the only explanation for this. The clay figures had a spell cast on them to crumble. I just checked them myself with my third eye. It was a subtle enchantment done by someone of excellent skills, someone very subtle. I can only assume that both figures were cursed to make sure they got Liam because he is... The headmaster must be told. We have a traitor in our midst. It is the only explanation for what happened. Get the Headmaster and tell him everything that has happened here. He needs to know now so he can put the right security measures in place," she told Stonefeather.

He rushed out of the room leaving Sian Boru and Liam alone. Once he was gone, she rushed to Liam's side and gave him a motherly hug. He felt better. In the hug he felt some of his energy return, as if he took it from her.

"What happened to Hollingsworth?" he asked looking into her eyes, which were tearing up.

"His soul is out there somewhere. I do not know where, though, because his body wasn't grounded; he wasn't attached to his body or anything else. He is a free spirit now. I couldn't contact him in order to lead him back to his body. I am afraid that he is lost," she replied.

"I have to help him."

"You can't help him, Liam. No one can help him now because he is no longer grounded. A soul must be grounded either to a body or to a place or else it loses its way. He must find a way to the other side on his own now without any help."

"I'm not sure about that, Sian. I don't know why but I feel like I will be able to help him someday. Maybe it's the knowledge Merlin gave him, or something else, but I know I will be able to help him some day. He isn't gone; he is nearby and his soul will stay nearby until I help him. He's too afraid to leave," Liam stated.

"I could talk to one of the spirit guides and see if they have some ideas. Maybe they can reach out to him before he can never be reached," she said.

"No, they won't be able to help him. He is not a spirit or a ghost, but a healthy soul whose body is lost to him. It wasn't his time yet."

"Liam... most of your classmates will be in awe of you now, even a little frightened of you now. What you did out there is considered impossible by many. They now know just how powerful and different you are from them. They will talk, spread rumors, even legends about you."

"They think they know, but they don't know what I am. If they did, they'd have a right to fear me."

"Why?" she asked.

"Because in his time Merlin, as much as he was loved by his comrades, was feared. He did things they didn't understand or couldn't do. It is hard to accept someone like that because we are told that great power corrupts a person that powerful, or so most people assume that. They don't understand that to some special people power doesn't really corrupt certain individuals, but is a burden they have to carry," he explained to her.

Sian Boru sat beside him on the sofa and took his hands in her own. His hands were cold and shaking. He was drained. For the first time she realized she cared for this young boy like a son.

"Liam, you teleported," she said with a smile.

"I know."

"Only Merlin has ever done that."

"I know."

"How did you do it?" she asked.

"The knowledge just came to me. Merlin said I would receive the knowledge, as I needed it. He was right."

"You will have to teach me how to teleport someday," she said.

"I will, Sian, I will teach you as best as I can. I have the feeling that it will come in handy for you someday to know how to teleport," he said then began to cry. He cried for Hollingsworth and for the fact that everyone now would know he was different. They had seen him teleport. It will be all over the school. He would never be thought of as the same, never be able to play a game of Conjurer's Maze either. All he had to do was teleport and he'd win. And an innocent boy died because someone wanted him dead. It wasn't fair.

Sian took him in her arms and comforted him as she had never comforted a child before. Patting and kissing his hair, she hugged him wanting to take all his problems away but knowing she couldn't. A warm feeling flowed through her, a feeling that made her believe she could stop anyone or anything to protect him. He had released all her maternal feelings and in that moment she wondered if he had just made her a better Triune Conjurer because she truly understood love now and its importance.

CHAPTER 14

With the tragic consequences of the Conjurer's Maze incident, Headmaster Fergus cancelled all trips into the town and off the island in general, unless it was to go home for a visit and you were chaperoned by a parent or guardian. Maol Stonefeather used an owl to find the lost soul of Thomas Hollingsworth. In his shaman tradition the owl escorted souls to the other side of life, but his owl was unable to find poor Thomas, whose soul seemed to be lost permanently. Wherever his spirit was, it was now floating free, ungrounded, and in need of guidance. Fergus had to make a decision. It was now apparent that his school and students were under attack from the outside and from someone on the inside, too. Yes, a traitor must be at Samhain. Fergus didn't want to believe it but there must be a traitor at his school.

The ban on visits to Fort Augustus and surrounding areas left a prevailing dour mood on many of the upper level students as their privileges were now limited to life on Samhain only. Going to Fort Augustus was a reward for students, a chance to go shopping for some things you couldn't get on Samhain, like CDs, and a chance to be normal for an afternoon. At least now it was Christmas time, and like every other Christmas season since the time of Merlin it snowed on Samhain leaving the island covered in white and everyone generally in a good mood. Merlin thought Christmas wasn't Christmas unless there was pure white snow covering the ground. Long ago he had made an easy peace with the Christian religion, which he slowly saw replace his own beliefs in his own land, and even learned to enjoy some of their rituals and holidays, especially Christmas. Christmas in Merlin's opinion was a time in which humanity almost achieved grace, and anyone who inspired that sort of behavior in humanity was worthy of respect. For the students of Samhain they had a three-week winter break during this time of year.

Most of the students left the island for home to be with friends and family during this time. All that remained of the student body and the rest of those who lived on Samhain were some of the cooks and cleaners, most of the teachers, who had come to think of Samhain as their home, Headmaster Fergus, and a few of the students, including Liam, Kieran and Selena, whose parents or guardians were too busy to celebrate the season, and those who, for all intents and purposes, didn't have a home. Walking from Morgana House to CuChulainn Liam was awed by the serene beauty, which the snow seemed to give the landscape. It covered the roofs of the buildings, leaves on the trees, bushes, and most of the ground giving the whole place an almost magical feel and look, which was a difficult effect considering this was a mist Isle. He felt like he was in a snow globe that had just been thoroughly shaken and had its fake snow dispersed through the watery scene. Getting to CuChulainn House he entered then walked into the common room, which was decorated with lush green wreaths, red bows, and white lights, where he saw Selena and Kieran sitting together on a leather sofa in front of a roaring fire.

"Join us, Bro, you look frozen," Kieran said.

Liam took off his winter robe to reveal an Irish Knit sweater and jeans underneath his school clothes. He draped the robe, which now had slowly melting snow turning it to water and vapor, on a chair near the fire then sat down on another chair on the other side of the warming fire.

"Dad will be here soon for Christmas vacation," he said.

"Oh," was Kieran's answer. Selena, though, perked up with the mention of Brian CuCullen's imminent arrival. He had saved her life and taken her into his family, which made her feel nothing but positive about him. Even though she hadn't spent much time with him, she had started to feel as if he was a father to her, a protector from the evil that was out there.

"Mistress Boru is planning a nice private dinner for us in her private rooms to welcome him. She said it is a family get-together, a gathering of the CuCullen and Boru clans," Liam stated happily.

"She's not really family, Liam," Kieran said.

"She is my private tutor, which makes her family to me, and she was ma's cousin, which makes her distant even if she wasn't my private tutor and mentor," Liam corrected his brother.

"I keep forgetting about that, probably because we never saw her before Paulette's funeral. You'd think family would stay in touch."

"That's not the reason you don't want to think of her as family, you don't like thinking of her as family because she is so beautiful. And you still haven't accepted Samhain as where you belong," Liam told his older brother, who looked at him as if he was talking about matters he didn't understand.

"Bro, don't lecture me. I'll get enough of that when dad gets here tonight," Kieran warned his brother. "I bet he can't wait to tell me how badly I'm doing here."

Liam fretted about Kieran lately. He knew his brother had a great destiny but he saw how Kieran fought against that destiny. Part of him wanted to tell Kieran what he knew, but he wasn't sure that would accomplish anything accept make his brother more adamant that he didn't belong here. Not even the last few month playing in the Ruadh league, where Kieran's team, the Aongus Misfits, was now in fourth place and in line to make the playoffs, made him feel at home at Samhain. He took to playing Ruadh not as a chance to be accepted but an opportunity to prove that he wasn't second rate. Kieran was so busy proving himself that he hadn't even noticed that most of the school now considered him one of the best Ruadh players.

"When will he be here?" asked Selena tentatively, though she couldn't hide the excitement in her voice.

More so than with Liam Selena had bonded with Kieran. Besides the physical resemblance to their father, Kieran also had their father's way of protecting people. She was drawn to this and treated Kieran as if she idolized him. But she was intuitive enough to know that Kieran and Brian CuCullen didn't exactly have an easy relationship, so she tried not to talk much about Brian CuCullen with Kieran. She saved all those discussions with Liam, who had become a bit of a family historian learning as much about his mother and father as he could from people and books at Samhain. He was filling in the blank spaces of personal history for himself and, eventually, for Kieran.

"Any moment. I know that Maol Stonefeather and Mistress Boru are on the beach waiting as we speak. They say Nessie is restless and that usually means that a Tiarnán is on the water. There are three Eadach keeping Nessie occupied tonight to make sure he doesn't get too cranky and makes the mistake of attacking dad. They treat him more like a pet than a demon, so they don't want him hurt. I was going to wait with them but they told me not to bother. Headmaster Fergus wanted to talk to dad privately first," Liam explained.

"Maybe he is in trouble with Fergus," Kieran joked, "that would be great. I'd like to see a different CuCullen in trouble for a change."

"I think that..." Liam started to say but stopped. He wasn't sure he wanted to speak honestly about what he knew in front of Selena. Kieran told him not to bother her with too many things because she had been through enough already this year.

"What is wrong?" Selena asked sternly.

"Nothing," Liam replied.

"That is a lie. I can sense it. I can sense many things since... tell me what is wrong with Brian CuCullen."

"Calm down, Sis," Kieran tried to calm her.

"I'm not upset. I just know that something is wrong. I can sense it. Tell us, Liam, tell us what you are hiding from us," she demanded.

"Go on and tell her whatever it is, Liam. She won't calm down unless you do," Kieran told him.

"Okay. From what I've overheard and from some other sources, I think that dad has had a tough time doing his job lately. The Illuminatii have been making a strong effort to kill him. They have him targeted for death."

"Of course, they have him targeted, he is a Tiarnán," Kieran said.

"No, not just the normal amount of danger that every Bene Lumen is in, or any Tiarnán deals with, but something more than that. The Illuminatii have made it a top priority to kill him in particular. It is part of some overall plan they have," Liam explained.

"They fear that he can stop whatever their plans are," Selena stated in a voice that told them that she was sure of what she said.

"Now, Sis..." Kieran was about to tell her not to worry when suddenly Liam saw that she was right.

"Selena, you're right. I can sense the truth in what you said. He is a problem to them. They fear him because he can stop them from succeeding at something, which they are planning. His death is important to them," Liam stated.

To Liam's surprise he suspected that Selena might have the power of discerning truth from lies, a truthsayer. He only recently found that he had the ability when he was told by a fellow student that he was wanted by the headmaster, yet he just knew that it was a setup because the truth sounded different from lies to his ears. He wondered if Selena had somehow developed this talent because of the werewolf bite.

"Calm down you two, Dad..."

"Dad is in constant danger," Liam interrupted his brother. "They are always trying to get at him now. We should try and make this as nice a holiday for him as we can, Kieran. He needs the time to rest, re-energize, and think, so lay off of him when he gets here. Be nice."

"Why are you telling me that?" asked Kieran.

"Because you are always fighting with him, blaming him for everything that has happened to us in our life. Try not to do that this time, Kieran," Liam said.

"Please, Kieran, be nice to him. This is his vacation," Selena pleaded with him.

"I...I," he started to defend himself out of frustration then thought of what he had told Liam about Selena. He didn't want to upset her more than needed.

"I'll be nice," he said.

Right then on the beach Brian CuCullen's rowboat broke through the mist and headed towards the sand. Once the rowboat hit the sand of the beach he stood up and deftly jumped out of the boat and landed softly on the sand. He was a different man from the man who had last come to Samhain. Sian Boru noticed this immediately once his feet touched the ground. It was more than the fact that his physical skills and gifts were once again working at peak form, but he was also a man who knew where he belonged in the world and what he needed to do. His whole being pulsated with confidence and a kind of contentment that he lacked on his last visit. The last time he came here, he was a man at odds with his fate. Much had changed for him.

Stonefeather gave him a friendly hug. Sian walked towards him. Ever since Siobhan died they had a distant relationship with her not wanting to infringe on his memories of Siobhan and him not wanting to feel anything but guilt of his wife's death. She had decided it was time to end this distance and walked up to him and hugged him also. It last for only a few seconds, but Sian and Brian felt an electric charge pass between them when they touched. They made no mention of it, though. Sian knew that the time wasn't right, and Brian was not ready.

"Mallory wants to speak to you in private right away," Sian said.

"Why?"

"Because of what you have gone through this past few months with six of your fealty dead, Jennifer Sult almost killed and you under constant attack from the Illuminatii and their associates. He feels that you and he should talk about it before you relax for the rest of your stay here. He is worried about you, Brian," she told him in a tone that implied that she was worried about him, too.

"I'm fine," Brian stated.

"Brian, you are a Tiarnán. Mallory understands what that feels like, the pressures and burdens you have to deal with. He also knows what it feels like to be under constant attack from the Illuminatii. Remember he was once someone they wanted dead more than anyone else. All he wants to do is talk to you in private, so indulge him. Indulge me, too."

"Okay, I'll talk to him, Sian."

"Good, I'm glad to hear it. I was afraid I was going to have to subdue you with my devastating moves and drag you off to his office in a headlock," Stonefeather said with a straight face.

Brian laughed. It had been weeks since the last time he laughed and meant it. Stonefeather slapped him on the shoulder and lead the way. Sian placed her arm tenderly through his and walked beside him. Though he was surprised by her gesture, he was also calmed by it.

"Liam is an amazing student. He already has the skills of a fifth year conjurer, a third year charmer and a fourth year caster. His abilities are blossoming quicker than I anticipated," she said to him.

"Have you found out who cursed the clay statues?" he asked with concern.

"No. Someone either has infiltrated Samhain or has found a way to visit without our noticing, which is very scary if you ask me. Either way Mallory has upped security measures and taken a personal hand in overseeing certain things, such as who is allowed onto Samhain. The idea of Samhain being susceptible to attack has been such a stress on him. I fear for him."

"He is that concerned," Brian said.

"Wouldn't you be?" she asked rhetorically.

"And Kieran... how is he doing?"

"He is slowly adjusting, though he still thinks of himself as an outsider. The one thing he has done easily is to accept Selena into the family. He is very protective of her," she told him.

"Good. How is Selena?"

"A special girl. I have talked with her several times about what happened to her. She knows that I had a similar situation as her. She wasn't surprised to hear that it was you who saved me from..."

"You saved me, I didn't save you," Brian gently corrected her.

"I remember it a different way, Brian. I remember the way it truly was," she replied.

"Has she asked about her family yet?" he asked another question about Selena, as if she needed his attention the most and not his boys. It also allowed him a chance to change topics.

"Once. We talked about it honestly and openly. All she wants to make sure is that they are not too sad and wished that she could somehow make them understand what has happened to her."

"What did you tell her?"

"That I could see what I could do about comforting them," she answered surprisingly.

"There is nothing you can do about that."

"Don't be so sure. You're son has taught me not to assume that you can or can't do something," she said then stopped. "We are here."

They were now in front of the Headmaster's house. Stonefeather was holding the door open for Brian CuCullen. Sian took her arm away from him now.

"You and your children are scheduled to have dinner with me tonight. I expect you at eight on the dot," she said and walked away. For a moment Brian watched her go then turned, slapped Stonefeather on the shoulder and entered the Headmaster's house. He knew where to go since he had made many trips to the Headmaster's office during his school days. He knocked on the closed door.

"Come on in, Brian," he heard Mallory's voice say on the other side of the door.

He opened the door and entered. Just like the rest of Samhain, the office was decorated for the holiday. Mallory sat behind his desk smoking a pipe and enjoying a glass of honey wine. He poured some of the wine into an empty glass he had waiting and placed it down in front on the front of the desk where an empty chair waited Brian. He took off his coat, draped it over his chair, sat, and took a sip of the wine. It warmed him.

"Times have been difficult for you lately," Mallory said to him.

"And for you," Brian added.

"Yes, we will talk about my difficult times in time. But let us first start with you," he said. "I heard that you have enlisted Caleb to aid you in gathering intelligence."

"Yes, I have."

"I remember when I worked with him for the first time, I found him surprising. At first I was scared of him, but I got used to his oddness and began to appreciate not only his situation but also his strength and willingness to carry his burden without many complaints. That has to be two hundred years ago. See what happens when you accidentally drink from the fountain youth, you get an extra long life in which to serve. That's what I get for being thirsty on a hot day in Gaul. How is Caleb doing?" Mallory asked Brian.

"He is Caleb. He is never really happy, yet he never truly succumbs to depression or to the darkness that calls to him. He seeks peace in a world that can't offer it to him."

"A remarkable man," commented Mallory.

"Yes, he is."

"How are you dealing with things, Brian?" asked Mallory.

"As well as can be expected. I've lost several key people and almost lost my top Lieutenant."

"Yes, I know. They want you dead and now."

"I've noticed that," he said with a yawn cracking open his mouth.

"Am I boring you?" asked Mallory amused by Brian CuCullen's seeming nonchalance.

"No, not boring me. I'm just exhausted. I have averaged about three hours of sleep a night with everything that is going on. Just last week I had a jann or was it a jinn attack me. I can't tell the difference between them. Luckily, I had a Maol, Father Raphael Majorca, staying the night. He was able to confuse it for a moment with Arabic chants then I was able to get to my weapons and do battle with it. Twenty-five minutes later it was returned to whatever hell it belongs in," he said in a matter of fact tone, as if this was a commonplace occurrence. But it wasn't commonplace, not even for a Tiarnán.

"Was it green or gray?" asked Mallory.

"Grey," he answered.

"Then it was a jann. I'll make a note of it, so there is no confusion in the records. We need to be exact when keeping our historical records. They are used to inform and teach."

"Well, if we are being exact then let's go over exactly what I have killed in the last two months: a nephilim, a shapeshifter, two vampires, a tengu, a wight, a ghoul, and now a jann. This, of course, does not include the human Illuminatii who have recently tried to kill me. Their last count was at seven. It's been a busy return for me."

"No wonder you are tired, my friend," Mallory said with a smile.

"What do you find so amusing?"

"Well, for someone who was gone for ten years you are making up for lost time, aren't you? I can't think of another Tiarnán who could deal with such a diverse group and lose so few fealties, or not be killed themselves. You are a remarkable man and a great Tiarnán."

"I don't feel remarkable or great," he responded to the compliment.

"What do you feel like?"

"Like a man who needs to know why they want me dead so badly," he said.

"Brian, I put this to you: you're son Liam was nearly killed here at Samhain in a strange incident while playing Conjurer's Maze and you are under constant attack. Do you think these two incidents are separate or connected?" Mallory asked.

"They are connected," he answered without much thought.

"Why?"

"Because Liam and I are connected. It is the obvious answer."

"More than likely that it is true, too. And this means we have a very large problem indeed. I should like to know immediately what Caleb finds out when you hear from him. I am afraid that your current situation is related to your son here. We must treat them as the same problem."

"Mallory, do you think they know about Liam being so special, even more special than we thought?"

"Brian, I think there is a traitor in our midst and I hope that whatever information Caleb gathers will tell me if this traitor lays with the Council or here on Samhain."

"Let's hope it is someone on the council and not here," Brian stated.

"I am in agreement with you. If it is here on the mist island, it means that they have found a way to get around certain enchantments which have protected this place for a very long time," Mallory explained. "I do not like to think of Samhain as vulnerable. My students have always lived here without fear, feeling safe which allows them to learn. I don't like the idea of those evil you know what's having a wolf amongst them waiting to pounce on us."

"Neither do I. I have two sons here and now an adopted daughter," Brian added.

"I know. And both sons are very special."

"Kieran, too?"

"Yes, Kieran is also a special student, though no one knows it but me, Liam, and Sian Boru, and maybe one or two others, who have looked past his current incompetence but have seen the fire inside of him. He doesn't even realize how special he is. I have a fondness for the boy. He reminds me of someone I followed and admired."

"Explain," Brian demanded sounding like a Tiarnán with a problem to solve.

Mallory laughed at his demand. He reached down and took his wine glass in hand and had another drink of the honey wine. After a moment to savor the flavor, he set the glass back down and looked at Brian CuCullen as a father looks at a son.

"Liam is like Merlin..."

"There's no mistaking this?" Brian asked quickly.

"No, he is a fulcrum of energy and history. He will be more than powerful, he will be important to history, a man for myth and legend."

"So what is Kieran then?"

"Another Arthur," answered Mallory with a smile.

"He's a champion, a special Tiarnán for the fulcrum to use to bring changes," he stated not for Mallory, who understood what being another Arthur meant, but so that he could hear it himself. It was stunning to think that both of his sons were so special, so powerful, so endangered. "They must be protected at all cost."

"I know," Mallory replied.

"At all costs," he said.

"I am well aware of that, Tiarnán. I have kept this school safe for many, many years."

"Does the council know about this?" asked Brian.

"No, they do not. I have kept this knowledge to as few people as possible. Believe it or not, Brian, but I don't trust many people. A long life has taught me to not trust easily. I have been disappointed too many times," Mallory said with a smirk on his lips.

"And I am grateful for that, Mallory. I want you to be overly cautious."

"I believe there are some on the council who have their suspicions, though. I cannot stop all teachers from reporting back to the council with news and facts. I try to encourage autonomy from the outside at Samhain, but word has a way of trickling back to certain people. It is frustrating."

"Teacher? Could it be...?"

"It could be anyone, Brian. That is always the problem with traitors. They are not obvious; they do not wear signs. Remember American History? Benedict Arnold was a hero of the revolution before he became a traitor to it. It could be me. It could be you," Mallory answered.

"Mallory, you don't think that I am..."

"No, I don't, but that doesn't mean you aren't the traitor, Brian. See I told you I didn't trust that many people, so you wouldn't want me to start trusting now," Mallory said with amusement in his voice. "Now let's change the topic and talk of other things. Drink your wine, relax while you are here and recharge your batteries. Your sons' security is my responsibility, well, mine and Sian Boru's."

"She has taken to overseeing their security, too?" Brian asked.

"Yes, of course. Liam is one of her private students and she cares for your family deeply."

"I feel better thinking she is also looking out for them," he said.

"I'll overlook the implied insult to this old man and focus on the fact that you are a concerned father. You see, Brian, I also care about your family."

"I know..."

"Now I hope to see you at the Christmas Eve tomorrow night. Father Mueller puts on a beautiful mass. I am always stirred by it."

"I'll be there with my boys and Selena."

"Good. Now drink your drink and tell me how you killed the Ghul. I always had trouble with them when I was a Tiarnán. It takes so many blows to slow them down enough for you to administer a deathblow. I found them very frustrating," he said then leaned back in his chair to listen.

"Do you really expect me to relax, Mallory?" asked Brian in a mocking voice.

"I expect you to at least pretend to relax for my sake and for your sons' sakes. They deserve a happy father for the holiday not a brooding warrior on guard. Act like you are enjoying yourself while you are here, Brian. Do it for your family, if not for your own sanity."

Midnight Mass was held in the great stone church located in the middle of Samhain's town square. It was used by many faiths from Russian Orthodox to Baptist, but on this night it was a strictly Holy Roman Catholic

Mass with Father Mueller as the main celebrant. Because of the stone nature of the building the acoustics were inspiring as the sound reverberated off the rock. But it wasn't just the acoustics, but the great stone church itself that was inspiring with its multicolored stained glass windows and Celtic influenced sculptures. Though the church was far from filled to capacity, which could hold almost the whole student body, Brian CuCullen, Liam, Kieran, Selena and Sian Boru sat in one of the pews, as Father Mueller performed the mass which ended with the playing of Christmas carols and hymns.

After the mass they strolled back to Sian Boru's private quarters where they were going to open a few gifts and enjoy some hot chocolate. Snow lightly fell as they walked and Liam and Selena got into a snowball fight with Kieran acting as referee.

"That was nice," Brian said to Sian as they watched the snowball fight.

"Yes, it was."

"I was surprised to see you at the mass."

"I have long ago come to an understanding with Christianity, we are friends now," she said.

"Really? That's a surprise," he goaded her. "I remember when you were against Siobhan marrying me because I was Christian."

"I was rash back then... and I had other reasons to treat you as I did back in those days. I was not completely honest with Siobhan or myself," she admitted.

As Brian was about to ask Sian what she meant some other students who had stayed for the Winter Break joined Liam's and Selena's snowball. Mallory strolled over to them to watch the snowball fight.

"I love Christmas. It's so festive and light of spirit," he commented.

"We know. You always were in a better mood during Christmas," Sian said.

"It's the eggnog. I believe in real eggnog, including a dash of some spirits," he replied.

"Would you like to join us at Sian's rooms? We are having a small Christmas gift opening party for the kids?" Brian asked Mallory.

"What? Aren't the children going to wait for Santa's visit? If I recall correctly he knows how to get to this mist island."

"Mallory, we know that St. Nicholas was Bene Lumen," Sian rebuked him mildly.

"Tomorrow morning I am planning a concert in the town square with hot chocolate, fresh hot sweet buns, non-alcoholic eggnog, and a choir of volunteers to sing songs. Maol Stonefeather has agreed to be the choirmaster for the event. He is probably preparing songs in his rooms as we speak. I hope to you see all there," Mallory said.

"We'll be there for it," Brian replied then Mallory strolled away.

"He is in a good mood considering all things considered that are going on here. It must be your presence. Having a Tiarnán on the island is like having an extra level of security," Sian commented.

"I know. Mallory told him he has scheduled an appointment with the Council of Guaire at the end of school year. He is concerned with the security here and his ability to deal with it. I feel Mallory thinks his time here is coming to an end."

"He has been headmaster for ... for two hundred and twenty-two years now," Sian said, "I think he is just feeling a little tired. That's all it is."

"No, it's more than that. I think he longs to die. Think about how many friends and loved ones he has seen grow old and die. It's more than being tired."

"Some didn't even have a chance to grow old either," she added.

"Exactly. He is not so much tired of his job, or unable to do it, but he is worn out from living so long. I think he is ready to die."

"When he dies is not his choice, though, is it? He knows that a greater power than him will decide when his time is," Sian expounded.

"Well, whenever his time comes, I for one will miss him. He is almost like a father to me," Brian said.

"He always had a soft spot for you. When you decided to leave the Bene Lumen he was broken hearted. When Paulette died, he was sure that you would finally see the light and return to the fold. He was right. The day we got the message that you would return, he walked around the school insufferably cheery."

"Sian, what did you mean that there was another reason why you didn't want Siobhan to marry me," Brian returned to the subject which Mallory had interrupted.

"Well, Brian, the answer is a difficult one. I'm not sure you are ready to hear, though I am ready to say it."

"Whatever it is, I can handle it," he said.

"Are you sure?" she asked.

"Yes," answered Brian.

"I didn't want her to marry you because I was jealous. I loved you

Brian and I still do," she said simply.

"Sian..." he began to say then was hit right in the face by a powdery snowball that exploded into flakes and ice. To his surprise Sian laughed at his discomfort.

"Hey, Dad, sorry about that," yelled Liam who had thrown the errant snowball.

Looking over at his children, he saw that Kieran, Liam and Selena were all laughing at his getting hit by a snowball. Beside him Sian continued to laugh. Not wanting to get angry, and still not sure what he thought about what Sian had just told him, he decided to join in the laughter.

"We should get going if you guys want to open your gifts," he said to his children.

"Come on sis and midget, let's open up some gifts," Kieran said prodded them to break off their snowball fight with the other students.

They herded together once again and headed back to Sian's rooms. When they got to Morgana's House she ushered them into her rooms, where she had a traditional decorated Christmas tree with strung cranberries, wooden ornaments and gold and silver balls. There was even silver tinsel hanging from the tree branches. Under the tree there were twelve wrapped gifts and on a wooden table she had placed a plate of chocolate chip cookies and a pitcher of hot chocolate and several mugs waiting to be filled. Everyone was pleasantly surprised.

"This is great," cried Liam sounding like a little boy, which was something he didn't sound like too often lately. Selena stood beside Brian CuCullen beaming with joy and even Kieran looked to be happy in his father's company for a change.

"The gifts have your names on it. So why don't you three go rummage under the tree and open your gifts. It is now officially Christmas day," Brian told them.

Liam and Selena hurried off to start looking at the nametags, while Kieran followed slowly behind them. As they divided the packages into appropriate piles, Sian and Brian walked over to the table where the cookies and hot chocolate sat.

"I can't believe you, Sian you got a Christmas tree? When I had the presents sent to you, I thought you'd have some ceremonial druid burning log or something like that. But you have a Christmas tree, this is a shock," Brian said.

"I thought they would like one," she said as she poured them each a hot chocolate.

"Still it is a surprise."

"Diarmund was very upset with me. Between the Christmas tree and telling him I was going to Midnight Mass, I thought he was going to yell at me, but he thought better of doing such a rash thing" she told him.

"What's his problem?"

"He hates how our religion recedes further and further behind the veil. Unlike my sister, the Lady of the Lake, he still thinks the Druid religion should be the religion of this land. He is surprisingly bitter about it."

"He doesn't seem bitter to me. He seems friendly and at ease," Brian said.

"Diarmund has always been able to hide his bitterness well to those who aren't druids."

Brian took a sip of the hot chocolate. It was the best Belgian chocolate melted down with a hint of mint and cream. He took another sip appreciating the flavor. Looking over at his children, he saw that Selena was wearing her i-Pod. He had Jennifer Sult download several dozen songs which she thought Selena might enjoy since she was more in tune with what was popular and what wasn't, then he downloaded a dozen songs, such as Bobby Darin, some classical music, and even a Gregorian Chant, he wanted her to like. When she noticed that he was looking at her she beamed a smile at him, which told him that she liked his gift. This made him feel content. As much as he loved his boys, he felt a responsibility for Selena that he had a difficult time explaining. If the boys were his children from Siobhan, then Selena was his child made by his vocation.

Liam had unwrapped ten Playstation games and his new Playstation and was starting to choose which one he wanted to play first. Months of being the next Merlin had made him forget what it felt like to be a kid, but these games were reminding him. As Liam made his decision on what game to play and Selena danced around and listened to her new music, Kieran unwrapped his big gift, a retractable blade sword made from Calibur, not unlike his father's. Once it was completely unwrapped, he looked at the weapon as if he had been given an unexpected though not unwanted gift.

"It is made completely from Calibur, which can only be found on Avalon and is the strongest, hardest metal in the world. There are few people who have weapons made just from Calibur, mainly Tiarnáns. It needs to be blessed, or it will be useless against most Illuminatii. Unblessed you could still use it against human Illuminatii, but even against some of them a blessed weapon is necessary," Brian said to her.

"I can do a blessing for you," Sian said.

"Really," Kieran responded, "I'd like that."

He liked the idea of having his own weapon. One that was no one else's but his own. Lately, he practiced swordsmanship with one of Talbot's old blade, or with a loaned one from Master Nagura. They were not calibrated to his likes and dislikes, though. He extended the blade and swung the sword. It felt perfectly balanced for him, like it was just for him.

"I told a sword maker on Avalon that my son needed a weapon of his own and he made it for me. His name is Matsuda and he is one of the great weapon makers in the world. Master Mifune recommended him to me. He makes all of Mifune's weapons. I recommend that you get more than one blessing. I find it helps the effectiveness of your blade against even the strongest evil," Brian added.

"Are you saying that my blessing isn't good enough for you?" asked Sian in mock indignation.

"You're becoming a troublemaker, aren't you," Brian replied.

"I think it is the influence of your sons," she stated then looked over at Liam, who was ignoring them and playing one of his new games. Brian stared at her for a moment. It had been too many years since she was so comfortable with him. Ever since Siobhan's death, Sian had become slightly aloof in response to his overwhelming feelings of guilt. But it appeared that she finally had dealt with her feelings, which meant that it was time for him to deal with his own feelings.

"Can you bless it now?" asked Kieran.

"I'll do it for you tomorrow. I'll also get Father Mueller, Rabbi Justiz, and Maol Stonefeather to bless it for you, also, so that it is properly empowered," she told him.

"Thanks," he said with a smile then returned to his other gifts.

"This is nice," Brian said to her.

"Yes, it is."

"It feels like a real family. The boys have been missing that over the years, you know, a female influence in their life. They've missed it. They've had to put up with my stoicism and hardness and have lacked the balance of a mother in their life. I've tried but I'm not really in touch with my feminine side," he continued.

"You've done well with them, though, Brian. Liam could not be a better boy and Kieran is strong and has a noble soul just like you. Just look at the gentle way he treats Selena and the protectiveness he has for Liam. He protects them. They are both good boys and Selena is comfortable with them. She wouldn't be if you were just all hardness," Sian said.

"Sian, you know what you said earlier about still being in love with me," he said in a whisper as he turned away from his sons and Selena.

"Yes, Brian," she said.

"I've been selfish these past ten years, very selfish. I've used my guilt over Siobhan as a shield to keep people away. But..." he said then stopped.

"But what," she gently encouraged him.

"But maybe it is time to put my shield away, not all the time, but sometimes," he told her.

"Then put it away, Brian, and rejoin life. I will be here to help you if you need it. We will take this slowly, Brian."

"Good. Slow works for me," he replied then they both turned their attention to the Liam, Kieran, and Selena.

CHAPTER 15

Caleb Keane truly hated Southern California. It wasn't just that the sun was too bright during the day, which caused him discomfort, or that the Illuminatii thrived out here, which disappointed him, but the truth was that he hated it there because he fit in so easily with many of the people who lived there. There were many out in Southern California who hid from the sun, though not for the same reason as him. They hid because they didn't want their skin damaged and wanted to remain youthful looking for as long as humanly, and sometimes inhumanely, possible. Many of the inhabitants there wanted to be eternal and powerful, two things Caleb understood all too well. He understood they were prayers you didn't want answered. Walking down Melrose Avenue with sunglasses on together with a light hooded coat and leather gloves hiding his skin from the sunlight, no one even bothered to give him a second glance. He fit in all too well into the Southern Californian scene.

Fitting into the scene was not a great comfort to Caleb, but, conversely, it was a curse to him. He didn't want to fit in there, or anywhere, just as he didn't want to be a vampire. Instead he felt better when people stared at him out of fear or curiosity, or ignored him as they did in New York City. To fit in was to be accepted in some way and he didn't ever want to be accepted, either by himself or by others. The Bene Lumen could think of him as good or even think of him as human, but he knew better than that. He struggled with the urge to drink human blood every day, like a drug addict struggled with their particular addiction. The overpowering desire to kill a human being and drink in their fears and memories along with their blood was with him every day and it never went away. Fitting in, feeling comfortable with himself, would lower his perpetual guard against his own evil nature and inclination, and he couldn't have that.

On Melrose Avenue near La Cienega Boulevard there was a well-known holistic healing shop called Green Tea and Monk's Hood, which was used by both Bene Lumen and Illuminatii alike, as well as the non-fat milk and organic honey crowd of Southern California. Caleb knew the owner fairly well. He was a strange man with white hair, a trimmed grayish beard, a handsome ageless face, which was dominated by intelligent dark eyes, who went by the name of Paris LaMent. It was a name that Caleb was sure was phony, a contrivance that he came up with to hide his true identity. LaMent's knowledge of both the light and dark arts of alchemy and potions was extensive. So extensive as to be considered a prize member by either group in their shadow war if he cared enough to join one of them. Yet, LaMent never took sides. He remained neutral assiduously working to make sure neither side deemed him an enemy or a potential problem.

The shop itself was beloved by charmers, alchemists, and others because of its extensive stores of ingredients and access to almost any flower, herb, or object needed in making the most complex potions. To most normal people Green Tea and Monk's Hood was a natural Tea Shop and holistic remedies store. LaMent kept his shop open by selling organic teas, natural cures to depression, sour stomachs, as well as books on holistic cures and Eastern philosophies. Entering the store, which had a small water fountain in the middle of it that was surrounded by a small Japanese stone garden, hardwood floors, glass windows tinted brown, and walls painted the color of a desert evening, Caleb's olfactory was overwhelmed by the smells of incense and herbs. Lowering his hood and taking off his dark glasses he walked over to the young woman, an earthy crunchy type who smelled of sandalwood and soy burgers, to ask for LaMent.

"Is Paris available?" he asked her.

"Oh, I'm sorry but he's busy in the back doing inventory. I'm not supposed to bother him when he's doing important work," she said in a singsong voice.

"Tell him it is Caleb Keane. He will see me," he told her in a voice that was both intimidating and gentle.

Caleb had long practiced the art of tone when talking to normal people. He was always shocked at how easily they responded to certain tones of authority or anger, even intimidation. It was as if human beings were so unaware of themselves and their surrounding that they constantly worked on animal instincts and the right tone punched certain of these buttons evoking an appropriate response.

The young woman reluctantly left her post behind the counter and went into the back. While waiting for her to return, Caleb looked about the store. In one corner there was several racks of teas with each silver tea canister having a written description of the tea's effects and cures. Along one wall there were two aisles of bookshelves filled with titles to appeal to those who visited the store. Then in the other corner was several racks of canisters of herbs, which had similar descriptions as the teas written on them. Of course this part of the store was nothing important, just a little bit of show. It was in the backrooms where Paris kept all the interesting items and ingredients.

Paris LaMent, dressed all in black, shirts, pants, and shoes, exited the black room area with the young girl in tow. She returned to her spot behind the counter, while Paris with his long, delicate right hand offered walked up to Caleb. They shook hands. The young woman watched them greedily, as if she suddenly knew that Caleb was an important person, one worth watching and overhearing.

"Caleb, it's a pleasure to see you again. How long has it been? No, don't answer because that will depress me to think of how much time that has passed between meetings," he said. His voice had a creamy quality to it as if he enjoyed hearing it. Gently, he took Caleb by his left elbow and began to escort him to the back rooms. Once they were out of earshot from the young woman, Paris smiled and spoke again.

"Isn't it a little too bright out there for your taste, Caleb?" he asked.

"Admittedly, it's not my favorite time of day, but I deal with it as best as I can," Caleb answered.

"Yes, I bet you do," he said then escorted him into his small office.

The office was carpeted with a royal blue colored rug, had a large mahogany desk, and beige painted walls which were decorated by various African tribal masks. There was an aesthetic cleanness to the way he had his office decorated. In the corner was a black leather love seat for visitors to sit in. Paris motioned Caleb to sit down, so he did so. LaMent walked over to his desk and sat down.

"So what can I do for the famous and mysterious Caleb Keane," he said.

"I'm not famous."

"Ooh, you are very famous in certain circles, aren't you? Just the other day an Illuminatii member of some importance was asking about you."

"And who would that be?" Caleb asked.

"Oh, Caleb, that would be telling and you know that I don't do that."

"Yes you do. You tell the Bene Lumen and the Illuminatii a great deal when you want. What you don't do is make yourself a problem, which is why you are still alive. Now who was looking for me?"

"Byron," LaMent answered with a devious smile.

"I never did like his poetry. He was too self-indulgent, too impressed with his own darkness," he said.

"Oh, that's just mean, Caleb. Lord Byron was a genius as a poet, though he was self-indulgent as a human being and still is as a vampire. Just ask him yourself, if you dare. He revels in his own self-indulgence. I mean the man dresses in leather and silk. Can you think of anything more self-indulgent?"

"He is rather fond of himself, thinks too highly of what he is and what he has done. Byron has no respect for good and too much respect for the effects of evil. So why did he want to know about me?"

"He wouldn't say. All he told me was that he was curious where you had been spotted, keeping tabs on you. I felt that it was important to him to know about your movements and whereabouts, but I couldn't help him. Though, I could enlighten him now since you are sitting in front of me," Paris stated.

"Paris, I have never found you very amusing. You know that, too. If I find out that you told Byron where he could find me, I will feast on your blood..."

"You don't drink human blood, do you, Caleb," Paris interrupted him.

"I never drink the blood of the righteous, the good or the innocent, but abominations and perverted souls' blood, well, that I enjoy drinking a great deal. It tastes like a good dessert wine to me and I have a sweet tooth, though I try not to indulge it too much. So don't push me too far, LaMent, or I will make you my dessert."

"You are scary. No wonder the Illuminatii fear you so much," he said then once again his devious smile made an appearance. "What can I do for you, Caleb?"

"I'm looking for some inside information on an Illuminatii plan, some of their machinations, which means I am looking for you to point me in the direction of someone I can talk to," he answered.

"By inside information, I take it you mean certain plans in which the Illuminatii are brewing and which you want to know about so that you can stop it?"

"Yes," he answered.

"Any particular plans?"

"Yes," he said then went silent. LaMent looked at Caleb waiting for more information, but none came. The silence filled the room for several minutes until finally Paris knew he had to break the silence.

"How can I know where to direct you, if you don't share more information with me? This is a game we are playing, Caleb, and games have rules. Play by the rules and you just might win the game. I give a little then you give a little."

"You are well aware that when a vampire drains the blood of his victim, he also gains the person's thoughts and memories along with his nourishment. Some vampires believe that is where they get their greatest strength from."

"Is that a threat, Caleb?" Paris asked in an amused voice.

"No threat, LaMent. I am merely pointing out that I have an alternative to a stalemate in this conversation."

Reaching into his desk drawer Paris took out a 14 inch silver cross and placed it down on the desk. This was his way of making a threat in return. Caleb laughed softly. He then got up off the leather love seat, walked over to the desk, and picked up the cross. Unlike all other vampires this holy object didn't cause him pain, or burn his flesh, or fill him with an urge to run from the room. Caleb had a soul and it wasn't a cursed one. He kissed the cross then placed it down on the desk.

"Some say that blessed objects don't bother you. So it's true," Paris stated, "you truly are different. No wonder they fear you. I take it a stake through the heart or cutting your head off does still work?"

"Yes, it does, but only if you are able to do it and I guarantee you won't be able to do it. You are not what you seem, LaMent," Caleb said then sniffed the air. He recognized that scent. It smelled not unlike Fergus. "You are older than anyone realizes. I can sense that about you. Yes, you are human, truly human, but you are no longer a normal human. But whatever you are, you aren't a threat to me."

"I believe you, Caleb. I also recommend you find and talk to Anna Hoffman. She is on the outs with the Illuminatii again and is hiding," he said.

Anna Hoffman was a vampire, who Caleb knew well. She had been turned to darkness over one-hundred and fifty years ago in New York City, the lower East Side to be exact, and had struggled with her fate every day since then. As the daughter of a devout and religious man, who moved to the United States to avoid religious persecution, she was a dark beauty who many a man lusted after. Unfortunately, one of those men happened to be Silas Dyre, a particularly nasty vampire, who pursued her and changed her into a vampire. For her first kill he had her drink the blood of her mother and father, those who loved her most in the world. It was a cruel act, which left her hating the Illuminatii, though she could never deny her bloodlust.

Since Dyre was a high-ranking member of the Illuminatii in the United States, he has always allowed her to rebel a little against them. He treated her indulgently, as if she was a spoiled child, even taking her with him when he moved out to the West Coast, though she knew he would have her killed immediately if she ever went to far in her rebellion against the Illuminatii. So Anna Hoffman, the dark beauty of the night, attempted to find the right level of rebellion and subservience. So far her worst transgression was to have a relationship with Caleb Keane, who they considered an abomination. Denied the love of a normal woman because of his bloodlust, Caleb fell in love with Anna, though it was a troubled love he regretted ever feeling.

"Where is she?" he asked Paris LaMent.

"Hiding."

"Where?"

"Maybe the subway system, it's a new spot out here for those who hate the light. It's almost as if L.A. built it for them. Or maybe the sewer system, though Anna hates dirty places. Maybe Hollywood Hills, or Echo Park, there is plenty of spots and food there. I'm just not sure," he stated.

"Why is she hiding?" Caleb asked.

"She killed a human member of the Illuminatii who was important to them. Silas was angered by this and swore to give her a punishment she wouldn't forget. You know Anna, she doesn't like being punished."

"Who was the human?"

"A movie producer with lots of contacts and money who financed some of the Illuminatii's more expensive work. He's replaceable, everyone is replaceable, but Silas didn't like losing his cash cow just yet."

Caleb sat in silence for a few moments thinking of Anna. Even before she became a vampire, she had alabaster skin, so when she did turn into a creature of the night, her skin took of an almost glowing quality. She was a beauty, but also a danger to him. One moment she could be very loving and the next scheming to hand him over to an Illuminatii hunting party. She could never control her urges or appetites, which kept her from completely turning away from evil.

"There is something or someone that has the Illuminatii spooked out there," Paris stated breaking the silence. "I'm not sure what it is, though."

"How do you know they are spooked?" he asked him putting thoughts of Anna into the background for the moment.

"Certain activities, like the forming of specialized hunting parties, as well as special requests for herbs and other ingredients from them. I keep my eyes and ears open, also. You may not believe this, but I am a fairly smart man, Caleb."

"What special requests did you get?" Caleb asked.

"I shouldn't be telling you this, but your charming ways have convinced me that it is all right. Certain alchemists have asked for hard to get ingredients', such as certain old and ancient roots. I mean one of them was a weed that grew in Jerusalem in biblical times and is now extinct. I had to get a fossilized sample of the root off of the Shroud of Turin and clone it."

"Do you have any idea what the ingredients are for?" he asked.

"The best I can make out is that they are trying to brew something which will allow an opening, a small opening, in a mystical barrier. It is a very difficult potion and the opening would only be open for a matter of seconds. You wouldn't be able to get anything of great size through it, though," he explained.

"What else?"

"Let's see... oh, yes, they have been acting skittish lately. I mean the Illuminatii owns the West Coast, yet they are acting as if they are under attack. I haven't seen them like this since..," he started to say then stopped himself and gave Caleb an enigmatic smile.

The rumor about Paris LaMent was that he was an alchemist of great power who had developed a potion to conquer death. No one knew his exact age, other than he seemed ageless. But Caleb recognized that smile. He was sure he had seen it somewhere before, somewhere in a painting. It couldn't be him, thought Caleb, then again he couldn't be a vampire but he was. To paraphrase Shakespeare, there definitely was more under heaven and earth than was dreamt in science and philosophy. And one of those things was an ageless artist who was revered by modernity, yet hid from himself.

"Leonardo Da Vinci, I presume," he said to Paris.

"Very good. What gave it away?"

"The smile. It is Mona Lisa's smile."

"Mona Lisa was an attractive young woman, but women didn't pose in those days and, anyway, she had the smile of a donkey in heat, so I gave her my own smile when I painted her. It was a bit of vanity on my part. Little did I know how much trouble that would cause me," he said. "Now that you know what you know what are you going to do?"

"I am going to ask you why you would want to live for so long?" he asked.

"I don't want to. I came across a potion to remove death in my studies and attempted it. It worked and since then I have regretted my curiosity. I thought God cursed me then I realized that He merely abandoned me, so I abandoned him. Over the centuries I have watched so much destruction and evil happen to humanity, and attempted to do something about it in a small way, but all my efforts were futile. Now I merely chose to sit and witness," he said.

"You stopped painting, haven't you?" asked Caleb, as he looked about the room noticing there were no paintings in his office.

"Of course, I have. Painting was something very personal for me. I worshiped at the altar of painting and science and was punished for that. Anyway, people wouldn't recognize my genius as a painter now. They are too enamored by the ideas of painting instead of the skill. I had skill. So what are you going to do with your information about me, Caleb?" he asked.

"Nothing. You have made your choice and you must live by it," he said then started to leave the office. He stopped at the office door and turned to look at the great artist behind the desk.

"Michelangelo was a better artist, maybe even a better painter than you. He never lost faith," Caleb said to him.

"But he was not a better man of science," Da Vinci replied.

"True, but look where your science has gotten you. We shall meet again," he said then left the office leaving Da Vinci to sit and think about his choices.

Brian CuCullen and Mallory on the astral plain...

"When Caleb informed me about this potion the Illuminatii were working on, I thought it best to let you know about it right away," Brian CuCullen told Mallory.

Though the astral plain continued to be Mallory's least favorite form on communication, he had come to appreciate its immediacy over the years. A small open in their mystical barrier could be a catastrophe. Too many demons had the ability to take another form, a smaller form.

"Thank you, Brian, for your help. Did Caleb mention Samhain?" he asked.

"No, but call it instincts or a feeling, I thought of Samhain immediately."

"I agree with you. And with that I need to return to Samhain right away. You understand why," he said.

"Of course, please go now and do what you must," Brian CuCullen replied.

Maol Stonefeather guided both himself and Mallory to their bodies on Samhain, while Brian CuCullen and his spirit guide returned to Cape Elizabeth, Maine. Once he was returned abruptly to his body, Mallory quickly stood up from his chair as if he had somewhere to go. In front of his desk sat Stonefeather, who also quickly stood up from his chair.

"What do we do, Headmaster?" asked Stonefeather.

"Alert all the Maols right away. I need them to be vigilant. They have to be alert twenty-four hours a day from here on. We may have a great problem brewing. A small hole in our defenses could allow in something small that can grow," he walked over to the window, which overlooked the snow covered main street.

"Why would they want to enter Samhain?"

"To cause havoc, to kill children who may one day grow up to be a problem, to..." Mallory stopped talking as he noticed a red humming bird quickly fly by his window. Samhain had many birds and animals that made their home there: rabbits, deer, doves, hawks, reptiles, even a few snakes, but no hummingbirds. The winters were too harsh for them to survive and migration was impossible off of the mist isle. With more speed than you'd expect or thought capable from an old man, even an ageless old man, Mallory turned away from his window and proceeded out the office door into the hallway.

"Headmaster," exclaimed Stonefeather, "what's wrong?"

Mallory didn't answer but instead grabbed a thick black cane from the container right by the front door where he kept umbrellas and this cane. He then ran out of the door and attempted to catch the bird. With his black robes flapping in the wind he chased the hummingbird. Students stopped and pointed as they watched their old headmaster run past them. It was a shocking sight to see Mallory Fergus expending so much energy and effort. He always seemed so calm, but now his face was flushed with excitement and something else, rage. Stonefeather followed closely behind him, not bothering to ask any more questions because he knew how Mallory was when there was trouble.

The hummingbird appeared to be headed towards the playing Ruahd field. Mallory knew that there were no games scheduled today, so he assumed that there must be a team practicing. He picked up his pace trying to run as he did as a young man, but his old muscles and bones wouldn't allow for that kind of speed anymore. Stonefeather caught up to him and ran by his side. The hummingbird suddenly dropped from the sky and disappeared. Mallory knew what this meant and cursed his own muscles for not having their old speed still in them. He continued as best as he could towards the field.

From the top row seats of the stadium stands Liam, Selena, Dani, Brigid were watching Kieran and his team practice. Tutu, Renoir, and Gunthar along with Kieran swung about at top speed tossing the corb to each other as they did. Though their overall game had improved passing was still a weakness for them. Kieran for one still had a fear of falling when passing, and Renoir tended to throw the corb either too high or too low. If they were going to make the playoffs they needed to win their last three regular season games.

"Liam, something is wrong," Selena suddenly stated.

"What is it, sis," he asker her.

"Evil," she said and looked up at a hummingbird which was slowly descending. As the bird descending its small perpetually flapping wings began to disappear, even as its body began to grow and change shape. From the stands Dani, Brigid, Selena, and Liam watched in awe, while Kieran and his team stopped practicing to watch. As the hummingbird lost its delicate shape and changed, Jan recognized it.

"It's a tengu," she yelled as she recognized the red face and long nose that dominated its head. Two well muscled arms and legs formed as the tengu dropped to the ground and scanned the area. It was a fierce looking creature with black eyes standing out in its red face. As his teammates remained frozen in surprise, Kieran dropped from the bars landing on softly on the ground. He began to run at full tilt towards the tengu, which was now moving towards the stands and Liam and Selena.

"Run," Liam turned to Selena, Dani, and Brigid and ordered, "Run now."

"But," Dani began to protest, but Liam glared at her. She immediately understood that he wanted them to get Selena out of there.

"I won't leave you," Selena stated, but Dani grabbed her arm and pulled her hard to turn around.

"We need to get help now," she told Selena, who realized that leaving was the smartest move but she didn't want to leave Liam or Kieran.

"Then go and get it, but I am staying with my brothers," she replied.

"Come with me," Dani demanded.

"It's too late," Brigid said calmly and pointed as the tengu easily hopped the fence and was now walking up the stands stairs towards them.

Unexpectedly, Headmaster Fergus and Maol Stonefeather came running into the Ruadh field area. When he saw the tengu Mallory pulled a thin sword from his cane and ran towards the tengu. The tengu turned to see the old man jump the fence and run towards it. Maol Stonefeather lowered his head and began a chant in a low voice which then got louder and louder until finally he turned his face towards the sky and released a plume of fire from his mouth that reached the sky. He then returned his attention to the tengu, which now readied itself for battle with Mallory. It was a heart pumping sight to see the old headmaster stand ready for battle.

"A champion," it said to Mallory, who was now a few feet away from it.

"Actually, an old headmaster and former champion of some skill," he replied sounding slightly out of breathe which was a remarkable feat considering all that had transpired.

Kieran ran past Stonefeather, who was once again chanting, as if he was summoning something, and headed towards Mallory and the tengu. He had no weapon, but he instinctively knew to protect his brother and his new sister, so he needed to join the battle. It was more than brotherly love that overtook him, but rather it was an overwhelming sense of duty that swelled up inside of him. This was what he was meant to do.

The tengu moved gracefully towards Mallory. His movements were faster than Kieran had ever seen before in his life. The headmaster was barely able to get out of the demon's way as it jumped towards him. When it landed, it had a large, thick bladed sword in its hand and swung it towards Mallory's head. Mallory lifted his thin blade up to stop it. To Kieran's surprise the headmaster's blade didn't shatter on impact, but it stopped the demon's blade easily. They began to exchange blows with each other in a blur of swings and counter swings.

"Old man, dead man, poor dead, old man," the tengu said in a singsong voice.

"Old man, huh? Well, you have a really big, ugly nose," Mallory replied.

Kieran jumped the fence and then stopped waiting to see if he could help the headmaster in any way. He wasn't sure how he could help, but he was sure that if it was possible, he would. The headmaster and the tengu exchanged blow after blow until the tengu surprisingly jumped up into the air, did a somersault in midair, and landed behind the headmaster, who turned quickly to defend his back, though not quickly enough. The tengu swung his large blade hard enough to dislodge Mallory's sword from his hand. It landed with the blade sticking in the ground with cane handle hilt up in the air near Kieran.

The tengu moved quickly towards Mallory to bring down a deathblow, but when his blade came down where the headmaster's head should be, Mallory had jumped aside, landing hard on the wooden seats. This took the wind out of him causing him to almost black out. Before the tengu could move in on the stunned headmaster, Kieran grabbed the blade and ran up the stairs towards the tengu. Everyone could hear the creature laugh as it saw the teenager run towards to help Mallory. It was a malicious deafening laugh meant as much to instill fear and to show amusement. Kieran heard the laugh and had the exact reaction to it as most. What he heard was a challenge and he didn't back down from challenges. He was the son of a Tiarnán; he didn't back down.

From his vantage point Liam saw that his brother was in trouble. He was about to summon up his powers, when he realized that he couldn't interfere with Kieran's battle. Kieran needed to fight this tengu without his help, so that he could realize just how powerful he was. Liam forced himself not to interfere, but instead took hold of Selena's left hand in his right hand. Her hand was sweaty and tense. She wanted to fight with Kieran, but Liam held on to it tightly.

"A baby," the tengu said, "I like killing babies. It makes me feel like a parent."

"Shut up, ugly, and fight," Kieran responded.

"Oh, a brave baby," it said then jumped at the oncoming Kieran.

In a move that was both faster and more graceful then Kieran thought he was capable of, he easily avoided the tengu and its blade. As the demon passed by him, he stuck it with his blade in its thigh causing it to scream in pain and anger. When it landed on the stairs below Kieran, he saw that blue blood was running from the wound he gave it. Kieran smiled at the demon, which angered it even more.

"I'm going to kill you," it screamed.

"You're all talk, no wonder you have such a large mouth," Kieran said.

The demon took to the air in another acrobatic jump that was meant to land on Kieran, but instead it landed on a patch on empty concrete. Kieran had rolled away and came up in a defensive position ready to strike the demon again. He thrust his blade this time into the back of the demon's left shoulder. This time the tengu's scream was blood curdling. It turned with blazing speed and slashed at Kieran, who was able to stop the demon's blade just inches from his head, but was unable to avoid the tengu's left leg which kicked him in the gut and sent him down the four rows landing hard on the stadium seats.

The tengu took to the air yet again in order to land on the stunned Kieran and kill him, but instead was met in midair by Mallory who used his body as a missile. The tengu and Mallory landed hard on the concrete stairs and rolled down until they hit the bottom. The headmaster lay on the ground barely able to move, as he was sure he had broken at least his shoulder maybe more than that. The tengu slowly got up, but before it cold compose itself several people came running into the Ruadh field area, including Diaghilev, Talbot, Sian Boru, Master Nagura, and many students, including Nadia. Stonefeather had finished his chant released a ball of energy from his spirit that sent the tengu flying away from Mallory. After releasing the ball of energy, Stonefeather fell to the ground exhausted.

The tengu struggled to get up. When it was on its feet, it saw that Boris Diaghilev, Talbot, and Nagura were headed for it, so it turned to run. As it turned, it came face to face with Kieran, who had finally recovered. A trickle of blood ran down his forehead and he looked as if he might have broken a few ribs, yet he stood his ground prepared to fight. The tengu swung its large blade at him. He blocked then parried. Everyone stopped moving towards them to watch as Kieran and the tengu fought. It was fascinating watching the young teenager grow in skill and ability right before their very eyes. As the fight became fiercer and fiercer, Kieran's response became calmer and more precise. With the help of Sian Boru and Nadia Headmaster Fergus got up off the ground and watched the young warrior discover his true potential.

222

"He is starting to feel his power," Mallory said between gritted teeth.

"Merlin was right about him, Mallory, he was right about Kieran," Sian Boru said sounding slightly surprised.

"I told you that I had a feeling about him," responded Mallory with a smile.

Nadia looked from the headmaster to Sian Boru then back at Kieran, who was fighting brilliantly. She then turned to see that many more teachers and students had come onto the field to see what had caused all the commotion. They were all enthralled by the battle between the teenager and the powerful demon.

"He is my rival now," she said to herself with a smile. Mallory heard her and smiled to himself. Kieran had finally taken a step forward in his development.

As the tengu became angrier and angrier, its movements became sloppier which gave Kieran openings in which to cut it. It now bled from over half a dozen wounds on its body, while Kieran had but a few. The last blow he gave it was a deep cut right on the right side of its ribs. This caused the demon to swing wildly in a fit of rage. Instead of backing away from the rampaging demon, Kieran stepped towards it knowing that he would be able to finally finish the fight. Avoiding and blocking swing after swing he stepped in close enough to the tengu to allow him a quick thrust to the demon's throat. His blade slid easily through its neck cutting completely through. Pulling the blade out he watched as the demon dropped its sword and reached for its neck. Before it could do anything else, though, he raised the thin blade and swung with all his might at the neck separating the tengu's head from its shoulders.

Just as the head rolled off to the side, the demon's body fell hard to the ground. Kieran dropped to his knees exhausted and slightly injured. As he attempted to breathe and calm himself, Kieran heard the Ruadh field fill up with applause. He raised his head and saw hundreds of students and many of the teachers staring at him from the field and applauding him. Liam and Selena finally reached his side.

"You did it, Kieran," Liam said.

"You were great," Selena added.

"Yeah, sure," he said. "How is the headmaster doing? Is he all right?"

"Fine, Kieran, he's doing fine. You can look for yourself," Liam said and then pointed at Mallory who was being helped towards him by Sian Boru and Nadia. When he got close enough to Kieran, the headmaster motioned for them to leave him alone and walked painfully to Kieran then offered him a hand to help him up. Kieran took his hand and got slowly up from his knees.

"You saved my life," Mallory stated.

"You saved mine," added Kieran.

"You know what that means?"

"No, sir, I don't."

"It means we are indebted to each other. As warriors that makes us close friends. From one Aongus Cathal to another saving each other is a debt of honor. It means that as long as one of us breathes we are friends and loyal to each other, Kieran. I hope that it won't be a problem having the headmaster as a loyal friend," Mallory told him.

"Sir, I was just doing what anybody..."

"You acted like a potential Tiarnán. Do not underestimate yourself any longer, Kieran. You have great potential," he said then leaned in close to him and whispered, "and you have a special admirer."

"Huh?" Kieran replied.

Mallory nodded his head towards Nadia, who was looking at Kieran with something more than respect. Kieran caught her dark eyes and blushed. She blushed, also.

"I think you like this school more than you let on, Kieran," Mallory whispered to him.

"Maybe."

"Maybe or maybe not, but starting Monday you will begin taking a few personal lessons from me. This is considered an honor because I give so few personal lessons. I have a great deal to teach you, Kieran, and I better do it before I am no longer here. You have a great deal to offer the Bene Lumen, and I believe I can assist you with your development."

"You'll always be here, sir," Kieran said.

"No, I won't."

CHAPTER 16

Good to his word Mallory arranged to give Kieran some private lessons, which meant some private time alone with him telling Kieran about his life and his experiences. Mallory's life was nothing if not a lesson to teach a would-be-Tiarnán the ups and downs, the hardships and responsibilities of such a life. Twice a week he was scheduled to go to the headmaster's office and receive this private tutoring. According to some of his housemates this was considered a great honor bestowed on very few students. His father and Paulette were the last two students he gave these private lessons. Knocking on the headmaster's office door, Kieran inhaled a deep anxious breath and waited for Mallory to give him entrance. The response came quickly in the form of a friendly voice.

"Enter Kieran," Mallory called.

Kieran slowly opened the door and entered the office. The last time he was here he ate sandwiches and drank wine and wished to be back in Maine. It was an enjoyable evening in which the headmaster treated him like a friend instead of a student. But today he was a student, not a friend, and the anxiousness in his stomach let him know that.

"Don't be apprehensive, Kieran, come in and sit down. Make yourself comfortable. I am not going to hurt you; I am going to instruct you. There is minor difference between the two," Mallory said.

Kieran walked over to the chair that was waiting for him in front of the headmaster's desk. Sitting down he looked at the headmaster, whose left arm was in a sling because the tengu had broken his left shoulder. Mallory seemed completely untroubled by his injury, though. He said that he was a quick healer, so the shoulder wouldn't be much of a problem. Kieran realized this must have been but one of many painful injuries he had suffered in his life.

"How is your shoulder feeling, sir?" Kieran asked.

"A little painful, though nothing really to complain about. I wake up every morning with more pain in my knees than in my shoulder. My bones are old and creaky and a tengu's body is almost as hard as Calibur, so I'm lucky I didn't do more damage to myself fighting that demon. I was very impressed by the way you handled that tengu, Kieran. Your housemates, who are more experienced, wouldn't have been able to handle the situation the way you did. You showed not only courage but innate skills and instincts that cannot be learned but are born with."

"I admit that I surprised myself, sir," Kieran said.

"Good. I expect you to keep surprising yourself. Kieran, you have a surprising and difficult future awaiting you, but it is a future which will have great consequence and we can't ask more than that out of life."

"You don't mind if I don't believe what you just said, sir," Kieran countered.

"I don't mind if you don't believe me. I understand what it feels like to not fit in or to not believe in yourself, Kieran, or what it feels like to feel like you don't want to be who you are or what you have become. I have felt many things in my time, many things, and the one which is hardest to overcome is not believing in yourself."

"I find that hard to believe, sir. You seem so sure of yourself, like your comfortable being who you are and have always felt that way."

"Unlike your teachers, my form of private tutoring is to instruct you by telling you intimate details of my life because I have experienced more emotions, more changes of mind, more crisis of the soul than just about any other human being alive. Sounds egotistical, doesn't it," he mused. Kieran knew this was a rhetorical question so he kept his mouth closed and waited for the headmaster to continue with his speech. He knew that he was about to hear things none of the other students will hear. This filled Kieran with pride. Nadia won't even know these stories, he thought.

"I use my own life because there are many, many lessons to be found there. I have made great mistakes and have accomplished great things in my time. The mistakes, though, are always more instructive than the accomplishments, and often time more fun to rehash. Do not worry I will also share a few of the accomplishments with you, as well. My actual name was Brennus and I was a great warrior for my Celtic clan, hence I eventually took the clan name Fergus, which means great warrior. I changed Brennus to Mallory when I took this position some 250 years ago because I thought it made me sound like an English headmaster instead of a Celtic warrior. Brennus sounds almost like a Roman centurion, which I never was. I've killed a few of them, though. I am very old, too old to even give you an exact age."

Kieran looked at his headmaster as if his hair was on fire and he didn't know. How could he have killed Roman Centurions? Mallory knew the look in Kieran's eye well and smiled.

"Long ago, on a very hot day while looking for Romans to kill in Gaul, which was a pastime of mine back then, I drank from a gush of water, a small ground well that sprang up. After I drank from the water the gush dried up before anyone else could quench his or her thirst. It turned out to be a kind of fountain of youth, a bit of..." he started to say then stopped for a moment until he found the right words, "a sort of curse from God. I found out much later that a truly powerful Triune Conjurer had created that gush for the purpose to create a warrior who would be able to fight the Romans for as long as they existed. The water changed me, made me into a sort of perfect immortal warrior."

"You fought the Romans, I mean those guys in the skirts with short swords," Kieran said with complete awe and surprise in his every syllable.

"Yes, I fought the Romans, and they wore tunics not skirts, and I won many a battle against them. I was part of a group of Celts who sacked Rome long ago. We stayed there for about a year, pulling patrician beards, taking their women, and demanding buckets of gold then we left and returned to our families and farms. The Romans were so upset by our sacking of their great city that Julius Caesar decided to conquer Gaul in order to prove how great Rome was. Now that man was a butcher," Mallory commented then fell back into his memories for a moment or two. "He killed many of my friends and much of my clan."

"I thought you were Christian?" Kieran asked.

"I am now. I was converted by Saint Patrick himself, another Roman slave, and I have been a Christian ever since. It was my conversion that gave my long life purpose and eventually introduced me to the Bene Lumen. At first I was this strange, even scary, outsider in the society, but eventually I became a Tiarnán and a valued, even honored, member of the society."

"Sir..."

"Call me Mallory in here, Kieran. Remember that you and I are bonded now. You saved my life," Mallory interrupted him.

"Mallory," Kieran apprehensively said using his name, "why aren't you dead?"

"Good question. You see that water changed my body chemistry. It changed it on a fundamental level. What it did was to cure me of most ailments, such as aging, sickness, as well as increased my body's ability to heal itself. Several times I have been close to death, receiving wounds that should have killed me, but my body eventually completely healed me. There will be a day, though, a day not too far in the future, when I will receive a blow I cannot heal from and I will gratefully die."

"Gratefully? You want to die?" asked Kieran sounding as if he didn't believe him.

"Yes, I look forward to my own death. It has been a long time in coming, Kieran, a very long time in coming. I have killed many, and seen many killed. I have lost loved ones, people who I believed I could never live without and those I never wanted to live without, but have had to learn to live without. I have seen friends grow old and die and seen other friends die too young. Death is ever present in my life, Kieran, and some day it will visit me and I will gladly embrace it," he said then silence filled the room as the young man and the old man thought about what was said.

"Now let me begin your tutorial with a story about one of the greatest champions and Tiarnáns ever known, Arthur..."

"Do you mean the King Arthur in those stories Liam likes to read?" Kieran asked.

"Yes, I mean the King Arthur of legend and myth, Kieran. Shortly after the time when Rome was starting to have problems with barbarians, after Hadrian built his wall in England, Merlin saw the opportunity to unite England under one Warlord, a Cairbre, a King to rule the other kings, who had sprung up to rule their own piece of land. As Merlin had gifts beyond the usual, even for a Triune Conjurer, he knew that his perfect champion, his great warrior, would be the son of a great warrior by the name of Uther. Legend and reality intersect many times when it comes to Arthur and Merlin and in the case of him being illegitimate and Merlin striking a deal with Uther, the legend and the facts are one and the same. Where they diverge is in how Arthur was raised by Merlin. Though Merlin constantly told him that he would be a great warrior, Arthur didn't believe him. When your father decides to give you to a stranger because they cut a deal, it leaves a deep psychological scar. Arthur constantly felt abandoned and lacked confidence. So in lieu of self-confidence, Merlin decided to train young Arthur harder than any other warrior has ever been trained and in doing so he discovered that Arthur had the ability to do more than any warrior he had ever seen. You see to explain it in modern terms Arthur was able to use up to ninety percent of his muscles capabilities without his body being unable to deal with the strain. From sunrise to sunset, he honed the boy's physical gifts, as well as tutored his mental ones. He pushed and pushed until that young boy grew in a young man and at eighteen he sent him to Avalon to receive Excalibur."

"I bet he didn't have to pull a silly sword from a stone," Kieran commented.

"Of course he had to, Kieran. Excalibur wasn't a silly sword; it was an enchanted sword and its true owner had to pull it from a large boulder. At the time, I served The Lady of the Lake, who placed it there herself. It was impossible to get out, too. I should know because I tried to pull the blasted thing out myself, but it wouldn't budge then this red mane youth comes walking up to the boulder and pulls the most beautiful sword I have ever seen crafted out of the rock. It was as easy for him, as if the stone was stuck in a vat of butter."

"You were a follower of Arthur's?" he asked half in awe and in disbelief.

"Of course I was. After seeing him pull the sword out, I left the lady of the Lake's honor guard and joined Arthur. He became my king. As a matter of fact Arthur was the first to treat me as if I was a friend instead of as a fiend from hell. At that time even the Lady herself was a little afraid of me. The druids knew what had happened to me and told their followers that I was the warrior who would lead them from Roman occupation, but I couldn't accomplish that so I eventually joined the Lady of the Lake's honor guard. For many reasons, some of which had to do with my unwillingness to accept my fate at that time, I made for a poor a leader. I was marked as more than a man, yet somehow because of my curse, less than human. People would follow me into battle but wouldn't invite me to dinner. Arthur gave me a seat at his table."

"And you followed him because of that," Kieran stated awed by the fact that Mallory had followed the real King Arthur into battle time and time again.

"So at eighteen this young pup gathered together warriors who would follow him into battle and slowly over the next ten years tossed the last of the Romans out on their arses, which I completely enjoyed. With the help of Merlin we were victorious. Then came our next problem: uniting England. Christianity was becoming popular, which, to say the least, annoyed the druids, except for Merlin who said that beliefs have a flow to them. I introduced Arthur to Christianity and, well, he converted. Of course he converted not because of me, but in order to marry Guinevere. Oh, Kieran, she was a beauty. She turned many of our heads, including my own."

"You loved her?" he asked.

"No, not really, but I was awed by her beauty and grace. It was hard not to be, but enough about her for now. Merlin knew that we would have a great problem uniting England than pushing the Romans out, so he recommended to Arthur that he use his newfound religious conversion to help unite the people. Well, you can imagine the problems this caused in the druid world. Morgana for one wanted Merlin, Arthur, and all who followed them dead for heresy against the druid faith. The Lady of the Lake remained neutral since she didn't believe in forced conversions to anything. She wasn't sure about Merlin's idea, though, but was willing to observe how it went. A sort of civil war pursued. It was a bloody war, too," Mallory stated then as was becoming his habit drifted into a momentary fog of memory.

"Well, the war lasted for another ten years with Arthur finally uniting England under him. So what we thought would be a time of peace, unfortunately, it became the beginning of the shadow war we fight today. You see those druids who had a proclivity towards the darker side of their arts sought out like-minded people and what they found living just under the surface of life was a world of abominations, demons, and humans who were individually causing as much havoc as they could. These dark druids, now called necromancers, were smart, so they united those who lived in darkness and founded the Illuminatii. Poor Arthur, my poor Cairbere, they hated him so, but he was a valiant and superior warrior and with Excalibur as his weapon he fought them. Merlin marshaled those druids and Christians who found the Illuminatii's vision of the world repulsive and became the bane of their existence. This was the beginning of the Bene Lumen. Someday, when the time is right, I will tell you the full story."

"Mallory, was Arthur born to lead like my father, or did Merlin teach him to lead?" asked Kieran.

"Good question. Are you born to lead or can you learn it? Arthur was an extraordinary man and he was born with extraordinary gifts, which Merlin honed. But Merlin couldn't hone what wasn't already there. Like you, Kieran, he was gifted, truly gifted. As a matter of fact you remind me a great deal of Arthur. You, too, have trouble believing in yourself, though, unlike Arthur, your father has never abandoned you. It was your mother who left you behind..."

"My mother didn't abandon me," Kieran replied with sharpness in his voice.

"Of course, she did. She didn't want to abandon you, but she did nonetheless. She died and that is a form of abandonment, a permanent form of abandonment. Let us be honest about that, Kieran."

"My mother... my mother died because of an accident. It wasn't her fault," Kieran stated defiantly.

"An accident?" Mallory repeated the words realizing that Brian Cucullen had never told his son the truth of his mother's death. "Yes, I guess you can say that her death was accidental; it wasn't her fault that she fell. But that doesn't stop you from feeling abandoned by her, does it, Kieran?"

"That's not true."

"I'm too old to argue with you. It's true," he said with a gentle smile on his lips, "so after the Romans and after uniting England under one rule, Arthur had to fight evil in many forms from the grotesque acts of abominations to the manipulations of twisted mages and necromancers. And he fought them successfully for many, many years. I remember the Lady of the Lake telling Merlin that Arthur's bloodline was as precious as Merlin's or her own. For a druid priestess admitting that a mere warrior, even one so great, was as precious as a druid priest or priestess was unheard of. It was then that Merlin arranged to keep track of Arthur's bloodline after that, as well as the Lady of the Lake's and his own. Would it surprise you to know that Arthur's, Merlin's and that particular Lady of the Lake's blood flows in your veins?"

"Really?" Kieran replied in shock. "All of them?"

"Yes, all of them. Someday I will take you to the library where we will exhume the ancient book of genealogy, so I can show you in writing. For now, though, you can take my word on it that Arthur's, Merlin's, and the Lady of the Lake's blood flows in yours and Liam's veins."

"That would explain why Liam is so powerful a conjurer," Kieran commented.

"And why you are powerful, too," Mallory stated.

Almost as if it was for the first time, Kieran realized what Mallory was saying. He, too, was powerful, maybe not as powerful as Liam was, but he was powerful. The legendary King Arthur's blood flowed through his veins. In his own way he was like Liam.

"You understand now, don't you," Mallory said seeing the light go on in Kieran's eyes. "You have no excuses for failure here, except the fact that you have started late and have a long ways to catch up to the rest of your housemates. But the rest of your housemates don't have a collection of honored bloodlines housed in their veins. In the modern parlance, I think I can sincerely say that you have superior DNA. If you were a racehorse, I'd bet on you in every race."

"But... but..."

"But nothing, Kieran. You are meant to be a Tiarnán."

"Does my father have Arthur's bloodline?"

"Yes," answered Mallory.

"And Merlin's?"

"No. You get Merlin's and the Lady of the Lake's bloodline from your mother. Your father's ancestors of note are Arthur and CuChulainn. Now you know why he is a great warrior."

"Does Liam know this?" he asked.

"Yes, he does. Young Liam as a matter of fact has met with Merlin himself, or, at least, Merlin's spirit."

"Liam has met Merlin's spirit," repeated Kieran feeling as if the world, or, at least, the history of the world was closing in on him.

"Yes, Merlin's spirit," Mallory repeated. "For many years Arthur and Merlin and all those who agreed with their way of life fought Morgana and the Illuminatii until outside influences started to weaken Arthur's ability to deal with the shadow war he fought. Those outside influences were Viking invaders. Between the Vikings drawing men away from him and the Illuminatii, Arthur was finally defeated. Part of the reason was that many thought that the Vikings were a greater threat than the Illuminatii. They chose to ignore the greater evil they couldn't always see or understand and fight the obvious invaders. Well, Merlin understood immediately what this meant. It meant that an army, a society even, needed to be built that dealt only with the evil of the Illuminatii, so he began the Bene Lumen and Samhain. Now, Kieran, do you see how important you are and how important it is for you to be here at Samhain?"

"But...I'm not even the best Aongus Cathal in the school. That is Nadia," Kieran said.

"Kieran, you have only scratched the surface of your potential. Don't judge yourself second until you give your best effort. Nadia is extraordinary, but I believe, no, I know, that you are extraordinary, too," Mallory told him.

Mallory got slowly up from his chair and walked around the desk until he was standing beside Kieran, who seemed to be almost in a state of shock. He placed his right hand on Kieran's left shoulder and patted him.

"I'm hungry. How about you?" he asked.

"I'm... yeah, sure," Kieran answered.

"Why don't I order us up some roast beef sandwiches and some mild ginger ale and I can tell you more about Arthur and Merlin and the relationship between a fulcrum and a champion. It is an important relationship, one that has meaning for you and Liam, even if you still don't believe me."

"Uh huh, sure," Kieran replied.

"Yes, you are very much like Arthur in deed," Mallory commented.

Liam finds Thomas...

Ever since his Conjurer's Maze game went wrong with Thomas Hollingsworth, Liam spent much of his free time both in the library seeking out certain books and quizzing Maol M'Tenga and Maol Stonefeather on the spirit world and its intricacies. He knew that his opponent's spirit, his soul and essence, was now unattached to its body, yet still out there somewhere looking for help and guidance, which no one seemed to be able to supply him. Liam felt great guilt over this because he was able to save himself but unable to save Hollingsworth.

Even though Sian Boru had become worried about his obsession with helping his distressed housemate, she decided not to interfere with his extracurricular activity. She understood that his obsession was tied to guilt and guilt was a powerful teacher. Her own guilt over Siobhan's death, over her feelings for Brian CuCullen, had only recently evolved from a self destructive and introverted parasitic feeling to a form of realization and enlightenment. Human beings could love more than one person. That wasn't wrong. She could never take the place of Siobhan in Brian's heart, but there was room in his heart for her, also.

Liam's obsession with Hollingsworth was as much based on his inability to save his mother, as with not being able to save his housemate. Yes, he was too young to do anything when his mother faced Baal and died, but the irrational feeling that he could have saved her didn't know logic or age. All it knew was that he lost his mother and that was wrong. And now he needed to save Hollingsworth somehow as a way of redemption. Gathering together a few items, which he had hid in his trunk that was in front of his bed, he waited for the right moment in which to try and contact Thomas Hollingsworth. Tonight there was a full silvery moon and the spirits were very attractive, so tonight was the night he would attempt it.

Liam waited until everyone was asleep in his dorm room then he put on his clothes, a pair of jeans, an Irish knit sweater, and his sneakers, and gathered the items he needed. Once he was ready, he used the knowledge and power Merlin had given him to teleport to the spot where the oldest tree stood in Samhain. He knew this spot well because it was Sian Boru's favorite spot to teach Dani, Brigid and him. All around him his dorm room became to elongate and fade, stretching into what seemed infinity until it was nothing more than a piece of fabric of time and space then it began to reconstitute, except now it was the spot where the old tree stood.

Liam was now standing in the snow beside the old tree. He felt his body's energy dip then quickly recover. The more he practiced teleporting the more quickly his body recovered from the experience. It had now gotten to the point where he could teleport again, if he needed to do so. He had taken recently to teaching Sian Boru how to teleport, but it was difficult for her to master and it drained a dangerous amount of her body's energy. She fainted the first time she did it and he needed to quickly put together an energy boost procured from nature for her. The next time she did it, her energy dipped precipitously but she didn't need his combination of herbs, grass, and leaves to regain her energy. Liam doubted that she would ever be able to teleport without her using some of his energy because she would end up draining herself of all her energy and risking death, but he was impressed that she was able to master the process.

Taking a votive candle, which had been blessed by Father Mueller, out of his backpack, as well as Thomas Hollingsworth favorite Manchester United shirt and some incense, which he had made from gathering some of Thomas' favorite things, like a few pages from his favorite book, *Dune*, as well as a few favorite items of his own, Liam prepared to contact Thomas' spirit guide or guardian angel, as Father Mueller called it. Through the effort of the guardian spirit Liam hoped to contact Thomas.

Sitting down on a snowless spot at the base of the tree, Liam prepared for the ceremony. He lit the candle, began to burn the incense then placed the shirt in his lap. Taking a few deep, concentrating breaths, he started to chant in the old, recently learned Celtic language an invitation for the guardian spirit of Thomas Hollingsworth to come to him. If he were correct a combination of his power and sincerity would draw the guardian spirit to him and allow him to ask for its help. Liam wasn't sure how long this would take but he was willing to do it all night and into the morning if he had to do so.

He chanted the invitation over and over again. Over and over again he entreated the guardian spirit to trust him and appear. Liam was unaware of how much time passed as he gave his full attention and energy to asking the spirit to visit him. Almost imperceptibly at first, the coldness of the weather warmed a bit. Not so much that Liam felt warm, but that the coldness no longer chilled him to the bone. This slight warmness grew and grew until Liam no longer noticed or felt the snow on the ground. He was warm, and not internally warm, as if from hyperthermia, but externally warmed as if he was being warmed by a guardian spirit whose aura emitted warmth and protection.

Liam opened his eyes and saw a white ephemeral figure with an orange aura about it. He knew this was the guardian spirit he had been waiting for.

"I seek the spirit of Thomas Hollingsworth and ask for your help to find him," he said calmly in a confident voice that was the opposite of what he felt.

"I know," the spirit answered without speaking.

"Can you help me?" he asked the spirit.

"Why?"

"Why help me or why am I looking for Thomas?" he asked.

"Yes," it calmly answered him.

Liam nodded his head in understanding. The spirit was looking to trust him, but needed him to supply the reasons for the trust. Picking up the Manchester United from his lap he held it in his hands as if it was totem.

"I am seeking Thomas Hollingsworth so that I may help him. It was because of me that his spirit became dislodged from his body, floating free and ungrounded. I am responsible for him and want to somehow bring him some peace," he said.

"You think highly of yourself," the spirit stated.

"No, well, maybe I do, but I, also, feel responsible for Thomas. I don't know how exactly how I will help him, but I have to try and help him."

"Why?" it asked again.

"Because..." Liam began to speak but stopped. He knew that his answer needed to be completely honest if the spirit was going to trust him. He took a deep calming breath.

"Because I couldn't help my mother when she died, but I believe I can help him. It is the right thing for me to do," he answered.

"Thank you, Liam," the spirit said. "Now why should I help you with Thomas?"

"Because you are his guardian spirit and you know the loneliness and pain he feels right now. You want to help him but I bet he won't listen to you, even though you mean him no harm. He is fourteen years old and not ready to go from this world. He knows me, maybe I can help him somehow."

"You are the fulcrum, Liam CuCullen," the spirit said, "I will help you."

The guardian spirit disappeared. Liam knew that it was now searching for Thomas Hollingsworth spirit in order to bring him to Liam. He still wasn't sure how to help Thomas. There were so few options to him. He could either assist Thomas to move on threw the caul into the next world; or he could let Thomas stay in this world until he was ready to go. If Thomas as an ungrounded spirit stayed too long, though, he would never be able to move on. He needed to be grounded to someone or something.

In his research he read of an Indian Shaman who grounded his deceased son's spirit to a wolf. This wolf became a protector to the tribe looking out for his clan. The animal lived longer than any of its kind and when it died the Shaman's son moved on to the next world. Liam wasn't sure if he knew how to do that, but he'd be willing to try if Thomas wanted. Or he would be willing to try something else, too.

The guardian spirit returned unexpectedly with Thomas Hollingsworth soul in tow. Thomas' soul looked just like him, except he was now dressed not in robes, as he was when Liam last saw him, but in his Manchester United shirt, jeans, and Nike trainers. He was as ephemeral as the guardian spirit, except he gave off no aura, merely a dull whitish glow.

"Liam. I bring you Thomas," the spirit said.

"Hi Liam," Thomas Hollingsworth's spirit said. Unlike the guardian spirit, who spoke without speaking, Thomas' mouth moved and words came from it. "Weird what happened to us, huh?"

"Yeah, it was weird," Liam, said.

"Do you know who did this to me yet because I'd really like to see that someone, you know, is hurt for doing this to me. I'd like to do hurt them myself," he said.

"No, I have no idea who did it. Do you?" Liam asked in return.

"Nah. I try to listen in on teachers and students looking for clues but I keep fading out. I can't control where I am or where I am going too well, either. It is really, really bloody annoying. I mean I wouldn't mind it so much being like this, if I could do what I wanted to do, but I seem to have no bloody control over myself."

"That is because you are ungrounded," the spirit said.

"Yes, I guessed that already, Liam. I know you are smart and powerful, but give me some credit, okay," Thomas said defiantly to the spirit.

"I want to help you, Thomas," Liam said.

"How?"

"I'm not sure how. How do you want me to help you?"

"You could place me back in my body," he said.

"I... your parents...well, you see..." Liam tried to explain.

"Yeah, I know, I know. My parents took my body away to be buried in our ancestral family plot in Somerset. They were very upset about me. My older brother cried like a baby. Do you know Colin?"

"No, I don't."

"He's an Aongus Cathal, fifth year. We didn't get along too well when I had a body. He was always showing me up. You know how it is - running faster than me, stronger than me, the whole physical thing. He was a real prat," Thomas said. "Your brother is Aongus Cathal, too."

"Yes, he is, but Kieran isn't a prat like your brother. He is protective of me."

"Lucky. My brother's a prat."

"I will leave you two now," the guardian spirit said to them. "Whatever you decide to do, Thomas, Liam can help you with it. Trust him, Thomas, as you trusted me."

Without any more words the guardian spirit was gone leaving Liam and Thomas alone to hash things out. Liam sat back down at the base of the tree and watched as Thomas sort of drifted back and forth. He assumed it was a spirit's way of pacing.

"Thomas, do you want to move on to the next realm?" he asked tentatively.

"No, not yet. I wasn't meant to die yet, so I don't want to go yet. I mean I can't explain it but I feel like I still belong here. If I was to leave now, I would feel like I didn't do something I was meant to do."

"Would you want me to ground you to an animal or a tree?" Liam asked.

"God, no. I'd hate to be a bunny rabbit or a puppy for the rest of my life. I mean the last thing I want to do is spend the rest of my existence popping in the woods. I don't think a tree is for me. Forgive me but I've never understood Sian Boru's telling us to imagine us becoming or being a tree. I mean I like trees, but I don't want to be one," he said.

"What are you, or should I say, what is your power: a caster, a conjurer, or a charmer?" asked Liam.

"Caster. I didn't have the right feel for nature to be a conjurer or a charmer. You know what I mean," he said then realized whom he was talking to. "Of course you don't know what I mean. Look who I am talking to, Liam CuCullen, a Triune Conjurer and a fulcrum."

"You know that I am a fulcrum," Liam said in surprise.

"Yeah. That much I did overhear. Actually, I heard the headmaster talking to your brother about some things. He's a bit special, too, isn't he?"

"Yes, he is."

"You see that's what I want. I want the chance to be special, to help in our fight. I don't want to just disappear without having helped or accomplished something. I want to leave my mark, also. Can you understand that, Liam?"

"Yes, I can, Thomas. I think I have an idea."

"If it's grounding me to a dog idea again, I swear I'll haunt you if I can."

"No, Thomas, it's not that. I have a different idea," Liam said then thought about what he was about to offer Thomas. It was a radical idea and he had no idea how it would affect either Thomas or him.

"Thomas, what if I grounded you to me," he stated.

"Huh," was Thomas' answer.

"What if I grounded you to me? Like some ghosts or spirits are grounded to a house, I can ground you to me. You'll be attached to me in some way. I think this will allow you to be able to move about without fading away because you will always have a home, me. It will give you control over yourself."

"Yeah, I guess, Liam, but won't it be difficult for you. I'll be part of your life. I mean I'll be really part of your life. You'll have no secrets from me," he said.

238

"I know. But I'll also have a friend who I can talk to whenever I need him," Liam said.

"I'd like that, Liam. I'd like be grounded to you," Thomas said. "How do we do it?"

"I have to perform a simple enchantment. Well, not that simple, when I think about it, but I can do it. This can work," Liam explained.

"Okay, let's do it," Thomas said then began floating back and forth once again in his form of pacing.

Liam stared into the candle's flickering flame and began to empty is mind, so that he could perform the enchantment. If this worked Thomas Hollingsworth would be with him, or near him, until he was ready to move on. This had some benefits, Liam thought, like Thomas would be able to scout for him and spy on people for him but it also meant that he and Thomas were one in some ways.

"Hey, Liam, will I be able to help you cheat on tests and such?" Thomas asked him.

"I don't need help cheating on tests," Liam said as he continued to prepare for the enchantment.

"Just thought it would be the right thing to offer. You know will be close mates now," Thomas said.

"Uh huh," Liam answered. He was ready for the enchantment. It was an ancient enchantment one, which many shamans, druid priests and others had used before him, though it was not used often now. It had been used as a curse to ground some evil person's soul to spot so that it could do no harm to another, or as a gift, such as the Shaman did with his son. Yes, it was a simple enchantment but it had complicated consequences, which now Liam would know first-hand. Suddenly, it occurred to Liam that he knew this enchantment because of Merlin. He performed the enchantment.

"It's done," Liam said.

"Really," answered Thomas.

"Yes."

"You mean I'm grounded to you know."

"Yes," Liam answered.

"What should I do?" he asked.

"You now have control over yourself, so why don't you go somewhere you wanted to go and then return and tell me about it," he said.

"Okay," Thomas said then disappeared.

For the first time since the Conjurer's Maze incident Liam felt good about himself. He had told Sian that he would help Thomas and he had. His powers had given the ability to find a solution to a problem and, in some way, he was proud of himself. Thomas reappeared looking disappointed.

"What's wrong?" Liam asked.

"Oh, nothing," he answered.

"As you said we are close mates now. What's wrong?"

"Just disappointed," he said then went silent.

"Were you unable to go where you wanted to go when you left me?" Liam asked.

"No, I was able to go where I wanted to go."

"Then what is it," Liam almost demanded.

"Well, I went to one of the girl's lavatories to, you know, see if anyone was taking a shower, but everyone was asleep," he admitted with a certain sense of shame.

"Thomas, really, you went to check out girls," Liam said.

"Yeah," Thomas stated.

"You are going to be trouble for me, aren't you?"

"Yeah, maybe, but we'll have fun," Thomas said then thought about something. "Liam, does this mean you will always be able to hear and see me?"

"Whenever you are around me I'll be able to hear and see you as clearly as if you were solid and alive. Now that you are grounded, you'll eventually be able to learn to appear to others when you want and move objects and the like, but no matter what state you are in, I'll be able to hear and see you," Liam explained.

"Oh, that's brilliant. We'll definitely be able to have a few giggles, won't we, Liam?" Thomas commented.

"I guess we will," Liam replied.

"What do we do first?" he asked.

"I don't know about you Thomas, but I'm going to bed," Liam said as he headed back to his house.

"I don't sleep," Thomas stated. "Come on, Liam, you're not tired."

"Thomas, I'm going to bed," Liam said.

"What a gyp!"

"Sorry," Liam said with a smile. Thomas was going to be a bit of an annoyance but he was glad to have him.

CHAPTER 17

It was once said that all roads lead to Rome, and for the Society of the Bene Lumen in many ways this was still true, which was why Brian CuCullen had traveled to this venerated and ancient city. Brian CuCullen didn't need any further attacks on his sons for him to act. Even though he had Caleb searching for answers in Los Angeles, he knew that he needed to take a more active role in regards to his children's protection, so he arranged a quick trip to the Eternal City in order to speak to the Council of Guaire, or to be more exact to a spot near Vatican City in order to demand action. He would need the council's permission to take over the security and protection of Samhain. It was a bold, almost arrogant, thought for him to think he should take over the school's security from the legendary Headmaster, but he didn't care how or what people thought of him. His children's lives were at stake.

After taking an Air Italia plane out of Logan Airport in Boston, he arrived in Rome and without delay took a taxi to his destination. In short time he arrived. This was mainly due to the earliness of his arrival that allowed him to avoid the famous traffic of Rome when the taxi crossed the Tiber to the Via della Conciliazione, which led into St. Peter's Square Vatican City. This was where the Society of Bene Lumen housed the Council of Guaire in an old building, which they had owned since the Italian Government had built this broad avenue for the Jubilee of a pope. Headquartered in what appeared to be a Travel Bookstore, the Council of Guaire had set up shop there after an attack on its headquarters on the Aran

Islands. It was thought for the longest time that an out of the way and rural setting was safest for their headquarters because it was easy to keep the council safe, but that mindset was destroyed on a night in 1948 when six wights, three zombies, two lesser demons, a necromancer in control of a succubus, and eight vampires boldly attacked their hidden away compound. The Ardal Cathal, who guarded the Council, put up a valiant and inevitably victorious fight, but many of them died along with three of the seven council members that night. It was decided afterwards to move the council to a less rural setting in order to give the council better protection. Eventually, Rome was chosen instead of London, mainly because the Vatican knew about and approved of the Bene Lumen and the Swiss Guard made for a nice backup armed-force in case of emergency.

The last time Brian had come here it was to tell the council that he decided to leave the Bene Lumen. In a combination of fury and grief he stood in front of the selected seven members and told them what he thought of their decision to send him on a wild goose chase against Azeral while his wife faced the more dangerous Baal and the creature Baal had raised on her own. She died because of his absence and their stupidity, he told them. Fiona Philbin being the Supreme Councilor of the seven accepted his resignation with some regrets, but also with a dollop of relief. The council had made a mistake and she knew it. She told him that he had the makings of one of the greatest Tiarnán and Cairbre, but some day his sons might make up for his mistake. He thought her response to his resignation just proved hers and the councils' arrogance. Brian CuCullen swore to her that they would never have either of his sons to exploit. When he left on that day, he thought he'd never return to face the council again. But like so many other things in life, the innate contrariness of living again proved him wrong. Now he was back in Rome.

"Just drop me off at the corner," he told his taxi driver in halting Italian. It had been years since he had spoken the language. Like Irish and Scottish, Italian was another language he hardly ever used once he left the Bene Lumen.

After paying the driver in Eurodollars, which he exchanged some dollars for in a bank in Boston before coming to Rome; he took his overnight bag and stretched his legs. One of the simplest rules the Bene Lumen had was never to be dropped off directly in front of any of the society's many safe houses and operation houses. This allowed you to spend a few moments making sure that you weren't followed. It was a simple security rule, though not everyone seemed to remember that it existed. In a war as long as the one the Bene Lumen fought against the Illuminatii and their like, some tended to either let their guard drop or to even regret, if not forget, that a war was being waged in the first place. Long wars, and this shadow war was indeed a long war, tended to put a strain on the will more than the body.

Brian looked down the Via della Conciliazione towards St. Peter's Square. There in Vatican City, as well as other places in Rome, the ancient and the antique mixed in an awe inspiring fluidity with modernity. St. Peter's Basilica was five hundred years old and it was still one of the newer buildings in Vatican City. The basilica wasn't even a thought in a pope's mind when the Bene Lumen first began their shadow war in full. How far they had come since then, yet how much ground they had lost.

Carefully checking up and down the Conciliazone, he made sure that no one was following him, or that no one seemed to be keeping an eye on him. He knew that there were demons and necromancers who had the skill to keep a close eye on him without needing to stare at him, but their unique gifts were useless on this avenue because of enchantments. Once he was sure he wasn't being followed he started walking towards the Travel Bookstore. Though it was early in the morning, too early for the store to be open, he rang the front door bell. Within a few moments two burly men, a black haired man with rich dark skin and a blonde haired one with red cheeks and skin that sunburned easily, dressed in casual clothes came to the door. The blonde haired man opened the door.

"Tiarnán, the password, please," he said.

"Shibboleth," he answered.

"Please enter. The council is not ready to see you yet, but they will be soon," he said and stepped aside, so that Brian could enter the bookstore.

"My name is Allen. Simon and I will be your guard while you are here," the blonde haired man stated.

"Thank you, but I don't need any guards while I'm here," Brian politely said.

"Regardless, you will have us as your guard while you are here. It is the council's order."

"It sounds like the Supreme Councilor's order."

"Yes, Supreme Councilor Rasputin was the one who now gave us the order," Allen replied.

"He's afraid of me," Brian stated.

"Not so much afraid of you, but he's all too aware of the mistake the council made in regards to your wife, Siobhan CuCullen," Allen told him. "He hopes that you no longer hold a grudge, but understands if you do and wants to be sure to have safeguards in place just in case."

"I hope Supreme Councilor Rasputin doesn't think I would hurt him or anyone on the council," Brian CuCullen said, "because I have no violent intentions towards them."

"I wouldn't blame you if you did wish us some harm considering your history with us," a strange voice said from behind Brian. He turned to place a face with this strange voice. Coming from the door to the back room was a man dressed in the black and gold robes of a counselor. Brian put the man's age at forty-five or six. He was six foot three inches with solid frame and long black hair that had a mere hint of gray in it. This was Stephan Rasputin, the current Supreme Councilor.

Stephan Rasputin was a distant relative of Grigory Yefimovich Rasputin, the evil Illuminatii who helped bring down the Russian Czar and his family and opened the door for the Communist Revolution and the bloody reign of Stalin. Where Grigory was renowned for his hypnotically evil ways and still held honored position in the Illuminatii's upper circle to this day, Stephan Rasputin was known as a talented empath, a tactical thinker, and staunch defender of the Bene Lumen way.

"Supreme Councilor Rasputin, I am Brian CuCullen..." Brian started to introduce himself but was stopped by a raised hand Rasputin.

"Of course, I know the great Tiarnán Brian CuCullen by look and by reputation. It is my honor to greet you here at the council's headquarters," he said in a slight Russian accent that became more discernible as he spoke.

"I was just telling my guard here that I have no ill intentions or need to bring harm to the council," Brian told him.

"Tiarnán, honestly, considering what the council did to your family, I would not blame you if you did want to give us a black eye or a bruise or two. But if you don't mind, I can read your feelings and clear this all up and put my security at ease?" he asked.

"Go right ahead," replied Brian.

Rasputin closed his black eyes and reached out towards Brian with his right hand. For a few moments he stood there with his hand in the air and his eyes closed then he dropped his hand and opened his eyes.

"You are dismissed," Rasputin, said, "he means the council no harm. He is here on serious matters but he is not here to bring any harm. Please go get breakfast and enjoy a quiet morning."

"Yes, sir," said Allen and the two guards exited through the doorway into the backroom.

"You are worried and anxious but not in a violent mood; though, you do still hold some ill will towards the council because of your wife's death," Rasputin said.

"I have a great deal on my mind, which is why I'm here to talk to the council. Any ill will I have is purely emotional and I am dealing with it in my own way. My reason for being here I believe is of great importance and needs a decision by the council," Brian stated.

"I beg you that you save your serious talk for the council then. It is only right that you make any requests in front of the seven of us, not just one of us, even if that one is me."

"Of course, Supreme Councilor," Brian said.

"Please, until we are in the council chamber, call me Stephan. I'd like some informality unless I can't avoid it. Too much formality breeds an exaggerated sense of self importance."

"Okay, Stephan. And please feel free to call me Tiarnán CuCullen," Brian said with a smile cracking his lips.

"Ha, ha, ha, you have a sense of humor after all, Brian," Rasputin said, "I was told that you were humorless, which I was sure untrue since the only truly humorless people I've met are members of the Council of Guaire."

"I can't argue with that, Stephan," Brian added.

"Good. And you shouldn't argue with me. Now let me take you to get some coffee. The council will not be ready to see you for another hour or so. To be honest one or two of the councilors are still taking their morning ablutions. Your visit to speak in front of the council was scheduled for an ungodly early hour. You and I can talk of the difficult time you have had the last few months over a cup of coffee," he said then motioned Brian through the doorway.

Once he was passed the doorway, Brian wasn't surprised to find that this simple bookstore was far from a simple bookstore. A maze of hallways met him. Stephan Rasputin brushed past him and led them down a hallway to an elevator. They entered the elevator and Rasputin pressed a button. None of the buttons were numbered, which meant you had to know where you wanted to go to get there in this building. The elevator doors closed and with a gentle jerk, Brian felt the elevator begin to descend.

"How many floors down are we going?" he asked.

"Ahh, yes, you haven't been here since we did the changes to our facility. With the help of the Vatican and some Italian politicians, we were able to make some renovations and we now go six levels under the ground instead of two. The Vatican has helped us unearth and excavate some catacombs which were long forgotten and which we are now utilizing with their permission for our own purposes. This has increased our ability for council members to live full-time in the building and also to supply operational guidance and help to Tiarnáns and security for the council."

"What level are we going to?" he asked.

"Six. It is the most secure level we have. That is where the council meets and where you can get the best espresso in the building, maybe on the whole block. Plus, it is one of the few rooms in this building that is not monitored. We councilors use it to discuss certain matters openly. Sometimes it is easier to have open discussion without monitoring than with it."

The elevator stopped with another gentle jerk and the doors opened. In front of Brian was a long concrete gray hallway. Rasputin exited the elevator and began to walk down the hallway, so Brian followed him.

"It's not much to look at but we have psychics, spirit sensitives, spiritual guides protecting the astral plain on this level and a host of highly trained Ardal Cathal providing the physical security, which includes monitoring devices," he said and made a light hand motion towards the ceiling. Brian looked up and saw that beside every overhead light there was a small camera that monitored the floor.

"The espresso room is in here," he said then opened a door on the left side of the hallway.

The espresso room was impressive. On the pale yellow walls there hung several pieces of art, which belonged in museums. Five antique tables with four antique chairs filled the room, except for a long thick oak table with a brass espresso machine, fine china cup and saucers, plates of pastries and biscotti, and a Waterford crystal sugar bowl and Waterford crystal creamer. Brian followed Stephan Rasputin as he poured himself a fresh espresso and took a few chocolate biscotti then went and sat down at a table. With espresso and pastry in hand Brian CuCullen sat down beside him.

"Now that we are alone, we can speak honestly and without interruption, Brian," Rasputin said.

"I thought we could speak honestly everywhere in this building, Stephan," Brian responded with wariness in his voice.

"I fear that someone either in the council or in this building has ears which listen for someone other than the Bene Lumen."

"We have a mole," Brian CuCullen stated cautiously.

"We may have a mole, a traitor. It is the only explanation I have for some incidents happening these past few months. Lately, the Illuminatii have been a step ahead of us on several important missions and specifically, missions that they should have known nothing about. Tiarnán, we have lost important people because of this, some very important people; too many in fact. Aongus Cathal, Ardal Cathal, charmers, conjurers, and others have died because the Illuminatii knew our plans. It has been a devastating time for us."

"Why are you telling me this?" Brian asked feeling as if the reason he came here for was already being undermined. He came to the council to ask their permission for him to take over the security of Samhain, to develop a new position, the Tiarnán of Samhain. But that request, which seemed so important to him just a moment ago, now seemed like a selfish concern. He was a father worried about his sons, but there were more important things to worry about at the moment.

"Tiarnán, I want you to find the traitor in our midst for me," Rasputin stated.

"Why me? Why not one of the other Tiarnáns, one who hasn't taken ten years away, or has a history with the council?"

"Brian CuCullen, you know that you are the best we have. The Bene Lumen was weakened in your absence. Why would I want to put the second best in charge of such an important mission," Rasputin stated.

"But...but my duties, the attacks on me lately, there is too much on my plate..."

"Tiarnán, I understand all of your concerns. I even understand your concern for your sons. But haven't you considered the thought that everything is connected: the attacks on you, the attacks on your sons, the failed missions, and the mole. I believe that they are all connected," Rasputin stated in a grave tone.

"They all could be connected," Brian agreed.

"If you want to protect your sons then find the mole who is causing all of this chaos in our ranks," Stephan Rasputin demanded.

"Is that an order?" asked Brian.

"No, but it is a request."

"How do you expect me to do this?"

"Jennifer Sult is healthy again?"

"Yes."

"She is very capable and would make a fine temporary replacement for you until we anoint a new Tiarnán to take your place. Put her in charge of your area while you seek the mole."

"Supreme Councilor Rasputin, you expect me to abandon my position once again?" Brian asked.

"No. I expect you to take on a more important position in our society. Instead of entering the council chamber today and making a request to take over the security of Samhain..."

"You know about my request," a surprised Brian interrupted Rasputin.

"I have my own moles, Tiarnán. A person doesn't become the Supreme Councilor without knowing how to keep an eye on the important pieces of the Bene Lumen."

"I tip my hat to you, Supreme Councilor Rasputin," Brian CuCullen commented.

"Instead of asking to take over the Samhain's security accept a special emissary position that I will offer you in council today. The position will be the Special Emissary of the Supreme Councilor and it will allow you to gather a small fealty together to ferret out this mole and expose them. Will you accept the position, Tiarnán?"

"Can I chose my fealty without interference or question?" he asked.

"Of course, you can."

Brian thought about the offer. He had just gotten used to being a Tiarnán in Maine and now this. But the offer was intriguing. It would afford him the opportunity to freelance a little, keep an eye on his sons, to stir the pot, and even to take the offense against the Illuminatii. He had been on the defensive too much lately. The offer had possibilities.

"Then I accept it. The mole needs to be found or we are all in trouble," Brian stated calmly, even though his heart raced and his stomach slightly turned. He felt as if he was once again abandoning his post, but he knew that was an emotional reaction to a difficult choice. No, this was a better way of helping and protecting his sons then being on Samhain with them.

"When do you expect me to start?" asked Brian.

"Immediately, if not sooner," Rasputin answered with a smile.

Brian CuCullen took a sip of his espresso and then a bite of his pastry. Here was an opportunity not only to make sure his sons were safe, but also to make up for his time away from the Bene Lumen, to make up for his time in his self-imposed exile.

"What if I find that the mole is a member of the council?" asked Brian.

"Well, then, Tiarnán CuCullen, I expect you will do what is right to protect the Bene Lumen," answered Rasputin.

"A council member gone bad will mean that we can't trust anything that the council has decided and planned recently," Brian stated. "Are you prepared for that?"

"It would be a travesty, but it is better to know and fix the problem than to allow the problem to become our demise. The Illuminatii have too many playing fields where they are winning the war. We must turn the game around or the Bene Lumen will no longer be able to preserve the balance. Evil will win. It has become that desperate for us."

"I'll find the mole, Stephan. You can be sure that I'll find him or her," Brian said firmly.

"I expect you to do so, Tiarnán. I chose you because you will succeed, Brian. I have made a study of your life and career and know that you are one of the special ones. With your help, Tiarnán, I intend on turning the tide against the Illuminatii."

"And become a legend in the annals of Bene Lumen history," Brian offered.

"Do you think that I am a vain man, Brian?" he asked.

"Let's just say you have a healthy ego."

"It takes a healthy ego to believe that you can come up against true evil and conquer it. Remember that."

Back at Samhain...

Slowly, Liam got used to Thomas Hollingsworth's constant presence in his life. It was like having a voice in your head, except that you had no control over it, no ability to turn it off when you wanted silence. The voice spoke when it wanted to and shut up when it chose. But Liam dealt with the voice because Thomas Hollingsworth proved to be both a friend as well as an annoyance, and Liam never had many friends in his life. Now he had a perpetual best friend.

His private tutoring suddenly stopped, as Sian Boru was called away by the Council of Guaire on important business. The rumors flew around the school that she had been given an important secret assignment, but no one, not even Liam with the help of Thomas, could find out the truth about where she went and why. Headmaster Fergus' office had an enchantment around it which didn't allow any souls or apparitions, grounded or not, to enter his office. Much to Thomas' frustration he just could not enter the Headmaster's office to do any spying.

Even though the tutoring stopped Dani and Brigid remained his constant companions when they weren't in class just as they promised Sian Boru they would. Before she left she told the two young girls to protect Liam with their lives if they must because he was important to the survival of the Bene Lumen. Since they both had seen Liam teleport they did not argue with her assessment. In their combined opinion he was another Merlin and that was good enough for them to risk their lives.

"Hey, Liam do you think Kieran will score the winning goal for his team?" Thomas asked Liam as he, Dani, and Brigid watched the Ruadh game. "I hope he does. He's my favorite player, Liam. I like the way he never gives up, and always gives as good as he gets. Hey, because I'm now sort of part of you, does that mean he is kind of like a brother to me, too?"

Floating above their heads as they sat in the viewing stand, Thomas seemed comfortable with his fate now. For the first two weeks all he did was complain about this and that, but once he started focusing and listening to Liam and he gained more and more control over himself and now was able to go off on his own, listen in on conversations, spy on the girls, and return to Liam whenever he wanted to return. Just one day earlier he actually moved a cup for the first time. The cup didn't move very far on the table, only a few inches, but it moved. Next he hoped to reach the ability to reach an apparition state so that he could haunt his brother.

"I think Kieran's team will win. Jan and Kieran are a deadly pair in goal scoring. It's like they can read each other's minds," he stated.

Since they were in public Liam didn't answer him or even acknowledge his existence. It took great self-control on Liam's part, but he quickly realized after being seen talking to himself in the Morgana common room, that he could carry on conversations with Thomas in public. People were already afraid of him, he didn't need to give them any further reason to fear him.

"Come on, Liam, don't be a bloody toe rag, talk to me. I feel like I'm cheering for the team all by myself, Mate. Throw me a bloody bone and say a word or two of encouragement to me," Thomas told him.

Beside him Brigid giggled quietly. Liam looked at her wondering what she found amusing about a game of Ruadh. She returned his stare and gave him a defiant grin as if to say she could laugh at whatever she wanted to laugh at.

"That Jan is a really big girl, isn't she," Thomas said, "I don't mean she's fat or anything, more like a body builder, all sinew and muscle like. I think she could kick everyone's butt on either team, except Kieran's. I know I wouldn't want to meet her in a dark alley at night and I'm a disembodied soul."

Brigid giggled again. Liam quickly turned his head and stared at her. This time instead of being defiant, Brigid blushed then shrugged her shoulders at him. Liam just didn't understand what she found funny about a game of Ruadh. Phillip had just been knocked from the bars and almost hurt himself, so what was so funny.

"Hey, do you think Dani would mind meeting me on the astral plain for a date, Mate. She's got a lovely body. If I tell her that she has a lovely body, do you think she will hold it against me?" Thomas asked Liam, but Liam didn't answer him.

"Come on and ask her for me, Mate. She's a looker and let's face it all I can do to her on this plane is look at her," Thomas stated.

Just then Kieran scored another goal giving his team the lead. Liam jumped up to cheer his brother. When he sat back down, he noticed that Thomas was now sort of floated just above Dani's lap, which made it look like he was sitting in her lap. This time it was Liam who giggled and Brigid who stared at him. He blushed and turned his head back to the game.

The time clock finally ran out and the game was over. Kieran's team won. Selena, who had become almost a mascot for the Aongus Misfits so she sat on their bench, gave Liam a big hug when he came down on to the field to see the team. After congratulating Kieran and his teammates, Liam chose to spend some time practicing his skills rather than celebrating the victory. From the Ruadh field he went into the forest exited the school and went into the forest with Dani, Brigid, and Thomas in tow.

"I wanted to go to the party, mate. I mean your brother's team made the playoffs. That's super, incredible even, if you think about how bad they were at the beginning of the season," Thomas complained.

The weather was chilly, but gone was winter. Liam wanted to go sit under the oldest tree and see if he could access any of the ancient knowledge that Merlin had placed in his subconscious. Even though Merlin advised him to enjoy being a boy and enjoy school, Liam knew that was impossible after his teleporting. Now even some of his teachers treated him as an equal, and his classmates treated him as almost a celebrity, but not a celebrity whose autograph you wanted instead you just wanted to point at them. Thomas hovered above them floating leisurely on his back as the others walked through the trees.

"I mean the playoffs. I hope he beats my brother's team. They're a bunch of bloody prats," Thomas stated as he amused himself with thoughts of interfering in the game and not letting his brother's team score.

"Hey, Liam, do you think you can help me later work on my apparition skills. I want to make sure my brother doesn't score any goals. I was thinking I could knock the corb out of his hands on occasion during the game?" Thomas pleasantly asked Liam, but no answer came.

"Come on, Liam, you don't expect me to wait until we are alone before you talk to me. This is torture, Mate, I mean real torture," Thomas told him sounding as if he was starting to get upset at Liam's silence.

Liam noticed out of the corner of his eye that Brigid looked up at where Thomas floated for just a moment then returned her gaze to the flower buds and other bits of nature that were beginning to grow once again. For a split second he thought that she might be able to see Thomas, also, but then decided he was only falling into the trap of wishful thinking.

"Liam, Mate, talk to me, talk to me or I will haunt you. I mean it, Mate," Thomas threatened Liam.

Brigid giggled once again. Liam stopped dead on their path to the oldest tree. He turned on Brigid and raised an accusatory finger and began to shake it at her.

"You can hear and see him, can't you?" he asked.

"I don't know what you are talking about, Liam," she replied in a blank tone.

"Don't act that way with me, Brigid, I know that you like to act distant and unattached at times, but it's all an act. You notice everything. And you can see him."

"She sees me, Mate, really. How do I look? Am I presentable?" Thomas asked Liam as he drifted right in between Brigid and Liam. Through the misty haze that was Thomas' image Liam could see Brigid smile as Thomas turned to look at her and gave her a big smile. She could see him, just as he thought.

"Brigid, I demand that you tell me the truth and remember that I can sense the truth when it is told to me," Liam said.

"What is going on here?" asked Dani.

"Hi, I'm Thomas and you are Brigid, right," Thomas introduced himself to Brigid.

"Yes," said Brigid.

"I knew it," Liam declared.

"Now I have two friends," said Thomas.

"Will someone tell me what is going on here right this minute," demanded Dani.

"I can see Liam's friend, Thomas Hollingsworth," replied Brigid to Dani's question.

"But he's dead," she said.

"Duh," Thomas responded to her comment and Brigid laughed. "She's a bright one, isn't she?"

"What are you laughing at?" asked Dani.

"Thomas," she answered, "he's funny."

"Will someone explain this to me," demanded Dani as she turned to face Liam.

"All right, I will explain everything," Liam said and as concisely as he could tell her all about him and Thomas Hollingsworth. When he finished explaining everything, Dani's face turned red as she looked as if she was about to explode.

"Liam CuCullen, are you an idiot. Of course you're not. You are special and important to the Bene Lumen and you risk yourself and your sanity for this Thomas Hollingsworth. That is reckless," Dani, lectured him.

"She's a bit of a wet rag, isn't she," Thomas said to Brigid who laughed.

"What are you laughing at?" asked Dani.

"Thomas," she answered.

"I wish I could see and hear this Thomas for myself," Dani said.

"He's working on that, Dani. I expect in another week or two he'll be able to appear to you and whomever else he wants to appear to. Just yesterday he was able to materialize one foot," Liam told her.

"Well, when he can appear to me on his own, I intend on giving him a piece of my mind," she said.

"Can she spare a piece?" asked Thomas of Brigid, who laughed again.

"Does he even know how important you are, Liam, does he even realize how important you are?" she asked him.

"Well..."

"Of course, I know how important you are, Mate. Besides being the fulcrum, you are my savior. Without you I'd be drifting on the breeze," Thomas declared.

"Fulcrum," repeated Brigid as if she no longer found anything worth laughing at.

"Fulcrum?" Dani asked. "Liam's a fulcrum?"

They both knew what a fulcrum was. Being a student of Sian Boru meant that you knew everything there was to know about Merlin. Merlin was a fulcrum and now Liam was. That explained just how important Liam was to the Bene Lumen and why they should give their lives to protect him, just like Nimue.

"Liam, you are a fulcrum?" asked Brigid with great concern in her voice.

"Thomas, I told you not to mention that again," Liam said to Thomas.

"Sorry, Mate but it just sort of just came out of my mouth. I didn't think about what I was saying. You know how it is, Mate," Thomas answered.

"Liam, this Thomas has to keep that sort of information to himself. I don't care if he is dead, he has to act responsibly," said Dani.

"I know that," Thomas said to her even though she couldn't hear him.

"He knows that, Dani. Thomas knows that he has made a mistake, so leave him a lone," Brigid said to Dani.

"I hope so," Dani replied.

"Liam, how did you find out that you were a fulcrum, how did you learn about it?" asked Brigid, leaving Dani to stare at a spot where she thought Thomas was standing. He was standing in that spot, though, but was now standing behind her making faces at her.

"Merlin told me that I was like him. He told me that I was a fulcrum," Liam said.

"Merlin," shouted Dani, "you've seen Merlin? You've contacted him?"

"Yes, I have. This past Halloween Sian Boru and I contacted him together."

"Why didn't you tell us about it, Liam?" asked Brigid, whose brow frowned and cheeks turned red as if she was going to cry, but she didn't.

"Sian Boru thought it best to keep my reaching out to Merlin to very few. It would cause a commotion in the student body if everyone knew I contacted Merlin."

"Well, she knows best," said Dani. If Sian Boru thought something was best, then it was best done that way in Dani's opinion. Sian Boru knew best.

"She doesn't always know what is best, it seems," replied Brigid, who seemed very upset that this secret was kept from her by Liam.

"I'm sorry, Brigid, but Sian asked me not to tell you guys," he explained. "It's not an excuse and I knew that it was wrong when she asked me, but... We are family, right? We should share everything. I should have told you. It was wrong of me to keep it secret."

Brigid walked over to Liam and with both arms wrapped around him gave him a long hard hug. She held on to him as if she didn't want to let go. Finally, she let go.

"Don't keep any more secrets from us, Liam," she said.

"Okay, Brigid," he agreed.

"I want a hug, too. This isn't fair," said Thomas. Both Brigid and Liam began to laugh. Eventually, even Thomas joined in with the laughter. Everyone laughed, except Dani.

"What is so funny?" she asked in exasperation.

"Thomas," answered Brigid.

CHAPTER 18

The often water deprived, sun bleached and yellowing rolling hills of Napa Valley zipped past as Caleb drove towards the town of Napa where Anna was in hiding. Gone were the dense groupings of green trees he had seen on his ride up to Northern California, instead, they were now replaced by a lone tree here and there standing friendless on a rolling hill. Occasionally, he'd pass one of the ever-present vineyards where the grapes waited for their leaves to turn from orange of winter back to the green of harvest season. Soon it would be sunset and soon he would be with Anna.

Because of her close relationship with the inner circle of leaders in Los Angeles Caleb believed she would know a great many things that would interest the Bene Lumen. Once he caught hold of Anna's scent through harassing fellow vampires and other Illuminatii, he followed her up the California coastline. Mainly traveling by night he took Route 1 up the coastline hitting certain spots as he went. In Carmel he met a necromancer named Nathan Payne, who knew Anna and helped her keep under the radar from Dyre. This necromancer didn't do this because he was kind, but because he hated Dyre. Anna spent a week with him in his estate, where he headed a New Age cult called of vegans who called themselves the Earthers. Payne used this cult as a front for him, while he slowly made inroads into usurping some of Dyre's powers.

Caleb took comfort in the fact that they fought each other on some level as much as they fought the Bene Lumen. The Illuminatii was filled with power hungry humans, abominations, and demons that wanted to be the most powerful, the most important. Caleb knew how to exploit their weaknesses, which were Greed, pettiness, and abuse of power. When Caleb got to Payne's estate, Anna had gone on to her next hiding spot. Payne wouldn't tell Caleb what he wanted to know, so Caleb had to resort to intimidation. The bold necromancer attempted to subdue the vampire with several enchantments, but they didn't work on him. Because of his soul what worked on most vampires didn't work on Caleb. He couldn't be made into a soulless servant by an enchantment, or bend his will with a spell. Payne fell victim to Caleb's attack, yet he still wouldn't tell him where Anna had gone. In the end he had to take those memories from him by drinking his blood. At first he intended to leave the necromancer alive, but as he drank in his blood and memories he realized just how evil this man was and finished him off instead of letting him live.

Caleb knew that what he did wasn't the act of a hero, but it was effective nonetheless. Brian CuCullen and men and women like him were heroes; he was not one. He wasn't even the good man that Brian told him that he was. What he was really was an instrument, a sharp instrument to be used against the Illuminatii. He didn't want to be an instrument, but that didn't change the fact that he was one. Unfortunately for him, Payne had no knowledge of why the Illuminatii wanted Brian CuCullen dead or who might the traitor be, but he did know where Anna was.

One hundred years ago in Newport, Rhode Island Caleb fell in love with Anna. Yes, he fell in love with her. Love was an emotion he never thought he'd be able to truly feel since his bloodlust almost became uncontrollable when he felt passion with a normal, human woman. Anna, though, was a vampire, like him. He found her in Newport hiding from Dyre. This was her first time she ran from him, the first time what was left of her conscience caused her to want to break away from the Illuminatii. He was enthralled by the fact that she felt some guilt that she wanted to leave the Illuminatii, so he helped her hide from them. Since he knew Newport well he arranged for living quarters for her with a wealthy Giolla who owned one of the great mansions of Newport.

Over a lugubrious hot summer he and Anna fell in love, or what he thought was love. She appeared to want to be free from not only the Illuminatii, but from the bloodlust which made her crave human blood. Caleb wanted to help her; he wanted to save her. She was a gift from God, he thought, but what she turned out to be was an abject lesson from God. By the end of the summer she had killed a maid and the grounds keeper for their blood in order to assuage her atavistic vampiric need to cause fear and for power. Her inherited by blood true nature surfaced and overwhelmed her desire to be free from the Illuminatii. Caleb couldn't kill her, though, because of his feelings for her, even if he no longer wanted those feelings, he had them. Yet he could no longer help her, either, so he drove her from Newport, a place he once thought of as home. Since then he had never returned there. After Anna he realized that he no longer had a place he could think of as home. She soiled Newport with treachery and death for him. But more importantly she showed him that he couldn't trust love, either. Love betrayed him.

Now Anna was hiding in a section of the town of Napa populated with old Victorian homes. It was a quaint neighborhood of old Napa, a reminder that the old town has been home to people of varying degrees of wealth for many years, along with laborers, and lost souls looking for a place to hide. In Caleb's opinion Anna was one of those lost souls looking for some place to hide more than an Illuminatii. Deep in his tortured soul he still thought of her as someone who could be saved, someone who could prove that it was possible to be redeemed, even after they did much evil.

Caleb finally reached the town of Napa. He drove into the heart of this town noticing a supermarket and the kind of squat flat top institutional concrete buildings that best suited stores, restaurants, and government offices. Past these buildings he continued in the Victorian home section of Napa. The last time he was here these homes were populated by families, but now all he saw were business signs hanging from the porches announcing either a real estate office or a lawyer's office. He didn't bother noticing street names or house numbers because he knew exactly where he was headed. Payne's memories supplied him with an exact map.

Parking in front of a well-kept and stylish Victorian home, the sun was now a red ball of setting fire in the sky, so he didn't bother with a hat or sunglasses. It was only an irritant on his skin now no longer causing him great pain. He walked slowly up the pathway. Once he got to the front door, he took several moments to collect himself. He thought of taking a deep breath, even though his lungs or body no longer needed oxygen. Caleb Keane rang the front door bell.

"Hello, Caleb, I've been expecting you," the pale beauty who was Anna Hoffman said as she opened the door.

"May I come in?" he asked her politely.

"Of course you can, old friend," she replied then walked into the old house leaving the front door wide open for him.

Caleb entered then shut the door behind him. At first he wondered if this was a convoluted trap of the Illuminatii to capture him, but there was nothing about a trap to be found in Payne's memories. If Anna was expecting him, it was because she knew him well enough to know he could help but to try and save her. But also because she knew she had information that Caleb would be interested in attaining.

He followed Anna, who was dressed in a light black summery dress, into the living room. The house was decorated with antiques and lush, soft fabrics. The furniture was old yet comfortable. In the living room he saw that she was reclining on a daybed wrapped in royal blue velvet. The room was lit by one single dull kerosene lamp since vampires saw clearly in the dark. It had all the hallmarks of a place where vampires came to relax, to recuperate, and to hide. He sat down on a soft love seat and stared at her.

As was to be expected Anna hadn't changed in the slightest since he first saw her all those years ago. Vampires aged, so to speak, by exposing themselves to harsh conditions, which in turn weathered them. Anna avoided harsh conditions, as she avoided most hard things. She was made by Dyre to be his eternal concubine and that was what she was most of the time.

"You're in trouble," he said.

"I'm...I'm in turmoil, Caleb, not trouble," she said with her voice sounding as if she was in some pain, though he knew she suffered no pain at the moment.

"From what I know, and I know everything since I killed Payne and drank his blood, you are merely avoiding punishment by Dyre. You can't fool me, Anna, I know you too well. Dyre won't harm you permanently, but he will hurt you badly. You are here to avoid pain and punishment, two things you abhor."

"It's more than that, Caleb, I'm avoiding being me, a killer, a damned soul. I am tired of being a vampire; I am tired of the Illuminatii and all their intricate schemes. I am even tired of the Bene Lumen and all their deadly good intentions. All I want is eternal silence now. I've had enough of life. I am tired, Caleb, just tired of being me."

"Like you were tired of being you that summer we spent on Newport," he said harshly.

"You can't hold that against me, Caleb. I was hungry, so very hungry. It was the first time I tried to deny real nourishment to myself, so I was so very, very hungry. I needed real nourishment, not another dinner of some pet rabbit or stray cat," she told him. "I needed to eat or I'd starve to death. You see, Caleb, I am not a mystic or an aesthete like you, who can deny what they desire most and find solace in that. I occasionally need to indulge my desires, or I need to find a way of stopping those desires."

"But your desire kills," he replied.

"I know that," she said sadly, "and I regret that in my way. It is harder for me to change than it is for you, Caleb. I don't have your soul, your good soul. I am empty inside."

"Not completely, Anna, you're not completely empty," he said then they went silent.

In that silence lived regret and wasted chances. Anna knew what she was and what she wanted to be. But she also realized how great a distance there was between the two of them. As for Caleb he knew who he was and knew the struggle he had to remain who he was and not turn into a dark creature. The one thing he couldn't allow for was to fall into darkness because he would then lose his soul and it was his soul, which supplied the only comfort he had in this life.

"I believe you have information which would help me," he stated.

"Help you?"

"It would help a friend of mine, then, not me. My friend needs the information I believe you can provide me."

"You have friends, Caleb? You have found friendship with mere mortals. Isn't it odd how Caleb Keane can find friendship with mortals but not with his own kind? I bet the reason for this is that you hate yourself and you hate those who are like you," she said exposing just a glimpse of the evil Anna that Caleb knew resided within her.

"I don't believe a Tiarnán is a mere mortal. I think he is an exceptional mortal."

"A Tiarnán. Which one? Oh, don't tell me let me guess. Let's see which of the Tiarnáns would you be friends with? Yes, course, you'd pick a strong yet tragic one. Is it Brian CuCullen?"

"You know that it is."

"Poor, Brian CuCullen, his wife long dead and his children in such danger. They will join their mother soon I think," she goaded Caleb with a laugh.

"I thought that you would know about the plan against the CuCullen Clan. What is the plan, Anna? Tell it to me."

"Against the CuCullens? Caleb, how prosaic you are sometimes? It must come from being hungry all the time since you starve yourself so much. It is not just against the CuCullens, it is a plan to cripple the whole Bene Lumen, cripple it and maybe even destroy it. The CuCullens are merely pawns in the overall plan that the Illuminatii has set into motion," she announced to him.

"If I'm so prosaic then tell me the whole plan, so I can see just how unimaginative I am. Show me the dark light of the Illuminatii, Anna."

She sat up from her daybed. Her once soft brown eyes were now yellow as it had gotten darker out and the room was almost completely in shadow. She stared at Caleb intensely then leaned back on the daybed.

"I'll tell you if you help me," she said. "I'll tell you everything I know if you just help me this one last time, Caleb. I think that is a fair deal, don't you?"

"Help you how?" he asked.

"Kill me," she answered.

"Kill you? What do you mean kill you, Anna?" he said sounding slightly agitated.

"I want to end this existence and I don't have the courage to do it myself, so I want you to do it for me. Kill me, Caleb, show me how much you once loved me and end this horrible existence for me once and for all. I don't want to live under the burden of the Illuminatii any longer and I don't want to become a pet of the Bene Lumen. Kill me," she pleaded with him.

"I... I don't know if I can do that," he told her in a voice that was almost a resigned whisper.

"The traitor isn't on the Council of Guaire, but is Councilor Kahn's chief assistant. It should be easy enough for you to find out his name, I can't remember it myself. I could care enough to listen to Dyre when he told me all about him. But what I can tell you is that he is a wight. About two years ago he went on vacation to Cairo and was killed by the Illuminatii then revived by a Voodoo priest, with the help of a very skillful necromancer. He was then trained on how to keep his secret about being a wight and told that his soul would be fully restored to him if he did as he was told. You see the necromancer had taken control over his soul. The Illuminatii had planned this out in minute detail. This wight has access to all council information because he is so trusted by Councilor Kahn. He was been feeding information to the Illuminatii ever since, as well as doing other tasks for them," she explained.

261

"What about a soul crystal? Shouldn't a soul crystal have exposed him?" asked Caleb.

"He has been with this councilor for twenty years. He hasn't been exposed to a soul crystal in fifteen years because of his trusted position. He is a man above suspicion. They always make the best traitors. But that is only one traitor; there is another one out there, too. Agree to kill me and I will tell you who the other traitor is, also," she said.

Caleb stood up and moved towards her, but before he could get close to her, she was up off the daybed and standing behind it. Caleb stopped in his tracks.

"Anna, I... I don't want to kill you," he admitted.

"Kill me and I will tell you why they want the CuCullens dead and who the traitor is who is manipulating the events to bring this about," she responded.

"Anna, I..."

"The second traitor is on Samhain, Caleb, so close to those two young boys. He is right under their noses on that damned island where they educate the brats," she told him.

"Samhain. He's near the CuCullen boys," Caleb said to himself. "Anna, tell me who it is now. Redeem yourself and tell me who it is."

"I don't want redemption, Caleb, I want death. Agree to give it to me and I will give you the name of the traitor on Samhain," she demanded now.

"But maybe redemption is something you should want," he retorted.

"Enough of this meaningless talk, this babble," she said and then walked out from behind the daybed and towards the table where the kerosene lamp stood. "Are you going to give me what I want, Caleb?"

"Anna," he said with anguish, "I can't kill you. I don't want to kill you."

"Then you are useless to me and you have condemned me to this damned life," she said then picked up the kerosene lamp.

"Who is the traitor, Anna? Tell me and I will help you," he said.

"But you won't kill me," she replied.

"Anna, I just can't, but I can try to help you in other ways. You can come with me. I'll protect you."

She raised the kerosene lamp until it was level with her face. Gone was her delicate beauty. The darkness in her had overcome what light there was. Her eyes blazed a sort of yellowish orange and her vampiric teeth where now protruding slightly from her mouth.

"I will no longer be a pawn for the Illuminatii and you will not help," she declared in a cold voice. "If I can't have an end to this existence then I will find a way to have freedom in this world from all of you. I will kill who and what I want and when I want and I will not be anyone's pawn any longer. You will regret the day you didn't kill me, Caleb."

"Anna, tell me who the traitor is and then come with me. I can get you help," pleaded Caleb.

"They think you are strong. The Illuminatii actually thinks you are strong. You aren't strong, you are weak," she told him.

"What do you intend to do?" he asked.

"Whatever I want, Caleb, whatever I want to do. Find the traitor if you can, kill all the Illuminatii if you can, I don't care. I can only give you one present now and that is this," she said then threw the kerosene lamp directly at him.

Caleb attempted to dodge the lamp but it broke at his feet and set his legs on fire. The fire quickly spread up his legs enveloping his lower body. Quickly, he knew he had to put the fire out. He was a powerful facing the front lawn. Landing on the lawn he began to roll about slowly extinguishing the flames.

Once the fire was out, he stood up. People who lived in the neighborhood were either staring out their windows at him or standing on the sidewalk staring at him. He imagined what he looked like to them with eyes blazing yellow and his vampire teeth fully extended. Turning to look at Anna's house, he knew that she would be gone by now. Gone and a danger to anyone she met. He turned back to stare at the people again. In the background he could hear a police siren racing towards the area. It was time to leave.

With graceful movements he ran towards the house, but instead of running up the porch steps he jumped up towards the roof of the house landing on it. He then concentrated all his energy and powers on his next move, which was to jump up into the air catching the wind and drifting like a bird in flight. Though some vampires could shape shift and fly, Caleb had learned to ride the wind when he needed to do so. It was dangerous to do, though, because he had yet to learn how to gain great height when doing this, so he hung in the air like a bird. Below him as he flew, he watched the ground looking for a good place to land.

Once he had gone what he considered a good enough distance from the neighborhood he landed on a deserted street and began to run at his stop speed. He wasn't sure where he was running, but he knew he had to put distance between him and Napa for now. All that he could do now was find a place to rest and recover. He needed to feed on some animal in order to regain lost energy and repair his body from the fire then he had to contact Brian CuCullen. Caleb didn't have the name of the traitor at Samhain, which Brian so desperately wanted, but he had at least one traitor for him.

Golden Gate Park would be the best place for him to recover, he decided. There were plenty of places for him to hide there for a day or two. When darkness fell, he'd take to the sky again and head for San Francisco. There he would feed and recover as quickly as he could. The Illuminatii needed to be stopped and Anna needed to be found.

Brian CuCullen faces a wight...

Brian CuCullen's latest fealty consisted of Sian Boru, the young Fiach William Running Deer, and himself. He kept it as small as possible because of the necessity of speed and secrecy. Plus, Caleb Keane was an unofficial, yet important, member of this fealty, which gave CuCullen an added level of confidence over the size of his chosen team. Caleb engendered confidence in others, even if he doubted himself. That confidence paid off, too, when Caleb contacted him to tell him who the traitor was within the council. Though, it did disappoint him that he couldn't find out who the traitor was at Samhain. But Brian didn't push Caleb. From the sound of his voice, Brian could tell that Caleb was in pain, more than physical pain, it sounded as if he was in emotional pain.

With a little research Brian found out that Councilor Kahn's chief assistant was Gibran Hamdan, a man so well trusted because of his dutiful service that it had been years since he loyalty was tested. Hamdan had complete access to the Council of Guaire headquarters and the records stored there. He was so trusted by Councilor Kahn in fact, that Brian doubted he would take his or Caleb Keane's word that Hamdan had been a wight in the service of the Illuminatii for the last few years. Instead of telling Supreme Councilor Rasputin that he knew the traitor, Brian merely requested a visit with the full council in chambers in the hopes that Hamdan would be present and he and fealty could expose him. He wanted to expose the traitor in front of the whole council, so that they all realized just how much danger the Bene Lumen faced. Sian Boru thought his plan showed an unnecessary flair for the dramatic, but she didn't argue too hard against it. She was enjoying the opportunity to once again work closely with Brian CuCullen.

"I hope Caleb's information is correct or this could be embarrassing," Sian stated as the three of them sat and sipped espresso in the sixth level espresso room, which Rasputin had introduced Brian to.

"If Hamdan is there all you have to do is produce the soul crystal and check him out. If he is a wight, the crystal will turn black or..."

"Actually for a wight the crystal turns a glowing yellow color," she interrupted him.

"Okay, the crystal turns yellow and then Running Deer and I will take it from there. There won't be any problems," Brian offered.

"I can handle a wight, Brian, if I need to without your help," Sian scowled.

"I know that, Sian. But slaying is more my job than yours, even if you can do it yourself. I need something to do," Brian said with a dollop of humor.

Being able to spend time with Sian Boru was the only thing about his new position that Brian CuCullen was comfortable with. After ten years of self-imposed exile Brian realized just how selfish he was being staying away from the Bene Lumen and from Sian. If he had let her into his life after Siobhan died, she may have been able to get through to Kieran where he failed. She was far more important to him than he ever admitted to himself. He just hoped that all that wasted time could be made up.

"I thought we were going to take him alive when we caught him," said Running Deer.

"We are, William. That is if we can take him alive. Some wights have been known to be ferocious fighters. They are strong and feel no pain and sense they are already technically dead you have to strike them in the right spots," Brian responded.

"And once we've taken care of Hamdan, what is next on our agenda?" asked Sian.

"My hope is Rasputin allows me to stay in this position and allows us to track down the name of the traitor at Samhain," Brian stated.

"I visited Mallory last night on the spiritual plane and told him that he might have a traitor on the island," Sian said.

"What was his reaction?" asked Brian.

"Calm. He told me that he expected that he had one. The tengu getting through the barrier has put him in a state of perpetual vigilance."

"Good," replied Brian then he sighed. "I hated taking you away from the island, Sian, but I needed someone I could trust completely to be part of this fealty."

"Brian, I am glad to be hunting traitors with you. That is the best way you can help your children. I trust that your sons will be able to take care of themselves. Kieran has killed a tengu and Liam may only be twelve but there are fifth and sixth level students who do not have his control over his powers. He is remarkable," she told him, though her voice did betray a slight anxiousness.

Brian could hear the anxiousness in her voice and he shared it. Even though he trusted Mallory to protect his boys and Selena, he would only feel comfortable if he oversaw their security personally. He took a sip of his espresso, not so much that he needed the boost, but because he needed something to do with his hands. William Running Deer shifted in his chair and yawned. Brian looked at the young man he had chosen to be his Fiach.

Just three years ago Running Deer had finished first in his class as a hunter from Samhain. Since then he had worked with Sylvia Hand the Tiarnán who oversaw England. She gave him the highest praise and told Brian that she had never met a better hunter. To look at Running Deer you didn't think he was a hunter. He dressed in a San Diego Chargers Football jersey, a display of hometown pride, faded and ripped jeans, and a pair of old New Balance trainers. His long black hair wasn't tied back, so he was perpetually throwing his head back to get his hair out of his eyes. Most hunters that Brian knew had eyes that seemed to be forever searching for something, but William's eyes merely appeared to drift about never focusing on anything at all, yet Brian realized his eyes noticed everything.

"Tiarnán, do you think Hamdan has accomplices here?" asked Running Deer.

"Probably not, but it will be up to security to make sure once we have exposed him."

Suddenly, the door to the coffee room opened and a man entered. It was Gibran Hamdan. He looked just like the photograph Brian had seen of him when he researched Bene Lumen files. Even though they were sure he was a wight, Brian, William and Sian could not discern it from his outward appearance. His hair was a light shade of gray with hints of its form blackness from through it. He wore the robes of the Ardal Cathal, a symbol of his background. His brown eyes were sharp and clear and seemed to be friendly in their expression. Though many wights became emaciated because of their lack of need for food, he didn't seem undernourished, and his skin had a healthy tan to it, which was in stark contrast to what they knew about wights.

"Greetings, my name is Gibran Hamdan. The council has sent me to inform you that they will see you in five minutes. Shall I escort you?" he asked.

"No, I know the way there by now. It's not my first visit here," Brian answered.

"Of course, it isn't. I was merely being polite. I will wait for you at the council door when you are ready to enter. Please, feel free to finish up your espressos. I wish I had time to enjoy one. They are delicious," he said then turned and left.

"He doesn't look like a wight," stated Sian Boru with the first hints of doubt popping up in her voice. She couldn't even sense evil on him, which disturbed her, also. He would have to be tested another way. "I realize that wights are difficult to spot but he looks completely alive. His skin doesn't even that lifeless quality that can give them away."

"Caleb said he was a wight, so he is a wight," Brian said. His faith in Caleb Keane was unchangeable.

"The tan's fake. I bet it's the kind that comes from a can you buy at a salon. You know the spray on kind of tan," commented William Running Deer.

"How can you tell?" asked Sian.

"On the back of his left hand there is a small patch, no more than the size of a large freckle, that he missed revealing his true skin color, which is the grayish white color of dead skin. I bet if I got a closer look at him I'd find some more spots he missed."

"Nicely done, William," Brian congratulated his sharp eyesight.

"I'm impressed," added Sian which made Running Deer blush ever so slightly.

"Well, let's get this over with," Brian said as he stood up. "Sian, once we are in the council chamber expose him to your soul crystal."

"Remember, we are looking for it to turn yellow if he is a wight," she stated.

The three of them left the coffee room and continued down the hallway. Once they got to the end of the hall, Brian turned left which led down another short hallway that ended in two large dark mahogany doors. That was the entrance of the council chamber. Waiting for them outside the closed doors was Hamdan. He gave them a friendly smile as they approached. Sian smiled back at him. She was slightly impressed at how well this man was able to represent himself as a living human being. He hid his evil behind some powerful enchantments. This took more than training this took the help of a powerful necromancer.

Brian CuCullen and his small fealty came to a spot in front of Hamdan. For a few moments no one spoke a word, but instead Hamdan sized Brian and his team up, while they did the same to him. It was an uncomfortable few moments in which Brian CuCullen thought he might have to act against Hamdan before he wanted to do so, but the silence soon passed.

"I have always wanted to meet you, Tiarnán," said Hamdan to Brian.

"Really, why?"

"Because you are a legend in many ways. Brian CuCullen is feared by many," he answered.

"I am a flawed legend if I am a legend," Brian said.

"That is what makes you even more interesting," Hamdan explained then opened the doors to the chamber.

The council chamber was meant to leave visitors with the feeling they had just entered an important room where deeply important decisions were made. It accomplished this illusion through darkness and starkness. A single overhead lighting source lit the councilors' Dias where sat all seven councilors in their black and gold robes. In the middle sat Supreme Councilor Rasputin, who had his head down as he reviewed some notes that laid on the surface before him. The councilors were the only thing to receive any direct light. The rest of the room was lit with small lights in the floor which gave off a grayish dull light, so that the small viewing stand, where observers and visitors could sit, the two witness boxes, where those who either gave witness or were under suspicion stood, or the special visitors table, where those who were invited to speak or inform the council sat, were almost hidden in darkness.

Entering the black box, which was the council chamber, Hamdan led Brian CuCullen and his small fealty to the special visitors table. As they reached the table, Brian nodded to Sian. It was a signal to her. She nodded back then her right hand disappeared into the sleeve of her free flowing dress she wore and emerged a second late with the soul crystal in it. Before Hamdan could leave them, she gracefully and quickly moved in close to him and placed the crystal to his forehead. The crystal, which appeared to be a plain glass bauble, turned a glowing yellow and Hamdan immediately let out a scream and tossed roughly Sian into the air. Before she could land hard on the floor Brian leapt over the table and caught her in midair leaving

Running Deer to face Hamdan alone. William running Deer began to move towards Hamdan.

Each councilor reacted with shock at what had just happened, except Rasputin, who smiled. He had chosen correctly in picking Brian CuCullen as his own personal Tiarnán. His left hand disappeared under the Dias in order to trigger a silent security and almost immediately eight security men and women came running into the chamber. Running Deer was about to tackle Hamdan when Hamdan screamed another blood curdling scream. If the first scream was one of shock and pain then the second scream was one of hatred and agony. Hamdan's body began to shake and tremble violently. Not knowing what to do, William stopped his attack and stepped back away from him. The violent shaking continued for what seemed like an eternity but was no more than thirty seconds then he stopped. As he stopped shaking his body released what appeared to be a greenish gas, which Sian recognized.

"William, hold your breath that is miasma he is releasing from his body. Breathing in too much of it will kill you," she warned him.

William took a deep breath and held it as he moved even further away from Hamdan. Sian removed herself from Brian's arms raised her arms into the air and began to use her considerable powers. The air around Hamdan seemed to become a vessel for the miasma, collecting it into a cylinder of poisonous fumes, containing it from spreading. As Sian contained the miasma, Hamdan's body began to implode until it was nothing more than the shrunken remains of a corpse then it dropped to the floor.

A new security guard entered the chamber carrying a container. He took of its lid and placed it on the floor. Sian moved the contained miasma over to the container and gently lowered it with her powers into the container, whereupon the security guard placed the lid tightly on it. Rasputin stood up and began to clap.

"Very well done. I see you have caught the traitor for us just as I requested," he said. "It's too bad we couldn't question him, though."

"What is going on here?" demanded Councilor Kahn, who had turned pale white and looked to be in almost a state of shock over the death of his assistant.

"Your assistant was a wight and a traitor, Councilor Kahn. The Tiarnán and his fealty, my special emissary, has exposed him for us," Rasputin stated putting special emphasis on the words my special emissary. "It seems our bad luck lately was not bad luck but was treachery. And your assistant was the source of that treachery, Councilor."

"I had nothing to do with this treachery. I didn't know he was a wight. I am as shocked and surprised as any of you here," stated Kahn.

"Of course you didn't know, Councilor Kahn, but I believe it would be best if you stepped down from the council for appearance sake, don't you? He was your closest assistant all these years. He was your responsibility," Rasputin said.

"I hate to agree with Supreme Councilor Rasputin on this, Kahn, but I think you should step down immediately and an investigation is started right away on you and your whole staff," added Councilor Dolores Balzac.

The rest of the council shook their heads in agreement as they sat back down at their place on the Dias. Councilor Kahn looked about at each of them for support, but found none. He was disgraced not so much because anyone believed he was a traitor, but because he never noticed that someone so close to him was a traitor.

"I will resign then. The Bene Lumen is too important for me to argue. I will not hurt the council or the society. I am loyal to both," he said and walked slowly out of the room.

Brian was reminded of a wounded animal limping away to die as he watched Councilor Kahn take his leave. For a moment he felt horribly used by Rasputin, but he could argue with the Supreme Councilor's decision to remove Kahn. Yet, what he witnessed was not justice, it was politics, dirty, simple politics. Rasputin was exerting control over the council. He might be doing it for the right reasons; he might be doing to save the society; but what he did was not just, it was the art of taking power.

Two security guards cleared the container from the room. Sian stood over the desiccated body of Hamdan. Lowering her head and spreading her hands out over the body she began to sense that what was at play here, what had happened to him. She turned and faced the council.

"An enchantment was placed on him to decompose if he was found out. The Illuminatii didn't want him questioned if discovered," she stated. "The necromancer who placed the enchantment was a powerful one, too, very powerful. I can only think of two or three with this skill or power."

"Who?" asked Rasputin.

"Morgana, Hecuba, or Lilith," she answered.

"Skillful and powerful indeed," said Rasputin. Those three names were the name of three of the most powerful and ancient necromancer ever born. They were so powerful that each had conquered death and aging and had caused many in the Bene Lumen to suffer.

"There is another traitor we have become aware of, Supreme Councilor," announced Brian CuCullen.

"Who?" asked Rasputin sounding surprised by the announcement of another traitor.

"We don't have a name, only a location where they are. Samhain."

A group gasp escaped the remaining councilors. Samhain was thought of to be as safe as Avalon. In essence a traitor in Samhain meant that nowhere was safe, nowhere at all.

"What do you suggest we do, Tiarnán?" asked Rasputin calmly, but putting such emphasis on 'Tiarnán' to let the rest of the council recognize that Brian CuCullen was his man.

"That we be allowed to continue our work as special emissaries and find out who the traitor at Samhain is. We have already informed Headmaster Fergus and feel the best way to expose this traitor is by gathering as much intelligence as we can."

"I will discuss this with the council, Tiarnán," stated Rasputin. "But for now I think we must retire to our private chamber and discuss what has happened here today and what we need to do in order to minimize the damage that has been done. Security will escort you and your fealty to some rooms that have been prepared. We will speak again soon."

CHAPTER 19

Talbot watched along with Nadia as Kieran crossed the obstacle course finishing line. Over the school year he worked tirelessly whenever he could to improve his time in this challenge knowing full well that Boris Diaghilev would not let him continue as an Aongus Cathal unless he made a better time. He collapsed to his knees once across the line and began to cough. Both Talbot and Nadia walked slowly towards him, allowing him to take a few moments in order to compose himself.

"This is the best run that you have done yet," Talbot announced to him with a proud tone in his voice.

"How fast did I run?" he asked in between gasps.

"Ahh, well, 14 minutes and 3 seconds," he answered sheepishly.

The obstacle course was still his weakness, the bane of his existence, at Samhain. It was the one thing that could hold him back from being an Aongus Cathal next year. He exhaled when he heard the time. The release of air in his lungs sounded almost like a sign that he was giving up, resigning to failure. He would never make the 13 minutes and 30 seconds that Diaghilev said he would need to remain an Aongus Cathal, which would mean that he'd be sent to the Ardal Cathal.

Kieran wasn't sure when exactly it had happened, but sometime during the school year he had begun to want to be an Aongus Cathal, to consider himself an Aongus Cathal. On many levels he still felt like an outsider in this strange school, but between Ruadh and a few other factors, he was starting to accept that he belonged there. Maybe it was fighting the tengu and winning, or the private lessons from Headmaster Fergus, or the unwritten competition he had with Nadia, but he had started to think of himself as Aongus Cathal, even as a potential Tiarnán like his father. But 14 minutes and 3 seconds wasn't Aongus Cathal time.

"Don't worry, Kieran, you still have time to improve. I still think you have forty or fifty seconds of improvement left in you. If you could just cross the ropes more quickly," Nadia gently said to him.

Instead of making him feel better her words annoyed him. She thought he had 40 seconds still worth of improvement in him. Here she was trying to break his father's record time, and she thought he could maybe do only 40 seconds better. Her words sounded almost as if she pitied him and he didn't want to be pitied by Nadia. He wanted her to feel something more than pity for him.

"It isn't fair," said Talbot. "You were too far behind the rest of the fifth years, Kieran, to start with. Maybe I can convince Master Diaghilev to at least give you the summer before being tested in the obstacle course. You just need more time to train your muscles to give you that extra ten or fifteen percent necessary to make up the time."

"I think that is a very good idea. Kieran needs more time. I will talk to my uncle, too," Nadia agreed.

"NO! I have the time left that has been allotted to me. I don't want special treatment," Kieran stated.

"I agree that you shouldn't get special treatment, but all I'd be asking is fair treatment. Kieran, you've had so much to make up this year," Talbot said, "that it is only fair that you get a few extra months. I can't remember someone who has made up so much in such a short time."

"You will have to earn being an Aongus Cathal, Kieran," added Nadia. "You will not be given a pass. No one is making this easier for you. We think it should just be fairer."

"I will run the course at the year end and my time then will be my time. I either do this now or never," he defiantly said.

"But Kieran..."

"No more, Talbot and you, too, Nadia. I've had enough time already. If I took this more seriously from the beginning I'd be running the course in 14 minutes flat. No, I don't want special treatment."

For a moment Nadia looked as if she wanted to argue with Kieran, but then her expression softened. Again, he thought he saw pity in her eyes and wanted to yell at her not to pity him. He had killed the tengu not her. And he would face this challenge and somehow overcome it because he was meant to be an Aongus Cathal. It was in his blood. He was destined to be one.

"Okay, I won't mention my idea again," Talbot, said.

"Good."

"And neither will I," mumbled Nadia.

"We were only trying to help, Mate. We weren't trying to shame you or anything," Talbot said then offered his right hand to Kieran to help him up off the ground. He took it and stood up.

"I should run it again," he said to Talbot.

"No, you shouldn't, Kieran" interrupted Nadia. "If you run it again, your time will only be slower than last time because you are tiring which will depress your mood and make this harder for you in the end. You need to be mentally and physically strong to do this. You also will probably feel a need to push yourself even harder this time and that could lead to an injury. You can't afford an injury now."

"I won't injury myself," Kieran responded with some heat his words. He was tired of Nadia treating him like a student of hers instead of...something more.

"Yes, you will, Kieran, you are getting unnecessarily angry," she responded to the tone of his voice.

"I know what I have to do and what I am doing," he declared to her in a tone that sounded harsher than he wanted it to sound.

"I...I do not want to argue," she said coldly. "I am going."

Without another words Nadia strode away from Talbot and Kieran. He watched her as she gracefully receded from view. She didn't look back as she went, though Kieran wished that she would. But Nadia now felt as angry as he did.

"Nice going," Talbot, said.

"What?"

"Nice going," he said again.

"What do you mean?" Kieran asked.

"Well, if I had a beautiful girl as crazy about me as she is about you, I wouldn't be pushing her away like you. I'd be accepting her help and seeing where our relationship ended up," Talbot said.

"You're crazy. She isn't crazy about me. I am competition to her and nothing more."

"Are you stupid?" asked Talbot.

Kieran didn't answer Talbot but instead bent down to retie his trainers.

He was now even more hell bent to run the obstacle course today.

"Excuse me, student, did you hear me ask you a question. I am your trainer so answer me," barked Talbot.

"Stop fooling around, Talbot," said Kieran.

"I am not Talbot now. I am Mr. Talbot right now and I asked you a question and expect an answer. Are you stupid, CuCullen?"

"No, sir," Kieran said reluctantly.

"You could have fooled me. That girl is crazy about you. I've known her longer than you and I have never seen her treat another student like she treats you. She treats you like an equal and Nadia does not think she has an equal here in the student body. You are hearing me, young man?"

"Yes, sir," he answered.

"Good," Talbot said then he relaxed his tone. "Kieran, she likes you and you are pushing her away."

"Because she pities me," Kieran said.

"Kieran, it is not pity, it is worry. She is worried about you. She wants you to be an Aongus Cathal next year. I bet she even wants you to give her a run for her money, maybe even be chosen for the Tiarnán program along with her. Boyo, she doesn't want to lose you."

"You really think that is what it is?" he asked Talbot.

"Yes, that is what I think it is. So what are you going to do about it?" he asked him.

"Apologize," Kieran said.

"Then go prove to me how fast you are and go apologize to that girl now," he commanded.

Kieran took off in the general direction where Nadia went. He wasn't sure where she was headed but he knew that he had to find her now. Running as fast as he could, he passed through the obstacle course fenced off area and into part of the school area. Looking about as he ran he didn't see a single sign of Nadia. But he did spot his brother and went running over to Liam.

"Liam, I need your help," he told his brother as he caught up to him.

"Sure, Kieran, what is it?" asked Liam.

"Can you send your friendly specter out for a look about for me?"

"What are you looking for?" asked Liam.

"Hey, I'm not a specter," Thomas said from his perch beside Liam. Even though he had mastered becoming an apparition, he preferred to remain unseen and unheard beside Liam's side.

"Shut up," Liam snapped at Thomas.

"Sorry, Bro, I didn't think asking for a favor was a big deal," Kieran said then started walking away from his brother.

"Kieran I wasn't talking to you. I was talking to Thomas. Of course we can help you," Liam stopped his brother.

"Great," Kieran exclaimed as he came back to his brother.

"What do you want?"

"Can Thomas take a quick flyover Samhain and find Nadia for me?" he asked Liam.

"I don't know about that, Mate, she's pretty thing but she scares me. But then again she can't see me now, can she? Maybe I can haunt her," he offered.

"Thomas, behave," ordered Liam.

"Hey, don't be a wet rag about it, Liam. I'll find her for your brother, but I just wanted to have a little fun," Thomas told Liam then took off into the sky and starting floating away.

"He's checking for her now," Liam said.

"Thanks."

"Why are we looking for her?" asked Liam

"I have to talk to her."

"About what?"

"Is one of your powers the ability to see into the future?" Kieran asked him.

"So far I have no ability to see into the future, or read minds, or any of that fun stuff," Liam answered.

"Good. Now to answer your question, it is none of your business," Kieran told him.

"Sorry I asked?" Liam replied. "Did you hear about Selena?"

"No, what's wrong?" asked Kieran with concern for Selena overtaking quickly his need to speak to Nadia.

"Nothing bad, Kieran, it's just that Boris Diaghilev has decided to let her stay in Aongus Cathal next year, too. He said that she has come a long way and wants to give her another year, even though her true skill is as a Fiach."

"Really," responded Kieran.

It appeared sometimes that Boris Diaghilev was willing to give everyone a break but him. This was why he refused Talbot and Nadia's offer to ask for more time for him. He wanted to prove to Boris and everyone else that he was just as good as his father and didn't need special favors to catch up.

"You ready to run the obstacle course for him yet?" asked Liam knowing that his brother needed to remain an Aongus Cathal. Kieran still didn't know that he was Liam's champion, his Arthur.

"Not yet, Bro. I'm still too slow. I need to take quite a bit of time off my run," he admitted.

"You can do it, Kieran."

"You think."

"Yeah, I think you can," Liam said then looked up to see Thomas in the blue sky above him.

"Yes, Thomas, where is she?" he asked his ghostly companion.

"Over at the Ruadh field looking like a sour puss," he answered as he came down right beside Liam.

"She's at the Ruadh field," Liam told Kieran.

"Thanks, Bro. And thank Thomas for me. Tell him I owe him one," Kieran said then took off towards the Ruadh field.

"Nice brother you have there," Thomas said.

"I know," replied Liam.

"I've started to haunt mine late at night. I take off his blanket when he's asleep and move his things around so he can't find them without a good deal of effort," Thomas stated with pride.

"Why?" asked Liam.

"Because he was a prat to me when I was alive."

"Thomas," Liam started to scold him.

"It's just a bit of fun," Thomas quickly said.

"Let's go, I have studying to do."

"Maybe I should check out what your brother is up to with the Russian Goddess," Thomas offered.

"No, you're going to help me study."

"I hate studying," Thomas commented as he followed Liam.

Kieran finally arrived at the Ruadh field. Looking around the nearly deserted seating stands and field he finally saw Nadia. She was sitting off high up on a stadium bench looking as if she wanted nothing to do with anyone. He ran to the stands then began to climb the steps to her. Nadia's face turned even less friendly as she saw him coming towards her. Kieran finally got to her.

"I just came..." he started to say but was stopped by her.

"To tell me to leave you alone because you know what you are doing," she snarled at him.

"No, I just came..."

"To say you don't need any help."

"No, I came..."

"To yell at me and make me feel foolish for thinking we are friends," she stated.

"No, I came..."

"To insult me..."

"To tell you that I am sorry about how I behaved and that I like you," Kieran yelled quickly before she could finish interrupting him.

The anger in Nadia's face vanished and her dark eyes once again became friendly. Kieran even thought he saw a hint of a smile on her lips.

"What did you say?" she asked him.

"I said that I am sorry for my behavior earlier. I was wrong for acting like a child. I need your advice and help, just like I need your friendship," he stated.

"Really, you need me," she remarked sounding slightly superior.

"Don't get carried away," Kieran cautioned her.

"You don't need me?" she asked.

He thought it best to think before he answered her question. If he said he didn't need her, he would not only be contradicting himself, but he would be lying. Yet if he admitted to her just how much he needed her, he'd be changing their friendship, changing their relationship. Nadia waited patiently for him to answer.

"I need you, Nadia. You are the best friend I've made since I came here. If it wasn't for you I wouldn't have improved in the obstacle course at all."

"We are just friends?" she asked in a way to prompt him to continue.

"Actually, we are friends and competitors. Since the first day I met you I wanted to beat you at something. You were so sure of yourself, so good at what you did, that I even forgot that you were the prettiest girl I've ever seen," he admitted.

Kieran thought he saw her cheeks turn slightly red in a blush, but the blush quickly faded as her lips and eyes hardened into anger once again. She liked and didn't like what he had told her, which was what he wanted. He wanted her angry to keep her off balance a little while he worked his way through this.

"We are competitors and friends. How nice for us," she sniffed.

"Yes, competitors and friends. At least that's what I thought we were at first but even those feelings have changed," he said and Nadia looked up at him with curiosity instead of anger.

"You see, Nadia, I didn't want to come here. I was a star jock at my high school and I had a great girlfriend..."

"Girlfriend," Nadia interrupted him to repeat the word as if she didn't like the sound of it.

"Yeah, a girlfriend."

"Are you still boyfriend and girlfriend?" she asked.

"No. We broke up before I came here," he told her.

"Oh," she responded.

"You see I didn't want to come here. Unlike you and other people I don't get along with my father all the time and I don't want to become him."

"He is a great Tiarnán," she stated in Brian CuCullen's defense.

"Yeah, I guess, but I didn't want to be him. Not everyone wants to follow in their father's footsteps, but... but then I started to train with you and play Ruadh and get to know everyone and I started to like it here. I even started to like being an Aongus Cathal and it wasn't that bad being Brian CuCullen's son."

"So you and I are friends and competitors and you like it here. How nice for you," she said sarcastically.

"I'm not through explaining myself so listen," he said then sat down beside her. "As time passed I realized that I admire you, that I liked you and that I wanted to be..."

"Yes, continue," she said.

"I'm looking for the right words," he explained.

"Just speak the words that are there for you," she told him.

"Okay, I will. After some time I realized that you and I are friends and competitors, which is nice, but I wanted to be more than friends and competitors."

"What is more than friends and competitors?" she asked.

"I'm not sure. It's hard to tell. You see if I fail as an Aongus Cathal, we won't be able to find out what is more."

"Yes, we will," she said.

"No, we won't. We might want to but I want to be your equal and unless I am Aongus Cathal and eventually a Tiarnán, like you will be eventually, then we won't be equals. I want to be equals, Nadia."

She reached over with her right hand and gently took his left hand in hers. He felt her squeeze it, not hard, but firmly. "Then work harder, Kieran," she said sweetly and sincerely.

Kieran smiled then the smile turned into a laugh. She was right he had to work very hard if he wanted to know what was possible with Nadia. She tried to pull her hand away from him, but he held it tight then reached over with his right hand and turned her chin to face him. He stared into her eyes and thought if there was a time to show courage, it wasn't when the tengu attacked but now. He slowly moved towards her. Nadia didn't back away, so he continued to move closer until he gently gave her a kiss on the lips. When he moved away he saw that she was smiling.

"You must work very hard to get your time down," she said.

"I know."

Caleb in San Francisco...

Without feeding on demon, abomination, or human blood it took a week for Caleb's body to repair itself. During this time he mainly hid himself from view in the hidden away spots of Golden Gate Park and occasionally took to living in the back alleys and less savory sections of San Francisco to seek out some nourishment from rodents. He chose San Francisco because he knew that he could mingle and hide among the city's ever present homeless population without too much trouble. With his slightly burnt clothes and scarred skin, he fit into the lost and forgotten of a society which didn't look too closely at their lost and forgotten.

Now that his skin had repaired from the fire, he knew it was time to resume his search for information. His first instincts were to find Anna, but he realized that she would be difficult, if not impossible, to find now. She was filled with the passion of hatred, which meant she was in full vampire mode. No one was safe from her now and he was at fault for that. He should have had the strength to give her what she wanted, but he didn't. And now he would have no choice but to kill her the next time they met. Yes, he didn't want to find her now.

No, he needed to find out either who was the traitor at Samhain or the name of someone who knew who the traitor was. With dusk setting in, he reached into his pants pocket and counted how much money he had. He had made it to the famous Haight-Ashbury section of San Francisco and now wanted to purchase some new clothes to wear. Caleb knew these hilly streets fairly well having spent time here many years back. It was odd how little the neighborhood changed in essence. Just like before it was still a haven for those who looked at life from different angles and with the expectations of a supplicant seeking enlightenment. Of course the rents were higher now. Noticing a used clothing store he entered and began to look around at the men's overcoat. The pretty sandy haired young sales clerk, who was dressed in bohemian chic, tentatively walked up to him.

"Can I help you?" she asked cautiously.

He knew his appearance must seem unseemly, if not suspicious. When Anna had set him on fire, it left his clothes in scorched rags. But he had no alternative but to continue to wear them since he would draw far more attention walking about the city naked. The sales clerk was lucky that his skin had repaired or otherwise she be calling the police out of fear.

"Yes, I need some clothes. You see there was an apartment fire and my belongings were destroyed. This is all I have to wear right now and, well, I don't think it's very fashionable," he told her in his most charming manner.

This lie seemed to satisfy her. He watched as her muscles, which were tense and rigid when he entered were now relaxed. She even managed a sincere sympathetic smile for him, which oddly enough warmed Caleb's non-beating heart. It had been a difficult week for him.

"Oh, well, it's closing time, but let me put the closed sign up in the door and you can shop. You can be my last customer," she said.

"Thank you," he replied.

She left to put up the closed sign. Even after all these years, humanity surprised him because people were capable of goodness and charity under most circumstances. Yes, humanity was also capable of greed, hate, and violence, but those moments of goodness made him remember why he struggled to fight his bloodlust, why he fought on the side of the Bene Lumen. He searched the clothes rack for a suitable overcoat. One after another he flipped through until he came to a long plain black raincoat. He took it off the hook and tried it on. It fit him like it was made for him.

"Found something," she said.

"Yes. Now all I need is a black shirt or sweater and a pair of black pants," he said.

"What about shoes?" she asked looking down at his feet.

His shoes looked as if he had left them in the fireplace then lit a fire. He smiled at her.

"They have seen better days. Yes, and shoes," he said with a smile.

"Let's find everything that you need and maybe I can even give you a discount considering what you've been through," she said then took him by the arm and led him around the store to collect everything.

When he left the store he was wearing the black raincoat, a black sweater shirt, black jeans, black loafers and a pair of black sunglasses. He was ready to resume his search and the first stop was a witches shop in he of in the area. Many, many years ago in the 1960s when San Francisco was a beacon to everyone who wanted to lay back and tune out the world, a real coven of witches moved to Haight-Ashbury. They were considered the Switzerland of witches remaining as neutral as they could in the shadow war, so they opened an occult shop in the city neighborhood and stayed out of the way of the Bene Lumen and the Illuminatii.

By the 1980s this coven, which had remained neutral in the shadow war, their occult store became a good spot to purchase exotic ingredients and information. Even though they mainly used their powers to keep the war at bay, to stay out of the fight, they knew they had to give both sides a reason to leave them alone. Like Paris LaMent, or Leonardo, as Caleb now knew who he was, they walked a delicately tightrope between good and evil trying not to take a side.

At present Caleb knew the witch who ran the store for the coven. Her name was Gundrun Ure. He first met her thirty years ago when she was six years old when he attended one of their 8 sabbaths, a meeting of the whole coven. She was a sweet child who even after being told that he was a vampire liked to sit in his lap and have him tell her stories. He saw her again ten years later when she had grown into a sweet young girl. Still, she was unafraid of him and still she enjoyed his stories. The last time he saw her was ten years ago. She had grown into a lovely woman with piercing green eyes and long blonde hair. By this time she no longer listened to his stories, but she had her own stories to tell him. They were stories about her experience in college, her discovery that her supernatural powers were impressive, and that she had fallen in love. He wondered what she would be like now.

The name of the store Caleb sought was Wicca Goods. Walking the streets of S.F. Caleb was surprised to see how little it changed in some ways, yet how much it changed in others. For reasons he always thought supernatural, San Francisco drew those seeking enlightenment along with those peddling false enlightenment. They became almost a symbiotic organism feeding off each other, and Haight-Ashbury was a central feeding ground for this organism. The city still had those types of people, but it now added those seeking expensive real estate, which they wanted to make even more expensive. The store stood where he remembered it was. It occupied the bottom floor of a three-story house, where several of the witches of that coven lived. He entered the store. A few people were milling about looking at the crystal, spirit catchers, books, candles, scents, clothes, and other items the store sold. Behind the checkout counter was a long blonde haired woman with her head down, as she appeared to be checking the store's account books. Flipping through what Caleb assumed were pages of numbers he stared at the woman inhaling deeply the stale candle and incense scented air of the store until he picked up the scent of Gundrun Ure. She was the woman behind the counter. He cleared his throat just loud enough to get her attention. She looked up.

"Caleb, Caleb Keane, is that really you," she said with a bright smile on a face that had aged comfortably into its natural attractiveness. She wore no makeup and her only jewelry was a necklace, which he recognized as a soul crystal. He approached her.

"Gundrun, it has been a long time," he said.

"Not for you," she countered with a knowing smile.

"Can we talk?" he asked her.

"Of course," she said then went to the back room for a few minutes before returning with a dark haired woman, who took her place at the counter. She then motioned him to come around the counter and follow her.

Caleb followed her through the door into the backroom then down a short hallway to a staircase leading to the second floor. On the second floor, which appeared to be a communal gathering spot for the witches, he followed her into a kitchen where a young girl, no older than nine, sat doing her homework. Gundrun kissed the top of the child's blonde haired head and motion Caleb to sit at the table. He did so.

"Hi, Mom," the child said.

"Una, this is Caleb Keane. I've told you stories about him," she said to the child.

"Oh, you're the good vampire, aren't you?" Una asked him.

"Good. I'm not sure about that," he answered.

"Yes, he is the good vampire," Gundrun said, "and modest, too."

Gundrun sat down at the table now. Una shut the math book she was studying and waited for her mother's orders. Gundrun patted affectionately her daughter's hair. He was surprised at how much mother and daughter resembled each other.

"Go upstairs to your room and finish studying," she told Una.

"Okay," she answered and picked up her stuff and left.

"That's wonderful, you have a daughter," Caleb commented.

"Yes, it is."

"Where is her father?" he boldly asked.

"Dead. He was a police officer, a man of integrity and courage. A thief shot him while he was breaking into a building near the Presidio. That was five years ago."

"I'm sorry," he said.

"Why? You didn't shoot him," she responded with a slight smile on her lips.

"He accepted that you were a witch?" Caleb asked.

"He accepted me," she said with a laugh. "He once asked me why my coven called ourselves witches instead of Wicca and I told him that if my sisters could be burned in Salem all those years ago for being witches then we can proudly call ourselves witches. He liked that."

"And he left you with a beautiful child," Caleb added.

"Yes, he did," she said then paused to consider something. "I often wondered why vampires are unable to have children."

"Physically, we can't because those reproductive organs can't support life, but we do have children in other ways. We spawn other vampires. They are our children."

"Are you still childless?" she asked.

"Yes," he answered with sadness in his voice. He had no children because he refused to turn someone into what he had become, though there were times he considered it. To spawn other vampires would have meant he would no longer be lonely. But he could never guarantee that those he spawned would have souls like he did, so he never attempted it.

Una places her right elbow on the table and used it to support her chin, as she stared at him. She looked almost as she did as a child to Caleb.

"Did you know that I had a crush on you when I was a little girl?" she asked him.

"I knew. I can see a great deal with these eyes, especially in the dark," he answered.

"Did you really know?"

"My senses are heightened beyond the human. I could hear your heart race, the blood flow quicken in your veins increasing your pulse. I knew."

"Nice trick," she said, "what can I do for you, Caleb?"

"You are the only coven I know of that still has the power to use divination through the crystal ball. I want you to answer some questions for me."

"What type of questions, Caleb?" she asked.

Before he could answer Caleb's vampiric sense warning of danger went off. Without knowing who caused the danger, he knew he was in danger. He closed his eyes and listened using his ears almost like sonar then inhaled deeply trying to pick up scents. The witch downstairs was dead, as well as those window-shopping. He could hear the rapid breathing of whatever killed those downstairs. Caleb opened his eyes and looked at Una. His expression told her that they were in trouble.

"Something has killed everyone downstairs. Is your coven in trouble?" he asked.

"No," she answered.

"Then I must have brought this danger to you by my visit."

"I need to get Una," she said and started to get up. Her chair scraped along the floor as she did. Caleb could hear whatever it was downstairs react to the sound. It would now come upstairs.

"It's too late for that," he said then suddenly the creature's scent reached him. "It is a Se'irim."

"A demon," she said but in a way that asked for assurance.

"Yes, a demon beast. They are mentioned in the Hebrew Tanakh. Azazel is their leader."

"How do you kill it?" she asked.

"They are tough to kill. You have to rip out their hearts. When he gets to us, I will take care of him. Go upstairs with your daughter. If you know of any magic to raise a spiritual barrier, I would do so. Hide behind it and hope it can hold him off if I don't kill him."

She nodded. They listened as the creature came up the stairs. It sounded heavy, but quick. The Se'irim made its way towards them. Caleb got up and prepared himself for battle. With a craning of his head to loosen his neck muscles he brought forth his vampire teeth. Two long fangs now appeared in his mouth. His yellow eyes narrowed and the nails on his hands slowly extended until he had talons. He was ready. Gundrun stood up and got behind him and waited for her chance to get to her daughter. They both watched the kitchen doorway waiting for the demon.

Finally, the Se'irim darkened the doorway. It was huge, almost seven feet tall, with a brownish fur covering its human-like frame. Under the fur its body appeared to be all muscle. On top of that muscled body was a large wolf-like head that seemed to almost have human features. Gundrun gasped. It hissed at her.

"Caleb Keane," it said, "prepare for judgment. You killed Payne, so I kill you."

"I don't think so," Caleb said then attacked the demon.

The Se'irim was quick but Caleb was quicker. He tackled the demon at about mid-body and drove it out of the doorway and almost through the hall wall. This gave Gundrun her chance to leave the kitchen and get upstairs to her daughter, as Caleb held it for as long as he could. The Se'irim recovered, though, and tossed Caleb through the air and all the way into the kitchen sink, which shattered from the force of the impact.

With water spraying out of broken pipes Caleb got up. The demon was on top of him before he could prepare himself and attempted to rip his head from his body. Caleb sunk his vampire fangs into its left hand and began to drink its evil and polluted blood. The demon screamed and attempted to toss him to the other side of the room, but he held onto the demon with his fangs and continued to drink its blood.

Being a demon the creature's blood reproduced at a remarkable speed, so he was unable to drain it and kill the demon that way. But the Se'irim blood strengthened Caleb. It increased his powers greatly as he drank. The demon finally decided to drive its left hand along with Caleb into all of the kitchen cabinets. One by one it smashed its hand and Caleb into the many cabinets splintering them along with many of his bones. Some of the splinters began to pierce into Caleb's back driving deep into his body. The pain and fear of having a splinter of wood pierce his heart caused Caleb to retract his fangs. The demon now tossed Caleb through one of the kitchen walls into the witches' living room.

Caleb landed on a sofa near the windows facing the street. He felt as if several of his bones had been crushed from the impact of going through the wall and from being used to smash cabinets. The demon, which appeared now to be raging with anger, rushed towards him to finish him off. He wasn't sure how to stop it, so he decided to use the demon's own momentum and force to his own advantage. The Se'irim ran towards him, so he reached out and flipped both it and him through the windows and wall facing the street. Since he was used to flying through the air, he shifted his body, so that the demon was on the bottom and he was on top, and before they reached the hard concrete ground he drove his right hand through the demon's chest, grabbed its heart and ripped it from its body.

As they hit the ground with a sickening thud, he felt all life leave the demon's body. He rolled off the dead Se'irim feeling as if he would not be able to move. People started to gather around staring at him and the slowly decaying demon. Within a few more minutes the demon would be nothing more than unidentifiable dust and he would be a badly injured vampire unable to get away. A young man in a business suit came up close to Caleb.

"You all right, man?" he asked Caleb.

"Been better," he mumbled.

"Get out of my way," he heard Gundrun's voice yell. He glanced and saw her and her daughter break through the crowd. They came over to him where he laid.

"Can you move?" she asked.

"Not sure," he answered.

"Be sure and move," she said, "my car is parked right there."

With both daughter and mother helping him they got him on his feet then deposited him into the back seat in the cab of a cherry red Ford Pickup Truck. Una got in the passenger seat and buckled up as her mother started the pickup and peeled out of her parking spot. With police sirens in the distance they drove away from the coven's store. Whatever neutrality the witches possessed it was now gone.

"Where are we going?" he asked.

"Somewhere safe," Gundrun answered. "How do you feel?"

"Many cracked and broken bones," he mumbled.

"We'll fix you up, right, Una?"

"Right, Mom."

"But I caused that horror back there," he said.

"No, you didn't, Caleb. The Illuminatii caused that. They entered neutral territory and destroyed it. The Coven of Salem's Blood has now joined this fight on your side," she told him and continued driving down the hill and as quickly away from San Francisco as she could drive.

CHAPTER 20

Tadhag Zheng stood in front of his class and frowned. This frown surprised many of his students, who were chatting away while they settled into their seats, since he was more apt to smile when imparting knowledge than to find the occasion to frown. Of all their teachers he was the most constant in his good nature. Liam wondered what would make one of their wisest and most insightful teachers knit his brow in consternation. Was it what he had to teach this day or was it why he had to teach it to them, he considered as he watched the gentle monk begin to pace the floor.

"This class could bore me to death, if I was alive, that is. Can I take off, Mate?" asked Thomas as he hovered behind Liam's seat.

"Sure," Liam answered trying to act as inconspicuous as he could when he answered an incorporeal Thomas.

"What did you say?" asked Ja' Rune, the student who sat beside Liam.

"I was just saying to myself that Tadhag Zheng sure looks upset today," Liam said in covering his answer to Thomas.

"Yes, he does," she agreed. "I have always found him to be one of our most calming teachers, but today he looks agitated. I hope there is nothing wrong with him."

"Jeez, she sounds like an old woman in a girl's body. What a wet rag! Well, see ya later, Liam. I'm going to check out the girl's locker room and see what and whom I can see, if you know what I mean," Thomas stated and took off.

Liam observed that Tadhag Zheng stopped pacing and appeared to watch Thomas slowly waft up to the ceiling and disappear. The wise old monk then cleared his throat in his usual manner to subtly tell his class that his lecture was to begin. Everyone began to settle down. Zheng's lectures had become almost everyone's favorite class with their mix of stories and arcane knowledge.

"For those of you who are conjurers, casters, and charmers, seers, prophets, and the like, today I will speak on a matter not related to the undead, but related to your counterparts in the Illuminatii," he said without his usual good humor. "I do this because I believe these are dangerous times we currently live in and you must know where the greatest danger comes from. I speak today of the men and women who have taken ancient and esoteric knowledge and perverted it for their own uses, for their own empowerment. Knowledge has no morality, it merely exists, but those who possess knowledge must use it morally, or else their knowledge becomes dangerous. There are those who seek to destroy the balance and become their own deity, their own divinity, and their own authority. I have faced these perverted humans many times and I tell you this, they may be human in form but in my opinion they are abominations of the worst kind."

"Tadhag Zheng, do you mean that they are humans who have changed into abominations because of their knowledge of the occult and dark arts?" asked one of the students.

"No, I mean that even though they remain human in form that the knowledge that they have cultivated and the way they use it has turned them into abominations. Their actions have made them abominations," he answered then stopped and frowned once again before he spoke.

"Some of you who study the supernatural and occult arts may have the choice some day between knowledge and balance or power and control. Your decision will lead you down two different paths. Choose knowledge and balance and you will be Bene Lumen, a warrior for the light, a source of goodness and righteousness. Choose power and control and ... and you will become one of many who has chosen to become abominations."

"You mean to become Illuminatii, Tadhad," young Talbot corrected Tadhag Zheng.

"No, not just Illuminatii but aligned with the Illuminatii, part of them yet separate from them. But this will become clearer to you as I describe them. Back in 1598 a man named Christian Rosenkruez traveled to China in search of what he considered esoteric and secret knowledge. He sought this knowledge at first out of curiosity since he was a man of great intellect. His first intention towards this knowledge was merely to possess it, as if you could merely possess knowledge. He had no idea of the true nature of this knowledge, of its great power. Rosenkreuz, you see, is a brilliant man, but he is a brilliant man, unfortunately, without a sense or right or wrong, without a moral compass. Once he gained access to certain knowledge, his mind became thirsty for any and all knowledge that would bring him more forbidden and dangerous knowledge."

"Sir, do you mean to tell us that this Christian Rosenkreuz is still alive?" asked Liam.

"Oh, yes, he lives today. In accumulating his vast knowledge he discovered a way to stave off death and to keep his corporeal state perpetually youthful. Yes, there are certain Triune Conjurers who have also accomplished this feat by perverting nature, but Rosenkreuz succeeded in doing this through a science of sorts: alchemy. Some say he discovered the formula for the philosopher's stone from Hermeticism, but if he had created a philosopher's stone his powers would be complete and he would have truly conquered death as well as all else. I tend to believe he hasn't so much conquered death than he has found a way to delay death by stopping the aging process. I believe that, thankfully, the philosopher's stone's secrets are still secret to him and his kind."

"But, sir..." began to ask another student but Tadhad Zheng raised his hand for silence.

"Let me tell you more before you ask any more questions. Rosenkreuz went from China, to Egypt, to Palestine, to Greece, to Rome, and other places collecting his esoteric and secret knowledge, like some boys collect baseball cards. Unfortunately, the more knowledge he collected, the greedier he became and the more he wanted. When he was through gathering enough knowledge to give him powers he had only dreamed of possessing, he started The AMORC, the Ancient Mystical Order of Rosae Crucis, or the Rosicrucians as they are more commonly known. Rosenkreuz combined the secrets of Egyptian Hermeticism, Gnosticism, certain Hebrew Kabbalah sects, as well as some sects of the druid religion, alchemy, and other occult knowledge and created an organization without a sense of right or wrong. This was an organization that only wanted to possess a sense of power and entitlement. There are those who believe that the Rosicrucians are a benign group, but they are not, they are soulless gatherers of dangerous knowledge. They are practitioners of the dark arts, and over the years they became allies of the Illuminatii."

"Allies but not members?" asked Ja' Rune.

"In a way yes. They are Allies who are members but maintain their own practices, their own agenda, and their own identity. They work with and in conjunction with the Illuminatii, but they have their own reasons for doing what they do. You see Rosenkreuz believes that once he has all the ancient and esoteric secrets there are to have he will be like a God and will no longer need the Illuminatii. Of course the Illuminatii holds certain secrets, which they will not allow him or his Rosicrucians to have. It is a game they play with each other."

"Is Rosenkreuz their most powerful member?" asked Ja' Rune.

"Not necessarily. Another member of this group is an Austrian physician of some historical repute, Franz Anton Mesmer. He, too, was a collector of ancient and dark knowledge, and he, too, has found useful Rosenkreuz's method to keep death a bay. But he had a unique gift, which Rosenkreuz admired, which was hypnotism, not the kind you see practiced today on TV shows, but true hypnotism, the control of another's soul and actions. Rosenkreuz gave Mesmer the gift of avoiding death for his knowledge of hypnotism. They became student and mentor and in some ways Mesmer is more powerful than Rosenkreuz because no one has mastered hypnotism like him. Now do you see why I frown, Master Liam?"

Liam was startled at Taghad Zheng's picking him out of the class and asking him this question. He always knew that Tadhag Zheng possessed a certain innate sensitivity towards people to go along with his vast knowledge, but now he had an even greater respect for this man's gifts.

"Yes, sir, I see why you frowned before class," Liam answered.

"Tell the rest of the class why I was frowning," he prompted Liam.

"You frown because of how deep the beliefs and agenda of Rosenkreuz has permeated modern life. Many people today seek easy, if not obscure, answers to their spiritual questions and he and his followers provide these people with answers leading them towards him and his beliefs, which in turn lead them away from balance and the light. From the shadows he has corrupted many, many lives."

"Very good, Liam. He and many of his Rosicrucians are abominations, just as I said. They have truly lost sight of the balance that needs to be maintained if the world is to continue. Without true balance the world will plunge into permanent darkness and whatever God, Gods, or Goddesses who believe in will desert this world. The fight then will not be between the Bene Lumen and its allies and the Illuminatii and its allies, but will be between the Illuminatii and the Rosicrucians and their allies. What a dark, sad, hopeless world it will be then. We cannot allow this. They must be stopped," stated Tadhag Zheng.

"Sir, you paint a bleak picture," commented Ja' Rune.

"Yes, I do. Yet there is hope in the darkness."

"What is the hope?" asked another student.

"Another Merlin, another fulcrum, can help restore the balance and keep us from losing our shadow war," he answered.

"But, sir, that is impossible," interrupted Athena Karras, a talented student who mainly remained silent in her opinions, "there is only one Merlin. He was unique in time and history, more than a Triune Conjurer, he was one of a kind."

"He was a fulcrum, Athena," Tadhag Zheng told her, "as well as a powerful Triune Conjurer. Do you know what that means?"

"No, sir, I don't know what that means. I've heard the term used before, but my parents wouldn't explain it to me," she answered.

"He had the power through his actions to change the course of history, which is a remarkable thing for one to do because once history sets on certain course, it takes truly great powers and energy to change that course. Merlin was a focal point of historical energy and change. He was able to see what needed to be done and powerful enough to change the course of history through his actions."

"And we need another Merlin," she interrupted him.

"Yes, we need another Merlin at this time, if we are to keep the world from plunging into darkness which the Illuminatii and its allies wish for," Tadhad Zheng said to her then glanced at Liam, who blushed.

He knows what and who I am, thought Liam. Tadhag Zheng must have guessed; he must have somehow guessed. Liam's mind raced. He wasn't sure if this was a good thing or a bad thing, then suddenly, he understood. Even a fulcrum needs teachers and those teachers will make themselves known to him in their way. Tadhag Zheng was making himself known to me, thought Liam. He is to be one of my true teachers.

"Yes, how will we know this new Merlin when he or she comes?" asked Athena Karras, the once quiet student turned chatterbox.

"You will know him or her because of their extraordinary abilities. Think of all those things that Merlin did that others couldn't do easily. He had several truly extraordinary gifts, which he couldn't hide even though he didn't flaunt them. Look for another with those same gifts and if that person also seems to not want power, you will know that he is a fulcrum," he told the class, who seemed to be shock by the comment.

Everyone suddenly became abuzz with talk and glanced from person to person with many a glance falling on Liam. He could feel their eyes were now on him, burning through him with their curiosity and unasked questions. Trying to hide his discomfort he stared at Tadhag Zheng who stared back at him. Tadhag Zheng merely smiled at him.

"Class is dismissed early today," he said. "I have given you much to think about, so go out and think about what I have spoken of. You are the future of the Bene Lumen and the only hope for the balance to be maintained."

Slowly and reluctantly one by one the students gathered their belongings together and left the classroom. As they left they glimpsed at Liam, who remained seated waiting for everyone to leave. Liam lingered continuing to catch Tadhag Zheng's eye as he dawdled looking for ways to stay behind to speak to him. He noticed that Athena Karras boldly got up from her seat and walked down to Tadhag Zheng. He followed her lead.

"Yes, Athena," Tahdhag Zheng said to her.

"Sir, I'm confused. Do you really believe that there can be another Merlin?" she asked him.

"Why shouldn't there be another like him? Was he so unique that God, or the Gods, broke the mold after he was made?"

"But, sir, Merlin..."

"Merlin is your idol, Athena, and a good idol to have. You know everything there is to know about him, am I correct?" asked Zheng sweetly.

"Yes, sir. I admire him so much that, well, I'm kind of obsessed by him. I've also thought that he would return to this world if we were in dire need of him."

"Then you should be thrilled that there will be another like him for you to become obsessed with," Zheng joked with her, but she didn't find it amusing.

"I can't imagine another like Merlin, sir," she said humorlessly.

"What is your particular gifts?" he asked her then glanced at Liam who waited patiently for their talk to end, so he could speak to Tadhag Zheng.

"I'm a caster and charmer," she answered.

"You have another gift, too, don't you," he prodded her.

"Yes," she said and blushed.

"A gift you keep secret from people," he stated. Liam became fascinated by their exchange, but wondered if he should now back away and give them some privacy. Athena didn't even seem to notice that he was there.

"I can sense truthfulness or falseness in everything that is told to me, sir," she said earnestly.

"A truthsayer. It is difficult being a truthsayer, isn't it? You know when people are lying to you, even your parents. You think it is a burden more than a gift."

"Yes," she said.

"Have you sensed any lies come from me today?" he asked.

"No," she answered.

"There is another Merlin. Now go and think about that," he said.

With her head down, as if she was deep in thought, she walked away. Liam came towards Tadhag Zheng, who stood smiling at him. The expression on his face was beyond a smile, though, it was as if Zheng knew what Liam had to say to him.

"Sir, you know who I am," he said to him.

"You are Liam CuCullen," the Tadhad answered with a smile.

"But, sir, you know what I am," Liam stated.

"You are a Triune Conjurer and a fulcrum, Liam. I know who and what you are. And I gave this lecture today because I believe that the Rosicrucians know who and what you are, too."

"How?" asked Liam a bit shocked by this comment.

"Because Rosenkreuz and Mesmer are too smart not to have divined who you are. Dear Liam, if you think I am smart, these two men hold enough knowledge to make even me jealous. They know who you are, I am sure of it."

"Have you told others that, sir?"

"Yes, but the Council does not agree with me. They prefer not to deal with problems until the problems become unavoidable."

"So you have decided to prepare me yourself for the Rosicrucians," Liam said.

"If I am not mistaken Merlin would have imparted certain ancient knowledge to you," Zheng said then noticed the shocked expression on Liam's face. "It is the way of one fulcrum to impart his knowledge to another. Do you know what Rosenkreuz would do to possess the ancient knowledge that is buried inside of you?"

"Where the illuminatii would want me dead; he would want me alive and in his possession, so that he could retrieve the knowledge I possess."

"Exactly, Liam. He probably believes that your knowledge is all he is missing to become divine, to become the god he wishes to be. You must be prepared to face him and his kind," Tadhag Zheng stated grimly.

"Will you teach me?" asked Liam.

"Of course, I will. Though, I'm not sure what a simple monk like myself could teach a boy your age who already accomplished the feat of grounding a soul to him."

"You can see Thomas when he is around?" asked Liam.

"And hear him. To think I always thought I was one of Mr. Hollingsworth's favorite teachers. I didn't realize I bore him. Remind me to tell Sian Boru to put an enchantment around the girl's locker room when she returns. We can't have Mr. Hollingsworth disturbing their privacy, can we? You see that I am not without my own gifts," he said mildly.

"I believe you can teach me a great deal, Tadhag Zheng."

"Let us find out."

Caleb and Gundrun

In Southeastern California Joshua Tree National Park laid two desert regions, the low Colorado Desert and high Mojave Desert. Its arid stark beauty, a mix of colors of the desert punctuated by the deep green of life, embodied a sense of the ancient, a primordial, antediluvian time from when time immemorial sprang ancient knowledge and arts. Gundrun's coven kept a safe house hidden amongst the junipers, palms, creosote bushes, octillo, cholla cacti, and Joshua trees, from where the park got its name.

From his vantage point under a blanket Caleb stared as best as he could out the car window at the Joshua trees, whose branches recall the arms of the prophet Joshua with spear in hand pointing up to the city of Ai in ancient Greece. Although this desert looked lifeless, even at dusk as it was now, he knew that it actually teemed with life. From coyotes to kangaroo rats to bobcats, golden eagles, tarantulas and sidewinders, there was enough food for him here to recover quickly. Even though he drank deeply from the Se'irim Caleb had been damaged too badly to be useful until he had time to repair. They had been two days in the pickup and Gundrun and Una were feeling the effects of driving and sleeping in a tight pickup cab. But they were almost at the coven's safe house.

"What will you need when we get to the house?" asked Gundrun to Caleb.

"You can come out from beneath the blanket now, Mr. Keane,"

commented Una.

"Call me Caleb," Caleb said.

Slowly he pulled the blanket off. His always pale looking face was now grayish in pallor from the damage he had received in battle. His yellowish eyes were also turning blood red from hunger. His appearance startled Una, who wasn't used to vampires and their ways, so Gundrun placed a comforting hand on her shoulder.

"He's merely hungry, darling, so don't worry. Caleb would never harm us. Think of him as a man with a disease in which there is no cure and he deals with his disease as best as he can," she said to her daughter.

"Okay, ma," she responded then looked at Caleb, as if to wait for him to assuage her fears.

"She's right. I would never harm you. I'm merely hungry, but you don't have to worry because I don't eat cute little girls" he said as comfortingly as he could, though he knew he must have sounded a little intimidating. Over the years Caleb had little practice speaking to children of any age.

"So what can I get for you when we get to the house?" Gundrun once again asked.

"A dark room and either some animal blood or a small animal or two," he answered.

"Easy as pie," Gundrun stated.

"Hmm, pie. I haven't had pie in several lifetimes," Caleb said. "My favorite pie used to be a simple Shepard's pie. I preferred Lamb as the meat."

"We can make you one," Una said.

"That would be nice, but I wouldn't be able to eat it. My stomach can't hold real food. Every time I eat, I end up throwing it up or doing something worse with it," he told her.

"Why?" she asked.

"Because I am dead inside, Una. My body just can't handle food."

"Oh," she mumbled starting to realize just how difficult a life it was for Caleb. Being young she had romanticized it, but now seeing him suffering from hunger and hearing what he had to eat, she no longer thought the life of a vampire, even one with a soul, was romantic.

"Maybe we can make him something special with animal blood, Una, so that he can eventually sit and eat dinner with us and not feel out of place," Gundrun stated.

"Sure, we can try that," she answered with some pity in her voice for Caleb.

He heard that pity. It struck at his dead heart. Pity for him, pity for what he had become. Only human beings were truly capable of pity, an emotion he used to abhor because it reminded him of what he was, but now it was an emotion he understood. If he could, he would pity himself, too.

"If you two don't mind, I'm going back underneath my blanket until we get to the house," he said then slumped down on the backseat and pulled the blanket up over his head.

Within a few minutes the ride in the backseat got bumpy for Caleb. He guessed that they had left the main road and were now on one of those off the beaten track roads heading for the coven's safe house. For the next fifteen minutes he got bounced about in the back until finally the truck suddenly stopped.

"We're here," declared Gundrun.

He heard the passenger door open and Una get out. Pulling the blanket off his head he pried himself out of the backseat and joined Una and Gundrun as they stretched their legs. It was a beautiful starry night in the dessert with a sky full of stars looking like diamonds hanging from a navy blue canvas. A light breeze blew giving cooling relief to Gundrun and Una. Even on Caleb's dead flesh it felt refreshing.

He looked at the smallish, wooden house that was the safe house. All around them was nothing but the sounds and life of desert. There were no other buildings or home to be seen just a few Joshua Trees.

"This will be our home for now," Gundrun said.

"It's a bit isolated, isn't it?" asked Caleb.

"It isn't even supposed to be here," admitted Gundrun. "The coven has placed an enchantment on this little patch of land so that when you step or drive on it, you get a horrible feeling of doom and sickness then are compelled to leave. No one will bother us here."

"Unless they aren't bothered by a horrible feeling of doom or sickness," added Caleb.

Una and her mother both laughed. Caleb followed them into the small house. While Una prepared the backroom for him by hammering sheets over the windows, he sat on the sofa in the living room. Gundrun went off into the kitchen to take inventory on what they would need to survive. Once the backroom was ready, she came for Caleb.

"Get back there and lie down. Una and I are going to drive down to the gas station that doubled as a general store and pick up a few things. When we get back I'll get you some food."

"There's only one bed?" he asked.

"Yup," she replied.

"You and Una should have it."

"You need isolation and time to regenerate. Don't worry once you are better we will take the room."

"I agree," he said and got up unsteadily on his feet. Gundrun quickly moved in and steadied him then led him onto the bed in the back.

"Sleep well, Caleb. Dream beautiful dreams," she said then left him.

Caleb settled down on the bed and closed his eyes. He thought about her words - dream beautiful dreams. When he first became a vampire all he dreamt of was about tasting human blood, of hunting down human prey, and draining it of its life's blood. After he conquered his longing for blood, though, his dreams changed. Gone were the hunting and killing dreams, as they were replaced by dreams he felt were even more disturbing.

His replacement dreams were of a life he would never have. He dreamt of a wife and children, of sailing the blue seas as a captain, of eating fine foods and drinking good wines, and even of having simple friendships. These dreams he considered nightmares more than those other dreams because they caused him to wake up in the middle of the day with the wish to walk into the sunlight and get burned. But even those dreams passed.

Now whenever he dreamed it was of being chased by werecreatures or slaying demons. The dreams became nothing more than an extension of what he had become: an evil creature who destroyed other evil creatures. His dreams and his life were the same, a nightmare, until this night. With Gundrun's words ringing in his ears, he fell asleep and in that sleep he began to dream.

There standing in the room with him was Anna. She was dressed in black so that her pure white skin stood out. He tried to reach for Anna but instead of grabbing her he grabbed hold of a powerful dark creature whose skin felt cold and wet and whose teeth dug into the back of his neck. With all his strength he tried to pull away from the creature but it wouldn't release him. Instead it kept drawing all of the blood out of him until he was completely empty. When he was empty, the creature released him and then suddenly, right before his eyes, it turned back into Anna and she began to laugh. Caleb awoke with a start. Gundrun Ure was standing at the foot of the bed holding a picture of what he assumed was dark red blood.

"Dinner is served," she said then offered the pitcher to him.

"What kind of blood is it?" he asked.

"Rabbit," she answered.

"Thank you," he said then took the pitcher from her. He hesitated for a moment before drinking the blood. Gundrun looked at him with confusion.

"Aren't you hungry?" she asked.

"Yes, but..."

"But what?"

"But I feel ashamed drinking this in front of you," he admitted.

"Why?"

"It's disgusting. I'd like to think that you didn't have to see me drink blood to live because only the vilest, most foul creatures have to live off of the blood of others."

"Tell that to the mosquitos," she said with a smile. "I'm not ashamed of eating in front of you, so don't be ashamed to eat in front of me, Caleb. I like to think of your drinking blood as merely a unique diet."

"But..."

"But nothing, Caleb. You saved my life and Una's back there in San Francisco. We accept you for what you are, which is a good man. Now eat up."

His hunger overpowered his wish for privacy, so he lifted the pitcher of blood to his lips and began to drink. The blood flowed down his throat. He could feel his body react to the blood. Some more sleep and some more blood and he would be back to full strength.

"I'm sorry that I took so long to get you the blood," Gundrun said as she sat down on the edge of the bed.

"I didn't notice; I was asleep. My body uses sleep and blood to regenerate. Some vampires will sleep for a year when they have been damaged enough. My bones mend while I sleep."

"Well, I'm glad you don't need to take that much time. While you slept, I had a talk with many of my coven," she said with sadness in her voice.

"How? Phone?"

"We have no phones here. I used my crystal ball to contact them," she answered.

"Is everything all right, you seem upset?" Caleb asked then took another drink of the blood.

"I am upset. The Ser' irim attack has done more than destroy our store and kill; it has torn us apart. We are splitting up as a coven. Half my sisters seem to want to blame the Bene Lumen and the other half of them know well enough to blame the Illuminatii. Of course you know whom I blame. My mother always taught me that when the time came for us to stop being neutral that we must join the Bene Lumen. Do you think they will take me and my sisters?"

"Of course they would, especially you. You are an extremely talented witch, Gundrun. They will be glad to have you."

"I'm glad you feel that way. I know that you are considered well by the Bene Lumen," she said.

"I am not a member, but they treat me like one."

"Good, that should make this easier. As a matter of fact I have a favor to ask you," she said.

"What is it?"

"Those of us who blame the Illuminatii want to contact the Bene Lumen as soon as possible to offer our allegiance. Can you help us with that?"

"Of course I can. I was going to invite Brian CuCullen here for you to do a crystal ball reading for him..."

"He's a Tiarnán," she commented.

"Yes, he is."

"He will be able to help us?"

"Yes, he can."

"Then I will be glad to do a reading for him, Caleb. If he can help my sisters and me then I will do whatever is necessary. How can you contact him?"

"Believe it or not I expect him to contact me any day now through this," he said then placed the now half empty pitcher down on the table beside the bed and reached into his pocket and took out of black crystal and held it up for Gundrun to see.

"That is a halo crystal. When it turns the colors of a rainbow it connects a person with another person who has the sister halo crystal," she described the crystal for him as a way of letting him know she knew what it is. "We witches have a talent with sacred crystals."

"I expect to hear from Brian any day now," Caleb said. "He will be able to make any arrangements that are necessary for you and your sisters."

"Do you think he can arrange for Una to attend Samhain? I hear it's a better education than public school for what she is going to have to face in this life," she said with a smile.

"She's a little young for Samhain, but I bet he can work something out for you and her," he told her then reached for his food.

CHAPTER 21

The day had finally come for Kieran's last chance to run the obstacle course and achieve the time that Master Diaghilev had set for him so as to remain an Aongus Cathal. Now that his relationship with Nadia was slowly evolving into something more than just being friends, he was even more determined to run the course in less than twelve minutes. But his determination and his running time were two different things. The last time he ran the course, he still fell short of Diaghilev's time by 45 seconds. 45 seconds doesn't sound like a great deal of time, but it was.

Master Diaghilev had arranged for him to run it alone, which was a mixed blessing at best for him. Running it with others would mean that he would be pushed to keep up with other Aongus Cathal, but it also meant that if he lagged too far behind as he ran that his confidence would fade as well as his chances to achieve his needed time. In general competition was good because it gave you someone to pit yourself against, but Kieran was feeling oppressed by competition lately. Too many of his classmates passed him too easily on the course, and he felt humiliated by his effort. Running the course alone meant he was his own competition. He ran against no one but himself.

Dressing in his workout clothes and putting on his trainers, he left O'CuChulainn House to be met by Nadia and Liam. It was a beautiful day, not too hot and not too chilly, with no humidity. Both Liam and Nadia appeared to be both excited and nervous for him. Everyone else who wanted to see him take his last chance to remain an Aongus Cathal was waiting at the obstacle course for him.

"Are you ready, Kieran?" asked Nadia.

"No, but I don't have a choice."

"How much time do you need?" asked Liam.

"45 seconds."

"That much?" Liam gasped.

"If you can overcome your fear of running across the tightrope you could make up some of that time that you need right there," Nadia told him.

"And if I can run faster and not be exhausted at the end of the course, I'd make up for the rest of the time. It can be done but I may have run out of time, no pun intended," Kieran admitted.

"Bro, you have to do this," Liam blurted out sounding slightly panicked.

"Hey, I'll try. Where's Selena?" asked Kieran.

"Waiting for us at the course. She's holding a spot up front for Nadia and I. Thomas is looking after her to make sure no one bothers her," Liam told him.

"Good. I'm starting to like Thomas."

"Bro, you have to do this. You have to be an Aongus Cathal," Liam stated.

"Do not put too much pressure on your brother," Nadia warned him, "he needs to remain centered and calm, if he is to do his best."

"Yeah, chill out, Liam," Kieran said.

"But, Kieran, you don't understand..."

"I understand. I don't want to be Ardal Cathal. You know me, Liam, I'm pretty competitive I like being the best I can be and nothing less."

"You don't understand, Kieran, I need you to be an Aongus Cathal," he shouted in anger wanting his brother to understand just how important it was for him to be Aongus Cathal, for him to live up to his potential.

Kieran stood and stared at his brother. Liam was never a shouter in the house. His father shouted on occasion, not too often, and he shouted, maybe too often, but Liam always tried to be calm. Liam shouting was a sign that his brother knew something that Kieran didn't know, but he didn't want to tell him what it was. He knew his baby brother well enough to know when Liam was keeping an important secret.

"What's wrong, Liam, what aren't you telling me?" he asked his brother.

"Kieran, it's just important that you remain an Aongus Cathal and fulfill your potential."

"No, it's more than that. You yelled at me. You don't yell, Liam, unless it's important or you are frustrated. What are you hiding from me?"

"You have to get going, Kieran. It is almost time," Nadia interrupted.

"I'm not going anywhere, Nadia, not until my brother tells me the truth."

Kieran stood his ground and stared at his brother. There was no softness in his stare, only determination to find out what the secret was his brother was keeping from him. For his part Liam knew that he needed to tell his brother the truth, but how much of the truth he wasn't sure. He could tell him everything from who he was to who Kieran was in the scope of things, or he could tell him a cold truth that their father had kept from them for many years. Liam somehow knew that the truth of their mother's death would push his brother to fulfill his destiny. He took a deep breath and prepared himself to tell his brother the truth.

"You need to be an Aongus Cathal in order to help me revenge our mother's death," Liam said knowing those well chosen words would have a strong effect on him.

With those words Kieran looked as if someone slapped him across his face. He took a step back away from his brother then looked to his right at Nadia. Even though she didn't really understand what Liam was talking about since she knew that their mother was considered a fallen hero, she saw the effect the words had on Kieran. She gently placed her right hand on his shoulder. Kieran looked back to Liam, who stood there on the sidewalk waiting to tell him the truth about their mother.

"Our mother died from a hiking accident. How can you revenge an accident?" Kieran asked.

"It wasn't an accident, Kieran, she was murdered by a powerful demon."

"What are you talking about, Liam, dad told us it was an accident. How can an accident become a murder?"

"Dad didn't tell us the truth, Kieran. He couldn't tell us the truth because he didn't want us to become Bene Lumen and be exposed..."

"He lied to us about our mother's death," Kieran shouted as his body filled with anger towards his father.

"How was he supposed to tell two little boys that their mother was killed by a demon named Baal while he was away fighting another demon? How could he tell us two boys that, Kieran? Would you have even understood what he was talking about? Our father didn't do anything wrong, except try to protect us from nightmares of our mother being murdered. But you can't protect people from the truth in the end, Kieran. You shouldn't be angry at dad you should want to kill Baal."

"Who is Baal?" asked Kieran.

"He is a very powerful demon, a sort of proto-demon, boss demon, who leads those demons who make it into this world. Baal has personally killed many Bene Lumen," Nadia told him as she stared at Kieran with concern.

"You need to fulfill your potential in order to help me defeat Baal and others like him, Kieran. Together we can do it," Liam told his brother.

"I can't believe that ma was murdered," Kieran said more to himself than anyone else.

"Kieran, it was because of her murder that dad left the Bene Lumen, so that he could raise us away from danger. He didn't want us to become part of the society, but then Paulette, who replaced him as Tiarnán, died and he owed her a great deal. Headmaster Fergus encouraged dad to come back to the Bene Lumen. He never wanted us to know the truth because he never wanted us to live this life."

"He was wrong not to tell us," Kieran simply stated.

"Kieran, you are going to be late for your run," Nadia said gently trying to get him away from his brother.

"Let's go," he stated and started walk towards the obstacle course area.

Liam knew what he did was difficult, maybe even risky, but it had to be done. Kieran needed a shock to his system to get him to give his best. He needed his brother to be his champion, which meant he needed to give his brother a reason to push through his insecurities. Revenging their mother's murder was that lever.

Kieran strode silently towards his challenge. Thoughts of his mother dying by the hands of a demon kept pushing all other thoughts out of his mind. She didn't have an accident; she was murdered. And their father knew. But Liam was right about their father he wasn't the problem. The problem for Kieran was finding a way to revenge their mother. He needed to remain and train as an Aongus Cathal and then become a Tiarnán.

As he approached the obstacle course paddock, Kieran noticed that Mallory, Diaghilev, and Talbot were waiting for him. He wasn't in the mood for advice or unnecessary talk. All he wanted was the chance to prove he belonged there. Mallory turned to Diaghilev and Talbot and said a few words. Both men walked away leaving Mallory alone. Kieran walked up to him, while Liam and Nadia continued walking towards the spot where

Selena with the help of Thomas held seats for them.

"What is wrong?" Mallory asked him.

"Nothing."

"Don't lie to me, Kieran. You and I are bonded friends now. Your burden is my burden," he told the young man.

"My brother just told me the truth about my mother's death," he stated coldly.

"Ahhh, your brother had an interesting sense of timing," Mallory said.

"Yes, he does, Headmaster."

"And I take it that you are angry and want to take revenge," Mallory stated.

"Yes, but I also want to remain Aongus Cathal, so that I have a chance to become a Tiarnán. I want the best training I can get," Kieran told him.

"Well, then, you are finally a true Bene Lumen. You understand the need for our ways and training for the enemy we battle. Are you ready to run this course?" he asked.

"Yes, sir, I'm ready."

"Good. Here is the advice that I give you then," Mallory said then took a deep breath. "You are filled with anger right now, so use that anger. A true warrior uses whatever is at his disposal in order to be victorious. Don't suppress your anger, but don't let it overwhelm you, either. Anger can get adrenaline pumping, which can then break down the final barriers that you have on your muscles. Do not hold back when you run this course today otherwise you will have regrets. Warriors leave all regrets on the field of battle. Let your bodywork to its fullest capabilities. You have it within you to be a great Tiarnán, Kieran, so trust that and let your instincts and body do the work. In other words turn off your mind, which tells you what you can or can't do, and let those gifts which God gave you shine through."

"Sir," Kieran mumbled, "why?"

"Why was your mother murdered?"

"Yes."

"Because she stood for balance and light, she stood against the Illuminatii, and that meant she stood in the way of someone like Baal, who wants to bring a new dark age to this world. She was Bene Lumen and proud to be so, Kieran, just like I am Bene Lumen and Sian Boru and all those Bene Lumen, who stand in the way of the Illuminatii. I hope you will feel this way someday," Mallory said then walked away leaving Kieran with his anger and his thoughts.

Kieran walked slowly towards Talbot, who waited for him at the starting line of the course. Mallory's words managed to take the heat out of his anger without removing the energy. He was as ready to run this course, as he'd ever be.

"I'm not going to ask what is wrong, but I do have something to say," Talbot said.

"Yes, Talbot," Kieran said resigned to hear what his private tutor was going to say.

"Leave whatever you have inside of you on the course. Don't run this today and then think later - oh, I could have done better. Give it all you have," he told Liam.

"I will, Talbot."

"Good," he said, "get ready."

Kieran began to loosen up. Now that his mind had taken in everything he had been told, he finally stopped to look about him. Temporary stands had been set up to allow for students and teachers to watch him run the obstacle course. The stands were filled to capacity, as was all the other areas around the obstacle course. It looked as if most of the school had turned out to watch him run this course.

Between saving Mallory's life and killing the tengu, Liam's standing in the school as a remarkable Triune Conjurer, and his Ruadh team making the playoffs and doing well, Kieran had become well known by the whole school. It didn't hurt that his father was Brian CuCullen, either. He wondered if they were there to cheer him or to watch him fail. Finishing his stretching he walked up to the starting line. Talbot patted him on the back then turned to Diaghilev who stood off to the side with Nadia by his side.

"He's ready," Talbot told him.

Diaghilev walked up to Kieran. Nadia joined him. Where master Diaghilev looked stern and patient, Nadia looked to be worried for Kieran.

"If you succeed young CuCullen, I have a reward planned for you," Diaghilev said.

"What is it?"

"I thought you, your brother and a few of your invited guests will be my guest into the town for a day of relaxation, maybe even a hike into the hills. Highlanders say that the Scottish hills are magical, that they give you strength," Diaghilev said.

"The headmaster has disallowed any off island trips unless it to go home," stated Talbot.

"Don't worry, Donovan, I have permission to reward Kieran if he succeeds. Now you have something to run for," Diaghilev said and then walked away.

"You have the best reason to succeed here today, Kieran: your family's honor. I know you can do this," Nadia said then leaned forward and kissed Kieran on the right cheek then joined her uncle.

With the feeling of Nadia's lips on his cheek, Kieran got into position at the starting line. He lowered his body into a sprinter's take off position then when he felt everything was perfect he took off. From the moment he placed his right foot down, he never felt faster. It was as if his anger was rocket fuel giving him a boost. He reached the boulders and lifted one onto his shoulder without a problem then quickly carried it to the podium and placed it on it. Returning to the other boulder he did the same thing then continued on. This was the best he had ever felt running the obstacle course.

Kieran legs moved easily without hesitation or effort. They were like two pistons powering him to go faster and faster. Deep inside he knew that the thought of revenging his mother's death was pushing him to trust the gifts that he was born with. He moved through the course better than he thought possible. Up the tower he climbed getting to the top in a matter of seconds. Once he was at the top he ran across the tightrope for the first time ever. It made sense and it was easy.

Once he was down from the second tower, Kieran took a deep breath filling his lungs with air and took off for the last leg of the course. He was sure he was going to improve his time enough to continue as Aongus Cathal. Onward his pushed himself getting to the jungle gym made of the thorns. He ripped through it this time not caring if his skin was cut open or not. Once through he lowered his head and got his legs pumping again running the last mile faster than he had ever run a mile before in his life.

When he got to the he drove across it rolling onto the ground. Suddenly, his lungs were aching for air and his body throbbed with pain. Whatever trance he had gone into to run the obstacle course had been lifted. All over his body he felt little cuts and abrasions from the jungle gym bleeding. As he started to get up, he heard what sounded like the whole school yelling and screaming his name. Liam, Selena, Nadia, and Talbot ran to his side.

"Bro, you did it," screamed Liam, "you've never run so fast in your life."

"Did it?"

"Kieran, you're amazing," Selena told him as she helped him to sit up.

"He is bleeding. I will get some bandages," Nadia said then took off.

Kieran wanted to stop her and thank her for believing in him, but she took off too quickly. He wondered why.

"You did it, Kieran, you did it," Talbot yelled over all the voices and cheering.

"What was my time?" asked Kieran between pants for air.

"9 minutes and 24 seconds. Can you believe it Kieran? You did it! You really did it. You are now second only to your father in the best time for this course. I must be a better trainer than I thought," Talbot told him.

Is that why Nadia bolted off so quickly? Was she mad that I bettered her time or had I become her chief rival and you can't date your chief rival, the person who could stop you from becoming a Tiarnán?

"Congratulations, Aongus Cathal, it looks like you have done it," Boris Diaghilev said admiringly.

Liam and Selena helped Kieran to his feet. Selena stood by Kieran's side squeezing his right hand in her left hand. Once Kieran appeared to be steady on his feet Liam and gave him a bear hug. He had not lost his champion, as he feared. His brother was sill on track to be another Arthur.

"You told me about ma so that I would run like this today," Kieran whispered into his brother's ear.

"Maybe," Liam whispered back but the smug smirk on his lips told his brother that he did it on purpose.

"Thanks, Liam."

"I need you, Bro," Liam replied.

"If you say so," Kieran said then noticed Nadia jogging back to him with a first aid kit.

Teachers and students from the crowd, including his Ruadh team, swept him up, though, and carried him off before she could get to him with the first aid kit. Riding on the shoulders of fellow Aongus Cathal he searched the crowd for Nadia but couldn't find her. She had disappeared in the crowd.

Brian see's Caleb at Joshua Tree

Brian CuCullen felt an overwhelming sense of nausea as he drove through Joshua Tree National Park. It was a hot sunny day, but he knew that the weather or the sun wasn't the cause of his nausea. The stomach churning he felt had no natural causes but was from an enchantment. In the backseat of their Ford Jeep he heard Running Deer moan as if he was fighting the feeling to vomit. Glancing to his left he noticed the nonplused demeanor of Sian Boru as she stared out of the passenger window.

"This place is breath taking," she commented.

"I feel sick," Running Deer moaned.

"That's Gundrun Ure's enchantment," Sian explained. "It's a wonderfully effective bit of work. The closer you get to the safe house, the sicker you feel until finally you can't take it any longer and have to leave," she said. "It keeps the place safe and hidden."

"I'm going to vomit," Running Deer exclaimed then bent over and started to heave on the backseat floor.

"Oh, please, don't do that," Brian pleaded as he felt bile begin to move up his throat towards his mouth. He fought it back, concentrating with all his mental power to keep himself from getting sick. Sian Boru turned to look at him. Her expression was more amused than concerned.

"As a Tiarnán you should be able to fight through this feeling until we get to this safe house then this Gundrun Ure can give you the potion she's prepared to lessen the effects of the enchantment," Sian told him.

"Why can't you help us?" asked Brian.

"I explained that already. I am able to make myself immune to this enchantment, but I'd need more time to find the correct ingredients to make a potion for you and Running Deer. From the pallor of your skin..."

"What color am I?" he asked.

"A light green," she said.

"Oh," he murmured.

"From your pallor, I'd say that we are almost there," she stated.

"Oh," Running Deer mumbled then vomited again.

"I wish you could drive," Brian said to Sian as he fought back another wave of sickness.

"I am a druid priestess who lives on the mist isle of Samhain, I have no reason to drive a car and no knowledge to do so," she stated then caught sight of the small wooden house they were looking for.

"There it is," she said.

Brian drove the car towards the house. He parked right beside Gundrun Ure's car. They all got out with Running Deer and Brian immediately bending over and vomiting on the ground. Gundrun exited the house holding a glass with a sort of pale green colored liquid.

"You must be Sian Boru," she said as she approached.

"I am."

"I have heard much about you. Your reputation extends even into San Francisco," Gundrun said and then offered Sian her free hand to shake. They shook hands. Gundrun then handed Brian the glass of pale green liquid.

"Drink half of this down quickly then sip the rest, it will stop your sickness fairly quick," she said. "Give the other half to your associate."

She turned her attention back towards Sian, who watched with a smile as Brian attempted to take a sip of the liquid. Brian tasted the liquid, which had the flavor of what he assumed old molded grass tasted like. He was sure he'd be able to drink it then another wave of nausea flooded his system, so he started to drink the horrible tasting liquid.

"The potion takes about ten minutes to take effect, and then they should start to feel better," Gundrun explained to Sian. "Can I invite you into the house for something cool to drink."

"I'd enjoy that," Sian said then turned to Brian. "When you stop vomiting, please join us."

The two women walked into the house. In the living room area, which had black curtains drawn so no light could get in, Caleb played cards with Una on the floor. Seeing Sian, Caleb got up so quickly and gracefully that it almost seemed like he appeared beside Sian. He took her right hand in his and held it.

"It has been years," he said, "and you are still lovely to look at."

"I was twelve the last time we met," she said.

"I remember. Where is Brian?" he asked.

"Outside with our Fiach, Running Deer. Both of them are feeling a little sick."

"They should be ready to come in soon," Gundrun interrupted.

"If it was nighttime I'd go keep them company," Caleb said, "but I don't feel up to be scalded by the sun at the moment."

"Una come," Gundrun said to her daughter, who got up from floor and joined them.

"Una, this is Sian Boru. She is a Triune Conjurer, which means she has powers which any witch in our coven would be jealous of," Gundrun introduced Sian to her daughter.

"Hi," Una simply said.

"Hello, Una. Do you mind if I place my hand on your forehead?" Sian asked her.

"No."

Sian placed her left hand on the child's forehead. Not unlike what she did with Liam she reached inside of the young girl to touch her powers seeing what potential she had stored inside of her. There nestled within her were her young, still sleeping powers. She smiled.

"Do you know what I just did?" asked Sian.

"No," answered Una.

"Do you want to know?"

"Yes."

"I touched your powers. And let me tell you, Una, you have wonderful potential," Sian told her.

"Really, I do," the young girl said excitedly.

"Will she be able to divine?" asked Gundrun.

"Oh, yes. She will be able to divine. And she has inherited her mother's potion making skills. But I also sense a Celtic power, an ability to partner with nature. Was her father a Celt?"

"He was Irish descent," Gundrun replied.

"Was he a druid?"

"No, he was a policeman."

"Well, he had druid bloodline. I would love to get you at Samhain, Una."

"I hope that she and I can both go there someday," Gundrun said.

Brian and Running Deer came bursting into the house. Both of them looked as if they had just gone through the worst experience of their lives. Each had pale skin and was sweating profusely. Sian once again smiled at Brian's suffering.

"Don't worry, you are both going to Samhain," Brian stated. "I talked to Mallory and he agreed. He is going off to meet with the Council of Guaire to settle everything in relations to those in your coven who seek the protection of the Bene Lumen. He will work out the details and present them to you. Until then all in your coven who wish our protection will be given a number of safe houses to go to where Ardal Cathal and conjurers will be waiting to take them in. I have the locations here."

Brian CuCullen reached into the left back pocket of his jeans and took out a folded piece of paper. Unfolding it, he handed it to Gundrun. On the paper was the location of six safe houses located in various parts of the United States and Canada. Gundrun looked at the paper for a moment then sighed in relief. Here was the chance for those in her coven who wanted to stay out of the reach of the Illuminatii to find safe haven.

"Thank you, I will let my sisters know," Gundrun said folded the paper and placed it in her own jeans' pocket then turned and gave Caleb a hug.

For a moment Caleb was startled by her intimacy then he returned her hug. He felt an almost paternal feeling towards Gundrun and Una. She broke the embrace off.

"When do we leave?" asked Una.

"First things are first," said Gundrun to Una, "go into the kitchen and get Running Deer, Brian CuCullen, and Sian Boru some cold lemonade."

The young girl went off to get the drinks. Gundrun motioned everyone to sit down. Running Deer still feeling the after effects of the sickness and the cure, decided to slump down against the wall not bothering to get a seat. Brian gingerly made his way to the sofa and sat down. Sian joined him. Gundrun and Caleb sat down at the small table where Gundrun and Una ate their meals.

"You need me to do a crystal ball reading," said Gundrun.

"Yes," Brian replied.

"Your coven has a unique ability of divination with the crystal ball. From what I've learned it is up to 94 percent accurate, which is remarkable. 73 percent is the best accuracy attained by our own diviners in the Bene Lumen," Sian Boru commented.

"Yes, but your divination is more far reaching. You can divine specific information such as asking if a certain person is in the process of committing some act or other. What our divination does is read the circumstances surrounding people. I can tell you if someone is in immediate danger or if not now if they might be in danger or not in the near future. If it is a truly strong reading I may get a shadow of the person who is causing the danger, but I won't get an easily read image. We read images the crystal ball shows us and interpret them," Gundrun explained.

"Which is what I need," said Brian. "I want you to do a reading about my sons. I know the Illuminatii are planning something against them, but I need to know if or when they will be in danger so that I can warn Mallory to plan security and a trap around them. If we can catch whoever they send to kill them next time, we might be able to get important Intel from them."

"You sound like a warrior," Gundrun said in a sad vice. "Warriors frighten many of my sisters. We have avoided them because of the violence around you. My coven has avoided violence for so long, thinking we could remain above the fray, but I guess it is unavoidable now."

Una returned from the kitchen with a tray of five empty glasses and a pitcher filled with lemonade and ice. She placed it down on the table near where Caleb sat. He gave her an uncharacteristic smile, which Brian and Sian noticed. Caleb appeared to be happy in the company of this witch and her daughter.

"Should I get you a bloody Mary?" asked Una to Caleb.

"No, I'm not hungry," he answered then reached over and took a glass and poured Una some lemonade.

"If you're playing mother, I could use a cold drink," Brian said to him.

"Sorry, Tiarnán, I'm no one's mother," Caleb retorted.

"I'll serve you," Gundrun said then began to pour everyone some lemonade.

"What do you need for a reading?" Brian asked her as she handed him a cold drink.

"I will need you, as their closest relative, and, if possible, an object or objects that they have touched. It is better if these objects have some importance to your sons," she said.

"In the car I have Kieran's football helmet and an old video game of Liam's," he said.

"That should do fine," Gundrun told him.

"What game?" asked Una.

"It's a game called Splinter Cell. He used to play it for hours upon hours. I never knew what it was about until recently when I found it and put it into his Playstation just to check it out," Brian said.

"Splinter Cell, that's a great game. Stealth and assassination," commented Running Deer after he drank down all his lemonade. "I played that until I mastered it."

"Well, if I knew what it was about I wouldn't have let Liam play it. But... but I never checked the games he played," Brian admitted.

"I wish my father was like you. He checked out my games constantly," Running Deer said then he got up from the floor and went to the pitcher of lemonade to pour another drink. When he got beside Caleb he stared at the vampire. Caleb finally looked up at him and bared his fangs for a moment, as if to tell Running Deer to stop staring.

"Sorry, dude, I've never seen a vampire this close before," he explained.

"Well, you should hope that you never do again because unlike me the rest of my kind would be going for a major artery right now," Caleb warned him.

"Got ya," Running Deer said then poured himself another drink and returned to his spot on the floor.

"So when can we do this reading?" asked Brian.

"First I would like to contact as many as my sisters as I can and give them the addresses of the Bene Lumen safe houses. I also want to prepare them for the fact that warriors will greet them. Once that is done, I can prepare for a reading," Gundrun told him.

"Can I help you with your preparation?" asked Sian.

"That would be lovely of you. Usually one of my sisters would help prepare me to reach the right level of consciousness for divining, but I am alone here. It would be wonderful if you could help me. I know that the druids have similar methods in attaining levels of consciousness as we do."

"It would be an honor, Gundrun. And maybe as we are getting you ready I can discuss the possibility of you teaching at Samhain. We can always use another instructor in the arts of potions and divination," Sian said.

"I am honored," Gundrun replied.

"Does that mean I can go to school there?" asked Una.

"Of course it means that," said Sian, "we also are always looking for good students of great potential just like you."

"And it doesn't hurt if they are cute like you," said Running Deer.

Una blushed then unexpectedly she turned to face Caleb, who seemed happy for Gundrun and Una. He looked at her and gave her a pleasant smile.

"You'll visit us at Samhain, won't you?" she asked him.

"Of course he will," replied Gundrun for him.

Caleb looked to Brian CuCullen for help on this matter. Brian knew that he swore never to pollute a place with his presence unless he had no choice. He had been asked there many times but had never gone to the Samhain or to Avalon. Brian did not speak up for him though. Instead he faced Caleb with a look of defiance as if to say - refuse this young girl who you seem to like and who seems to bring out your humanity.

"I'm sorry, Una, but I've never been to Samhain and I'll never go," he told her.

Una looked at him with confusion. She couldn't understand why he would not or could not visit them on Samhain. Gundrun decided to speak for her daughter.

"Why?"

"Because, Gundrun, it's not a place for the likes of me," he answered.

"Why?"

"Because I am a product of evil."

"No, you aren't," Una exclaimed.

"I am a vampire, Una. That is an abomination in league with darkness. Sounds evil to me. A vampire is evil," he stated.

"But you have a soul," the little girl countered.

"That does not change the fact of what I am," he replied.

"But your actions do, Caleb," Gundrun stated. "You have proven to be more than your nature. You are not evil, Caleb, so stop living behind a lie. If you don't visit us at Samhain, you will be evil, though."

"I couldn't have put it better myself, Gundrun," added Sian.

"Brian, help me explain this to them," Caleb pleaded with Brian CuCullen.

"I've learned never to argue with women, especially when they are right. You would think that someone as old as you would have learned that lesson by now," Brian told him.

"But..."

"But nothing. You will visit us. End of argument," Gundrun said then turned to Sian. "I need to contact my sisters then we can get ready for the reading."

"I look forward to having you at Samhain, Gundrun. You will be like a breath of fresh air. I'm afraid that the old school has too many rules and you strike me as a rule breaker," Sian commented.

"I've been known to bend a rule or two," said Gundrun.

"My mother has always told me that you should speak your mind and do what you feel is right," Una interrupted.

"Yes, you will be good for the old school. Isn't that right, Caleb?" Sian asked him.

"I'm afraid to answer in case I say the wrong thing," he answered.

"Good choice," Brian answered.

"I hate to be a buzzkill, but we have a traitor to find and, you know, a plot against the Bene Lumen to uncover," Running Deer declared, "shouldn't we get to work."

"Yeah, it's time to get to work," Brian agreed.

CHAPTER 22

Boris thought it best to take a nice hike before allowing his wards to enjoy the sights and comforts of the town. In his opinion it was best to get some exercise in before they enjoyed some leisurely pursuits, just so that you keep your muscles and your senses fine-tuned. Even on vacation trouble was never too far away for a Bene Lumen, so you must always be prepared. Boris planned on an overnight stay in a local Inn for him, Kieran, and his chosen guests: Liam, Selena, Jan, Jean Pierre, and Philippe, and Nadia. They would have a nice dinner at a restaurant in Fort Augustus, a good breakfast in the morning, some shopping, maybe even a movie, and then return to Samhain. Kieran earned this reward, he thought as he walked along a tree. Boris had yet to tell Kieran, but he had never seen one student make such a great improvement in one year in all his time at Samhain.

It was a gorgeous day to roam the hills around Loch Ness. With no humidity the weather Master Diaghilev thought it perfect for a hike in the surrounding verdant Scottish hills and mountains. Ever since he had come to Samhain as a boy he had loved these hills with their large clusters of thick trees filling up much of the hillside then stretches of treeless grassy space. Once they exited the trees entering into one of the treeless areas, he turned to stare down at the waters of the loch through a patch a morning haze. From his vantage point he could see the ruins as well as an Inn and hotel along the shoreline where tourists stayed, and the beauty of the countryside he had come to love. With some efforts he even could see the crumbling remains of Urquhart Castle. He turned and continued his hike.

Diaghilev would have preferred a more strenuous bit of exercise like running the Scottish Highlands, but this would have to do for the students as exercise. He did promise that this would be a vacation, a reward, not another training exercise he forced them to do. Looking over to his left he saw Liam, Selena, Jean Pierre, Philippe, and Jan leaving the lower tree line as they straggled along at a slower pace. Liam also wanted his two close friends, Dani and Brigid, to come, but Boris wanted to keep this to as few students as possible. He didn't like the idea of having to keep a close eye on too many. To his right he saw Nadia and Kieran hiking together in the open grassy area. They appeared to be in deep conversation not even bothering to enjoy the sights and sounds of nature. Though, he didn't mind Nadia making friends with Kieran, he didn't want him to interfere in her training to become a Tiarnán. He wondered what they were talking about with each other.

"I hope you are glad that I'll be Aongus Cathal next year," Kieran said to Nadia.

At first she didn't answer but instead looked about at the beauty of nature about them. This was the first time she and Kieran had a chance to talk since he ran the obstacle course in such brilliant fashion. When he invited her on this trip, she was with some other students and told him that they would be able to talk later. It was now later.

"Kieran, I am very glad that you will be Aongus Cathal, also," she responded, though he wasn't sure that she sounded very glad. Of course, he often had trouble discerning her emotions from her accent. Although she didn't have a heavy Russian accent, she had enough of one to make her sound either slightly detached or bored when speaking English.

"Are you really very glad for me?" he asked letting a little sarcasm enter his tone. "You don't seem glad, or happy, that I did it, that I succeeded. What is it, Nadia? Did I run it too fast for your taste?"

"No, Kieran," she said sharply, "it is not that. The problem is something different. You just don't understand do you, Kieran? You don't understand me."

"Help me understand the problem then! Help me understand you. Come on, Nadia, you owe me that much. I thought over the last year that we had become at least friends."

"Now that we are rivals I am afraid that you won't want to train with me anymore, or to be with me like we have spent time with each other," she said quietly trying to make sure that no one could overhear them. What she didn't know was that Thomas was hanging over them as they spoke listening to every word they said.

"That's stupid," he exclaimed.

"Stupid! Are you saying that I am stupid," she snapped.

"No, so don't get your Irish up..."

"Irish up?"

"Yeah, it's an expression my father uses to tell Liam and me not to get angry too quickly. What I meant was that what you said was stupid, you are not stupid, you know that you aren't stupid, I know it," he told her. "Of course I'll want to continue to train with you, Nadia. I like spending time with you. You're one of the reasons I wanted to remain an Aongus Cathal. I like training with you; I like being with you. I mean... I think you know how I feel about you."

"No, I don't," she said coyly, "how do you feel about me, Kieran?"

"You know... I like you."

"Like me?"

"Yes, like you."

"What is like me?"

"Like you means that I want to be your training partner; I want to be your friend; I want to be your best friend, your boyfriend, maybe," he said while looking down at the grass.

"Really?" she asked with a bright smile on her face.

"Yeah..."

"Watch out," yelled Boris in his most authoritative voice from a short distance away from them.

Emerging from the tree line was a gargoyle-like demon and it was headed in their direction. The demon was well over six feet in height, but made to look taller with it human-like upper body and satyr-like lower body, with blackened skin that appeared to have scales all over it. The face of the creature was hideous with red carbuncle eyes; long yellow fangs protruding from its mouth, and its hands had long feline claws, which he swiped about itself as if it was limbering up to do battle.

Boris came running up beside Kieran and Nadia with his sword, which he had hidden in his knapsack, drawn and ready for battle. He was looking about trying to judge what would be the best thing to do with his students. Kieran and Nadia fell into defensive posture behind him.

"No, you are not staying here to fight with me. You must get everyone out of here, get them to safety," he said.

"But we can't leave you here," Nadia said.

"I am the only one with a weapon. You have to leave me here and protect the rest of the group, get them to safety. It is your duty. Kieran, Nadia, this has been a setup. You must also let the headmaster know that somehow someone has set this up. There must be an Illuminatii mole at Samhain."

"What is that thing?" asked Kieran.

"It is a Nain, a Celtic demon," Boris answered.

"From Scotland?" Kieran asked.

"No, it makes its home in Brittany not here. It should not even be here at all, which is why I know that we have been setup. Someone had it lying in wait for us," Boris stated.

"How do we fight it?" Kieran asked.

"We don't fight it. I fight it. Besides being impervious to most metals, except Calibur, he is very, very strong and also has some magical powers. Calibur is immune to its magic, which negates the Nain's power of casting. Calibur can cut through all of its defenses, including its thick ugly skin," he explained.

"Uncle your sword is not Calibur," Nadia stated. "You didn't bring your Calibur blade."

"I know that, Nadia. This demon is too powerful for you and Kieran. It is too powerful for me alone. You and Nadia must take the rest of the group and get out of here while I occupy it and give you time."

"Uncle..."

"Nadia, I am a trainer of Tiarnán and Aongus Cathal. To die in battle will be an honor, considering how many I trained to die in battle, so don't make it a wasted honor by staying here and getting yourself killed," he said gently to her.

"Uncle," she said in a low voice, "I understand. I will do what you want."

"I don't understand," Kieran stated.

"We must go," she said and pulled him away to where Liam, Selena, Jean Pierre, Philippe, and Jan stood transfixed by the demon's appearance. Reluctantly, Kieran went with her. He wanted to stay with Boris, not just to prove that he was worthy of Aongus Cathal, but that he was Brian CuCullen's son, a Tiarnán's son. They finally reached the others, who were all in a state of tense preparation.

"Liam, is Thomas with us?" he asked his brother.

"Yes," Liam said calmly as he stared at the ugly demon that Boris was now facing down.

"Send him back to Samhain for help," Kieran ordered.

Liam looked up in the air above his head where Thomas hovered. He, too, was transfixed by this demon. Liam cleared his throat to get his attention. Thomas looked down at Liam.

"Go to Samhain and get us help," he said.

"Liam, I shouldn't leave you," Thomas said, "you might need my help, Mate. I know I can help you."

"I don't think you'll be able to scare that thing away, Thomas. Get help for us. They will be the best help you can give us right now," he said.

"Okay," Thomas replied then took off in the direction of Samhain.

"Oh, God," Nadia whispered as she watched the Nain growl a few words turning Boris' sword into a piece of wood then it attacked him.

Boris attempted to dodge the Nain's attack, but it was faster than he expected. Although Boris trained Aongus Cathal and Tiarnán, he had very little field experience. As a young man he was chosen to be a trainer of warriors but not a warrior. As the Nain galloped towards him with a slash from its right then left hand, the demon left Boris, who unsuccessfully dodged the blows, bleeding deeply from several deep wounds. It then raised itself up on its front legs and gave him a mighty kick with its back legs sending him hurtling through the air. Both Nadia and Kieran knew that Boris Diaghilev must be done for.

"Nadia take everyone into the woods and try to hide them until help arrives. This thing will be on us in seconds unless one of us stands our ground to slow it down," Kieran said then whispered to himself, "I wish I had my sword with me. It's made of Calibur."

"I should face it not you," she told him. "I have better training, better skills than you."

"I'm not going to argue that with you now. You'll be the second line of defense in case it gets by me. Now go," he ordered her in a tone that made him sound like his father.

"Bro, I'm not leaving you. Together we can face this thing. You and I are meant to face these things together. Believe it or not, it's our destiny," Liam interrupted them.

"Liam, I know you are a badass conjurer, but you need to survive this and for reasons I don't understand. Go with Nadia," Kieran said.

"None of us are going. We are Bene Lumen; we do not run from demons, we face them and fight them," Jan stated.

"Yeah," said Jean Pierre and Philippe together.

"Thomas has gone for help, so all we have to do is last until they get here. We can do that," Selena said.

"But Master Diaghilev had a weapon and he didn't last that long against this demon," Kieran said.

"He trained us to last long, though," Nadia said proudly of her uncle.

The Nain turned and looked at the Samhain students. He laughed to himself. It was a horrible sound, a mix of pitiless gargling with base satisfaction. They watched as it prepared itself to charge them, but before it could Boris, who had unexpectedly gotten up from the Nain's kick, came up behind it and jumped on its back. He tried to ride it like a wild bronco, but the Nain reached behind itself and with its talons dug its left hand into his back and spine. He screamed with great pain, as the Nain picked him up and tossed him aside.

Nadia gasped. Her Uncle was now truly dead. Kieran put his right arm around her and gently squeezed her shoulders. She stiffened to attention as he did this. Nadia was now ready for battle.

"It's our turn to stop it," he said to her.

"I know."

"What do you have in mind?" Kieran asked.

"I was thinking that you and I would be the first line of defense. Jan and Nadia the second line of defense, and Jean Pierre, Philippe and Selena, the last line. Hopefully, this will allow some of us to survive and also offer the demon a different set of attacks to deal with each time," Liam said.

"Sounds good to me," Kieran said.

"But not to me," added Nadia.

"Nadia, you and Jan get ready in case Liam and I fail," Kieran ordered, though in a gentle tone. "Please don't argue."

"But if we all attack at once," Nadia countered, "we might..."

"Get some of us killed quickly," Liam said. "Nadia, this is the best way. Kieran and I need to do this together. Trust me."

"Kieran," she said in almost a whisper.

"Please, Nadia, go get ready in case we fail," he told her.

Nadia turned and joined Jan, who was staring at the Nain with hate in her eyes. She looked as if she wanted to be the first line of defense, though she took Kieran's orders. She had gotten used to taken Kieran's orders since he was the captain of their Ruadh team.

"What do you have in mind, midget?" asked Kieran trying to sound as if this wasn't a tense situation.

"Well, Bro, I was thinking of using some of my powers on it, while you think up a way of trying to hurt it," Liam said.

"Sounds good to me," Kieran said then watched as the Nain began to charge them.

Gundrun and Una find a home and Caleb finds a family...

"Are we all ready for the reading?" asked Gundrun.

Around the table sitting about a large crystal ball that sat in a crystal holder were Sian, Brian, Gundrun, and Caleb. On the sofa off to the side watching the reading sat Una and Running Deer. With the help of Sian Gundrun had reached the proper level of consciousness in order to read her crystal ball. She now touched Kieran's football helmet and Liam's video game. Once she had absorbed whatever of them remained on these items, she took her hands away and reached for Brian's hands.

"Think about your sons, think of what they look like, of how they act, on what are their favorite foods, think about them both, the good and the bad," she told him.

Brian took a deep breath and thought about his boys. He remembered holding them as babies, of bathing them, feeding them, changing their diapers. Memories of their childhood flooded his consciousness. Good memories, such as first steps and first words, of little things he had almost forgotten, like Kieran's need to sleep with him after having nightmares, they all came back to him. Then the bad memories started to return. The endless hours of crying from both his sons after their mother died, Kieran's growing resentment of him over his mother's death, and Liam's growing solitude, these memories always entered his mind.

"Excellent, Brian," said Gundrun, "you deeply love your sons. This will help me find them and do this reading. Strength of emotion helps."

She let go of his hands and placed his hands now on the crystal ball. Sian leaned forward slightly watching intently at what Gundrun did. Gundrun now rubbed the crystal ball gently, allowing it to absorb all that she had leaned about Kieran and Liam. Slowly, the clear crystal ball started to turn a shade of lavender. Gundrun began to caress the crystal ball gently.

"Brian CuCullen, I can feel your sons," she said. "Now you must ask me a question about them. I am ready."

"Are my sons in danger?" he asked.

Gundrun continued to caress the crystal ball, as if it was an organic life form instead of crystal, as if it was a pet and not an inanimate object. As she did this she peered into the lavender mist which now undulated in the ball. Sian watched this with great interest. Divination for a druid was far different. It involved reading runes, cards, or stars, but this was fascinating to watch. Gundrun's approach was worth studying and learning from.

"I can feel their presence. They are strong, very strong. Your son Liam is exceedingly strong in the supernatural arts. He is worthy of your opinion, Sian. And Kieran... he is like you, Brian," she said.

Brian squirmed ever so little in his seat. He wanted an answer to his question now, not a reading about his sons strength and such. This was nothing more than wasting time and he somehow knew that he had little time to waste.

"All the tension between and you and your son Kieran are part of who the two of you are. This tension will not go away easily, but an understanding is possible between the two of you. As for Liam, his future holds great, great dangers. But Kieran will face them with him, even after you no longer can," she said.

"Are you seeing Brian's death coming soon?" asked Sian with great concern.

"No, not his death. I cannot see his death, but I see changes. Your life, Brian, has some unexpected changes in store..."

"What about my sons being in danger now," he barked.

She continued to caress the ball. As she did this, Gundrun lowered her head until her forehead was touching the crystal ball then she became to moan. The moaning began as a low hum, but it began to build and build until she started to sound as if she was in pain.

"Mom, are you alright," cried Una from the sofa.

Brian stood up and reached for Gundrun, but Sian stopped him with a hand motion. He sat back down. Sian now placed her right hand on the back of Gundrun's head and closed her eyes. She now began to moan. Her moaning began to build and build until suddenly....

"Pain, danger, pain, danger," Gundrun screamed as both her and Sian jumped back away from the crystal ball. Caleb rushed to Gundrun's side in the flash of an eye and took her into his arms, while Brian did the same to Sian.

"Mom, are you alright?" Una, asked again.

Gundrun put her hand up in the direction of her daughter, as if to tell her that she was fine, then she nodded to Caleb and he released her. Sian gave Brian a gentle kiss on the cheek and he released her. Both Sian and her needed time to regain their senses. Finally, Gundrun spoke.

"Your sons are in danger right this moment. They are under attack from a demon," she said.

"What do you mean? How? Where?" demanded Brian.

"I know where," said Sian.

"Sian, where?"

"Off Samhain," she said.

"You need to get to them now," Gundrun said.

"How?"

"I can do that," said Sian slowly. "Liam has been instructing me in teleporting. I don't have the power to do it yet, but I think I can with Gundrun's and Una's help."

"How can we help?" asked Gundrun.

"I have the power to tap into others preternatural gifts. If I tap into yours and Una's I will have the strength," she explained.

"Is it dangerous?" Gundrun asked.

"I would not place you in danger. It will tire you, other than that there will be no other effect," said Sian.

"What about you?" asked Brian.

"I'll be fine," Sian told him, even though she knew that teleporting for her might deplete her energies enough to kill her. But the lives of Liam and Kieran were too important for her not to do this.

"Will you?" he asked again.

"Trust me," she said.

"Then let's do this," Brian said then turned to Running Deer. "Get my sword out of the trunk of the car."

Running Deer got up of the sofa and ran out of the house to the car. As he did this Sian motioned Gundrun and Una to gather closely around her. Once they did, she lowered her head and placed her left hand on Una and her right hand on Gundrun. Caleb walked over to Brian.

"I wish I could join you, Brian," he said.

"I wish you could join me, also, but I have a feeling that transporting herself and me will strain Sian enough."

"Agreed," he said then stepped aside as Running Deer ran back into the house with Kieran's retracted sword in his hand. He gave it to him then also stepped aside. Sian finally raised her head.

"Thank you," she said to Gundrun and Una. "I have connected to your power. Let's hope I have learned well from Liam."

"I'm ready," Brian stated.

"Good. Will everyone step back? Brian I need you to hold my hand," she said.

Brian stepped over to Sian and took her right hand in his left hand. Again Sian lowered her head. Reaching deep into herself she started to do what Liam had taught her. Yes, Liam, a teenage boy had taught her, a Triune Conjurer. She teleported several times with him, each time with him in charge and using his powers to make sure it went without a problem. This would be her first solo attempt. Reaching deeper and deeper she tapped in Una and Gundrun's powers causing each of them to shudder, then she went through every step that Liam had taught her until finally she felt the world begin to implode. The room, all the people in it, all matter seemed to be drawn in on itself. The teleporting was working.

As the Nain charged towards Liam and Kieran, Liam now reached out and requested nature for its help. Nature agreed to help him. Suddenly, the grass under the Nain's feet grew longer and stronger and knotted around his hooves. This slowed down the Nain, but didn't stop him. It broke through the grass with a quick enchantment causing the grass to dry up and wither away and then continued forward, so Liam this time caused an earth wall to spring up in front of it. The Nain ran into the wall and stopped dead.

"Nice work, Liam," Kieran said.

"It won't stop him for long, but I have an idea," he said. "I'm going to summon Master Diaghilev's sword and change it back. Once it's a sword I will change it into Calibur."

Suddenly, he knew what Calibur was and how to came into existence. He understood even how to make it.

"How can you do that?" he asked.

Before he could answer Liam noticed that the Nain had gone around the earth wall and was coming after them again. This time he raised up four walls of dirt that kept growing until then formed a roof trapping the Nain.

"We have a few minutes," he said. "Calibur is nothing more than metal which has been endowed with some supernatural power by a powerful Triune Conjurer. Merlin and a Lady of the Lake created Calibur on Avalon, which is why it can only be found there. They knew they would need this special metal to combat evil."

He then reached out and summoned the piece of wood, which was Boris Diaghilev's sword. The log rolled across the grass at great speed towards him then stopped at his feet. He then bent over the log and began to chant a few words, what has been done can be undone, over and over again in an attempt to change the wood back into a sword. As he did this the earthen jail which trapped the Nain began to crack from the force of the demon's ramming against it.

"Hurry up, Liam. I could use that sword real soon," Kieran cajoled his brother.

The wood morphed back into a sword. Now Liam knelt down beside the sword and placed his hands on it. He reached deep into the cellular level of the sword and started to methodically change its makeup turning it into Calibur. Liam knew where that the information on Calibur came from and how to change metal into Calibur came from Merlin. This was just a little more of that ancient knowledge coming into his mind just when he needed it. The sword was changed into pure Calibur.

"It's all yours, Bro," he said to Kieran, who picked up the sword and began to swing it about to judge its weight and balance.

The earthen jail finally gave way. Before Liam could conjure more obstacles to impede the demon, the Nain growled a few words in what sounded like ancient Celtic, pointed at Liam and sent him up in the air with a blue streak of electricity that shot out of his left forefinger. Kieran turned to see his brother bounce on the ground and roll over. He wanted to go check to see if he was alive or dead, but he knew he didn't have the time.

Turning just in time, he saw the Nain was almost upon him. Rolling to the left he swung out his sword and caught the Nain on his back left leg causing it to scream in surprise and pain. It wasn't expecting a sword that could hurt it; it wasn't expecting a sword made from Calibur.

"Your sword is Calibur," he growled.

"Yeah, ain't that cool. Hurt, didn't it," Kieran said as he got to his feet.

"It won't help you," he said.

"We'll see."

The Nain again growled some odd sounding words and then sent a streak of now red electricity from his palm straight at Kieran. Instinctively, Kieran blocked the burst of electricity with his sword, which absorbed it easily. The sword in Kieran's hands as well as his arms tingled from the red electricity but it did no other harm. This angered the Nain, who now charged Kieran.

Just then the air cracked in a thunderously loud bang and Sian and Brian appeared. Once they completely materialized Sian fainted. Brian caught her with his left arm as he extended his blade with his right hand. The demon stopped in mid charge. Brian gently placed Sian on the ground then took off in the direction of the Nain with a blood-curdling scream.

"Tiarnán," the Nain growled.

"Nah, he's not a Tiarnán, he's my father," Kieran said then charged the Nain.

The Nain instinctively ran towards Brian CuCullen knowing that he was the greatest threat. Kieran ran after the Nain. Brian met the Nain halfway jumping over it as it jumped towards him. In midair he ripped open a wound on its back causing it to bray in great pain, then he landed on his feet and turned to battle more. Kieran ran up to his side.

"What took you so long?" he asked his father.

"I was a continent away," he said.

"Excuses," Kieran said.

"I'll take him high and you take him low. We strike together at the same time so that his injuries are deep and grave and he can't recover from them. All you have to do is follow my lead. We'll give him no quarter."

"You sure this will work?" he asked his father.

"Nain are tough but inherently stupid. Your sword Calibur?"

"Yes," Kieran answered.

"Then we have the right tools and skills for this job."

"Good," Kieran agreed.

Just then Mallory, Stonefeather, and Talbot came running through some trees. A visible Thomas was leading them. When Thomas saw Liam lying on the ground, he broke away from those he was leading and went directly to Liam's body. Selena, Jean Pierre, and Philippe were attempting to help him, while Jan and Nadia stood guard.

"Liam, buddy, wake up," Thomas screamed. "I need you, Mate. Don't be dead."

"He's not dead," Selena told Thomas.

"I'm okay," Liam mumbled as he slowly opened his eyes. "How's Kieran?"

"He is doing great," said Nadia admiringly, as she watched father and son face the demon.

The Nain once again charged them. Working in tandem Kieran and Brian charged the Nain. When Brian made his move by taking to the air, Kieran made his move by striking low. Together they each hit their mark cutting deep into the Nain. As the cleared the demon, it fell to the ground and began to screech in pain until it stopped then began to quickly decay and dissolve.

"Nice work," Brian said to Kieran.

"I know," Kieran replied.

"What is happening here," Mallory bellowed in a rough, gruff voice as he neared them.

"I'll explain later. Stonefeather help Sian. She fainted after she teleported us here," Brian commanded.

"I'll check her, Tiarnán," Stonefeather said then rushed off to Sian.

Brian followed him with his eyes as Stonefeather came up to Sian and knelt down. After taking a moment to check her, he looked up and gave Brian the thumbs up sign. Brian sighed in relief. With the help of Nadia and Selena Liam limped over to them.

"Now, can I ask what has happened here?" Mallory said.

"Yes," Brian replied, but before he could answer Kieran stepped in.

"Sir, we were attacked by a Nain. It killed Master Diaghilev," he said and pointed to where the prone, lifeless body of Diaghilev laid.

Without asking Talbot rushed off to the body of his one time teacher. Once Nadia had transferred Liam to Kieran, she joined Talbot. Together they respectively moved the body of the trainer of Tiarnán.

"You definitely have a traitor here," Brian told Mallory, who looked off in the direction of Boris, a man he had known since he was eleven and came to Samhain.

"I know," Mallory mumbled.

"We have a great deal to discuss, Headmaster," Brian said.

Mallory watched as Nadia and Talbot gently picked up Diaghilev's body and began to carry it down the hill.

EPILOGUE

The whole school gathered in the Hall of Heroes. They were there for several reasons, but the most important reason was to honor Boris Diaghilev. In the first row sitting with teachers Nadia sat beside Kieran, who placed his right arm around her shoulders waiting for her to cry, but she did not cry. She had been trained to be strong. In Diaghilev's death Kieran finally realized that the only one to blame for his mother's death was the Illuminatii. He and his father were not without issues, as Liam put it, but he no longer blamed him for her death. Mallory stood at the front of the Hall with Brian CuCullen on his right and Sian Boru on his left. He cleared his throat, which silenced everyone.

"It is a great honor to be memorialized in this place, a great honor indeed. But it is an honor that comes with a great price; you must die a heroic death. It is with sadness that I bestow this honor on Boris Ivan Diaghilev, trainer of Tiarnán," Mallory stated.

With those words Donovan Talbot walked onto the stage carrying a covered painting. He stopped near Mallory, who walked over the painting and in removing its cover exposed a portrait of Boris Diaghilev. In the portrait Boris was not represented in battle, but in training students to become Aongus Cathal and Tiarnáns. For all her strength and training Nadia finally broke down and cried when she saw this painting. It was what her uncle would have wanted as a memory of him. Mallory returned to his position standing between Sian and Brian, while Talbot stood supporting the portrait. The headmaster looked older somehow, as if the weight of the events of the past year had weathered him even more.

"Boris saved many lives because of his training. Although he appeared gruff and rough on the outside, a Russian winter of a man, he was actually a worrywart who fretted over all his students like they were his own children. May he find comfort now," Mallory intoned then bowed his head for a moment of silence.

Everyone in the hall bowed their heads even Thomas who floated about Liam. There was a palpable sense of loss and sorrow in the great room. Mallory finally raised his head and looked over the crowd.

"There will be changes here next year," he stated. "With the authority of the Council of Guaire an eighth Tiarnán post has been created, the Tiarnán of Samhain. This position will be fulfilled by Brian CuCullen."

A rush of excitement quickly changed the mood of the hall. Liam, Selena and Kieran already knew this news, so they remained reserved as their father asked. A Tiarnán on Samhain was an amazing thing, but it could only mean one thing: there was danger on Samhain, a danger only a Tiarnán could handle. Whispers began to break out through the crowd, as the students reacted. Mallory allowed this to continue for a few minutes. Brian CuCullen for his part could not help but be reminded of the deal he made with Rasputin. He could be Tiarnán of Samhain, just so long as he remained a special emissary for him, also. He agreed to this because he wanted to protect his sons, but also because he wanted to keep an eye on the Supreme councilor.

"Yes, a Tiarnán," Mallory said quieting those gathered. "He will be in charge of security as well as some other matters. He will not be here to help those who want to be Tiarnáns with insights and stories. You should keep that in mind. With the passing of our great trainer of Aongus Cathal, his position will be fulfilled by Donovan Talbot, the trainer of Ardal Cathal."

With the unexpected news Talbot looked, as if an electric shock passed through his body. He looked at the headmaster with a deep expression of confusion and sadness. Mallory smiled gently at him then nodded his head as if to say, yes, it's true.

"Master Diaghilev told me the night before he died that he had never seen a better job of training done than the training of Kieran CuCullen. For that effort he wanted him promoted to full faculty. I have done what he has requested and a little more. Let us all give a subdued bit of applause to Master Talbot."

A mild wave of applause swept through the hall. Talbot looked into the audience at Nadia and Kieran. They both smiled at him and applauded. A tear formed in his right eye.

"With Master Talbot moving up we need a new trainer for Ardal Cathal. We have found Jennifer Sult to fill the position. Ms. Sult will also be Tiarnán CuCullen's right hand person," Mallory announced and the crowd began to look about the hall for Jennifer Sult, who was nowhere to be found.

"Ms. Sult will join us once a new Tiarnán for Maine has been chosen," he explained. "This has been a trying year, a remarkable year, an eventful year. But I fear that next year will bring even greater trials for this school and the Bene Lumen. We are in a difficult time of change and upheaval, a time where evil seems to have the upper hand. Do not fret, though. In times such as these providence often supplies us with those we need to restore the balance, so that the harmony can exist on this earth. Those special leaders just might be in this room now, too. Pay attention to your fellow students, know them, trust them, and look for signs. They say that Arthur and Merlin will return when we in the Bene Lumen need them most. Dear students, they may already be with us. So my advice to all of you is to keep this in mind: every storm has its aftermath and every battle its casualties. We must now weather the storms to come and know that there will be more casualties to bury. Do not fear, though, because as long as you, my students, fight the good fight, the war is not lost. School is dismissed until next year."